The RAKE'S HANDBOOK

{ INCLUDING FIELD GUIDE }

SALLY ORR

sourcebooks
casablanca

Published by Sourcebooks Casablanca, an imprint of Sourcebooks, Inc.
P. O. Box 4410, Naperville, Illinois 60567-4410
(630) 961-3900
Fax: (630) 961-2168
www.sourcebooks.com

Printed and bound in Canada.
WC 10 9 8 7 6 5 4 3 2 1

My heartfelt gratitude to the intelligent and funny ladies of the message board. Special thanks to Rosy Thornton, who asked me if I ever considered writing a novel. Thank you, ladies.

One

Cheshire, England, 1821

"DID YOU ESCAPE THE CROWD JUST TO PEEK UNDER that man's fig leaf?"

"No!" Elinor Colton jumped back from the statue of Apollo Belvedere standing in the vestibule of the Macclesfield Assembly Rooms. A green elm leaf had been tied with a rope to cover the replica's private parts, and she had reached out to straighten it. "No, I would never…" Turning in the direction of the deep voice, she saw a tall stranger with a soft gleam in his eyes.

He tilted his head and grinned.

Elinor had escaped to the empty vestibule after the orchestra played the first notes of her late husband's favorite Scottish reel. Perhaps the tall stranger noticed tears shimmering in her eyes when she passed him on the assembly's floor. Then, with good intentions, he followed her and asked his impertinent question to shock her out of her melancholy. She pointed to the bright green leaf tied around Apollo's hips. "It's crooked, so I just tried to straighten it. Any woman would naturally straighten a crooked leaf."

The stranger bent his broad shoulders forward to examine the statue. "Seems Apollo's leaf is not a fig. An embarrassing situation for any fellow." He turned to address her. "Did you give him the wrong leaf?"

She managed a small smile. "Apollo wore a stone fig leaf when we chose him from the catalog. But after his arrival, he appeared to be an exact replica of the fifteenth-century statue. No stone leaf, and a broken…" She gulped. "It's an elm because there are no figs in Cheshire—no trees in Cheshire—no fig trees in Cheshire."

"No fig leaves, eh?" The soft gleam in his eyes transformed into a wholly mischievous one. "Even though he's missing most of his gentleman's area, the elm is not big enough to cover what little remains. Do you think it's big enough?"

She instantly gaped. *Under no circumstances would she answer that question.* As a widow recently out of mourning, she should have replied to his outrageous question with a proper set-down. Instead, she stood fixed in place with her mouth open. No doubt similar to the comical expression observed on people's faces earlier that evening at the statue's reveal. When seconds after the drop of Apollo's shroud, the entire town had resembled a school of openmouthed trout.

The tall stranger ignored her silence and peered through the vestibule's open doors into the dark night. "I seem to remember a splendid tree next to this very building. Perhaps a larger leaf can be found?"

"That tree is a pine."

"No, you are right. A pine needle would be too small."

She laughed—couldn't help it—then realized it was her first laughter since her husband's death. For the last month, she had eagerly anticipated tonight's assembly, but despite her best efforts to enjoy herself, she repeatedly became overwhelmed by grief in public. Tears pooled in her eyes, and she found herself sad in the middle of a happy crowd. Nothing could be worse. Now able to laugh again, the iron cloak of mourning began to lift from her shoulders. She flashed the stranger a grateful smile before leaning over to finally straighten Apollo's troublesome leaf.

He reached out at the same time, and his hand lightly covered hers.

She froze, conscious only of his warm palm.

With a soft chuckle, he squeezed her hand.

"Oh!" Glancing upward, she saw a sable forelock hanging over his forehead in a charming manner that for one second lured her with the tender thought of gently sweeping it back. The boisterous noise from the dance floor seemed to fade, and she heard herself gulp. Not wanting to be observed touching a stranger, she yanked her hand away.

"Allow me." Wearing a wry grin, he adjusted the statue's leaf to the left before a slight correction to the right. "Apollo doesn't really need a leaf. A long time ago he probably fell forward, and his…part broke off. Someone found it and…" He nodded several times. "We still need a leaf, though, but I can't think of a single leaf that would do the job properly. Tragic our British leaves are unsuitable."

She laughed, then bit her tongue to stop an improper exuberant reply.

He laughed too, until something over her shoulder caught his attention. "I beg your pardon. Please excuse me. I've an appointment to keep, but I'll be sure to ask the Master of Ceremonies for a proper introduction later." He stepped closer. "I promise. The delightful sound of your laughter is even more desirable than a fig tree in Cheshire." He bowed gracefully and strode toward the dancers visible in the main assembly room. His broad back soon disappeared into the merry crowd.

Elinor lifted her face to the brisk wind blowing through the vestibule's open doors, hoping to cool the heat sweeping across her cheeks. *Heavens, what an impertinent man.* Once her blush faded, it dawned on her that he had initiated their silly conversation on purpose. He knew his leaf nonsense would banish her tears and make her laugh. In an instant, her opinion of him changed. No longer an impertinent stranger, he was a gentleman she must find again to convey her gratitude for lightening her spirits and saving her evening.

She returned to the overheated assembly rooms to observe the large number of couples twirling in a country dance. The gentlemen's dark coats complemented the ladies' light-colored gowns. The shimmering skirts worn by many of her friends spun in beautiful, fluttering waves that left her unconscionably giddy and sparked a sudden desire to dance with every gentleman in the room. She then spent a delightful hour standing up with several gentlemen of her acquaintance.

When exhausted and needing to catch her breath, she rested against the wall and noticed her late husband's cousin, Henry Browne, approach.

Henry strode to her side, then held his arm out toward a group of oak chairs. They sat as far away from the noisy crowd as possible. "Are you enjoying this first foray out into society now that your mourning has ended?"

"Yes, everyone has been very kind." She held out her arms to emphasize her gown, a dark overdress of plum-colored silk. "Even though I'm dressed like a veritable dowd."

"I speak for many when I say you're as lovely as ever." A handsome blond attorney, Henry rarely sought the joys of society, but when he did, he purchased expensive attire to reflect his consequence. Except the numerous concerns of his clients took precedence over his tailor's desire for proper fittings. Therefore, his new garments always possessed some fault. Tonight his shirtsleeves were several inches longer than his coat, resulting in a furtive tug on each coat sleeve to cover his shirt's giant cuffs.

Since Henry's assistance had proved invaluable in settling her late husband's affairs, she sympathized with his sartorial misadventures and even considered them endearing.

Henry moved his chair closer to hers. "I am delighted to find you at last. I have important news to communicate. Evidently a fox has come amongst the chickens."

"Pardon?"

"It seems your new neighbor, Mr. Ross

Thornbury, has finally joined his mother to reside at Blackwell Hall."

"Wonderful!" She glanced around the assembly. "There are so many gentlemen that are unknown to me. Is Mr. Thornbury in the room now or lost in the crush of people here tonight?"

"I'm not acquainted with the man, nor have I ever seen him in person. As your closest relative, I must insist you speak to Mr. Thornbury only in my presence."

"Why?"

"The man is an ugly customer."

"Pardon?"

"A man about town."

"I don't understand."

Henry waited until the elderly couple standing near them strolled over to join a reel before he spoke. "I apologize. I do not wish to sully your ears, but I must mention a vulgar fact. The circumstances demand it. The man is a well-known London profligate, a libertine—a rake!"

She pursed her lips to smother a grin.

He peered left, then right, probably to determine if anyone was listening. "Haven't you heard about the infamous Rake Thornbury?"

"No. His mother told me he is a respectable, dutiful son. In fact, it was his concern for her welfare that he purchased Blackwell Hall. He knew it would make her happy, you see."

"That might be true, but"—Henry leaned toward her and whispered—"rumor says he's a Swell of the First Stare, and beautiful women swarm around him to gain his attentions. I don't comprehend why, since I understand from Dr. Potts that he is not out of the common way." He lowered his voice. "I gather he's usually observed in the company of... mistresses." His eyes widened from the shock of his own words. "Dozens of them. I wonder if he brought a mistress here into the country. Now that would be truly scandalous."

She grinned. The presence of a notorious rake might bring additional liveliness into the local society. She would enjoy watching him charm a lady or two. "How many female admirers do you need to earn the honor of being a rake?"

Henry huffed. "Being a rake is not an honor. One or one hundred mistresses would not make any difference. A rake to one lady is a rake to *all* ladies." He yanked on his right coat sleeve. "There are scores of scandalous stories about him circulating since his arrival. I even heard about a Mrs. M. who pounded on his door and handed him a baby...or a cabbage... my informant was not clear."

"Not a baby or a cabbage. It must have been a baby from a *carriage*. Unless Mr. Thornbury is fond of cabbages."

"The point is," he continued evenly, "this event preceded Mrs. M.'s ruin and forced isolation in Devon, and that's just one story too. I wonder how many women this vile seducer has ruined."

She doubted any man—even a rake—could be so charming that sensible women would risk censure for the excitement of a few masculine charms. "Surely the ladies bear some responsibility for their ruin."

"Not when the man is an expert at seducing ladies into forgetting their obligations. This Thornbury also wrote the very book on the subject of female persuasion, *The Rake's Handbook.*"

"Have you read it?"

"Of course not. I doubt our lending library acquires such villainous, profane books."

"Is the handbook popular with gentlemen? Is it fiction or a true handbook? Since he will be my neighbor, I might like to read a copy."

He sighed. "I'll wager the Portico in Manchester is the only library within a hundred miles with a copy of such a vulgar book." Henry leaned close to whisper. "I also heard Thornbury caused his brother's death. I don't know the details, but it's obvious the man is a rogue. I'm worried about you, since his estate borders yours."

"Pray, what could happen if I encountered Mr. Thornbury alone?"

He tugged his right sleeve. "If you are surprised by him, you might be forced into repelling his advances."

She spoke in a low, conspiratorial tone. "When I first meet him, even with proper introductions, do you believe he will consider—ravishment?"

"Please." He yanked his coat sleeve again, resulting in the sound of ripping cloth followed by an ungentlemanly grunt. "As a consequence of being a man, I understand the true nature of rakes."

"You *do*?"

A beet-red blush climbed from under his high collar to the top of his cheeks. "Listen to me. My status as your nearest relative means I am the proper person to be your advisor. You must trust me as you would a husband. It is unsafe for you to be seen in this man's company. Indeed, I am confident any lady observed in his presence will be shunned by decent society."

The thought of any lady isolated from Polite Society because they were discovered in one man's company seemed unnecessarily heartless. "I defer to your innate manly wisdom then, but I refuse to believe he had anything to do with his brother's death. If he did, why would his mother agree to live with him? What nonsense. I also cannot believe he is hiding a mistress. The countryside is not like London. So he can't set her up in the neighborhood discreetly, nor could he keep her at Blackwell with his mother in residence. In my opinion, this rake rumor is nothing but twaddle, and the magnitude of Mr. Thornbury's transgressions probably increases the farther one travels from London."

Henry hesitated. "I don't know about that, but London rakes are still dangerous. Besides, maybe his mistress is well hidden."

She lost her fragile restraint and openly laughed.

He slapped his thigh. "You must stop this levity. I had hoped we'd seen the last of your improper high spirits. You can no longer behave as you did when William was alive. Society demands widows to be staid in their behavior and exhibit deference in regard to their loss."

A group of older ladies stopped their conversation and stared after her outburst. The candlelight from the wall sconces fell upon their faces and exaggerated their masklike frowns. Some of the matrons gestured toward her, while the elderly dowager, Mrs. Harbottle, lifted her nose.

Elinor sat unmoving, acutely aware the matrons would consider her outburst of laughter indelicate. Because she was a young widow living in a small village, she could no longer give free rein to her high spirits in public. She must do her best not to burst into either riotous laughter or spontaneous tears. Otherwise, social invitations might be withheld—her worst nightmare. If only the matrons realized she was trying to behave like a dignified widow. She had to, not only for her sake, but for the sake of William's good name. Except the dowagers demanded society's widows to present solemn manners, like an aloof cat, while hers had always been more like a friendly hound.

Henry grabbed her arm and appeared to say something, but the orchestra's boisterous music overcame his words. Seconds later, the orchestra stopped playing, leaving his raised voice to boom across the hall. "I see you have made several conquests tonight." A brief hush claimed the room, and more than one head spun in their direction.

"Please, I'm not seeking conquests," she said in a whisper. "You know I have counted the days until this evening. And despite what everyone says, I still fail to understand why mourning requires forced seclusion. Vibrant society and the company of my friends is what I need to survive my loss."

"Yes, but standing up with Dr. Potts three times. You also danced twice with Mr. Mabbs and twice with Mr. Burton, then you—"

"I've simply enjoyed an hour or two dancing with

several of my neighbors. Since you and I have waltzed, you must approve of dancing."

"Yes, but your repeated dancing may create public expectations."

"I'm sure nobody but you counted. All of my friends know of my everlasting commitment to William, so no expectations of a future marriage will arise." Once again after the mention of William's name, unshed tears pooled in her eyes. The liquid transformed her silk gown's iridescent shine into a dancing rainbow. Her husband's loss was one catastrophe, but the isolation expected of first mourning became another blow. For the past year, she felt like a cloistered prisoner in a dark closet, unable to breathe, forced to listen to happy conversation just outside the door. She needed to hear laughter again, not only from her nephew or the housemaids. It sounded silly and unimportant, but laughter and good company banished her grief for a moment. Today that transient reprieve meant everything to her. Recalling the lively conversation with the impertinent stranger, she wiped her tears away and glanced around the room.

She discovered him standing on the opposite side of the floor, lounging against a marble mantelpiece and speaking to a group of gentlemen unknown to her. Dressed predominantly in black, he wore a white stock of small pleats instead of a knotted cravat. The sole embellishments to this otherwise stark attire were garnet waistcoat buttons that caught the candlelight and twinkled from across the room. After this first clear glimpse of him, she dismissed his dark garments as too simple. But upon reflection, she couldn't find a single feature not to her taste. His elegant evening wear was so flawlessly cut and hugged every inch to such perfection, the other gentlemen around him appeared disheveled, like their tailors had been the worse for wine.

The stranger caught her staring and grinned. Then with a straight face—probably feigned—he spread his fingers wide on one hand and nonchalantly held his "leaf" low in front of his trousers. This gesture was followed by a leisurely turn sideways in mock modesty.

"Oh." She swallowed a chuckle, a most embarrassing sound. She focused on the purple embroidered roses covering her slippers until she regained her composure. When she looked up, she discovered his eyes sported that mischievous gleam again. She tried to frown in proper admonishment but ended up grinning instead.

He flashed a smile of such radiance; it left her breathless.

"We must find this Mr. Thornbury." Henry patted her hand. "I should warn you that there is another reason to be on your guard. It seems Thornbury's investment group plans to erect a foundry to build small steam engines. The foundry will be constructed on his property, but he will need your property too." He pressed up the limp ends of his sagging collar tips. "Of course, the subject of a foundry is men's business and should not be discussed in polite company. As your attorney, I insist you inform me at once if Thornbury is seen near your land. Then I can officially warn him off."

"Why does he need my property?"

"He'll need an established waterway to move his engines to market, so he will have to travel across your land to the river." He patted her hand to gain her complete attention. "Now for the worst part. Since his foundry will likely obtain its power from a steam engine, the coal soot from the chimney flue might destroy your home."

She clutched his arm. "Destroy—"

"This is not the time to worry." He squeezed her hand. "After Thornbury declares his intentions and provides specifics, we will consult the current law and make our objections known."

Were Henry's comments nothing more serious than an attorney's usual suspicions? *Could her home be damaged or even destroyed?* William had built their Gothic-style house, Pinnacles, as a wedding gift. Today the house was the remaining tangible evidence of their happy past. Just yesterday she caught herself staring at the mezzotint on the bedroom wall, and recalled William carefully hanging the little picture just so. Now every inch of the house triggered a fond memory, and she vowed never to leave it. If the gossip proved true, she would do anything to fight a large steam engine with its smoky chimney near her home.

"Rum business, foundries," Henry said, running a hand through his blond hair. "Besides the destruction of Pinnacles, life for the whole neighborhood would change, including people of quality. Whenever a foundry, mill, or soot-belching factory moves into a populated area, the men of rank move away within a year or two. For those who remain, their lands will become worthless." A scowl marred his handsome face. "I've no inclination to leave my property."

She pictured her home's cream-colored stones blackened by soot, and words tumbled from her mouth. "When the steam engine at the Stockport colliery hauls coal to the surface, it belches enough sulfur-smelling smoke to dim the sunlight. Sometimes I feel those chimneys must be pipes straight up from Hades. With all that foul air, it would be like living in Manchester. Citizens in that city become ill when they walk down the street." She bounced her leg in a rapid, unladylike movement.

He watched her for a minute or two. "My dear, after further consideration, I've changed my opinion." Reaching out to imprison her hand, he pressed her palm on her knee for a brief moment to stop the bounces. "I now believe this man's information about Thornbury's foundry was false, since it was secondhand."

She silently dismissed his solicitude. Manchester was over twenty miles away. Yet new mills and factories were built in nearby towns every day, spreading outward like black soot-covered roots expanding into the verdant countryside. She clutched his arm. "But if the rumor is true, how can I stop Mr. Thornbury from building his foundry? What if my home began to smell of soot?" She bounced her leg again. "What if the smoke turned my windows black? What if smoke fills my lungs when I stroll in my garden? What—"

"Yes. I am now confident this foundry business is only a rumor. Please ignore my earlier concerns."

A long sigh escaped him. "A gentleman like Mr. Thornbury must be aware of the detrimental effect an iron foundry would have on your house and our small village. As your man of business, I will attend this matter. Don't worry." He spoke in a conciliatory tone. "You must realize that in company like this public assembly, some men enjoy spreading scandalous misinformation solely for their own amusement." He patted her hand. "There is only one way to end this reckless speculation. I'll go and inquire after Thornbury now, so we can resolve this rumor." He rose, tugged on both coat sleeves again, and soon disappeared in the direction of the card room.

Anxiously waiting for Henry's return, she refused all requests for a dance. She even refused her favorite, La Pastourelle, and its lively finale.

A long hour later, as the last midnight chime echoed around the room, she surveyed the assembly. Smoke hung in the air from the guttered candles, and half of the revelers had left for home. The remaining townsfolk conversed in small groups, a few discreetly rubbing their feet after a long night of dancing. She turned to find Henry bearing down in her direction.

He narrowed his eyes in a troubled expression. "I discovered Mr. Thornbury in the supper room." He held out his arm to escort her. "However, I had no chance to speak with him in private. This foundry nonsense has certainly spread. Some madcap fellow claimed the whole region would be choked with soot-belching chimneys before the year's end."

"Heavens."

"Come, come. Mr. Thornbury is ready to leave.

Let's have a private word and clear up this flummery now. Hurry." He clasped her arm and marched forward.

Once they were outside on the assembly steps, the light proved too poor to distinguish anyone clearly. The dark coats of the disordered crowd blended with the black sides of the carriages jostling to retrieve their passengers. The noise of restless horses and coachmen's shouts added to the chaos.

Standing on his toes to survey the crowd, Henry yelled, "There he is." Releasing her arm, he ran to the left.

Elinor lifted her skirt and hurried after him.

He stopped to point at a large carriage, and she quickly reached his side.

Under the dim lamplight, the impertinent stranger bid farewell to his friends before he entered the vehicle. The carriage lurched forward and soon disappeared into the thick nighttime air.

She gasped. "That's Mr. Thornbury? He's not a vile seducer. He's a kind…flirt!"

Henry seized her hand. "Remember my warning. If you are seen in the company of that scoundrel, your reputation will be at stake. Moreover, if you encounter him without an escort, well, who knows what mischief he is capable of. Under no circumstances should you meet this Thornbury alone."

Two

ELINOR SQUINTED AT THE DAZZLING SUNLIGHT SPILLING in from the windows as she entered the breakfast parlor.

"Did you enjoy the assembly last night?" asked Elinor's seventeen-year-old nephew, Berdmore Deane. "From what I saw, you were much admired and stood up with every eligible gentleman in the county." Berdy failed to hide his knowing smirk. "Any fellows you'd like to tell me about?"

The light shining from behind Berdy's head transformed his blond hair into a corona of gilt curls. This golden vision reminded her of his arrival nine years ago, after her sister's death. Berdy's gamester father had been unwilling to live with a small child in London and delighted to leave the boy in Cheshire. She remembered the young Berdy sitting quietly by the window, his hands clasped in his lap, and his hair lit from behind like today. She chuckled at the comparison of the child half listening to William's calm reassurances back then to the aspiring dandy before her now.

"I am just pleased you had such a wonderful time,"

he said, still chewing his bacon. "It was good to see you dancing and happy for a change."

"Thank you, I think." She sat in a slow, purposeful manner, then poured herself a cup of black tea. The air soon filled with a smoky, heather-like aroma.

"I am also surprised you received such marked attentions from every unmarried gentleman in the county. You must be flattered."

"Yes. I was very grateful for their kind attentions."

"You're too young to hide yourself in this Gothic pile," he said, waving a fork. "William has been dead for over a year. I worried you might marry Henry, but now with so many gentlemen vying for your favor, you will have your pick of beaus. Of course, the trick will be to find a beau who loves you, and not just your fortune."

"I am not interested in beaus." For some reason unknown to her, everyone—even Berdy—believed she would eventually wed. Why didn't they understand William's love filled her heart forever? *She could never marry a second time.*

She glanced around at the lovely room decorated in bright yellow. William had thought the color too bold, but he painted it that hue to please her. Now, after a restless night and two cups of strong tea, she faced the uncertainty over the future of her home. Her first instinct was to march over to Blackwell and demand an answer to the foundry rumor, but she owed Henry the chance to inquire about the foundry alone. Mr. Thornbury might reveal more detailed information to a gentleman than he would to an anxious widow like herself.

"If you are not interested in beaus, then what did

you think of everyone's dress at the assembly?" He rolled his eyes. "Henry's sleeves were too long, and his collar points became limp after the first dance. For the rest of the evening, his collar flapped like giant bird wings—"

"Yes…wings." Since patience was not one of her virtues, she devised a plan. If she visited Blackwell's grounds today, she might get lucky and meet one of Mr. Thornbury's employees. Maybe a groom or under-gardener could confirm or deny the industry rumor. If that failed, she would call upon Mrs. Thornbury and discreetly inquire about her son's plans.

While Berdy continued to describe every waist-coat at the assembly, she peered out the window to the bright July sky and recalled William had always enjoyed fishing at Blackwell's lake on warm days. Perhaps she could use fishing as an excuse to meet a Blackwell employee, and casually ask about the rumor. "Would you like to go fishing at the lake today? We can ask Cook to pack a picnic."

Berdy grumbled after finding jam on his yellow-striped waistcoat. "Picnic? Fishing? Dash it all, Elli. Look at me. Where do you expect a fellow to sit?" He surveyed his mint-colored pantaloons for more wayward jam.

She tapped a finger on her teacup. "On the ground, silly, or on a rock."

"Sit on a rock. That will ruin m' new trousers. Indeed, what if I catch a fish? I might spoil m' third-best waistcoat. A huge risk. Anyhow, I must go to town. I'm expecting a significant delivery from London soon."

"A delivery? What is it?" Curiosity seized her, but she tried to sound casual and not overly interested.

His jam-covered grin grew. "It's a surprise. A surprise of *great* import."

She was not going to inquire further. Hopefully, his surprise involved nothing more than a new hat or waistcoat. Any article of dress would be preferable to what she silently called a "Berdy Rash Scheme." She stood then pushed her chair back into place. "Very well, it's such a beautiful day. I'll go fishing by myself."

Once upstairs in her bedchamber, she changed into a blue dimity gown and tucked her guinea-gold curls into a tight chignon. She grabbed her gloves and biggest leghorn bonnet, and headed out to fish.

The small lake nestled on the grounds of Mr. Thornbury's estate, and she had acquired permission to fish there anytime she desired. She sighed after her first sight of the serene, secluded fishpond. Dense woods shaded one side, while on the other, large rocks glistened in the full sun. She inhaled deeply; the damp morning air tickled her nose.

Since William's death, she visited the lake often to recapture happy memories. Sometimes a sight—such as a random reflection in the green water—triggered a priceless remembrance of him. Today the calm pool evoked the memory of his tender smile as he proudly watched her bait her line.

Choosing a flat rock half-submerged, she sat and removed her gloves. She hooked the bait she'd brought from home and cast her line. It hit the water with a delightful little plop. Once she wedged her fishing pole against the rock, she opened her novel,

The Necromancer, and began to read. *The hurricane was howling, the hailstones beating against the windows, the hoarse croaking of the raven bidding adieu…*

A twig snapped. She looked up to find the impertinent stranger from the previous evening rapidly approach. He strode with determination, like a man confident he possessed rights to everything in his domain. In the morning after the assembly, she had wondered if Henry identified the wrong man in the crowded darkness. But the man's presence here confirmed that Mr. Thornbury was indeed that kind, flirting *smiler*.

His broad thighs, encased in tight riding breeches, then drew her attention, before it naturally moved to his fig-leaf region. Horrified he might catch her looking *there*, she drew her gaze upward until it fixed upon his gold watch fob. This ornament hung down below his waist and, with each stride, mesmerized her with a rhythmic back-and-forth swing.

She gulped awkwardly.

Forcing herself to glance even higher on his person, she found a broad-shouldered man with a lock of near-black hair falling over his brow. He held his hat under his arm, and with a single movement of his hand, he brushed his forelock aside. He had a prominent nose, framed by a jaw shadowed by close-shaven dark whiskers. Smartly dressed in a bottle-green coat and elegant buff-colored waistcoat, this almost-handsome man flourished another one of his radiant smiles.

She glanced back at the swinging watch fob and blushed. No. *Almost handsome* was incorrect. When he smiled, his whole person transformed into an uncommonly handsome man, indeed. She also harbored no doubts that he was completely aware of the power inherent in his captivating smile.

"Good day, Miss Leaf. Hope I haven't frightened your fish. Since I did not get the chance to formally introduce myself to you last evening, please allow me to—"

"Oh, yes, good day." His striking good looks caused her sudden embarrassment, which resulted in an overly cheerful wave. "You must be Mr. Thornbury. I've heard so much about you from every…from your mother."

He stopped at the edge of the rock. "You heard all about me from Mother? I am disappointed. I had hoped my reputation would be *just*."

She grinned. Was he alluding to the stories of his amorous conquests sweeping the village? Thankfully they were not in public, so she could ignore Henry's warning and speak freely. "I don't know if it is just, but your reputation precedes you. You are a scandalous—oh!" *Where had her manners flown?* Best not to speak about the rumors or any question about his supposed handbook. She still needed his sympathies and friendship to persuade him not to build his foundry. So she must remain ruthless and keep her mind focused on discovering his business plans. "I apologize. I meant no offense, and Lady Helen never called you scandalous."

"I sincerely hope not—not from Mother, at least. Although she has called me other names."

"Your mother described you as a much-loved son and touted your successes in business. Feats I consider admirable in a gentleman. She also mentioned Acts of Parliament and canal construction, or was it turnpikes? Whatever the details, I understand your business endeavors are varied and have served the public well. Since we are neighbors, I hope one day we will be great friends." Caught again by his steady gaze and all-too-handsome countenance, she took awhile before she realized her babbling. She must collect her wits and ask him about the veracity of the foundry rumor. "Mr. Thorn—"

"You need a man." He nodded.

"Pardon?"

He pointed to her fishing rod. "A man to help you fish. Ladies require a man to place the worm on the hook, then afterward to unhook the fish." An expression of sham solemnity crossed his face. "You thought I meant?"

She smiled, took a deep breath, and resolved to keep to her purpose. "I do not need a man, and I can bait my own hook, thank you. Now, I have some questions about your future plans. I'd like to ask you—"

"To take one off the hook?"

"A fish?"

He laughed. "What else? Take some man off your hook?"

"No!" Elinor met his sky-blue eyes, the same color found only on days warm enough to lie in the grass and look heavenward.

"May I join you?" He sat next to her on the rock without waiting for her reply.

Ignoring him was impossible. She felt his body's

warmth. Turning to ask him to move to a respectable distance, she found herself face-to-face. A nearness only lovers knew, certainly not strangers.

She froze; her pulse erratic.

He pressed his lips together in a terrible job of hiding his efforts not to laugh. Leisurely crossing his legs, he reached over her lap without touching her, and pulled on her fishing line. "So my new neighbors have been discussing me, have they?"

She smoothed the wrinkles on her blue skirt in an exaggerated movement to innocently push his arm back to his side. "We live in a small village, so your arrival has been anticipated ever since you purchased Blackwell Hall. You were also the subject of conversation at the assembly last night. Of course, you must expect a little tittle-tattle about your famous exploits."

"You seem to know me well, but I know nothing about you. Mother has not described anyone like you residing in the vicinity." He turned to examine her briefly, yet quite thoroughly.

Fighting to dampen a blush caused by his perusal— *the devil*—she straightened her shoulders and focused on the foundry. "Mr. Thornbury, in regard to your property, may I inquire whether or not you plan—"

"To let you steal, er...liberate my fish?"

"Liberate? In my defense, I've a long-standing arrangement with Blackwell's steward. No crime has been committed." Hoping he wouldn't drag her in front of a magistrate for poaching, she stole a sideways peek to judge his response. "Do you mind if I fish here?"

"No." He chuckled. "I don't mind if people purloin

my pike. However, I plan to make a new rule and confine fish thievery on my estate to lovely ladies only."

Glancing up at his face, she couldn't help but smile. She liked friendly people with frank speech and open manners. She even enjoyed his teasing banter when they were alone, since she felt free enough to be herself and tease him in return. But he was too close for a stranger of such short acquaintance. Someone might catch them sitting together and start an irresponsible rumor. She searched for a possible path around him, but the routes were blocked either by the lake or his all-too-solid figure. "Please, Mr. Thornbury, if you would remove yourself over to *that* rock." She pointed to another rock five feet away. "We would both have plenty of room to sit, and you might be more comfortable."

He rocked his hips and ended up an inch or two closer. "This stone is exceedingly comfortable, soft, and has plenty of room. Tell me, what is the forfeit"—he grinned—"for letting you fish in my lake?"

"Forfeit?" What could he desire from her as a payment? One glance at his knowing smirk and her cheeks heated. *The most forward man she had ever met.* So the numerous stories were true—a famous London rake. How exciting! She'd never met a real one and suspected all those rumors of rakish seduction were false. Nothing more than masculine boasts meant to impress other gentlemen in taprooms or their clubs. Yet she couldn't stop herself from wondering how far he might go. They were on his property, alone. Surely he wouldn't try to ravish her on a rock, would he? "You, sir, are very forward." She took a peek at his face. "Someone last evening even called you"—she did her best to suppress a smile and dropped her voice to a whisper—"*a rake.*"

He lifted a solitary brow. "My dear fish thief, call me anything else, please." His grin faded. "Especially in front of Mother. How about a charming cove or a bang-up blade?"

"I don't understand. What's the difference between a bang-up blade and a rake?"

He stared up at the cloudless blue sky for a full minute without responding. Then the stunning smile she first encountered at the assembly appeared, followed by a wink. "Well, a rake *is* vile: drinking, wenching, gaming." He leaned close and spoke in a deep rumble. "A most unsuitable lover to the lady involved. While a bang-up blade is a freethinker." He looked skyward and chuckled. "And in amorous relations, a man who is truly *upstanding.*"

She tried very, very hard not to laugh at his inappropriate innuendo. "Sir, you are *the* most forward man—ever." The gossip she heard at the assembly must in fact be true. Publishing a handbook of questionable taste, reckless wagers over females, multiple mistresses, and maybe even a lady handing him a baby on his doorstep.

"Only harmless words, dear lady. If judged by my actions today, you will find I am a proper gentleman."

"You call sitting scandalously close to a lady you have just met proper?"

"Touché. But this rock is small, and I've no intention of sitting in the lake."

"Are you telling me that you are no longer a rake,

and thus do not seduce women? What about your infamous wager with a Lord Parker over a fly? I heard a beautiful lady was somehow involved. Was that story false?"

"We were mere youths. Besides, that fly was a private wager. My scoundrel of a fly was smaller than Parker's oaf of a fly and more likely to leave the window first—or so I thought. I had nothing to do with the brawl afterward, but nevertheless, I paid the lady innkeeper for her five windows." He lifted his chin in mock indignation.

She laughed heartily. "Yes, I understand how that tale might be misconstrued as gaming." She attempted a serious expression. "Clearly spirits were not involved. I am glad you are not a rake, because now I won't have to fend off any attempts at seduction."

His grin was a mixture of expressions, half amusement, half devoid of shame. "A proper gentleman always gives a lady what she desires. I would be honored to have you fend me off, but I didn't hear a *please*."

"Oh, no. I just meant to teas—"

"The rakes I know don't seduce *innocents*. Spoils one's reputation. Besides, too much talking involved, explanations, flattery." He uncrossed his arms, leaned back, and rested on his palms. "I wrote all this down in a book, of course. The title is *The Rake's Handbook*." Another unnatural and wholly wicked grin spread across his lips. "*Including Field Guide*." The silence stretched. "Have you read it?"

"No, no, of course not."

"I know the words by heart. For your amusement

and pleasure, I'd be honored to recite the first chapter for you now."

She should be affronted, not amused, but she laughed anyway. "That is not necessary, I can assure you." Was he trying to shock her or determine if she was married? Either way, he was an expert tease and a devilishly clever man. "I'm a widow, so I'm not in your book."

"Yes, you are, my fetching female. I included widows in the handbook section, the first part of the book. My friend, George Drexel, penned the second part, the field guide. In that section, Drexel praises widows in great detail." He let out a warm, deep laugh. "It's rather shocking, but Drexel lists widows under the heading 'Houses to Let.'"

"Oh." His brazen innuendo proved unstoppable. Since his conversation and good looks had a profound effect upon her heart rate, not to mention her clarity of mind, he must be a professional seducer. If so, she might be fishing in a lake far too deep to be safe for a respectable lady.

She tried to crawl around him, but he kept his focus on a butterfly spiraling over the tall reeds for a full minute, so he failed to move his well-muscled thigh, and blocked her exit. Then he leaped to his feet and held out his hand to assist her. Without thought, she accepted his offer. The warmth of his palm caused her breath to catch, and she expected him to let go.

He did not let go.

"You really are a rake," she whispered, the sight and feel of their joined hands warming her cheeks. "A proper gentleman would never hold a lady thus.

I have been warned about your charms. Perhaps I too should write everything down. Pen a handbook to instruct my widowed sisters about what to expect upon attempted seduction and how to fight it."

"Factual or satirical?"

She bit her lower lip to stop an indelicate reply.

"I could write that handbook too."

His boast made her smile. "I seem to have found another trait of a rake."

"Humph. I'd be delighted to show you *all* of my traits. Perhaps start with chapter one?" The determination in his voice indicated he was quite willing to comply.

"Please do, sir," she replied in a facetious tone, tugging her hand free. "But I can already tell that I'll stop reading your book after the table of contents. You know, all of those funny pages in the front of the book numbered *v* and *i*."

He chuckled softly, then stared at her until he captured her gaze. "My handbook starts with fine eyes." He reached up and swept back a ringlet that had fallen over her eye and carefully tucked the curl under her bonnet.

Her heartbeat raced.

"The eyes are followed by a notable vee." His gaze lowered to the upper edge of her bodice and lingered in the center.

"Oh my, if that's the table of contents, I don't dare read chapter one."

"I'd be pleased to read you all of the chapters. There are a total of..." He glanced at her leisurely, from the top of her leghorn bonnet down to her sensible half boots. His focus returned up to her neck—almost. His chest broadened as he inhaled. "Ten."

"Ten!"

He gave her a smoldering look from under heavy lashes. "Ten in volume one," he continued in a silky baritone. "Let's start with chapter one." He leaned forward slowly, staring at her mouth as if he might take liberties and kiss her. The distance between them shortened to inches. Close enough to feel his warm breath.

"Enough." She stepped backward. "Enough of chapter one. I am finished with your book." She resisted covering both burning cheeks with her hands. "I'll return home now. I seem to be a little heated from the sun." She avoided his gaze and reached for her book.

Henry was right. Since Mr. Thornbury's rakish charms were beyond what she expected, she should never again speak to him alone. He certainly would not have attempted liberties with Henry standing nearby. However, even with Henry's presence, she might not be able to negotiate with him. He was a rake: not pure and not simple. His smiles, chuckles, and smoldering glances intended to blank female minds on purpose. *Curse his boots.*

"I see I've upset you. Apologies, my lovely fish feaster."

"I can assure you that your reputation is *just*," she said, her voice sounding higher than normal.

"A reserved gentleman with exemplary manners?"

"Never…never have I been so late returning home. Please give your mother my respects." After a brief curtsy, she snatched her fishing pole and punctured her finger on a fishhook. "Ow!"

He held out his hand. "Let me look at that."

She shook her hand vigorously. "No, thank you. I will consult my doctor for the proper treatment." She sucked on her finger.

"You should go home and treat that immediately," he said, sounding distracted and staring at her mouth. "Do you own any medical books?"

She withdrew her finger and felt the cool air ease the pain. "My late husband's study is full of medical books, but they are very detailed and use words I am not familiar with. I read only poetry and novels."

"I suggest you consult your husband's books. I have confidence you can find the best treatment yourself."

She nodded, sucking on her finger again.

His eyes focused on her lips and brightened, like a cat that had just spotted a bowl of cream—unattended. "I suggest you start by looking up puncture or—"

"Yes. Yes, I will. Good day, sir." She grabbed her fishing rod, gloves, and book, and hurried back up the road toward Pinnacles.

Once he was out of sight, her racing heartbeat slowed from immeasurable to fast. Halfway home, the beat slowed to normal. She had made a total cake of herself and failed to get an answer about the foundry— the future of her home. How could one very forward rake distract her so easily?

She put down her load, plucked a daisy, and snatched every petal off.

Obviously her wits had flown. Best to pinch herself hard the next time she met with Mr. Thornbury. Then the pain would halt the onslaught of his attractive figure, his seducing smile, or his laughing blue eyes.

Elinor grinned when she remembered one of her bracelets—shaped like a snake—that hurt whenever she wore it high upon her arm. The armlet felt just like a pinch. So the next time she planned to meet with Mr. Thornbury, she'd wear the bracelet and let the pain focus her mind. She exhaled a long sigh of relief.

Tossing the daisy over her shoulder, she grabbed her equipment and started to run.

Now she had a good plan; William would be impressed. Armed with her painful bracelet, she'd keep her wits sharp and persuade this Mr. Ross Thornbury not to build his foundry. A clear triumph over this charmer who enjoyed making females suffer that...*gentle panic.*

How could she possibly fail?

Three

THE SECOND ROSS THORNBURY STEPPED OVER HIS drawing room's threshold, his mother asked him a question.

"Well, what do you think?" The sound of Lady Helen Thornbury's voice filled the cavernous room.

Ross cringed. Variations of the same query had vexed mankind for centuries. "What do you think?" could easily be interchanged with "How do you like it?" A gentleman had an easier time finding the correct answer if the object of the inquiry was revealed, such as, "Do you like my gown?" Unfortunately, the luxury of knowing the subject of her question eluded him.

"What do you think of my alteration?"

The question sprang from his mother's lips, so to make her happy, he must find some object that had changed. "Give me a minute." He inhaled deeply and began his search with the most likely place—her person. Her needlework dropped to her lap as she watched him approach, her pronounced features softened with fondness. To Ross she appeared to have lost at least a stone within the last year, and the small

wisps of hair escaping her lace cap were no longer
jet. *Was the cap new?* Doubtful. Next he checked her
gown. She wore a black wool gown gathered at the
neck with no frills and a paisley shawl wrapped around
her shoulders. They both seemed vaguely familiar;
therefore, it was a safe bet the alteration did not refer
to her current dress. Now he faced the greater task of
finding the object of change within the vast room.

The loud click from his boots reverberated in
the expansive space as he turned a full circle several
times to survey the mostly vacant drawing room. He
searched from the wood floors to the plaster ceiling,
but nothing altered stood out. Shifting the pretty blue
box he held in his arms, he noticed the movement
briefly caught her attention.

"Well, what do you think?" She sat straight upon
the new brocade sofa delivered last week.

"Hmmm…" The yellow sofa, a wing chair, and
four bobbin-turned oak chairs faced the fireplace,
leaving thirty feet of bare room behind them. She
wore an expectant expression, so he redoubled his
efforts to discover what she changed. Finally, at a loss
to provide the answer, there was only one thing he
could do now to make her happy—bluff. "Very nice,"
he said, with a cursory inspection around the entire
room. Having done his best to please her by general
praise, and a glance that must have encompassed
whatever object had changed, he attempted to divert
her. "How are you today, dear?" He placed the box
on an ornately carved mahogany table in front of her
and kissed the top of her head.

She grabbed his hand and squeezed it. "I am well,

thank you. I am glad you approve of the robin's egg blue. The color perfectly suits our new yellow sofa."

After a fleeting grin, Ross peered up to the newly painted walls. The light blue accented the white plaster garlands nicely. For the life of him, he could not remember the old wall color, but the blue did look well now.

"So what is in the box?" She gazed at him fondly.

"A gift for our mantel. Go ahead, open it."

She opened the box and pulled out a Staffordshire figurine of a shepherdess. At first sight of the two-foot-tall statue, her glorious smile appeared. "Oh, how wonderful. Isn't this lovely? And look at the detail. Even the little sheep have painted pink noses."

He took his accustomed place on an old upholstered chair facing the sofa, delighted that his gift made her happy. He would always do his best to please her, but any man would draw the line when it came to voluntary admiration of pink sheep noses.

She cradled the shepherdess in her lap. "How was your first day touring the property? Did you meet with Mr. Douglas this afternoon? Did he take my side and agree we must stop the farm improvements until we furnish the house?"

"We had a long talk. I'm impressed with our steward. The home farm is well maintained, and the estate books are in good order. I also examined the terrain where the surveyor suggested we erect the foundry. The ground at the site is elevated, so next week we will dig three wells. If there is no groundwater at a depth of twenty feet, then the site is a good one for a foundry. Imagine it. Once our

steam engines are available for sale, Blackwell will
generate twice the profits it is currently producing.
With all that money, I'll be able to keep my promise.
You can then furnish this place with acres and acres
of the mahogany furniture you desire, even Gillow's
overdecorated firewood."

He winked at her. "However, before any capital
is committed, we must obtain a lease to move our
engines across Mrs. Colton's land. My calculations
show the foundry will be profitable only if we use a
waterway to obtain fuel for the blast furnaces and haul
our small steam engines to our customers. Since you
are acquainted with our neighbors, you must have
met this widow Colton already? What is her situation?
Does she need the money?"

Lady Helen stared at his muddy left boot. "Mrs.
Colton is a high-spirited lady who is financially inde-
pendent due to a considerable jointure. She lives in
that newer Gothic house in the direction of Knutsford,
the one with the lovely view of the river. She is not
old, but not young, and has no children from her
marriage. She is currently raising her nephew, a Mr.
Berdmore Deane. That young coxcomb lacks modesty
and is full of silly levity. Indeed, both aunt and nephew
are frivolous creatures."

Ross stared into the fire. "Even if she doesn't need
the funds, I can't imagine her refusing the extra capital
she would earn from the lease."

"I wouldn't wager on it. Her late husband left her
well provided for."

"Then I'll call upon her soon and ask for our lease.
I've one month to make the first payment to reserve

the steam engine for the foundry. If not, I may have to wait months before the next one becomes available."

A slight haze settled close to the tall fireplace. He strode to the opening, grabbed the poker, and stabbed the fire. "Bloody fireplace! Look at all this smoke. The whole damn house smells smoky. Remind me to have the chimneys cleaned." A piece of soot landed on his nose, forcing him to wave his hand and step backward.

She shook her head. "I believe they are clean. The smoke is due to the shortness of the chimneys."

"Excuse me?"

"The chimneys are too short." She wiped a piece of soot off the ornate table. "To retain the classical elegance of the Palladian style, the chimneys end after they emerge from the roof. The builders considered tall chimneys undesirable, because they would mar the roofline."

"*Hell's fire.*" He stomped back to his chair.

Her lips pursed before she placed the shepherdess on the ornate table and picked up her needlework. "Where was I? Oh, yes, evidently cleanliness is the price to pay for classical simplicity. What are overworked servants or soiled linens to architectural grace? Grand houses come at a cost, you know."

"I can fix that problem."

"You'll lose the elegance of the classical facade."

"Damn the elegance."

"That's your third use of bad language, young man."

"Forgive me." As a duke's daughter, his mother preferred grand and old-fashioned houses. One of his goals was to bring her fully into the nineteenth century by modernizing Blackwell, but he did not want to pressure her all at once with his planned changes. Every shilling the estate earned he set aside to fund either his share in the foundry or to bring Blackwell abreast of the times. Once these improvements had been implemented, he expected a higher income within the next couple of years. At the moment, he kept her happy using the irregular profits from the sales of his handbook to buy her furniture and gifts. He leaned forward to retrieve his teacup and decided to please her with a proven method to lighten her mood—rouse her feminine curiosity. "I was held up today by some *pretty* estate affairs."

Her needle stilled, hovering over her work. "Can you tell me the nature of your *pretty* estate affairs?"

"Maybe you could help me out on that score. A truly restorative sight on a sunny day: a beautiful country maid, widow, curly blond hair, brown eyes, dark lashes, and ample…lashes. Has a remarkable talent for a female—fishing. She learned of my business interests from you, so she must be one of your boon companions."

"Fishing! The countrywomen around here have the oddest hobbies, so fishing shouldn't surprise me. But from your description, I think you refer to our neighbor, Mrs. Elinor Colton."

"That's Mrs. Colton?" He dropped his teacup on the chair, splashing his knee with the scalding brew. "*The* Mrs. Colton I need to sign our lease? From your earlier description, I expected a daft, gray-haired clergyman's widow, not a young maid in a dimity gown."

"She *is* a clergyman's widow."

"Clergymen's widows don't look that live—"

"Look that what?"

"Ah…look that alive." Instantly his thoughts diverted to the memory of the pretty widow's backside walking home. Her hips swayed an infinitesimal degree detected only by men, a universal siren's call to all men with a pulse.

"That woman has no poise or dignity to speak of. Granted she is lively, but spirit does not compensate for a plump figure and a plain face. How she ever caught the eye of Reverend Colton, I will never understand. Don't tell me you are…you know… interested in her."

"No, I'm not *interested* in her." He remembered her lips, and the dimple that played in the corner of her mouth whenever she smiled. He retrieved his teacup and sat forward in his chair. "I gave you a vow… I have changed my actions, but don't expect altered manners and a different man. Besides, a gentleman should meet his new neighbors, and her lease will be crucial to our success. So tell me all about her." Next he remembered what the widow wore, an unfortunate recollection. Recalling the memory of her gown led to the mental image of him *removing* the gown. Followed by those quick calculations men make without conscious effort, like the time needed to remove every skirt and stocking and stay. He eased back in his chair. *You promised Mother to reform, no dalliances.* He shifted on the chair's cushions before resting his boot on his knee.

Lady Helen appeared animated now. "I have met Mrs. Colton on several occasions locally and have even been her whist partner once. I first met her at the house of Mr. Henry Browne, a relative and local attorney with whom she may have an understanding or is expecting an offer of marriage." She frowned at the carpet's faded roses under her feet. "Maybe I'm confused. Could it be Dr. Potts, our notable physician, with whom she has an understanding? He distinguished himself in the war, you know. Of course, those offers are probably all rumors, since I cannot imagine her receiving any on account of her frivolity. What gentleman would want a silly wife? I am pleased to hear you're not interested in her. Now that you have taken up permanent residence at Blackwell, you are the catch of the county. There are several local ladies I wish you to become acquainted with. All of them young, not like Mrs. Colton. Why, she must be at least thirty."

"Need I remind you I'm almost thirty?"

"No, you can't be. That would make me…wise. You must do as I ask and marry soon. I want many adorable grandchildren."

"Stop, please. I just wanted to know who Mrs. Colton was." He rose and stood with his back to the fire, discreetly watching her mood. Since his alluring fisherwoman was Mrs. Colton, he'd have to quickly apologize for his forward behavior at the lake if he wanted her to sign his lease. The foundry's success and mother's future happiness depended upon the widow's goodwill.

Lady Helen's eyes narrowed. "If you continue to frown in that manner, those wrinkles on your forehead will become permanent. Then no sensible woman would want to be seen in your company, much less accept your addresses. You must wed soon. Please, I want you to find a wife and have children." She paused to consider something for a moment. "I am too young to be called 'grandmother,' therefore, the moppets shall address me as 'aunt.' Of course, we will tell the children the truth once they have reached the age of discretion."

"I never reached the age of discretion."

She clicked her tongue. "At the rate you are going, you'll spend your life alone. Men need affectionate female company and children hanging on their boots. You are dear to me, Ross, and I would love to see you settled."

"Humph." When mothers demanded grandchildren, a gentleman's only recourse was to change the subject. "Do you believe this Mrs. Colton has reasons to refuse our lease and the extra profits it will generate?"

A knowing glare indicated she was not fooled by his diversion. "She has no reason to sign it. Her late husband's fortune came from his father, a wealthy ship owner, and she had a significant dowry too. So she can afford her taxes and life's luxuries. You should see her lovely mourning brooch…diamonds all around."

"You deserve a diamond mourning brooch. Shall I purchase one?"

"Don't be foolish. Diamonds would only remind me of John's bright…"

"But I owe—"

"Don't…" She struggled to complete the sentence, failed, and remained silent.

He wanted to kick himself. Two years earlier, his younger brother, John, had met with an accident. John's extended suffering unsettled his mother to such an extent, she took shears to her hair. Ross feared she would fade into madness if she remained in London. So last year, upon the advice of her physician, he sent her to live in the country with a promise of John's eventual recovery. Six months ago John died. Now all Ross desired out of life was to see his mother's spontaneous smile. A shadow of her old smile had greeted him upon his arrival, but he longed for the brilliant one. He glanced toward the fire but discreetly kept his attention upon her, trying to discover if time and distance away from John's suffering had cured her eccentricities.

"I know other mothers whose sons…" She dropped her needlework and tugged on the lock of hair escaping her cap. "A mother should stay with her ill son, not flee to the countryside like a coward, shouldn't she?"

His jaw tightened. She spoke of painful feelings, a subject he refused to openly discuss. "Please, let's not speak of it."

"Yes. I cannot bear it. Not a word, not a whisper. Too much…"

Ross could not bear it either. His exaggerated reputation as a rake, most likely created by boredom in London's clubs, coupled with a reckless moment where his behavior reinforced that reputation, had led to his brother's death. No amount of nursing on her part could have saved John. Now both he and his mother were living a fallacy—both pretending they would recover—both hearts broken. For all his supposed expertise with females, in reality he knew very little. Perhaps her desired furniture or grandchildren would preserve her sanity. For him, the promise of iron and steam engines to build England's future was the only thought keeping him sane. He rose from his chair and stood behind her. He hugged her, then let his cheek rest upon the top of her head. "We'll never mention this again. Period."

A taut silence ruled, and the room filled with an unspoken pain that hung in the air.

Once her breathing calmed, he strode over to the console table, poured himself a brandy, and returned to his chair. He peered at the amber liquid dancing from the reflected light, took a long gulp, and savored the brandy's trail of fire down his throat. Meanwhile, the stillness lingered, except for the ticking of the mantel clock or a random hiss from the coals in the fireplace.

His mother's expression, which had been light for most of the evening, remained blank.

He needed to say something to divert her thoughts from dwelling upon her grief. He planned to tell her his good news at the end of the week, but he'd rouse her from low spirits by telling her tonight. He expected her reaction to be a happy one, so he watched for her smile. "I have news for you. I've started negotiations with Charles Allardyce, the major contributor of the funds for our foundry. Next month he will visit Blackwell with several of his daughters. You know the family." He inhaled deeply. "It is not settled yet, but I plan to wed his daughter, Lucy, if we suit."

"Marriage?" Her face lit up with the famous family smile. "Grandchildren!" She clapped her hands. "I can hardly wait—boys—I so hope they are boys. I'm not quite sure how to spoil girls. Do you know how to spoil—don't answer. Why didn't you write me about your betrothal earlier?" She picked up her needlework then immediately put it back down.

He grinned, his victory complete with her smile. "I wanted to witness your surprise. But I'm not betrothed yet. Don't make plans for the wedding breakfast anytime soon." He hooked his forefinger under his tight collar and tugged it loose.

"Do you love Lucy?" Her insistent tone indicated every detail of the courtship was important to her, and she expected answers.

"Allardyce has given our investment group funds for the initial construction. Better yet, his share of the profits will only amount to five percent per year. He conceded these favorable terms upon my agreement to wed Lucy. With ten daughters, six still at home, his goals are not solely profit."

Her smile faded. "Ross," she whispered, "what about love?"

With his hands clutched behind his back, he started to pace before her. "Don't ask for the impossible. I will fall in love the minute your shepherdess here herds cows instead of sheep. Besides, with this marriage I will finally meet Father's demands. He was disappointed I didn't marry at twenty."

"Yes. Your father pushed you to wed for money, but now with your success, I want you to marry for love."

"Humph." Love—*the* ultimate female word. Many of his friends had found love, yet that seemingly violent emotion had never claimed him. The general consensus was that no love could be as powerful as the one you felt in your twenties. Now almost in his thirties, he was too old, too cynical, or perhaps his heart didn't work like other men's. He had every intention of respecting his wife and being fond of her and any children they might produce. But that *feeling* that drove men to behave like asses and ruin good capes by laying them in mud puddles for My Lady, he had no desire to find.

"After…" He paused. He needed to choose his words carefully to avoid another silence. "I gave you a solemn vow to change my behavior, and I have. I will try to act like the perfect gentleman you want me to be, but it is too much to expect romantic…attachment."

"Ross," she said with a slight shake of her head. "If you are not happy, I will—"

"The only way I can move forward is to put one boot in front of the other and do what's right. Since this marriage is desirable by all parties involved, it's settled. Anyhow, how could I be bereft of affectionate female company when I have my handsome mother near?"

"Oh, Ross." She gave him a small, sweet smile. "While I enjoy being first in your affections, it's a crime to waste a fine gentleman like you hidden away up here in Cheshire with only his mother to flatter. I wish you happy with Lucy Allardyce, and I hope you'll marry soon. She is the prettiest of the sisters, so you must wed immediately. Before a younger buck— who doesn't need her father's funds—presses his suit."

"Thank you, Mother. I'll present my offer of an

ancient buck before a younger buck can even ask her to dance."

"You don't know she will accept your addresses. We must not depend upon her father's friendship, and make sure of your engagement. I suggest you turn on that famous charm you seem unable to tame."

He chuckled warmly. "Yes, dear, if you wish it. Indeed, I look forward to marriage. It goes without saying that I will do everything in my power to make Miss Allardyce happy. So to insure the future success of our family, I'll give her an irresistible broadside of charm."

Four

A SHAFT OF DAWN'S RAYS ILLUMINATED THE DUSTY BLUE cupboard in the corner of Elinor's bedroom. During the night, sleep eluded her, because her home's fate remained in doubt. She lifted her sore finger up into the shaft of sunlight. Sure enough, it appeared bright red and throbbed like the devil. Within hours after returning home yesterday, the fishhook puncture gained the hue of burning coals and felt equally hot. She resolved to find the appropriate poultice before her immediate journey to Blackwell. At the first minute society considered a polite hour to call, she planned to directly ask Lady Helen about her son's plans for a foundry.

Once downstairs in William's book-lined study, she pulled several medical books from the tall shelves and spread them over the polished mahogany desk. Since the wound was not serious enough to call Dr. Potts, common sense suggested she should follow Mr. Thornbury's advice and teach herself the best method to cure an infected wound.

Her housekeeper, Mrs. Richards, entered the study and handed her a note from Henry.

After a quick perusal, Elinor discovered Mr.
Thornbury had not been at home when Henry called
at Blackwell yesterday. Her handsome neighbor spent
the morning charming her by the lake, so she wasn't
surprised. Henry promised to pay a call again within
the week and make inquiries about the foundry.

She moved aside the Trafalgar memorial inkwell—
replete with weeping lion—and pulled the largest
medical book forward. After deciding to start with
"cuts," she began to read the entry when Berdy came
into the room.

He must have been experimenting with cravat
knots, because he silently struck a dramatic pose on
the Axminster carpet's center medallion of roses. Thus
staged, he lifted his chin for her approval, but his smile
faded without her immediate praise.

"Please, love. A young man in your situation
cannot support himself as a London dandy. If you
married, how would you provide for your family?"

He waved a hand in the air. "Not now. I've plenty
of time to choose a profession. I thought you'd be
excited to see m' new knot." He turned to give her a
side view. "I call it *The Circumbendibus*."

"Why do they name cravat knots? It's not as though
they are pets."

"Elli. This is important. When we go to London for
the Season and I'm seen wearing *The Circumbendibus*,
I'm convinced this knot will be even more popular than the *The Bungup*. Then all of London will
acknowledge me as a gentleman of elegance and style."

Glancing at the wide-eyed expression beaming
from his smiling face, she cherished that eager look.

It first appeared when Berdy was nine, seconds before he ran toward a dangerous horse, his arms open wide, repeating the words "horsey hug." The first of many panicked moments she experienced in the role of his mother. Now, almost nine years later, she worried she would never fulfill her late sister's last wish to guide him from adolescence into a mature, responsible man. "With that enormous bow, can you look down?" She doubted he could move anything above the cravat.

He huffed and attempted to lower his chin. He couldn't place it on his chest—the giant neckcloth blocked his forward movement—so he tilted his head to the side. "Of course, I can look down. You are… are you pressing flowers?"

"No…books are used for reading." She closed the lexicon and gave him her full attention.

"Very amusing. You know at school I'm considered a great scholar."

She examined his figure from his head to his Hessians. Today he did not dress like a scholar. He wore ivory pantaloons below an apple-green waistcoat. His curly blond locks were brushed forward in a disheveled appearance called *à la Titus*. "Scholarship is more than knowing which tailor produces the best waistcoats, and which draper sells the finest silk. Scholarship means reading books, too."

"I read books that are…thick." He picked up the biggest, turned it around, and read the spine aloud. "*Quincy's Lexicon Physico-Medicum Improved: or a Dictionary of the Terms Employed in Medicine, and in such Departments of Chemistry, Natural Philosophy, Literature, and the Arts, as are connected therewith.*" He paused to take a deep breath. "That title is so long, I must have learnt something already."

She grinned. "William admired *Quincy's Lexicon* and said the book is a dazzling piece of scholarship. It was written in the last century and still contains important information, but William loved to laugh at the silly entries that somehow escaped revision. Of course, medical knowledge is much more advanced nowadays." She got up from the desk and sat on the large-cushioned chair by the arched Gothic windows. Relieved the subject of conversation changed from frivolous cravats to books, she picked up her needlework.

Berdy cleared his throat in obvious preparation to read. "A medical dictionary." He opened the book to a random page. "Let's see what it says... *Breasts, in men they are very small, and chiefly for ornament.*" He glanced at his chest. "Very true. Let's try another." He flipped the pages. "*Generation, Parts of, proper to Women...*" Shaking his head, he stopped reading aloud for a couple of seconds. "Evidently this female feature *affords a great deal of delight.* Hmm, I don't understand that entry. Perhaps I should start at the beginning." Turning back to the front, he examined each page. "*Acephalos. This is applied to monsters born without heads, of which there have been instances.*" He looked up at her. "All of these medical terms are confusing. I think I'll stick to reading the entries on diseases." He read silently for several seconds. "*Acne, a small pustule which arises usually about the time that the body is in full vigor.* No! I understand that disease." He pointed to his cheek. "I have acne.

It must be so, because I have a pustule, and I am in full vigor."

She kept her head down. "You are not full of vinegar."

"This is important information for a fellow to know. Silly rhymes are not necessary."

Her chest constricted as she indulged in a favorite memory of William's response to one of her silly rhymes. He once asked, "How about a rhyme for the word orange?" While she had searched for an answer, his expression softened before he swept her into his arms and twirled her around. She answered, "Porange, gorange, torange," in a whoosh of held breath and giggles. Her fists gently pounded his chest. He replied, "Fooled you, there is no rhyme for orange." With a glorious smile, he dropped his head back and rolling laughter overcame him. That's why she still played her rhyming game; with every silly rhyme she could hear William's laugh.

"What is the next disease? *Acor, it is sometimes used to express that sourness in the stomach contracted by indigestion, and from whence flatulencies and acid belching arise.* No!" He slapped the page. "Last week, I suffered Acor after eating mutton pie, remember?" Lines of concern appeared on his forehead, and he quickly turned the page. "I have Agheustia. I have Aglutitio. Without doubt I have Agonia."

"Berdy, please."

"Elli. I have every disease mentioned so far, and I'm not out of the *A*'s. At this rate, by the time I reach the *D*'s, I'll be—*D*—for dead."

Tossing her needlework aside, she leaped up and

snapped the book shut. "There, a simple cure. Now you will have to live." She smiled like a mother witnessing the shock on her baby's face after his first failure to stand. "If you have every disease in the book, it must be a great comfort to know you cannot get any sicker than you are today." She gave him a rocking hug. "With your good nature, I'm certain you will live for a long time."

"I'll certainly do m' best to live." He covered his cravat knot with his hand to protect the folds from her hug. "But if I am called to Edinburgh, I must let the physicians give m' diseases a poke or two for the betterment of mankind."

She ruffled his hair. "Are you interested in the practice of medicine? Maybe a physician would be a good profession for you to consider, if life in the church doesn't suit your tastes. Next week, when Dr. Potts and his daughter come to dine, we can discuss medicine as a possible living."

He pulled away from her embrace and restored the random curly locks framing his face in the Venetian looking glass. "You promised me we would live in London for the Season, before I choose my living. Come to think of it, maybe I'll marry well and won't need a profession to become a gentleman of great consequence."

She exhaled a long here-we-go-again sigh. His ever-changing expectations of future success caused her many restless nights. At seventeen, he could support himself on his living of one hundred pounds, complemented by whatever winnings his father sent when his purse strings were loosened by guilt. But this amount would never support a large family. So she could be a desperate mother and parade him around local young ladies, fishing for a sizable dowry, or steer him into a profession. One glance at the apple-green waistcoat confirmed the wiser choice was to find him a suitable living. "Please, love, gamesters like your father don't win forever. Someday your additional funds might be cut off. You must obtain a profession to support yourself and not depend upon marriage."

He turned sideways to check the hair on the back of his head in the looking glass above the fireplace. "Yes, but if I marry well, I won't be stuck in some boring profession. I'll be able to use my wife's fortune to become a gentleman of leisure and style." He tucked and untucked a single curl in front of his right ear.

The expected professions for an impoverished gentleman included the army, navy, church, or law. The first two would take him far from Cheshire, so they were out of the question. Instead, she would ask Henry to recommend law, and Dr. Potts to suggest suitable positions in medicine.

She silently tallied all the other gentlemen of her acquaintance, who might be of assistance, when Mr. Thornbury came to mind. His interests were varied and included the construction of canals, turnpikes, and manufactories. He was also rumored to be financially successful in the City on the exchange. But somehow she didn't trust him enough to give an impressionable young man practical advice. Even if his handbook was written solely for the amusement of gentlemen in their London clubs, the vulgarity of the presumed content brought his taste into question. So while she couldn't wait to watch all of her female friends fall under the spell of his masculine charm, she certainly did not want Berdy to emulate his successful flirting. Mr. Thornbury was therefore out of the question. "I have asked Henry to show you around the magistrate's offices sometime next week. Please, you must refrain from using the word 'boring' in his presence. And remember, a respectable occupation will give you options, and options are always a good idea."

"Yes, yes, don't worry. Once I spend the Season in London, I'm confident m' future will be a great success." He resumed reading the lexicon.

Returning to William's chair, she let her restless gaze move to the tall bookshelves before it continued upward to the white plasterwork of the ornate Gothic ceiling. Her sight locked on a line of the ceiling's tracery. She followed the line under and over the other plaster lines until its path became lost in a jumbled Celtic knot.

She might lose Berdy after his stay in London. He'd fall in love, marry, and reside in the City close to his wife's family. Since she would always remain at Pinnacles, close to her memories of William, she feared her future might be spent in isolation. She'd return to endless hours of "keeping busy" or staring outside at the rose garden. Doing her best to fight overwhelming melancholy whenever she spotted a drooping rose, its petals gone and the bud bare with age.

Berdy must have noticed her despondency, because he strode over and gave her a peck on the cheek. "I'm sure you'll be delighted with m' new surprise. Guess what it is?"

She used the small amount of her remaining optimism to grin.

"I knew you would never guess my surprise. It's a new *dandy horse*."

"What!" She clutched his arm. "Pedestrian curricles are dangerous."

"No, that flummery is just a rumor. I mean, what is the worst that could happen?"

Now she could no longer manage even a grin. "You might be killed." The words escaped in an unsteady whisper.

"Oh, please forgive me." He swiftly hugged her. "I did not mean to distress you with old memories. Besides, the dandy horse is not a real horse, so it won't behave like an unpredictable brute that can kill a fellow. The dandy horse is a *machine*. And gentlemen like m'self can control machines."

෴

Once Berdy finished lunch, he fled the house in the direction of the village to retrieve his dandy horse. Custom-made to his exact dimensions by Mr. Rosson of London, the vehicle failed to arrive yesterday, so he knew it would arrive on today's mail coach.

A brisk wind blew grim clouds overhead, but he believed providence would not let it rain until he had a chance to ride his new pedestrian curricle. By the time he reached the inn, the coach had arrived, and a large box bearing his name rested on the courtyard's cobblestones.

For two agonizing hours, he paced to and fro while Smithy assembled his machine. Then the most technological conveyance made for a single gentleman—a gleaming yellow-and-black dandy horse—beckoned him to mount. The machine had two large in-line wheels, with the front wheel and attached handlebar pivoted for steering. The lucky owner straddled the center bar and sat upon a leather seat. He then propelled himself forward using his feet, rather like running while sitting down. Not even the largest stallion could compete with this two-wheeled machine as fashionable transport. The dandy horse was not a mere animal, but a machine crafted by man and made for gentlemen like him—a man who appreciated style and machinery.

After an hour of practice, during which the faces of the inn's patrons turned from pointed curiosity to stifled merriment, he became confident in his control of the steering bar to turn the front wheel in the direction of home.

The return trip to Pinnacles proved more difficult than traveling the paved pathways of town. He feared the deep ruts on the road home made him look less than elegant. Luckily, he would not have this problem when he rode the smooth streets of London.

Minutes later, he suffered a small accident accompanied by a great deal of pain, the type of pain felt only by men. Of course, Mrs. Symthe happened to walk by as he was going to grab—but he refrained and gave her an innocent smile.

Mrs. Symthe quickened her pace toward town.

Once he reached the road along the Blackwell estate, he noticed a tall, unknown gentleman on a dappled gray and decided here was his chance to impress a typical appreciative bystander. No doubt one similar to admirers he might find in London. So he lengthened his stride—to present a clean line from his hip to his toe—and looked up to wave. "Ho-ho." The wind blew the ends of his cravat over his eyes. Unable to see the road in front of him, he hit a rock. "Ho-ho-up!" he yelled, catapulting over his dandy horse. Both man and machine flew into the air and landed with a heavy thunk.

Five

EARLY THE FOLLOWING MORNING, ELINOR STOOD before Blackwell's giant front door and repeatedly slammed the brass lion knocker.

The Thornburys' butler, Rowbottom, greeted her, a twinkle in his steel-blue eyes. He then swung the door wide and stepped aside for her to enter.

"Good morning, Rowbottom. How is Berdy today?" After Berdy's accident, Mr. Thornbury had taken him to Blackwell and called the local surgeon. Later that afternoon, he also informed her friend, Dr. Potts, and invited him to visit. The doctor assured her Berdy's injury was nothing more than a bad sprain and perhaps a fracture of a small bone in his foot. But today Elinor worried if Dr. Potts might have been wrong, and Berdy had a more serious injury. What if his injury had festered overnight, and her cherished nephew denied the chance to reach manhood? An active imagination: the bane of all mothers.

Rowbottom took her grass-colored shawl, straw bonnet, and buff kid gloves. "Mr. Deane is well, and you will be delighted to hear he has improved since yesterday. He ate a significant breakfast and is now sleeping. I understand from Mr. Thornbury that Dr. Potts is expected here sometime this morning."

"Oh, I don't wish to disturb him, but I must take a peek though. Is that all right?"

Rowbottom nodded, a smile of approval crossing his once handsome, aquiline face. He led her upstairs and opened the sickroom door.

Berdy was indeed asleep, and even from across the room, she could see a healthy blush upon his cheeks. Now with Berdy safe and her anxieties lessened, she resolved to find Mr. Thornbury. Yesterday, she lacked the presence of mind to adequately thank him for Berdy's rescue, so today she must give him proper thanks. He saved a young man, fetched the surgeon, then opened his home to strangers. One expected no less from an English gentleman, so she doubted he would repeat his forward behavior again.

Maybe Henry and society had misjudged him? In the excitement of believing the man to be a scoundrel, they failed to give him appropriate credit for his actions that revealed a heroic character. All this famous rake business might be an exaggeration arising from his inherently droll conversation and outrageous charm. Two of her friends had expressed doubts about the mistress rumors, as well. So if the right moment arose—she did not want to offend him—she would ask about the foundry rumor. She even took precautions and wore the snake bracelet today, though she probably would not need its painful pinch. "Is Mr. Thornbury at home, Rowbottom?"

Rowbottom indicated his employer was engaged in pistol practice on the lawn. Walking in the measured slowness appropriate in a good butler, he led her to Blackwell's vast library and swung open the double doors.

Elinor stepped out onto a stone terrace with a commanding view of the Cheshire countryside on a sunny summer's day. White cotton clouds marched overhead in unison with their dark shadows rolling across undulating emerald fields. The faint sounds of cowbells rang in the distance. Her spirits lightened from the stunning prospect before her.

Rowbottom announced her, nodded respectfully, and returned to the house.

Mr. Thornbury held a pistol up, aimed in the direction of a straw target, and turned his head upon her approach. His wine-colored coat, gray wool trousers, and a shirt the color of the richest cream gave him a casual air.

By now she knew him well enough to realize the dark forelock covering one eye was habitual. He probably had no idea that—for some unexplained reason—the sight made her throat dry. "Good day," she called. "I understand Berdy had a good night?"

He grinned broadly. "Welcome, Mrs. Colton. Yes, you will be pleased with your nephew's improvement. Dr. Potts is expected here sometime soon, so we'll get a report on his condition."

"I'm delighted to hear that. I also wish to thank you for—"

He fired the pistol.

She leaned sideways to get a clear view but saw no

evidence of a hit. "If you had taken the time to aim, you might have hit the target."

"I think you'll find that shot satisfactory," he countered in the barely perceptible tone of an affronted male.

Was he boasting? She marched toward the target placed a hundred feet away, and he followed. Once she drew near, she discovered his shot had hit dead center. "Why, you did aim." She turned to face him. "You have an excellent eye."

For a brief second his radiant smile appeared. "Yes, and not only for targets."

The all-too-familiar heat from his rakish innuendo began to simmer on her cheeks. She gulped and found her throat dry. *Heavens*. She told herself she was safe from his palpable charms, because she wore her snake bracelet. Not the best of her ideas, but it was her *only* idea. "May I take a shot?"

"You can shoot? When did pistol practice eclipse singing as a feminine accomplishment?"

"When my father didn't have a son. With no son to teach manly pursuits, he taught me instead. Unfortunately, there are unpleasant consequences of my unique upbringing. I'm very poor at needlework, you see."

"Regrettable tragedy." He rubbed his chin. "Explains your fondness for coarse fishing. Although you must possess some of the requisite accomplishments." He lazily surveyed her. "Can you sing?"

"Ah, a common question." She flashed him a sly smile. "When you squeeze a frog, I can sing the exact tune."

He chuckled. "Sounds harmonious. Can you play?"

"After you squeeze the frog, his arms stiffly shoot out—"

"Your technique?"

"Precisely."

He laughed freely, a happy, rumbling sound.

She laughed too, and they started back to the terrace. The day was warm, calm, and a bird chattered somewhere close. Gazing up at the rear of Blackwell Hall, she delighted in the house's situation. All it needed was a garden to complement the scenery. "I find it strange the back of the house has just a lawn and lacks a garden. Imagine how beautiful a formal rose garden would look. In the evening, you could sit on a willow bench while enjoying the perfume of China roses warmed by the day's sun. Do you know why no formal gardens were planted?"

"No," he replied, his arms moving in a slight swing as they walked back uphill. "Mother has yet to mention the landscape. She is interested only in new furniture and her tasty weeds."

"Pardon?" She caught the laughter playing in the corner of his eyes.

"Pineapples. Mother is making use of the pinery glasshouse to grow pineapples."

"Oh." Her arms swung in a rhythm matching his, so she clasped her hands behind her back. "Mr. Thornbury, I cannot thank you enough for your hospitality while Berdy recovers at Blackwell."

He halted too and appeared to be considering his next words.

She faced him directly. "Also, I cannot forget your

quick actions immediately after the accident." She unclasped her hands. "When you rescued Berdy and brought him here, I mean. I'd hate to think of the outcome had I found him by myself."

"I'm glad he's feeling better. No thanks are necessary." He paused. "I understand you are rearing your nephew."

"Yes, ever since my sister's death. She had hopes of him entering the clergy, rather than following in his father's footsteps and becoming a gamester."

"His father is Mr. Ralph Deane?"

"Yes, are you acquainted with him?"

He stared at his boots. "Not well. A passing acquaintance. I've seen him gaming at Brook's. Still, I'm surprised he's not raising his son."

"My sister married for love and discovered later that her fortune had more to do with Mr. Deane's reasons to wed. Once she was with child, he abandoned her on a small estate in Yorkshire and returned to his life in London. Before she died, she asked me to care for Berdy. I cannot tell you how surprised I was when Mr. Deane appeared delighted to be spared the trouble of a child about his house. He even called Berdy *baggage* once."

She leaned over to restore the dandelion she had just trampled to its upright position. "Recently, I rather foolishly agreed Berdy could attend the Season in Town before he settles upon a profession. I hope his notion of being a dandy will tire when he discovers he is not the center of attention. I also fear his father leading him into the ways of a gamester, but thankfully Mr. Deane has shown no interest in him."

"What does young Deane hope to accomplish in Town?"

"What do all seventeen-year-old gentlemen desire in London? Gain attention? Find a rich wife?"

The beginning of a smile teased his lips. "Let's see… at seventeen, I thought about females and then more females, and I never considered marriage. That's what I wanted at seventeen. It infuriated my father." He bent sideways to peer directly at her face. "Are you shocked?"

She laughed. "No, although now I understand why people call you a rake."

He gazed down at his boots again, the smile gone. "Please never repeat that word in my mother's company."

"Oh," she cried, brushing her arm. "Something bit me." She examined the small red spot closely. "I fear the creature may have taken some blood—a flea?" She rubbed her arm vigorously, a gesture that attracted his scrutiny.

"A flea?" he said, his lighthearted tone restored. "Reminds me of a Donne poem of the same name. Do you like poetry? I do, and I find Donne refreshingly honest in a veiled sort of way." With a mischievous grin, he began to recite aloud in a deep, carrying voice:

> *Mark but this flea, and mark in this,*
> *How little that which thou deniest me is;*
> *Me it sucked first, and now sucks thee,*
> *And in this flea our two bloods mingled be—*

"Oh!" She gaped, heat claiming her cheeks. Only

a *bona fide* rake would know Donne's metaphor of improper relations.

"I see you are familiar with that poem. Your blush gives you away. As neighbors, I hope in the future we can become friends and discuss our favorite poems. I look forward to that." He grinned, his blue eyes alight.

Her heartbeat started to climb from his all-too-obvious charm, so she needed the snake now. Under the pretext of brushing off another flea, she pushed the bracelet up her arm. Several of the reticulated scales dug into her skin. She glanced at Mr. Thornbury to discover if the snake's painful pinch rendered his rakish charms ineffective and found her wits remained intact.

The bracelet worked. *Thank heavens.*

"Tell me. Why does a respectable lady such as yourself know Donne's wicked poetry?"

"My husband enjoyed Donne and owned a complete collection of his works."

His devilish grin appeared. "The reverend enjoyed naughty poetry?"

"No—no, of course not." A blush instantly claimed every inch of her skin. "He told me he read only the sermons—the book was for Donne's sermons—he spoke on Sundays—needed sermons—heavens." She frowned in irritation, because he accused William of enjoying vulgar poetry any sensible person would ignore.

"That still doesn't explain why *you* know the elegies."

Her mind blanked. "I—I like to read." With her wits flown, she glared at the traitorous bracelet. The snake hissed in silent mockery at her defeat.

"Ah, don't we all." His lazy grin appeared.

"However, it's unusual you understand the meaning behind the wicked verse." He paused, watching her. "Let me immediately apologize for upsetting you. In fact, I also owe you an apology for my behavior at the lake. No disrespect was intended in either case. Please believe me." He stared at his boots.

Unsure of the reasons that prompted these apologies, she decided not to inquire further. "Um…an apology is not needed. I know you meant no disrespect. Your manners are just open and naturally charming."

He examined her expression carefully. "Thank you." He cleared his throat—twice. "Mrs. Colton, may I speak to you about an opportunity that would benefit us both?" His speech quickened. "One of the improvements I plan at Blackwell is to build a foundry for the manufacture of strong-steam engines. To be profitable, my raw material and finished engines must be transported at a low cost. My proposition for you is to grant me a lease to your property on the riverbank, so my engines can travel to market via the river. For the particulars, such as the amount paid to you, my man of business can meet with your man. This plan will be to your benefit by providing a handsome income. What do you say?"

She stood speechless. *The rumor was true.* He thought a foundry would benefit her. "No, I don't want an industrial chimney near my property, nor do I need the income. You are familiar with Manchester. People in the city can go for days without seeing the sun, and the smoke damages everything. Think of my home—my home. I know it sounds silly, but you must have seen the destruction soot can cause. I heard a rumor you planned to build a foundry, but I hoped it was a false one."

He stepped backward; his brow furrowed. "You're mistaken, madam. The foundry would be only a small one, with a modest number of steam-hammers. The smoke would not resemble Manchester's in any way. Besides, the wind is usually from the north, so I doubt soot would blow anywhere near enough to damage your house."

"Can't you build your foundry elsewhere?"

"No. The location is the only place on my property close to economical transportation for the raw materials and shipping the engines. Please reconsider."

"Sir, I must refuse. I fear my home's destruct—"

"No? But we would both profit."

"Not if I have to sacrifice my home. It is all that remains… I cannot take that chance."

An uneasy silence ensued. Their stares held until he began to fidget like a teakettle demanding action. "You overestimate the smoke." He slapped his thigh. "Promise me you will consider it."

"No," she said in a steadfast voice, hoping he would drop the distasteful subject forever.

"No?" He took a quick step forward until a mere inch separated them. "Not even at a later date reconsider your neighbor's wishes?"

Her heartbeat escalated. With no desire to observe his expression, she focused on his snowy cravat rising and falling with each breath. They stilled for what seemed like minutes. She moved first when her bracelet chose this—of all times—to fall to her wrist. Using a single move, she shoved the ornament far up her arm until it pinched her skin and remained in place.

Mr. Thornbury shifted his position to stare at the golden snake.

She felt it slipping again, but did not dare move.

The bracelet fell.

"Please, madam. I appeal to your generosity and request you visit a similar low-pressure steam engine in person to witness the smoke." He reached out until one hand held hers, while his other hand enclosed the offending bracelet. Using his warm palm, he pushed the snake up her forearm. When it easily stopped, he inhaled sharply. "Come with me to see the smoke from a similar working chimney at a nearby coal mine, yes?"

"No." She held her breath.

"Allow me." He forced the bracelet higher with a sudden push.

"Oh!" She stared at his mouth, attempting to calm her thoughts.

His chest rose from ragged breaths, and she felt the moisture he exhaled on her forehead. "Don't deny me," he whispered. His focus returned to the golden band cinching her upper arm, while his deft fingers surrounded the bracelet. He rocked it back and forth for several moments until she was breathing hard. Wrapping his forefinger under the gilt circle, he caught her gaze and slowly pulled the band down to her wrist. Her skin tingled along every inch from his touch. They stood for minutes, both staring at the gold snake resting around her wrist.

She tried to stop her rapid pants. The scoundrel

was trying to influence her with disingenuous, rakish charm. That realization didn't help her, because she remained fixed in place regardless.

"No?" he asked again in a rough whisper, raising her hand close to his lips. He didn't kiss her, but his breath warmed her fingers.

She became dizzy, expecting her legs to collapse.

"No? The foundry will help others, provide employment."

Speech eluded her. His fervent blue gaze forced away all semblance of reason.

He brushed his lips across her knuckles, while the stare from those sky-blue eyes never left her face. Then a gentleman's kiss graced the top of her hand before he turned her palm up and leisurely kissed its center.

Her control of the situation escaped, and she feared her insides might boil. *Going mad? Possible. Fainting? Certain.*

He wore the wicked smile of a male certain he would succeed. Still holding her hand, he pulled it behind him and took a step forward to close the distance between them.

She stood dazed, unable to move, her breasts touching his waistcoat. All she could think of was a simple chant: do not faint, do not faint, do not faint.

"No?" he repeated in a quiet, rumbling baritone. "Consider my request, or consider the consequences."

She raised her hand to his chest to push him away, but instead her palm traveled over his coat's rough surface and clutched his wool lapel.

He must have taken this gesture as a "yes," because he leaned forward and kissed her neck. The slow caress of his lips led her into a familiar current, where she instinctively flowed with the tide. He cupped her backside and pressed her against his solid frame, while his hot breath warmed her sensitive neck.

Summing up Herculean strength, she pulled herself out of the sensuous daze he created. All she had to do was repeat that he was a true rake and reaffirm that William would forever remain her only love. Armed with this truth, she found the will to push him away.

"Please," he said, "will you consider my offer?"

"My turn to use the word." She smiled with a certain measure of pride. "No."

Now *he* gaped. Half a minute passed before he chuckled and planted a swift kiss on her cheek. "I will explain the advantages of my plan later. You win... but only for now."

Dr. Potts shouted, "Sir!"

Startled, they both took a quick step backwards to put distance between them.

Dr. Potts strode up and for a moment remained silent, his face reddening. A tall widower with a military bearing and his short hair styled *à la Brutus*, he straightened his posture even more rigid than usual. The doctor struggled to contain his words. In rushed speech, he explained that he had examined Berdy, found the boy well, and offered to immediately escort her home.

"I will remain at Blackwell, thank you," she said. "But I'll see you off. I would like to hear more about Berdy's condition." She joined the doctor, and they started to walk toward the house.

Mr. Thornbury remained behind, unmoving.

Dr. Potts's face had become scarlet. "I witnessed that scoundrel kiss you. Shall I go back now and give the villain a few strong words? Call the man out?"

"Please, no, not today."

"The swine." Dr. Potts tugged on the bottom of his waistcoat. "Has he made advances before this? You know I have your best interests at heart. In the future, I will accompany you when you speak to him. Tomorrow I will join you bright and early. Don't worry. I will protect you."

"Thank you." Since she had failed twice to control her response to Mr. Thornbury's seductive manners, and the bracelet failed to preserve her wits, in the future she must speak with him only in the company of one of her knights, Dr. Potts or Henry. While grateful for the doctor's offer, she decided it would be best to ask Henry to explain to Mr. Thornbury why she could never sign his lease.

Dr. Potts mumbled on about his efforts on behalf of Berdy and reassured her of the young man's eventual recovery.

Thankfully, he needed no reply. She barely understood him anyway, because there was a buzzing in her ears. What ailed her she didn't want to consider, much less look up in a book. She turned to catch a final glimpse of Mr. Thornbury.

That gentleman held his arm high in farewell and in a raised voice said, "In regard to my handbook, we've read chapter one, and today we finished chapter two. I promise you even greater pleasure when we read *chapter three*."

Six

ON THE FOLLOWING DAY, ROSS ENTERED BLACKWELL'S stables to admire his new filly, Charybdis. Purchased using the profits from his handbook, the horse was his sole self-extravagance, an equine vision in jet black. Even in the brightest sun, her eyes, coat, hooves, and mane appeared a uniform black and could be differentiated only by texture. Her heart, too, was all you would expect in a two-year-old filly—fearless and fun. He pictured the races she'd win one day, and the admiration to follow. Stroking her soft muzzle, he swiftly kissed her firm cheek.

. As he stared into her fathomless black eye, his mind strayed to his dream of the previous night. *Naked*. He dreamt a sweltering red fog swirled around Mrs. Colton as she opened her arms and skipped toward him—laughing and naked. He tried to capture her, but she spun and disappeared into the boiling fog. He chased her, only to find her bending over with her pert, round backside offered to him. The thick fog seared his ankles before it rose to blind him. He reached out, and his hands found her rear, but upon his touch, together they went up in flames.

Females. Last thing he needed was unsettling, carnal dreams.

His gaze traveled to the stable yard outside. A light rain transformed the yard into a hazy mist. He must ask Lucy's father to let them marry soon. That way he could escape this damn lust, and merry widows with ample backsides would no longer beckon from within his dreams.

Females. If only he knew the name of Mrs. Colton's man of business. Then *his* man could discuss terms with *her* man, and no distracting backsides or dimples would intrude upon the negotiations. He congratulated himself upon his clear understanding of commerce. Men dealing with men always ensured success. So with a newfound confidence that he would eventually change the widow's mind, he held his filly's rear leg up to inspect her new shoes.

Ten minutes later, Rowbottom stepped inside the stable doors to announce the arrival of a Mr. Henry Browne and a Mr. Mabbs.

Ross straightened and turned to greet the gentleman. Browne was a handsome man and appeared prosperous. Yet he projected a stiff manner, in all likelihood due to his overstarched cravat and tight gold brocade waistcoat. While Mabbs wore the serviceable brown attire of a tradesman, his less than straight nose indicated a possible pugilist.

Charybdis snorted.

The sound halted the men's approach.

Browne stood with the general air of a man who

did not brook opposition and spoke first. "Mr. Thornbury, may I present myself. My name is Henry Browne of Gracehall, a local attorney. I am your neighbor to the south by the Holiday farm. This is Mr. Mabbs, the owner of the large cattle herd to the southwest of your lake."

Ross never expected a morning call this early, but perchance the men were fellow sportsmen. "Welcome to Blackwell, Mr. Browne, Mr. Mabbs. Since entering the county, I plan to call upon all of my neighbors, but familiarizing myself with the estate has kept me busy. I've taken possession only within the last year, so there is a great deal of deferred business to address. Are you perchance sporting men? Do you shoot?"

"No, sir," Mabbs said, shuffling his feet and appearing discomfited by the invitation.

A fly buzzed past Browne's nose, and he waved his right hand in front of his face. "No, I, too, rarely have time for such trivial pursuits."

Ross raised an eyebrow and leaned against the stall. "Are you gentlemen here on business, or is this a social call?"

Browne glanced around the stables. Leaning on a support post with a similar casual air, he jerked his elbow close to his chest, like the post was a column of fire, before carefully brushing his coat sleeve. "I guess you would call it a matter of business. Since Deane's accident, you've probably made the acquaintance of Mrs. Colton. Did she mention the rumor of great concern to our little community here?"

Ross started, unsure of the meaning behind Browne's question. "I understand there have been many rumors."

"It is our understanding you intend to construct a steam engine manufactory on your estate near the river."

"And?"

"And we want to know if it is true."

"Why?" He wondered why these gentlemen felt it necessary to make Mrs. Colton's concerns their business.

"So we can put a stop to it, of course." Browne's reply sounded like the slow intonation used to teach children one plus one equals two. "We don't want our rivers befouled, and if that isn't bad enough, the smoke emitted by your foundry has a pernicious effect upon healthy living no gentleman could be unaware of."

Charybdis pranced restlessly, loudly bumping the stall with her rear flank.

Ross moved to stroke his filly's quivering neck. "Shh." He waited until the horse calmed before he replied. "Perhaps you've traveled far, Mr. Browne, but in England a gentleman still has a right to use his property as he sees fit."

Browne's eyes widened before narrowing into slits. "I grant you have the right to build a foundry, but you have no right to foul the river or darken our homes with soot." He took a quick step forward. "Clean water is *publici juris*—"

"You are a good attorney, sir. Since your words make the law incomprehensible."

Mabbs snickered.

"Yes, and because I am a good attorney, I recommend you heed my advice. I gather you are determined to build this foundry?"

Ross shoved his fists into the bottom of his coat pockets. "Yes. Nuisance from either smoke or effluent into the river is not likely from the operation of our foundry. Mrs. Colton's home will not be destroyed by smoke. The house is too far away from the proposed chimney, and the wind too strong." Ross believed her house would not be affected, except for, at the very worst, a slight haze when the wind was just right. Why then did this stubborn widow believe her home would be destroyed?

"You don't know that for sure," Browne said.

"You don't know that for sure," parroted Mabbs.

"Then my engineers must all be wrong. You gentlemen are aware the foundry will provide jobs? Both the profits and the employment created will benefit the entire county."

Browne pointed his finger. "I tell you nobody will care if workers benefit. We do not want coarse, unlettered, and unkempt workers in our rural community."

Mabbs widened his eyes. "Steady on."

"I'll wager the workers care," Ross replied.

"Now, Mr. Browne," Mabbs said, "Our concerns are about the smoke and turning our water foul, nothing more."

Browne turned to Mabbs. "Yes, of course. If you would please excuse us, Mr. Mabbs. I have some private matters to discuss with Mr. Thornbury."

Mabbs hesitated and appeared to weigh the situation. "As you wish, sir. I came to express my opinion in regard to the water, and I have. I take my leave of you now. Mr. Thornbury, thank you for hearing my concerns." He bowed. "Gentlemen." Mabbs left the stables.

"I warn you." Browne shook his finger at Ross. "There will be consequences of your recklessness. The gentry in this vicinity will *not* be pleased. Moreover, your neighbors have vowed to stop construction of the foundry by any means possible. It also goes without saying that you will be shunned by decent society. Indeed, invitations have already been withheld because of your famed libertine propensities expressed in that handbook of yours—scandalous— just scandalous."

"Have you actually read this scandalous handbook, Mr. Browne?"

"Of course not. I never read vulgar books. I understand from many in the local society that the book is scandalous."

"The local lending library has a copy then?"

"You insult our library, sir," Browne replied.

Ross reached the limits of his patience. The man's conversation consisted of insults and veiled threats. Either Browne would have to leave, or he would. "Shunned by society and nibbled by ducks. I worry about both."

Browne took another step toward Ross, his wide stance like a boxer ready to unleash a facer. "You leave me no choice. On behalf of Mrs. Colton, I will indict you at the quarter sessions for nuisance."

"Indict!" Ross stepped toward Browne. "Nibbled by ducks *and* indicted for nuisance, very troublesome. I'm surprised Mrs. Colton approves of your suit." He paused. "Or did she suggest it? Still, the foundry is not even built yet. How can you indict for nuisance?"

"Well…I know it *will* become a nuisance. Despite

what your engineers tell you. So I will indict on the first day of operation." Mr. Browne tugged on his waistcoat again. "One more matter of business. I've been told Mrs. Colton and her nephew are residing under your roof at present."

"Yes, young Deane damaged his foot and will remain at Blackwell until he recovers." Ross wanted this man to leave his company before his civility escaped him entirely. He strolled toward the stable doors hoping Browne would follow.

Browne shuffled after him. "I must make a matter of some delicacy understood. Since I am Mrs. Colton's nearest relative, she is under my protection. Since the death of her husband, I myself provide for her needs and dispense the objective male guidance all females require. She now depends upon me as she would a husband, and shows regard for my opinion in all matters."

Ross turned to stare at him and met a defiant look from narrowed eyes. If Browne was Mrs. Colton's man of business, his plans would be damned forever, and the foundry lost. "I understand you well, sir. Although your relationship to Mrs. Colton is not my concern." He never anticipated this topic of conversation, and it kept him from having Browne immediately escorted off of his property. He'd seen Mrs. Colton at the assembly with several gentlemen, but he did not recall her in Browne's company. His mother had mentioned something about their possible engagement, but he failed to remember her precise words.

Browne huffed. "You, sir, are an unmarried

gentleman of a…certain foul reputation, and Mrs. Colton is a widow young enough to require protection. Her residence here without a chaperone may compromise her reputation."

"Compromise her reputation? You—"

Charybdis kicked a board lining her stall with a resounding crack.

Ross strode back to quiet her and compose himself. It seemed ironic now that he had once expected to be free of unfounded rumors and find peace in the countryside. "You are wrong, sir. Mrs. Colton spends only the day here, and she has company with her, as my mother is in residence. Even Deane is old enough to be a competent chaperone. Your widow holds no interest for me except as a neighbor." He turned his back to Browne, grabbed a brush, and eased his frustration by grooming Charybdis.

"There has been talk already," Browne said. "I recommend, for her sake, you avoid being seen in her company. She suffered greatly from the seclusion required of mourning, and it is my duty to prevent further isolation due to some reckless scandal of your making."

Ross stilled his hand, the brush resting on Charybdis.

Rowbottom then entered the stables to announce Mrs. Colton's arrival. He also indicated that she went immediately upstairs to check on her nephew.

"Ah, Rowbottom, please escort Mr. Browne to Mr. Deane's room," Ross said.

Browne glared at him first before following the butler out of the stables.

Once Browne left, Ross resisted the urge to jump

up and make a fresh attempt to change Mrs. Colton's mind in regard to the lease. Before he approached her again, he'd have to regain his composure. Then think of a new plan or better enticement to win her consent. Anyhow, yesterday's refusal still stung. He expected her to agree to his proposal, and had even apologized for his previous behavior, so there should have been no impediment to his request. One glance at that taunting dimple and the pink flesh swelling around that insufferable snake, and his reason had become ambushed by lust. As a result, he'd strayed from the "proper gentleman's" handbook and returned to his old ways of dealing with females. In the immediate future, it would be best to avoid her like a contagion, until he could lure her into reconsidering his proposal, or perhaps persuade her to visit a working steam engine to witness the smoke for herself. So for the next couple of days, he resolved to visit the sickroom only after she had left. Besides, this morning he could not tolerate failure at the hands of a dimple.

Ross threw the brush into a corner of the stall.

Now he must instruct his man of business to investigate nuisance law. The Earl of Northwold had an iron foundry to the east, close to the Derbyshire border, so there had to be precedent. He would also instruct his man to examine the cost of building a canal or using wagons to haul materials to the turnpike. He sighed, shook his head, and sat on a bale of hay. Clearly his neighbors were backward louts if they didn't understand the amazing revolution happening around them. Small, low-cost steam engines were needed for the manufacture of goods. And here around the Midlands, they had a front-row seat to witness England's industrial future.

Charybdis nudged his back.

Ross turned to pat her broad neck. "Well, pretty girl, how does a respectable gentleman negotiate business with a reluctant female, especially if it would be to her advantage? Do you know? Because I have no damn idea."

A loud snort from Charybdis answered his question.

Ross decided to learn more about Mrs. Colton's acquaintances, such as her relationship with Dr. Potts. Perhaps he might find a local man, other than Browne or Mabbs, to convince her of his lease's benefits. Then this Browne person, and whoever hired his services, could be stopped from filing a lawsuit. Nevertheless, after his forward behavior to her yesterday, he'd have to apologize—again.

Brushing horsehair off his coat, he stomped to the stable doors. That abominable Browne hinted he was a scoundrel of the worst sort toward women, and that this behavior took place with his mother nearby. Well, yes, there was that one moment where he kissed her neck, but that moment was more like an accident, really. In the future, he'd be more circumspect. This respectable behavior would put an end to his torrid dreams, as well.

Damn dream. Damn dimple. Damn kiss.

Once outside the stables, he caught the rancid smell of fresh horse dung.

What exactly did Browne mean when he said, "providing for her needs," or her "dependence upon him as a husband"? If Mrs. Colton possessed a considerable jointure, as his mother had suggested, what were her needs? The only needs that came to his mind were improper ones.

He felt his foot slide and looked down to discover he had stepped into a pile of fresh horse manure. *Hell's fire.* Lifting his shiny black boot free, he cringed at the revolting, sucking sound. He chuckled in acknowledgment of his well-deserved retribution for mentally sullying Mrs. Colton's honor. No doubt his mind was mired in the proverbial muck.

Still, Browne's assertion of providing for her needs puzzled him. Surely Browne—Mr. Proper Gentleman himself—was not suggesting immoral behavior? However, Ross acknowledged he knew very little about her. Perhaps she emulated some of London's widows and enjoyed discreetly luring the local gentlemen with her feminine arts and displays of swelling flesh—it seemed plausible. So for his mother's future happiness, he planned to watch Mrs. Colton carefully. If she betrayed any manners that strayed from those expected of a respectable minister's widow, then he might behave in the same manner and get his lease signed using a proven method. A few words alone, straight from his handbook, all delivered with a touch of charm, should be just the ticket to...*persuade* her.

Seven

THANK HEAVENS. WHEN ELINOR ARRIVED AT Blackwell four days after the accident, she found Berdy alone, the casement windows open, both curtains blown outside, and his bedcovers in a muddled heap on the floor.

"Elli. I'm glad you have come. There is so much to tell you," Berdy chirped, twirling his cravat in the air.

Even yesterday, while watching him sleep, she had wondered if morbid matter might be spreading without her knowledge. Today he appeared almost normal, with the exception of a few bruises and a cut on his nose. "Good morning, love." Rushing to his bedside, she kissed him on the cheek. "How's your foot today?" She covered him with the counterpane and tucked it under every inch of his side.

His brows puckered. "Very poorly, m' leg hurts something awful from m' foot to m' knee. But Ross was here earlier to cheer me up, and we had a serious discussion about life, you know—man to man."

"Man to man?" Since one man was a reputed rake, the other an innocent lad, she suspected, for her own peace of mind, she better not pursue the subject. "You'll be happy to hear Dr. Potts will be here soon, so he can give us a date for removing you home."

"Gad, no hurry there. Ross is very supportive. He's such a complete hand. I like the fellow. He's not at all what I expected. You know, an old museum piece." Berdy leaned over to whisper into her ear. "He wears a banyan with an open shirt around the house in the morning, so I suspect he's rather wicked."

She patted Berdy's hand and sat next to his bed. "Yes, wicked." *Heavens.* She couldn't help but imagine Mr. Thornbury in an open shirt. She was not going to think about him in an open shirt or wonder if he, like William, had that seductive little hollow in the throat. *No, she was not going to look at his throat the very minute he walked into the room.* "Considering the number of stories I've heard, he certainly is talked about by other gentlemen. Still, I want you home, under my care."

"That Ross is a great gun. Knows everything a gentleman should know, from finance to gears. Someday maybe I'll be just like him." Berdy tapped his forefinger on his cheek, apparently lost in thought. "Maybe I should become a rake? It certainly does impress other men."

"No!" Elinor jumped out of her small cane chair, knocking it over. "They're shunned by Polite Society. Please, anything but a rake." She righted the chair, sat, and smoothed out the wrinkles on her apricot-colored skirt.

He continued in a reflective tone. "I plan to meet with Father when we are in London, and I'll ask his opinion on the subject. Maybe I can be half a rake, or at least one not shunned by society. You know, a rake people only whisper about, like Ross. He is the greatest of fellows. I wish you would let him build his foundry. I mean, what's a little soot? A house is just a house. He's a neighbor, and William always said to help your neighbor, right?"

Clearly Berdy considered Mr. Thornbury a friend, so she didn't want to disappoint him by forbidding the association. Instead, she decided to carefully observe their host's behavior, before she considered him a suitable companion for her nephew. "Yes, helping your neighbor is important, but—"

After a swift knock upon the door, Dr. Potts entered the sickroom. "Good morning, Mrs. Colton, Deane. How is the patient today? Much better than yesterday, obviously." He strolled to the bedside to evaluate Berdy's temperature and pulse.

"I'm glad you're here," she said. "Berdy claims he wants to become a rake. Please warn him in private later about the personal…what it means to be a rake and why it is unsuitable." She glanced at Berdy. "Man to man."

Ignoring the immediacy in her tone, Dr. Potts completed his examination, replaced the white linen bandage, then pulled up a chair. "A rake? Why not? He will have to move to London then, since the City is the best place for a young man to make a name for himself."

She knew the doctor objected to rakes and libertines; then why didn't he condemn it outright? "Sir, you cannot honestly advise Berdy to become a rake."

The doctor flushed. "No, Polite Society cannot tolerate such behavior, but don't worry, Deane is not serious. He dresses like a dandy, not a rake. Take that monstrous cravat he invented, for example."

Berdy instantly sat upward, a wince crossing his features. "It's not monstrous. Rakes must have stunning cravats to impress the ladies. I'll ask Ross. You'll see."

Dr. Potts ignored Berdy's indignation and addressed her. "I understand Thornbury is intent upon building his foundry. As a medical man, I plan to confront him about the public health hazards."

She feared her host might be offended over any unpleasantness about his foundry's plans. Then send Berdy home prematurely, his wound not yet properly healed. "Not today, please," she said. "We can all discuss this foundry at a later date. Mr. Thornbury has gone to a lot of trouble to see to Berdy's care after the accident. I don't want to seem ungrateful for his rescue."

"Ungrateful?" The doctor scowled. "I suppose that *gesture* he made was mere gratitude then, or should I call the man out today?"

"I heard of a similar incident in regard to you and the widow Taft." She paused, shocked by her accusation. "I apologize. We can never understand another person's motive for their behavior, can we?"

"My dear Mrs. Colton," Dr. Potts said, still wearing the scowl. "Mrs. Taft is a relative, nothing more. Now let me handle Thornbury today. I've your best interests at heart. I am also pleased that you have given me the honor of being one of your confidantes. I go so far in saying that in the future I cherish—"

A knock on the door stopped Dr. Potts from completing his sentence.

"Please, not now," she whispered. The doctor and his daughter regularly dined at Pinnacles, and for the last six months he had dropped several random hints of a possible marriage between them. Perhaps he thought her loyalty to William's love would fade with time, so she might consider marriage. Since that would never happen, in the future she planned to stop the doctor's hints altogether and inform him of the impossibility of a second marriage. For the moment, she just wished he would not speak of the kiss he witnessed or mention a subject that might insult their host. "For my sake, say nothing about the foundry. We owe Mr. Thornbury thanks today."

"Yes, but don't worry. I will be here to protect you."

Mr. Thornbury entered the sickroom, greeted his guests, and strolled to the bedside.

Of course—she looked at his throat. Thankfully, a snowy white cravat covered his neck, surrounded by a lovely dark green coat with a velvet collar.

Berdy beamed and twisted around to face him.

"How's the old foot now?" Mr. Thornbury asked.

"Awful." Berdy drew everyone's attention with an overloud sigh. "Sorry, m' whole leg still throbs something fierce."

Mr. Thornbury fetched another chair. "I'm afraid you'll have to stay here for at least another week or two. Bad luck that, having to remain still. Anything you'd like, a book?"

"A book," Berdy exclaimed, glancing in Elinor's

direction. "You sound just like Elli. Lately, she's books this and books that—a regular look-it-up lady."

She gave Mr. Thornbury a wry grin. "I'm not that bad—really. I merely read about puncture…as you suggested." He winked at her, lifting her spirits. Gratitude swelled in her breast for his charitable attentions to Berdy.

"Ross, I was wondering," Berdy said, "do rakes need fashionable attire to be successful? You know, must they wear a stunning cravat to impress the ladies?"

Dr. Potts huffed. "What is your experience with the ladies? Cease this foolishness, Deane. Mr. Thornbury and I have serious adult matters to discuss." He turned his chair, so he could confront Mr. Thornbury directly. "I know Mrs. Colton objects to discussing the foundry today. But I have a responsibility as the town's physician to inform you of its dangers. Our farmers will not be pleased if you poison the water with soot-filled effluent. People like Mr. Mabbs depend upon clean water for their cattle and sheep. Can you build your foundry elsewhere on your estate? A place far from the river and Mrs. Colton's house. Perhaps—"

"Let's discuss this some other time," she said, giving the doctor a hard stare before rising to slam the window shut.

Mr. Thornbury's gaze followed her to the window and back. "At its current location, the works are far enough upstream that foul water will not be a problem to livestock."

After a minute of awkward silence, Berdy said, "Ross, surely a fine knot is the uniform of the rake."

"Berdy, please," she pleaded.

"I'm sorry to disappoint you, young man, but I am no longer a rake. When young"—Mr. Thornbury glanced at her—"I was...associated with a famous opera singer. Because we were seen together in public, I earned the title Rake. The word is overused, in my opinion, and seems to have several meanings. From behavior that is nothing more than public flirtations to more libertine propensities. So learn from my mistakes. The reputation men make in their youth— whether ill or good—follows them for a lifetime. Being a rake is a bad business all around, and that behavior can have disastrous effects upon your family. Today I get pleasure from my business endeavors. For example, our new foundry will be a success for all of its investors, provide employment, and power England into the future. I'm convinced of that. But I suppose young men will always spend their time thinking about females."

Berdy squared his shoulders. "I don't think about ladies all of the time. I think about a number of important subjects." He paused. "Subjects like knots. Success as a man must include how well a fellow ties his neckcloth."

She made no attempt to dampen his enthusiasm, since he appeared to improve in spirits minute by minute and felt happier discussing knots rather than his leg. She'd save more serious discussions about the lease to a later date.

Mr. Thornbury settled back in his chair and crossed his long legs. "Do ladies notice cravats? I thought they might glance elsewhere first."

She widened her eyes and refused to reply to his outrageous comment.

"Just a thought," Mr. Thornbury said, noticing her blush, "from recent personal experience down by the lake."

"Oh." *The nerve of the man.* Her previous glances had been spontaneous and quite normal. Should she laugh or crawl under the bed in mortification?

Berdy slapped the counterpane. "Yes, ladies notice. A man's neckcloth is everything. When I go to London, I'm sure the ladies will be impressed by m' new knot. There's no better way to achieve recognition than sartorial excellence."

"I see—a new Beau Brummell," Mr. Thornbury said. "Well, I emulate the German students I encountered on the Grand Tour and often enjoy an open shirt in private."

"An open shirt," Dr. Potts exclaimed. "What a shocking lack of propriety. I feel for your poor mother."

"I'm sure a mother who loves her son would never censure an innocent pleasure," Elinor said.

Mr. Thornbury inhaled deeply, held her gaze, then grinned.

Berdy continued without pause. "Why don't you take satisfaction in a stunning neckcloth? Have you read *Neckclothalotta*?" Berdy's features brightened. "*Neckclothalotta* illustrates many fine examples of the more challenging knots. For my current favorite, you need a high collar up to the ears and at least seven folds. It's called *The Liberator*."

"Sounds restrictive," Mr. Thornbury said.

Elinor hiccuped and furtively glanced at Dr. Potts. Unfortunately, that gentleman failed to appreciate Mr. Thornbury's humor and seemed to be formulating his next confrontation with their host.

Mr. Thornbury chuckled. "I cannot believe someone wrote a book on neckcloths. It's satire, I hope?"

"Satire?" Berdy furrowed his brow.

Dr. Potts pounded his fist on the arm of his chair. "Honestly, Deane. Mr. Thornbury and I have serious matters to discuss. Now, since you intend to proceed with your foundry, I must inform you every gentleman"—he glanced at Elinor—"womankind too, has a right to the flow of water without alteration." Dr. Potts's expectant expression appeared to seek her approval for his badly timed speech. "Here in England, my fellow physicians brought about these laws to stop the construction of privies over streams."

"Dr. Potts." She nodded in Berdy's direction, a clear hint to end this offensive discussion once and for all.

The doctor ignored her. "Let me finish. I—"

"Do you realize," Mr. Thornbury said, "the foundry will also be for the public good? At least sixty to a hundred men will be given employment. Many of our poor will find work and no longer have to depend upon the charity of our parish."

"That is of no consequence," Dr. Potts stated. "Our poor can find work if they put their minds to it." He picked up her hand. "Now don't be worried about the cost of prosecution. Mr. Mabbs, I'm sure, will help you share the costs of—"

"I insist you stop this discussion now." She yanked

her hand out of his. "We will speak of the matter at a more appropriate date." The good doctor, in her opinion, had become too presumptuous.

A tense silence followed.

She and Mr. Thornbury held each other's gaze, like old friends who could communicate their feelings with a mere glance. The empathy expressed in his eyes convinced her that he understood her exasperation created by the doctor's attacks.

"*L'Americaine*," Berdy said, reclaiming everyone's attention. "It's a favorite knot of mine. A difficult tie to get just right. First, you hold your head up and then scrunch the linen down fold by fold, like this." Berdy raised his chin and wrapped his soiled cravat around his neck. "You lower your chin thus to achieve each perfect fold." He concentrated on slowly lowering his head. "Not too fast. Your chin is not a hammer." He then took a full minute to produce one perfect crease. "The other difficulty is that, with so many folds, it takes an hour to tie."

Mr. Thornbury chuckled. "I can think of many things I'd rather do with an hour." He grinned at her. "For example…reading a good handbook."

"Oh." She coughed on purpose to mask the eruption of a spontaneous giggle.

"It's not a good idea to waste time on a knot," Mr. Thornbury continued. "You're too young to remember Viscount N. One morning he took so long to tie his cravat—he missed his own duel. Reputation ruined, of course."

"No," she said, laughing freely. He really was a complete hand.

Berdy calmly continued, "Did you know m' favorite knot is—"

"Cease!" Dr. Potts exclaimed. He jumped to his feet and yanked on the bottom of his puce waistcoat. "If you continue to speak flummery, no one will heed you. A mature gentleman must be able to converse upon every subject, but that does not include neckcloths. Now, Mr. Thornbury, perhaps you can move your foundry south."

"Dr. Potts, please stop." She stood to face him. "Enough."

"Stop? Why? After that behavior I witnessed on the lawn, do you have some understanding with this man?"

"No! Of course not. You are being offensive. Please stop."

The doctor turned to Mr. Thornbury and continued. "If you change your transportation plans to include wagonways to send your engines to market, it will lessen the adverse effects on the river. Perhaps I should make our objections known to Lady Helen. She will support our suit, I'm sure."

"I'm warning you. Leave Lady Helen out of this matter." Mr. Thornbury seemed to dampen his rising temper and spoke evenly. "Let me repeat again: the site cannot be moved. Wagonways would be difficult, because we'd have to cut through the high rock on the east side of Blackwell."

Her host's carefree smile vanished, so she tried to appease him. "That sounds expensive."

"Yes," Mr. Thornbury said. "The profits would quickly disappear in transportation costs."

She could not bear him being put upon any longer. Maybe in her panic at the thought of Pinnacles' destruction, she had been unjust. Now that she had witnessed his kind behavior toward Berdy, he seemed like a reasonable gentleman. He even warned Berdy about the ease of losing one's reputation.

As for his previous kiss on her neck, he must have been surprised by her refusal. So she decided to forgive him. She still had doubts about the foundry, but at least she could show her gratitude by agreeing to his earlier request and join him to visit a working industrial chimney. Together they would observe the amount of smoke and then come to a mutual agreement whether the soot might damage her home. "In appreciation for your efforts on Berdy's behalf, I will agree to visit a working steam engine with a similar chimney to the one you plan—if your offer still stands. This is not a formal agreement of your lease, you understand. I merely want to view the situation for myself."

Mr. Thornbury did not say anything at first. After scanning her expression, perhaps to determine if she was in earnest, his stunning smile appeared. "Thank you. I'll make the arrangements."

"I'm sure you want me to escort you, of course," the doctor said.

"No," she said with a firm voice. "Thank you, but I'm old enough that an escort is not necessary, and I don't want to take you away from your patients." Granted, she had a few doubts about whether she could resist Mr. Thornbury's charm on the journey, but if she remained steadfast, there should be no future loss of proprieties and certainly no opportunity for him to kiss her.

"Take my advice. You need an escort. Don't you understand this man wrote *The Rake's Handbook* and cannot be trusted around women?"

Berdy brightened. "Did you write a handbook, Ross? I'd dearly love to read it if it is all about how to be a rake."

"Deane, you are too young to read such a vulgar book," the doctor snapped.

Berdy sat straight in excitement. "Have you read it, sir?"

The doctor cleared his throat. "Of course." He glared at Berdy. "Well, let's just say I looked into the matter after I witnessed your aunt—"

"Now I question whether anyone in Cheshire has read it," Elinor stated.

"Is it amusing, Dr. Potts? Tell me all about it." Without a reply from the doctor, Berdy turned to Ross. "Do you have a copy of the handbook? I'd be immensely grateful if you let me borrow it."

"No, I did not think of bringing a copy here to the countryside," Mr. Thornbury stated. "I apologize."

After an awkward silence, Dr. Potts held his hand out to her. "You know my concerns. I'll take my leave now, but we will speak of this later. May I escort you home?"

Mr. Thornbury rose from his chair, headed for the door, then turned to address Berdy. "After the doctor leaves, I'll return with more cravats, so you can teach this old dog a trick or two about the perfect knot."

She smiled at him before giving her hand to the doctor in farewell. "Thank you. But I prefer to stay with Berdy while he is feeling poorly."

"Very well," the doctor said. "Deane, you and I must discuss your intentions later. Real intentions, none of this vulgar rake nonsense. Thornbury, I'll take my leave of you for the present. But unless you want to meet before the King's Bench, I suggest you stop your plans for a foundry." He bowed slightly, and Mr. Thornbury followed him out of the room.

Berdy fussed with his neckcloth in preparation for his return.

Judging from Mr. Thornbury's ability to keep Berdy from fretting over his leg, she gained confidence that he would see to Berdy's eventual recovery and amusement while he remained at Blackwell.

Berdy held up his long white cravat. "The rain after the accident must have washed out the starch. Look at this—limp—dead. A fellow can never be caught in public with a neckcloth like this."

She began to harbor guilt that the doctor's accusations had offended Mr. Thornbury. It was difficult to tell, because even after threats, his lighthearted banter remained. Mr. Thornbury's patience and charm were an admirable aspect of his manners, and she liked this side of his character. In the future she hoped they would become fast friends. The other side, the flirtatious rake side, she knew how to keep in check now—a simple, firm "no."

Mr. Thornbury returned with his arms full of white neckcloths. "My current cravat inventory is scandalous. Will these do?" He laid the neckcloths at the foot of the bed, picked up the top one, and handed it to Berdy. "Show me how to tie *L'Americaine*."

Berdy leaned forward to grab the tie. "Ow!" He

crashed back onto the pillows, the cravat pile spilling across the floor.

Mr. Thornbury, without comment, picked up the spilled neckcloths. He folded them neatly into an orderly pile on the counterpane. Pulling up the ends of his collar, he took the tie from Berdy's clinched fist. "I hope *L'Americaine* doesn't require a whale bone. I don't wear cravats with stiffeners."

Yes. She was glad she had agreed to visit a mine's chimney, a small token of thanks for his attentions to Berdy. She doubted she'd find the smoke acceptable, but that knowledge might be useful in persuading others against his foundry. He might even see the impossibility of chimneys near a residence and change his plans. The trip might also be to Berdy's advantage. The journey would give her the opportunity to appeal for his assistance in acquainting Berdy with the industrial gentlemen of the age. Gentlemen who earned livings as successful engineers, factory owners, and canal builders.

The subject of neckcloths lessened Berdy's distress, for he opened his eyes and started to speak without a grimace. "No stiffeners, lightly starched will do. Just bring the first pass around under your chin. Yes, like that. Now jut out your jaw and nod your head down to put a purposeful crease—not a vulgar crease—in the center."

"How is this?" Wearing a sly grin, Mr. Thornbury faithfully executed the young man's instructions.

Berdy tilted his head to observe the side view of Mr. Thornbury's cravat. "You want the folds to look spontaneous. Like they just fell into place. A true spontaneous effect requires a great deal of practice."

"Then why don't you tie a square knot and be done with it?" she said.

"Ladies don't know anything about neckcloths," Berdy countered.

She exchanged smiles with Mr. Thornbury, thankful for his efforts to divert Berdy's mind from his foot. "I don't see the crime in having an eschewed cravat," she said. "Sometimes a roomful of crooked cravats makes the company merrier."

Mr. Thornbury winked.

Berdy's eyes widened. "You can't be serious. A fellow can have the shiniest boots and the finest coat, but it is all for naught if he exhibits a fatal cravat."

"I agree," Mr. Thornbury said with a sham-serious expression. "If I ever presented a fatal cravat in public, guilty conscience would force me to avoid society." He pivoted to face her. A twinkle of glee shone in his blue eyes as he repeatedly lifted an eyebrow mockingly. "Even Polite Society."

She burst into laughter and looked forward to his friendship very much.

"Don't move," Berdy huffed. "You'll have to start all over again to tie *L'Americaine* properly."

"My fault, young man. I promise to move only under your direction." Unwinding the flawed cravat, Mr. Thornbury turned his back to her.

Her sight riveted on the contrast between his white shirt collar covered by the ends of his sable hair. The difference startled her, since it was so unlike William's light hair. She couldn't recall gazing upon her husband's hair resting over his collar, but she must have done so at some time.

Examining the tips of Mr. Thornbury's hair, she felt an overwhelming urge to press his dark locks against his snowy collar. What would his hair feel like if she raised her hand to the top of his head and stroked the glossy brown waves down to the ends? Coarse? Silky? She gulped loudly. What movement would his hair make if she ran her forefinger through the bottom of his short locks and watched them separate and join? Her palms dampened from the desire to touch. What would his hair smell like if she buried her nose in the depths of his midnight locks and inhaled? Soap? Cigar? A restless energy settled in her nerves, and she knew whatever perfume his hair possessed, she would recognize it.

Suddenly she became aware of Mr. Thornbury facing her, wearing a devilish smile. *Heavens*. The knowing fire in his eyes jolted her out of her fantasies. How long had he been staring at her?

He stepped toward her and whispered, "Reading my handbook, dear lady?"

Caught in nothing more than an innocent daydream, she felt her treasonous cheeks burn.

His wonderful smile broke across his face. "You must have really enjoyed those earlier chapters of my handbook, since you seem to be reading them a second time. Hurry up. It's time to read chapter three."

Eight

ELINOR GRABBED HER GLOVES BEFORE STEPPING OUTSIDE to wait for Mr. Thornbury's arrival. A chill wind circled under her bonnet and sent it askew, causing her to remonstrate to the dark cloud directly above her. "Make up your mind. Rain or don't rain." The evil cloud teased her by aiming a solitary drop on her forehead before it scooted away. Leaving the over-bright sun to shine upon Mr. Thornbury's carriage as it breezed up to her front door.

Yes, she was grumpy. She had been grumpy all morning, for that matter. Why did Mr. Thornbury insist they visit the mine today? She had asked Henry to join them, but this morning he had called off, citing an urgent need to consult with a client in Hale. Since she owed Mr. Thornbury for Berdy's care, she must keep the appointment. Somehow she suspected this journey, to view the smoke from a steam engine on the east side of Macclesfield, would not alleviate her grumps.

Mr. Thornbury bounded up to greet her, handed her into the landau, and joined her on the seat facing the horses. His tall frame seemed to fill more than his share of the carriage's interior.

She wouldn't feel so close if his shoulders were narrower—she peeked over and examined him—by at least a half a foot. William had perfect shoulders, at least four inches less, and would have moved to the opposite seat before imposing upon a lady of such short acquaintance. Then one minute later, she remembered Mr. Thornbury's speaking voice was a warm baritone. Lower than William's clear tone by at least five notes. She supposed her life would be like this now. Whenever she was in the company of another man, she couldn't help but compare him to the wonderful man she had lost.

She grabbed the carriage's handle, and the scenery outside soon blurred as the coachman drove, if not to the inch, at least to the foot.

The reckless speed seemed to have no detrimental effect upon Mr. Thornbury's spirits, as he whistled a lively tune.

"You are very happy this morning," she said.

"How can I not be? You are here, and in a few minutes we'll reach the coal mine. There you will see a working ten-horsepower steam engine in situ. A machine similar to the one purchased for our foundry. You'll then discover the truth about how much smoke is actually produced. It's only just that you witness this for yourself and not depend upon hearsay." He winked at her.

Elinor focused on his bright gilt-colored waistcoat and tried to capture some of his enthusiasm but failed. Like every person suffering from the grumps, she was quick to anger after witnessing the happiness of others. "Why is this lease so important to you?"

He examined her face, possibly because he couldn't believe anyone could ask something so foolish. "Many reasons. Foremost, Mother will be pleased. The profits from the foundry will allow her to furnish Blackwell to her taste and…don't ask me to explain, but it's essential for her happiness."

Even though it did not seem possible a minute ago, her grumpiness increased. If she rejected his lease now, it would cause his mother grief. She would never willingly cause sorrow in another human being, but she still had her reasons to be skeptical about the foundry. So in case the day ended in disagreement, she resolved to plead on Berdy's behalf before they reached the mine. "I have a favor to ask of you. I'd be grateful if you would introduce Berdy to your business interests, since I'd dearly love for him to find a respectable occupation that will keep him in Cheshire."

He inhaled deeply and scanned her face. "Perhaps, although this month I'm busy. My business partner, his daughters, and several of my friends will be visiting Blackwell for a house party. I want to introduce one of the daughters to my mother. There will be many parties and amusements to entertain everyone. I'll invite the whole neighborhood, so I hope both you and Deane will join us."

Elinor nodded and repeated his vague reply. "Perhaps." The news of his obvious sweetheart did little to alleviate her grumpiness. If he married and brought a wife to Blackwell, she should be pleased that a new female friend would reside within such an easy distance, especially if Berdy left Cheshire permanently. Except all she could do this moment was stare at him. Was he a man in love, and would he spend the journey talking about his sweetheart? Now she discovered a mood below grumpy, called "unjustified anger," and could not determine its exact cause. After all, Mr. Thornbury meant nothing to her other than a future friend.

Seconds later, he acknowledged her brazen stare with a lifted brow. She had no desire to turn away or blush, so she examined him closely for any betrayal of affection concerning his sweetheart, and he made no move to stop her perusal.

Without warning, the carriage stopped, throwing her forward toward the opposite seat. She stretched out her hands to brace herself, but a strong arm wrapped around her waist and pulled her back. She found herself sitting on his knee, and he failed to let her go. Holding her breath, she waited for him to release her.

Still holding her fast, he lowered the window with one hand and called to his coachman. "George, why did we stop?"

Snorting noises from outside the carriage indicated George was having trouble with the horses. "Sorry, sir, a rabbit," replied a booming voice from the direction of the coachman's seat. "Hercules is mighty afeared o' rabbits when they hop."

Mr. Thornbury raised the window and lifted her to sit fully upon his lap. "Mighty Hercules, indeed." The carriage jerked forward on its journey.

Aware of her scandalous situation—his warm body underneath her—she began to pant.

He readily observed this. "You're not like other

clergymen's widows, who would immediately take a seat on the opposite side. Since we are alone, and you have not moved, shall I read you chapter three? The title is: 'A Witty Lady Becomes Witless.'"

"You just mentioned a sweetheart. So your rake's handbook is obsolete." Elinor smiled at his startled expression. "You will be writing a new handbook, of course." She relaxed, her lack of response to his handbook and swift change of subject worked well. Yet, for some inexplicable reason, her grumpiness vanished, and she found herself quite happy sitting where she was. They were alone in a carriage, so she saw no immediate reason to change.

He rolled his eyes. "And that handbook would be?"

"Why, *The Handbook of Marital Happiness*."

"*That* book, madam, will never sell."

"You are right. As the author, you must think of a more appealing title. I'm sure the handbook will prove very popular and published more than three times too. Let's see, the titles of chapters one through four will describe the courtship: 'Gifts of Roses,' 'Whispered Promises,' 'Alluring Blushes,' and 'Stolen Kisses.'"

He lifted her over to sit on the opposing bench facing him. "Is this road too rough? I fear it is making me ill."

She laughed, even though she regretted the loss of his warm lap. "The titles of five and six will describe the thrill of being presented to society as a couple: 'The Tender Betrothal,' 'Private Winks and Giggles.'"

"Humph, a mile longer on this road and we will both be ill."

"Chapter three—"

"*Hell's fire.* How many chapters does this handbook have?"

She fanned her face and batted her eyelids. "Ten."

"Ten!" He frowned at the repetition of his own words spoken at the lake. "No, like you, I plan to stop reading after the table of contents. Unless the pages *v* and *i* stimulate further reading." Now he sported a wily grin—a mocking challenge.

Time to teach him a lesson. She leaned forward and traced the vee forming the edge of his gold waistcoat. She made sure the pressure of her finger was hard enough for him to feel. "Your favorite page is not a *vulgar* one, is it?"

With one swift motion he grabbed her wrist and pulled her toward him.

She found herself on his lap again, her face within inches of his. She held her breath.

"No, the vulgar pages are the main text of the handbook and always come after the table of contents," he said, focusing on her mouth, then inhaling once before engaging in an unyielding kiss.

Desire instantly claimed her from the movement of his lips. She recognized her urgent need for what it was—a disarming effect created by a masterful rake. She took courage in that thought, but—to her chagrin—found she was not offended. Surprisingly, she rather enjoyed the sudden excitement. A full minute passed before she lifted her lips. She needed to gulp air, stop her racing blushes. Heavens, if he still didn't wear that victorious grin.

"I enjoy our handbook discussions." His grin expanded into a broad smile. "Let's talk about books some more." He enclosed her within a tight embrace. "Binding." He kissed her once again.

Smiling, she shoved him back. "*End* papers."

He softly stroked her lips with the back of his forefinger. "Rubbed."

She shoved his hand away and pointed to her forehead. "Unbound."

He leaned forward in an attempt to kiss her again. "Broadside."

"Spine." She giggled and pulled away. "Your endpapers are definitely cut. Berdy was right. You *are* a complete hand." She composed herself, ignored her blushes, and felt no guilt about the kisses whatsoever. All this flummery meant nothing more than a professional rake playing females like a fiddle to get whatever he desired. In this case, a fun exercise, like six-year-olds holding hands, but not any action of significance. She wondered if he would cease his teasing games once he was wed. "The number of chapters in the book of marriage are endless," she said, stopping any further action by sitting as far from him as the landau would allow. "Don't you agree? My love for William will never die." The carriage turned a corner behind a row of cottages, and a busy colliery loomed ahead. She took a deep breath to compose herself. "We've arrived."

"Just in time too," he said in a wry tone. Glancing out the window, he pointed. "Look."

In front of them rose a spinning flywheel at least ten feet in diameter. Next she caught sight of the steam engine's rocking beams, all moving together in a choreographed cotillion of iron. Lastly, probably because it didn't move, a brick chimney belching smoke riveted her gaze. The soot-tinged smoke rose in a powerful plume before the wind proved stronger and pushed it to the south. The entire colliery emitted a symphony of clangs, whistles, and hissing steam.

"The chimney is smaller than I expected," she said, "but the smell—"

"The flue is a standard height, so you will smell the smoke only close to the mine."

～

After a brief tour of the workings, they walked to a small hill overlooking the colliery. Even at a hundred yards from the flue, the smoke made the sun look like a disk without rays. This and the smell of sour steam convinced her of the impossibility of a similar chimney close to Pinnacles. If she asked him now, would he end his plans to build a foundry?

Mr. Thornbury pointed to the brick chimney, directing her attention back to the colliery. "I trust you observed the smoke. This Watt engine is similar to the steam engine I expect to purchase, so you can see that with a machine of this size, the smoke clears rapidly. The best part of our plan is that we expect to generate profits approaching ten thousand per year." He chuckled. "I cannot wait to give Mother carte blanche with the house." The boyish expression now crossing his features might be as fatal to some ladies as his remarkable smile. "You should be pleased. My foundry will have little impact on the surrounding area."

Once again she glanced at the gray plume spewing from the colliery's chimney, and the acrid smell somehow grew worse. She remained silent and unmoving until a piece of soot blew into her eye, forcing her to remove it with her finger. "How many chimneys do you need? Will your chimneys be this size or smaller?"

"One of this size. We are closer to the smoke here than your house would be. But even at this distance, the air is fresh, and the smoke is barely noticeable."

She decided her ears were defective, either that or his nose. She stared in disbelief, unable to formulate a coherent sentence. Without a word in response, she started back to the carriage.

Nearing the landau, she found a small boy of eight or nine years petting the horses. He carried a sack, tin cup, and inky soot clung to every inch of his person. She bent to face the child at eye level and struck up a conversation.

Within minutes she learned the child rose at two in the morning and worked twelve hours standing still in the dark. The bright lad explained that the mine was built like a ladder, with two long pits representing the ladder's frame. Cool air went down one pit, while hot air rose in the other after being heated by a fire. To get air all the way down to the miners at the bottom, doors were closed at each rung. His job as a trapper was to keep his door shut, so air flowed to the lowest depths. The closed door he tended also stopped the spread of firedamp, the major cause of lethal explosions. He opened his door only to let the coal wagons pass on the burrow-ways. For six days a week, the boy stood in his small alcove. He was one of many boys doing the same job. In the blackness. Alone.

Her heart sank, and she became close to tears. She had no idea the type of jobs the children undertook.

Like others of her acquaintance, she assumed they worked close to their father or attended the pit ponies. What kind of future would England have if a large number of her children engaged in labor? Reaching into her reticule, she gave the boy two shillings. "Here's a shilling for you," she said, captivated by his wide white eyes shining from his soot-covered face. "And another shilling for your mother, because of her son's fine answers to my questions."

The boy tugged on his forelock. "Thank you, mum." Then he held up his pants with one hand and ran toward the row of cottages.

She glared at Mr. Thornbury.

Slapping his gloves on his thigh, he raised his voice. "Don't give me that female how-could-you look. In some families, a son may be the only source of income, so mining is better than starving."

Her thoughts became disordered and distracted. "Is it? Yes, of course it is." She resolved to spend more time considering the consequences of steam engines upon others. She then attempted to formulate the appropriate words to explain she was incapable of reaching a decision today. "Will children work in your foundry?"

"Boys are usually employed as ironstone-getters." He gave her a hard squint. "Maybe someday children will not have to work to put food on the table. Then everyone will live in wealth. Our steam engines will lead us to that future, I'll wager."

She made no comment, and they stood for several minutes without speaking, the distant rhythmic sound of the engine surrounding them. She noticed a piece of sod that he had absentmindedly kicked was blackened only on one side. What first appeared to be uniform dark earth on the surface, revealed itself to be coal soot on top and brown dirt underneath. Two years of this colliery's operation had smothered the ground in a blackened mantle. She wondered if her lovely garden would become blackened too. He noticed the black sod, and her spirits lifted a little. He must now see the impossibility of building his foundry close to her home.

He pulled his hat's brim lower upon his brow. "The mine is exciting, is it not?"

She swallowed. "Exciting? No. Look around. Smell the air. The expression on people's faces. Are you blind?"

"I do not understand. The smoke is tolerable. Perhaps if I show you some figures of the estimated profits, the number of men employed—"

"Children, you mean." She experienced one of those moments when women instantly look around for an object to throw. Since they were alone in a field, nothing presented itself. She stomped back toward the carriage.

He hurried after her, caught her arm, forcing her to face him. "Excuse me. You are refusing my lease then?" His voice choked on the end of his question.

Elinor resisted kicking his shin. "Sir, please." She begged him with her eyes not to continue the subject.

He panted and said nothing.

"My home is everything. You have a future. Family—"

"Madam, a house is a house."

"No!" Her anger escalated, a knot forming in her chest. "My home is a place to hold my memories of

William, a place for Berdy's future children to play around my hearth."

"A house is a pile of stones. It's not a family or a future."

"How can you say that when your mother feels the same about her home?"

"You mistake me. If you knew my mother better, you would understand. She's heartbroken over your refusal. To her it's not the house, it's a way to stop…" He paused and removed his beaver hat to brush the nap smooth with his elbow. A muscle in his jaw tightened; he looked down.

Sadness? Did she truly see sorrow in his features? Instantly mortified, she asked for his forgiveness. "Sir, we have both said enough. Perhaps I do not understand you, and I had no intention of causing Lady Helen distress, but let me make myself clear. My husband died over a year ago now. A mourning brooch, a marble bas-relief in the church, and our home are all I have to remember him by." She paused. "All I have, except for Berdy. I cannot agree to your lease, and I prefer we leave here this minute. For Berdy's sake, I wish to put this unpleasantness behind us. I offer you an olive branch, Mr. Thornbury. Will you take it?" She offered her hand and held her breath.

"No!" He stared at her, his stormy blue eyes as turbulent as the plume of billowing smoke. "I've the right to justly develop my land as I see fit for the happiness of *my* family. I will build my foundry as planned, and you are correct, madam." He pointed to the distant chimney. "This chimney flue is too small. My stack will be bigger—much bigger."

Nine

ROSS STOOD ON HIS PORTICO WATCHING A MUD-covered traveling chaise pull into Blackwell's circular drive. Inside the carriage, two of his closest friends could be seen in profile. One of them caught sight of Ross and attempted to lean out the window, but stopped when his hat was knocked off.

After the carriage came to a full stop, a tall, lanky man with curly brown hair and jesting green eyes jumped out first. Lord Boyce Parker violently shook Ross's hand before slapping him on the back several times. "Yes, yes, hallo, hallo."

"Good to see you," Ross said. His friends had arrived in time to join Lucy Allardyce, her father, and her younger sisters for a dinner party the next evening. Later in the week, more guests were expected, then a large house party would formally get under way. The monthlong festivities would end with an extravagant ball, the entire county invited to attend.

Parker glanced up to Blackwell's imposing facade and whistled. "Nice pile of stones here, old man." He stretched his arms high with exaggerated movements.

"Never thought I'd live through the journey. Did we miss the ceremony? Banns read, vows spoken, breakfast ready?"

"If the negotiations with Allardyce are successful, first of the banns read in a month." Ross anticipated he and Allardyce would negotiate a marriage settlement agreeable to all parties within the next week. Then once Ross and Lucy got to know each other better— and both consented to their betrothal—he would officially announce their engagement at the end of the ball. He returned Parker's enthusiastic backslap.

Parker rubbed his belly with both hands. "How about an early sample of the wedding breakfast then? I'm famished."

Behind Parker, Mr. George Drexel exited the carriage. Of sturdy build and darkly handsome, Drexel wore a frown that suggested the type of man who would not step aside on a narrow street to let you pass. Today, however, Drexel strode forward with a wry grin.

Ross had known both men for twenty years, so he knew the smallest of grins on Drexel's sardonic face equaled the brightest smile on any other man.

Drexel extended his hand. "Thornbury."

"Drexel." Ross grabbed Drexel's forearm and pulled him forward to slap him on the back. "Good journey?"

Drexel nodded in Parker's direction. "By North London, I thought I'd expire from that fart machine."

Parker leaned close to Ross and purposefully moved out of Drexel's reach. "Remind me to tell you all about Drexel, the honey, and the serving wench." He looked at Drexel. "Failed there, my lad."

Drexel's dark eyes narrowed. "Bracket-face."

Parker straightened. "Diddle-poop."

"Squeeze-crab."

"You're the baby."

"Ha!" Ross exclaimed. "I'm overjoyed to see you both." Ross initiated another round of masculine back pats. "Mother is delighted over the festivities, and with all the excitement, she seems like another woman. I can't tell you how pleased I am that you are all here."

❧

The following day, Ross and his friends spent the day shooting. Ross laughed, told jests, and his peace of mind succumbed to the healing power arising from the company of his friends. When his mind did stray, he thought about his readiness to meet Mrs. Colton at his supper party. The disastrous incident at the coal mine had been his fault, of course. Hindsight revealed his stupidity in showing her a smoky chimney at a relatively close distance. He should have taken her to a house a similar distance away from the flue, as her home would be from his foundry. Then she could have seen for herself that the smoke was not a nuisance.

So for the immediate future, he must devise a new proposal to change her mind, a seemingly impossible task. But first he needed to dampen his resentment and return their relationship to the friendly ease of their earlier meetings. The day after their disastrous visit to the chimney, he took the first step toward reconciliation by sending her a letter in which he politely requested her forgiveness, a simple act any proper gentleman must do. This evening he planned to be polite, nothing more, hoping to hide his residual anger enough to be friendly, so as not to offend her.

That evening, Ross and his mother stood in the hall and greeted Mrs. Colton upon her arrival for the supper party. The widow looked particularly fine tonight, Ross noted. Her hair, styled in a Grecian goddess-like fashion, tumbled in ringlets upon one shoulder, while a gilt, close-fitted gown revealed her comely figure. A shape more comely than he remembered, if truth be told.

Mrs. Colton gave an apprehensive glance toward his mother. "Thank you for your gracious invitation, Lady Helen Thornbury, Mr. Thornbury. I am delighted to hear your guests this evening will include Mr. Allardyce and Mr. Drexel, both successful engineers. Mr. Deane will appreciate the chance to question them about gears and steam engines."

Ross caught his mother slighting the widow by failing to acknowledge her comment. Holding out his arm, he nodded for Mrs. Colton to join him to the side. In a low voice, he said, "Please say nothing to Mother about our journey to the coal mine. I do not want her upset tonight."

"Yes, of course." Mrs. Colton twisted the chain of her reticule. "You've inspired Berdy's interest in engineering, so he wants to discuss gears and engines tonight. Am I correct in using the plural? Are there more than one type of engine and gear?" She flushed. "I want to thank you…excuse me." She hurried to join the other guests milling close to the drawing-room door.

Once the assembled party had been seated for supper, Ross observed his mother's strained countenance every time she glanced in Mrs. Colton's direction. Lady Helen's continued resentment had not abated after the widow's refusal to grant their lease. As a result, his mother placed her as far from him as possible, close to Dr. Potts and Drexel. She had even ordered a wide arrangement of flowers in the silver epergne, so if he wanted to catch sight of Mrs. Colton, he would have to perform a noticeable lean to the side.

Conversation amongst the guests was sporadic before the first remove, as many were becoming acquainted with the person next to them. Ross caught the tomfoolery of his friends, Lucy's nervousness over being separated from her younger sisters for the evening, and his mother's pointed glares at Mrs. Colton.

After the guests were served the roasted fillet of beef à l'anglaise, he found an excuse to lean sideways—to grab the saltcellar—but he quickly looked away. Mrs. Colton, while lovely, seemed subdued. Missing was the bubbling laughter that simmered under her barely contained propriety. He downed another two glasses of claret. He regretted the loss of the laughing widow fishing in his lake, or the happy lady in his carriage, blithely sitting on his lap and lecturing him about her imaginary handbook of marriage.

Meanwhile, his mother failed to remember that his engagement to Miss Allardyce had not been officially settled. She must have been so pleased by the thought of his marriage and grandchildren that she forgot about her promise to keep the subject private. Lady Helen asked Lucy numerous veiled questions to gather information in regard to their future engagement. "Where is your official parish, dear?"

Lucy's unwavering stare at the wineglass in front of her meant she probably had never been served wine, so the experience of dining in the company of adults, other than her family, might be new. "Our parish is Merton, mum," Lucy answered, glancing at her father for approval before returning to stare at her glass.

On his left, Ross spied Deane adamantly following Drexel's Banbury tale of the day's shoot.

Ross asked the young man, "How would you like to join us tomorrow? Your leg should not be a problem. A footman can give you a hand outside. We will have some good sport, and you can tell us about your interests."

Mrs. Colton leaned sideways to look at Ross, forcing him to concentrate on carving his beef joint.

Young Deane turned toward him and smiled broadly. "Yes. I'd like to join the gentlemen tomorrow. I'd enjoy watching the shooting, even though I cannot participate. It's of no concern anyhow, because I'm not much of a shot."

"Neither am I," Ross said, leaning to his other side to catch a glimpse of Mrs. Colton's widening eyes in the mirrored looking glass above the sideboard.

Lady Helen ignored him and addressed Parker. "Mr. Deane will likely mature into a singular young man, quite the surprise really, when you consider how he is raised." Her deprecating words were matched by an exaggerated shake of her fork.

Mrs. Colton's head lowered a fraction of an inch, and she appeared to have difficulty chewing her food.

Now his mother's resentment had gone too far. The lad had nothing to do with their troubles. "Yes,

Deane *is* a singular young man," Ross announced to his guests. "If you need to know anything about cravats, he's your man. He is also forward thinking and has a stunning appreciation for machines. You should see his dandy horse—amazing, really."

"Is that one of those rider thingamabobs?" Parker asked, followed by a loud gulp of claret. "Saw a half dozen the other day in Hyde Park. Don't think it will replace the horse. Too much physical exertion for me."

Deane swung around to face Parker. "It is strenuous exercise, but the challenge is worth it. Too bad it's not steam powered though. Then the work would be zero."

Most of the company chuckled at this remark. Except for Dr. Potts, who fixed Mrs. Colton's attention by bragging about his latest winning strategy at the local races. His mother also remained unamused and took several additional opportunities to glare at Mrs. Colton.

"Actually, not a bad idea," Ross said, brushing his forelock back. "But steam engines are too heavy. Perhaps a pulley around the rear wheel to power it with your legs would do the trick."

Parker waved his wineglass in the air. "No, no, that would never do. The work would be the same as if you were pushing with your feet, so you wouldn't save any effort."

Deane addressed the gentlemen much older than himself without hesitation. "I think Mr. Thornbury is right. A mechanical advantage might be had by a gear. This would multiply the energy generated from the rider, allowing for greater distances to be covered with the same amount of work."

Ross patted Deane on the back. "See, I'm right. A singular young gentleman, indeed." He ignored his mother's basilisk stare. "You'd make a fine engineer."

Deane's grin grew more pronounced than his overlarge cravat.

For some inexplicable reason, possibly due to the effects of ingesting a second bottle of claret, Ross wondered if he would have a son. Would his son be singular? *His son.* He chastised himself with a swift mental kick to his arse. He'd leave the responsibility of raising a son to his wife. Otherwise, he'd more than likely muck it up, the way he had with John's life. He slammed his glass of claret down on the table, making the dishes dance and everyone turn. Wearing a false smile, he started a lighthearted conversation with Deane, while his insides turned sour.

After the dinner's final remove, the ladies withdrew to the vast drawing room, and Lucy's father took his leave for the evening. Ross watched his mother take Lucy's arm to lead her away—all but ignoring Mrs. Colton. That lady followed the others alone. It occurred to Ross that the men shouldn't sit with their brandies for too long and should rejoin the ladies as soon as possible.

Once the dining-room doors closed behind the women, the men passed around crystal decanters of brandy and claret. Everyone helped themselves to large glasses. Parker and Deane continued their discussion of the dandy horse, and before long, Ross needed to request two more bottles of brandy.

Drexel leaned back in his chair and blew smoke rings into the air. "I say, Two," he said, using Ross's nickname, "heard you've had a run of luck lately. First you earned a packet on some canal investment. Then last month at Newmarket, the horse you bet on won. Goes without saying your horse was much better than Whip's bag of bones."

Parker appeared offended. "That filly was a promising two-year-old. The odds of winning too high to pass up." He slid the brandy toward Drexel, hitting several dishes in the process.

"Yes, my horse did well," Ross replied. "Even better than Stanford's filly."

"Too bad about Stanford," Parker said, shaking his head. "Have you heard? Got the news last week. He got caught in a difficult situation—like John. News is he'll recover though. The wound apparently is not deep."

Drexel frowned and wagged a forefinger at Parker.

"Oh," Parker said, furtively glancing at Ross. "Yes, yes, sorry ol' man."

Ross stopped himself from breaking the table with his fist. His jaw tightened as he reached for the brandy. Filling the glass to the top, he drank it all with a quick toss of his head. With any luck, within minutes he'd forget about John, forget about his past. Become drunk enough, so his only remaining memory would be his own name.

"Right. Speaking of fillies, how game is yours?" Drexel asked Ross, a subtle leer tainting his voice. "Is she good in harness?"

"Tom-m-morrow," Ross managed with a

brandy-addled tongue. "Show you her in the stables…
morning." He poured Deane another glass of brandy.

"Not *that* filly," Drexel said with a wicked leer.
"The intended. You know, the ol' lady wife to be."

Parker unsteadily addressed Deane. "That old
Two in Hand, he's quite the devil of a fellow with
the ladies."

Deane's eyelids sunk halfway across his eyes. "Two
in Hand? That's a cravat knot, right?"

"No, no," Parker said, "it's one of our nicknames
we earned after the publication of our book, *Rake's
Handbook: Including Field Guide*. We use these nicknames in jest, because they please the ladies no end.
Drexel here wrote the *Field Guide*—it describes female
types in detail—so he's called The Jockey. Ross here
penned the handbook, and he's called Two in Hand.
We shortened it and just call him Two." With both
hands, Parker made a gesture of lifting his breasts. "Get
it? I'm the publisher and editor of the tome, so the
book is a success because of me, really. Therefore, the
ladies call me The Whip."

"Right. You're called The Whip in your dreams,"
Drexel said. "Most people still call you—"

"Even your slow wits must realize that horrid
nickname is forgotten." Parker leaned over the center
of the table to conspiratorially address the entire group
of men. "Mentioned my *real* nickname, The Whip,
to the widow Crew the other day. Boy did her eyes
get big. Methinks she's interested, yes sireee, *interested*.
So I sang her an old favorite from the Coal Hole,
sealed the deal." Parker stood, swayed, and began to
recite an introduction. "This tune is called 'Roger

Rakes a Bower on Top of Thigh Lane.' I'll just sing the chorus."

"No!" Ross grinned.

With guffaws and choking laughter, each man raised his hand in a unified gesture to stop.

Parker dropped his jaw. "You're missing quite a song."

Deane appeared excited, fidgeting in his chair. "Will I get a nickname someday? Who gives you nicknames?"

"The handbook earned us the nicknames," Parker said. "Don't know the fellow who came up with them, though. We first heard our new names mentioned at Tattersalls. Yes, yes, so pen a book, my lad. Maybe I'll publish it." Parker turned to Ross. "Meaning to ask you fellows. The handbook has been out for almost two years now. Profits are beginning to slow. How about a second edition? You know, package it up in a fancy cover, maybe just this side of proper. Sell hundreds in a month. What do you say?"

"No," Drexel said. "Lately, that handbook has become nothing but trouble. Your additional profits could never be enough to fully fund my engineering projects. Now I need to impress respectable gentlemen when I seek investors, so a questionable book in my past hinders that ability. I imagine it's the same for Two here. He needs honorable, upstanding connections to invest in his canals and such. We both want that book well in our past and forgotten."

"But—" Parker said.

"Wait a minute," Drexel said. "You have successfully hid the existence of the handbook from your father for two years? I expected you to be hanged in the public square or at least transported by now."

Parker winked. "The Pater never leaves his club, handy that."

"Let's play the card game Drexel requested earlier in the day," Ross said, eager to change the subject. Like Parker, he had kept the publication of the handbook from his mother, not wanting to upset her. So as far as he was concerned, the subject of another edition was permanently closed. Eventually, the handbook's profits would fade altogether, but by then, he expected to use the profits from the new foundry to make her happy. He motioned toward the library, and the other men followed. Except for Dr. Potts, who took his leave and mentioned his intent to join the ladies. After an unsteady stroll across the hall, Ross recognized he was not in a suitable condition to be seen by either his mother or Mrs. Colton, so he regretted his inability to rescue the widow from the tedium of his mother's behavior.

Drexel dealt the cards with amazing dexterity, smug indifference written across his face.

Ross tried to remember what game they were playing. With his back to the fire and the nearest lamp having a red shade, a reddish light tinted all of his cards. Consequently, he could not easily determine the face count of the red cards. *Hell's fire.* He could barely see any of the cards because of the chimney's acrid smoke filling the room, but it really didn't matter. He was a trifle too disguised to play well.

"Right. I cannot wait for tomorrow's sport," Drexel began, appearing less affected by the brandy than the other three.

It didn't take long before Deane suffered a brandy-induced sleeping disease, and his head rolled back as far as it could go. Just when Ross thought his neck would snap, the young man woke. "We were...cussing?"

"Cussing?" Parker said. "No, no, we were dis-*cussing* tomorrow's sport." He passed the bottle of brandy to Drexel.

"Sport as in widow, Mrs. Colton?" Drexel asked, the firelight dancing in the center of his eyes.

Ross restrained himself from challenging Drexel to fisticuffs. Holding his finger up to his lips, he nodded in the direction of the lad. "Shh. Not that sport." He wagged his finger back and forth in front of his nose, making himself dizzy. "Shooting. Guns. *That* sport."

"A man does like to shoot his gun," Drexel said.

After second of silence, laughter erupted.

"Yus, yus, a man sure finds relief shooting a bird," Parker added, grinning.

Everyone chuckled, except for Deane, who appeared momentarily confused.

"And he likes to shoot all fetching birds," Parker continued. "Pack his powder vigorously, gather up his balls, go off with a bang, what?" He held out both hands. "See, I *am* a poet. That Byron fellow can't beat my romanticism."

"An original poet, too," Ross said, trying once more to blink away the red fog obscuring the cards in his hand. His attempt to focus was interrupted when Parker fell off his chair onto the rug. Parker's rolling laughter mixed with irreverent song indicated that his friend was not in immediate difficulties. A relief, since he wouldn't have to attempt a risky move—like rising from his chair—in order to set the situation to rights.

Suddenly, Mrs. Colton invaded the library. Standing behind Deane, she glanced at Parker on the floor, her lips pinched, and her expression grave. She grabbed Deane's arm. "You need to rest your limb. Time to go upstairs."

Deane looked up at her with his eyes closed. "Shelli, greeslings." He waved his hand, which promptly fell to the table with a thud.

"Mr. Thornbury, he's just seventeen," she said, keeping her gaze on the top of Deane's drooping head.

"Old enough to be out of leading strings." Ross's bitter retort came as a surprise, even to himself. His angry words left a rotten-egg taste in his mouth, due to some justice in her accusation. He tried hard to appear sober, apologized for the excess brandy, and attempted to stand, but changed his mind and remained seated. The fewer movements he made the better. He nodded in what he hoped appeared like a gracious farewell, instead of trying any tricky movement like a respectable bow.

Deane also moved to stand but failed.

Mrs. Colton remedied the situation by heaving Deane up. "Sorry, gentlemen. Thank—thank you." With Deane transferred to the shoulder of a footman, she led them out of the room.

"Yes, yes, he's in shrouble," Parker said, crawling back to his chair. "Foxed in front of Mater. Don't think we'll see him at the smack of yawn…crack of dawn."

"No, the widow Colton will probably interfere with our sport," Drexel said, slapping his cards against one another. "Maybe we should make the widow our sport. What do you say?"

"You're gonna shoot the widow?" Parker exclaimed.

"No shooting window—widow—Mrs. Colton," Ross said.

"Let's wager who will give her a green gown first?" Drexel pondered. "Rolling in hay counts as well as grass."

For some reason, Ross felt like punching everyone. "Leave the minnow—widow alone. No rolling in the green grass, hay, or any other female rolling. Listen. I need your help to change the minnow's mind."

"Right, a kiss will do it," Drexel said. "Widows will do anything for a kiss. Grant leases, whatever: Never failed in my experience. That's it. Let's wager which one of us will kiss the lovely widow first. Parker, you in?"

"Yus, yus, kiss the widow," Parker agreed, leaning toward Ross. "So glad we are not shooting widows. Remember the fly bet? Great bet. Great bet."

"Rules are on the lips," Drexel said, "no hand nonsense. Two, you in?"

"No," Ross exclaimed. "Bloody awful plan. Besides, intended here, remember? Plan to kiss—intended." *Hell's fire, what was her name?* Her father was his friend too. "Tomorrow plan to kiss intended woman."

"Just us lucky lads then, Whip. What's the prize?"

Parker struggled to remain on his chair, much less make a decision. "Same bet, same bet, what?"

"Agreed, last to kiss the widow pays a round for all

at the local establishment," Drexel said, jumping to his feet in a motion to run out and kiss Mrs. Colton.

Ross fervently hoped she had returned home by this time.

"Agreed," Parker echoed, catching Drexel's hand for a robust shake, which consequently upset his balance. Parker's head hit the table first before he slithered down onto the rug. "I mus' kiss widow first."

Ten

"MR. THORNBURY, WHAT IS YOUR OPINION ON RUFFLED sleeves?" Lucy Allardyce asked Ross as they paused on an isolated garden path. It was the afternoon of Blackwell's first garden party, and the fine weather had brought out the entire neighborhood. She repeated, "Ruffled sleeves?"

"Yes," Ross said, busy watching Lucy's ample bodice rise and fall with each barely audible breath. Like other gentlemen, he noticed bodices—Mrs. Colton's came to mind—but he had not seen her among his guests for the last twenty minutes. Maybe she too had escaped the noisy crowd gathered on the rear lawn to wander Blackwell's grounds. However, since he had reached an agreement with Allardyce over the marriage settlement, Lucy would soon become his wife. Now if he truly had reformed into a proper gentleman, he must try to appreciate only his wife's bodice.

Lucy held out her left arm and tugged on her red muslin sleeve. "I expected you to rightly insist upon me wearing ruffled sleeves when we are married."

The word *married* drew Ross's full attention, since it was the one word likely to penetrate the mental fog created by discreet bodice-watching. "I'm sorry; you caught me admiring nature's symmetry. Why in the dev—why would I insist upon ruffled sleeves?"

Lucy's scowl caused wrinkles on the top of her freckled nose. "These days, it's a serious error if your puffed sleeves are not appropriately ruffled for your wedding costume. Of course, one has to decide between furbelow, flounced, or ruched sleeves—such a difference. Which do you prefer?"

If Ross wanted to be a good husband, he must learn how to discuss womanly subjects like sleeves. It occurred to him that in her seventeen-year-old world, ruffled sleeves might be as important as sun and planet gears. Simple fairness dictated that if he must be aware of ruffles, she should be aware of gears. But he was not married yet, so he'd practice his matrimonial skills by first attending to her sleeve concerns. "Who could fail to like them all?" He cleared his throat in the sound universally acknowledged to be the male pronouncement of the final word upon the subject. "Without doubt, I prefer *flounced*."

Her brow contracted. "Really? I would have thought...ruched."

Ross inhaled sharply. "Yes, ruched is what I meant. I often admire ruched sleeves." He heard a soft snicker, looked around, and saw only a hedge of tall yews. By all appearances, they were quite alone, but his uneasiness that they were perhaps watched created an urge to return to the others soon. "Right then, sleeves it is." He offered Lucy his arm.

"Ah, but your mother told me she likes *flounced* ruf-fled sleeves," Lucy said, ignoring his outstretched arm.

Picking up her hand, Ross placed it on his forearm. He then started back toward his other guests. "That is only on Tuesdays. For important occasions, she requests the…the other sleeves."

"Since she is to be my mother-in-law, I should please her and pick flounced." Lucy stopped on the path.

"Good plan."

"But I cannot. Taste demands ruched sleeves or… corded tuck?"

Ross halted and peered upward for a brief second. Now after his first chance to have a long talk with Lucy alone, he contemplated the possible difficulties in achieving a happy marriage. Since Lucy was to be his future "My Lady" wife, he had wondered whether or not their temperaments would be sympathetic, or if they shared the same interests, like poetry.

Lucy alternately fluffed each sleeve.

He also considered Lucy's feelings and whether she'd come to love him. Without answers to his questions, he decided to rely upon the old adage. He'd wait to know her better before he made a pronouncement upon their suitability. Ross saw no reason why their union should not be a success. And romantic love? Doubtful, more likely impossible; he lacked that capacity. Giving her a tender smile, he said, "I'm stunned by your sartorial sagacity. Now I fully understand the crucial role of taste in your *final* choice of ruched." This time he was positive he heard a noise, followed by rapid footsteps on the gravel path. "Tell me, Miss Allardyce, I'm fond of poetry, are you? Any of Donne's works, for example?"

"No, I don't like the latest poetry by Donne."

"He hasn't *done* anything lately."

Lucy scowled. "Is he dead then?"

"See, I'm right." Ross gave her hand a pat and began to stroll.

"Mr. Thornbury, I have one more question to ask you, besides my wedding costume, but equally as important."

Ross stopped and glanced toward the house, steeling himself for her question.

"He-he, are you not going to ask me?" She beamed.

"I'm sure I could not give your question the justice it deserves."

She patted his arm, pleased with his response.

He stared at her hand.

"I recently overheard several of the ladies talking. Sounded amusing, so I moved closer. I was very careful that Mrs. Harbottle did not see me, as she reminds me of Nurse, who—"

"What did the ladies say?" He glanced upward. "Compliments on that very pretty gown you are wearing?"

"They said," she began to whisper, "that you wrote a handbook about—about gentlemen and women— you know, together. And I gather the relations described were"—her voice lowered even more— "not con-nu-bial."

Ross inhaled deeply.

"When we are married, you must read me your book, of course. I want to learn all about—you know." She eagerly smiled. The effect lacked even a whiff of maidenly modesty.

He stared at her in stupefying horror, the thought of reading his book to a woman of her expertise utterly farcical.

"Well?"

Up ahead, two gentlemen strode up the garden path toward them. Mr. Mabbs owned a cattle farm and large cheese factory, while Mr. Burton was the master of a nearby cotton mill. Both men resided close to the border of the Blackwell estate. "Ah, there you are my good fellow," Mabbs shouted.

Ross provided the introductions to Miss Allardyce.

After his bow, Mabbs straightened his garish brown hat. "We have come to discuss business, but I see you have more charming company. Perhaps later, the three of us can discuss the river's use? Lady Helen does not appear to know anything about your plans on the subject."

Ross stared at the man. He must keep any opposition over the foundry away from his mother. "Gentlemen, I will join you in a few minutes, after I leave Miss Allardyce here in her father's care. I'm confident we can then come to terms."

❧

Elinor ran down the gravel path, clutching her side while trying to postpone an outburst of laughter. Upon hearing voices approach, she had hidden in the tall yews. Mr. Thornbury's deep masculine voice intoning "sartorial sagacity" over his bride's decision to wear ruched sleeves on her wedding costume sounded so silly, she held her breath to avoid discovery. Once she was far from the garden, she laughed in whoops. His rampant drollery softened her current negative feelings toward him. Negative because he still planned to build his foundry.

When she stopped laughing, she discovered herself on the gravel path that began the short walking circuit. The previous owner of Blackwell had built numerous ornamental bridges and new ruins for the enjoyment of his friends and family. Unfortunately, he died soon after, and the estate was sold to pay his debts.

She headed toward a delightful wooden bridge she remembered from a previous visit. The bright red bridge straddled a small stream that flowed into a distant mere. She ran to the highest part of the bridge and peered into the rapidly moving water. Bubbles created by the churning stream hid any identifiable fish, so she gazed across the emerald valley to the distant hills in the direction of her home.

Would a new foundry change this landscape forever? Would the undulating green fields before her now one day frame a soot-covered valley? Mr. Thornbury impressed her as a man who admired machinery and viewed factories as examples of man's progress. Moreover, during the supper party, he had emphasized that a new foundry created many employment opportunities, and families could earn a better living working in his foundry than as tenant farmers.

By her own experience, working with the poor of William's church, she had seen children suffer from hunger when their parents could not find work in the fields or mills. Even though her home meant everything to her, she began to harbor doubts as to denying Mr. Thornbury his lease. The choice between Pinnacles' stones blackened by soot or knowingly allowing children to go hungry, or even die, didn't seem like much of a choice. Perhaps she should discuss this point with Mr. Thornbury and get his opinion. Of course, if she eventually agreed to his foundry, she must insist no children were employed.

Thank heavens the sun shone today, something rare in this part of the country. Elinor peered again at the gurgling stream below. She took a long, deep breath. Contemplation of puffy clouds reflected in meandering streams appealed to her more than difficult decisions regarding steam engines. Still, she could not ignore the issue forever, so she resolved to have a rational deliberation of these thoughts with Mr. Thornbury today. Perhaps she might have a word in private when she thanked him for his attentions to Berdy.

Elinor's musings ended when she heard a shout.

"Yes, yes, Mrs. Colton," Lord Boyce Parker yelled, advancing with long strides. "I see you too plan to enjoy this fine day. Spot any fish?" He bounded up, bowed, and leaned over the railing beside her. His casual bottle-green coat and buckskin breeches revealed his expectations to spend the sunny day outdoors.

"Your lordship, good afternoon. Do you plan to fish or take in the circuit?" They leaned over the railing in unison to stare at the water.

"Um, fish, I think." He grinned. "Actually, I have been looking for you. I say, is that a tench?" He pointed to the left edge of the stream.

She peered left into the rushing water.

Lord Parker grumbled. "No, sorry, over there." He pointed to a half-submerged boulder on the right.

She turned right to focus on the water close to the rock.

He briefly looked back toward the house before chuckling. "No, I believe the devil's over there by those rushes." He pointed to her left again, his arm crossing over hers.

When Elinor turned left to follow his gaze, he swiftly kissed her on the cheek with a loud *smack*. She jumped back; surprise rendered her speechless.

Lord Parker beamed. "I won. Oh, I mean I guess we missed the fellow." He returned to survey the stream, eagerly searching for his elusive tench.

"Sir!" Mr. Thornbury yelled. "Stop this nonsense, understand?"

Charging up the path were Mr. Thornbury and Mr. Drexel. Mr. Thornbury's thunderous countenance was contrasted by Mr. Drexel's wry grin. Without waiting for an answer, Mr. Thornbury confronted Lord Parker. "Apologize, sir," he said with restrained force.

She looked at Mr. Thornbury and sharply inhaled.

His chest broadened in response.

With the shock of Lord Parker's kiss abating, she felt relieved that someone, at least, had enough sense to demand an apology. Mr. Thornbury's fierce request made her giddy, and she refused to think about why.

"Apologies, ma'am," Lord Parker said, followed by the briefest of bows. "Couldn't help m'self, sunny day and all."

Men! That was the second "sunny day" excuse for

improper behavior Elinor had received. What was wrong with the gentlemen of today if mere sunshine turned them into bussing half-wits? "Your lordship, I insist you behave like a gentleman, please."

"Yes, yes, of course," Lord Parker replied in a tone without a drop of contrition. "Drexel, m' lad, guess I won." A remarkably wide grin lingered upon his boyish face.

"Pardon?" she asked, now aware of some secret the men shared that she had no part in. Uncertain and uneasy, she longed to escape and return home. With any luck, this incident would soon be forgotten, and the men decent enough to check their tongues. Otherwise, Lord Parker's indiscreet behavior might give rise to rumors she had become a "fast" widow.

"Don't count, Whip, and you know why," Mr. Drexel said, followed by a swift pat on his cheek.

Mr. Thornbury glared at Lord Parker, then held out his arm. "Mrs. Colton, may I escort you back to the house?"

Mr. Drexel and Lord Parker exchanged knowing smiles.

Eager to be free of all gentlemen today, she took Mr. Thornbury's offered arm, and together they began walking. Peeking up at his stern face, she noticed he failed to meet her eye. This formality surprised her. Today she was beyond understanding all gentlemen, but somehow she felt like she had been judged. "What was that all about?"

Mr. Thornbury said nothing at first and then, "You could have avoided that scene."

"Avoid? How? Jump in the stream?"

"You didn't have to stand there so he could kiss you," he said in clipped tones.

"Yes, I always stand ten feet away when I engage in conversation. And it's not as though you're innocent of similar behavior. You especially seem to enjoy acting the role of a professional seducer. In my opinion, the three of you gentlemen must have aspic under your hats."

Mr. Thornbury paused, grinned, and caught her indignant stare. "There is some truth in that." He no longer appeared angry, and a crinkle grew on his forehead, probably reflecting deep thought.

After a few minutes of silence, she hoped he had taken no offense from her comment. For Berdy's sake, she tried to lighten the mood between them. "I met your intended, Miss Allardyce. She is lovely, and I expect your marriage will be a success."

"We'll be well dressed."

"Pardon?"

"Success for Miss Allardyce means her husband's gift of a few new gowns—"

"She's young, remember."

He raised a solitary brow. "Are you telling me all women don't enjoy new gowns?"

"I know that when William presented me with a new gown, my enjoyment was due to the appreciation of my husband's kindness."

He chuckled. "Come, be honest."

She smiled. "Well, *after* I rejoiced in his kindness, the gown made me happy."

"Happy?" he said, staring at his boots. "Yes, that's the relevant word." They continued for several minutes in silence, except for the crunch of gravel under their feet.

Puzzled by his change in mood from light to reflective, she kept her eyes on the sculpted hedges while he gazed straight ahead. She considered whether to begin their discussion about families employed at the foundry, when he interrupted her thoughts.

"Forgive me," he said, removing his hat and sweeping his forelock back into place. "I must ask. I recently had a word with Mr. Mabbs and Mr. Burton. Both expressed their objection to my foundry, and they have incited opposition amongst the townsfolk. They even approached Lady Helen with their concerns. Mother is…has retired for the remainder of the afternoon. I wondered if you were the person who encouraged our neighbor's objections."

She ignored his accusation and focused on his concern for his mother. Mr. Thornbury, for all his charms and faults, desired his mother's happiness first—an admirable son. Lady Helen had impressed her as being occasionally frail in spirits, and she understood his wish to protect her. "I can assure you. I told only Mr. Henry Browne, my attorney, about my refusal."

"Ah, Mr. Browne." He paused to put on his hat; a muscle tightened in his jaw. He held his arm forward in a motion for her to continue walking. This time he strolled behind her and kept a sizable distance between them.

Once they reached Blackwell, they turned in unison to face each other. Elinor thought he looked confused, and she didn't know what to say. She absentmindedly glanced at the landscape and waited. Finally, he sighed and politely mentioned how pleased he would be to have her attendance at his upcoming ball. Without another word, he took his leave.

Even though he appeared unconvinced about her suspected influence upon Mr. Mabbs or Mr. Burton, she was pleased he did not withhold an invitation to the ball. It might reflect badly, not only upon herself, but also on Berdy. Yet he had not requested a dance and was quite put out over his friend's impetuous kiss. *So a kiss was the wager.* What else could it be? Mr. Drexel must have been Lord Parker's partner in the bet.

Heavens. Did Lord Parker's kiss on her cheek count? *Her cheek.* That was why Mr. Drexel patted his cheek. With two men possibly attempting to kiss her on her lips, she picked up her skirt and ran toward the others at the house party. Any discussion about the foundry would have to wait for a more convenient moment. In the future, she vowed to avoid both Mr. Drexel and Lord Parker. Moreover, she planned to arrive at Mr. Thornbury's next soiree after the sun had set, so it would no longer be a *sunny day.* She stopped. Was Mr. Thornbury part of the wager too? Was his thunderous countenance due to her supposed incitement of their neighbor's opposition or because he had lost the wager? Did he want to kiss her? In front of witnesses?

⁂

Elinor still felt unsettled about attending the private dance held at Blackwell on the following Saturday. Did the wager to kiss her remain? Regardless, she expected the Thornburys to continue their resentment over her refusal to sign the lease of her land. But Berdy had been home for two days and was eager to return to visit his new friends. The very reason she had agreed to attend the private dance.

Upon their arrival, Mr. Thornbury warmly received them as welcomed guests, while Lady Helen ignored her salutations. Thankfully, with such a large crowd in the hall, her cut went unnoticed.

Elinor marveled at the transformation of Blackwell's gallery into a suitable ballroom. Dozens of chairs had been pushed to the walls, and a small orchestra played at the far end. The room possessed no portraits or paintings, so Lady Helen must have seen to the large swags of mustard-colored fabric draped upon the light blue walls. Golden cording framed the fabric, and gilt tassels hung in the center of the swags.

Sitting alone on the side, Elinor was forced to play matronly wallflower more than she would have liked, due to the lack of older gentlemen wishing to dance. Nevertheless, she hummed along with the music and tapped her feet. A flash of Berdy's yellow waistcoat caught her eye, and she saw him lean on his good foot in the middle of the dancers. Lucy Allardyce was his partner, and Berdy merely stood in place as she went through the steps around him. Both of them gaily laughed; however, by the expression on his face, his leg must have been causing him considerable pain. Nevertheless, he clearly enjoyed drawing everyone's attention.

Mr. Thornbury conversed at the far end of the gallery with a local cotton master, Mr. Burton. On several occasions she met his glance, but he immediately looked away. This behavior puzzled her, and she did not know what to make of it.

Next she spotted Lord Parker. That gentleman wore an unruly grin upon seeing her, so she resolved to flee if he took even a step in her direction.

When the dance was completed, Berdy led Lucy to a chair next to her. "Elli, you'll never believe this, but Miss Allardyce thinks these walls are too dark. Just like I told you."

A flushing Lucy nodded. "Yes, I think the blue is very drab. They should be patent yellow—like a spring daisy."

"Capital thought, Miss Allardyce," Berdy said, silently asking Elinor for permission to stand up with Lucy for another dance. "Patent yellow is the preferable color for all grand rooms, as it never fails to make a fellow's spirits soar." He addressed Lucy. "May I have the honor of the next reel?" Both Berdy and Lucy stared at Elinor for her approval.

Unable to say anything that would dampen Berdy's rampant smile, she nodded. "Of course." Since this was a private party, hopefully no one noticed her failure to curb his enjoyment.

The two young people returned to join the other couples assembling on the floor for the next dance, and she witnessed Lord Parker approach her from the opposite side of the room. She didn't think he would try to kiss her in front of everyone, but she had no intention of testing him, so she hastily exited the ballroom in the direction of the hall.

Pausing by the central staircase, she looked up to find Mr. Drexel descending the stairs. *Heavens*. He

must be a partner in the wager too. She opened the
door to the servant stairs tucked behind the grand
staircase and flew down as fast as her elegant slippers
allowed. Once she reached the bottom of the stairs,
she heard heavy footsteps descending behind her.
Taking no chances Mr. Drexel might find her, she
entered the closest room and shut the door.

She found herself in Blackwell's salting room. Once
her eyes adjusted to the dim light in the cool room,
she recognized pickled joints, wrapped in muslin,
hanging from hooks overhead. The confined air
smelled faintly of saltpeter.

The door latch lifted; the door opened.

Mr. Drexel entered, and Elinor backed to the far
side of the room. *Heavens*.

He ducked past a hanging row of salted meats, and
the room seemed to shrink as he straightened his tall
figure before her. Tonight, only the top half of his
body was clad in a formal black coat and waistcoat.
All in dramatic contrast with his white satin evening
breeches. His bright eyes never left her face, while at
his side, his fingers moved in a rippled wave.

She scurried to the opposite end of the salting table.

Mr. Drexel paused before placing his open palms
on the slate table. "What happy circumstance I should
find you here, Mrs. Colton. I have come to request
the next waltz." He ambled to her side of the table.

She hastily moved around to where he had been
standing. "That is very kind of you, sir. However, I
no longer wish to dance this evening." She matched
his continued stride around the table.

After two laps, he responded, "But you are the only

female I wish to partner tonight. I would be sorely disappointed if you refused." He continued to stroll toward her with a barely perceptible increase in speed.

She quickened her pace. "I am sorry to disappoint you, but let's be honest with each other. Your presence here is related to your wager with Lord Parker, isn't it?"

He feigned innocence. "And what wager would that be, madam?"

"Come now, sir. You and his lordship have some sort of bet in regard to me. Admit it." By now his long legs were moving so fast—she needed to run.

"And if we did, surely you don't suspect me of winning the bet when there is no one around to witness the fact?" He broke out in a run. Within seconds, he caught her arm and spun her to face him. "Really, madam, I'm hurt you don't trust me."

"I trust you as much as I trust Lord Parker." She tried to step back, but he reached out and held her with both hands. He waited a minute—then tilted his head to catch a distant sound. The noise grew louder.

Next he focused on her mouth. "Mrs. Colton, I believe you have something caught in your hair." He started to pull her close.

She tried to struggle free, but his grip held fast.

Mr. Thornbury flung open the door.

Eleven

"MADAM…" MR. THORNBURY TURNED BACK TOWARD the hallway.

"Mr. Thornbury!" Elinor took advantage of Mr. Drexel's momentary release of her arms and ran to her host. "Some sort of farce is being played here, and I'm the target. I request that you escort me back to your guests, please."

A muscle in Mr. Thornbury's jaw twitched as he examined her face. He moved sideways to glare at the other man. "Drexel?"

Mr. Drexel appeared relaxed, yet impassive, tapping several fingers on the slate table. "Thornbury."

Mr. Thornbury held out his hand in a motion for her to lead the way. "At your service, madam."

Elinor left the chill of the salting room and started back to the party, while the two men followed in silence. Did Mr. Thornbury believe she orchestrated this rendezvous? He must be aware of the wager, surely? At the top of the stairs, she waited until a grinning Mr. Drexel ambled off toward the drawing room, before she addressed her host. "Sir, being followed has left me a little unsettled. I'd like to return home now; however, I do not wish to interfere with my nephew's enjoyment. May I request the use of your carriage and a servant to accompany me home? Berdy can return to Pinnacles in the gig when he is ready."

Mr. Thornbury avoided her gaze. He peered at the paneled wall, then kept his focus on the Persian carpet while he said, "Ah, of course." A frown appeared under his knotted brows as he turned to stare down the hallway in the direction Mr. Drexel had taken.

She caught a note of foreboding in his tone, suggesting perhaps this farce was not over yet. Maybe Lord Parker, even now, hid in the carriage, ready to kiss her as she climbed in, a well-paid footman grinning nearby.

"Mrs. Colton," he whispered, taking a step closer. "Please accept my apologies…"

She gave him a questioning gaze, but she could not discern the sentiment expressed upon his face.

He moved directly in front of her and paused. "Dunderhead schoolboy…friends."

She waited for an explanation.

"I don't want this incident to endanger…" Using the back of his hand, he softly stroked her cheek. "Forgive me?"

She felt comforted; his touch she regarded as an expression of kindness.

"I don't want you unsettled," he said. "I want you happy and…" He kissed her tenderly, his lips barely touching hers.

First she lost herself in pleasure. Seconds later, she

tried to understand his gesture. It was not a kiss of persuasion, nor one of fun, but a kiss heralding the beginning of fondness between two people.

When the kiss ended, he leaned on the wall, supporting himself with one arm and an open palm. He looked down at the carpet, his constricted expression troubled.

She stood unmoving, but remained close enough to feel his warm breath upon her face. The stringent taste of brandy lingered on her lips. There were no witnesses about, so his kiss could not be part of the wager. His kiss must have been a spontaneous gesture to ease her distress, perhaps a behavior that came naturally for rakes. While she did not understand men like him, his anguish concerned her, because she owed him so much for Berdy's recovery. To show him she felt no ill will, and firmly acknowledged their friendship, she kissed him on the cheek—a tender kiss of regard. She gazed into his questioning blue eyes. "Thank you, for all you have done for Berdy."

The troubled expression in his eyes transformed into their normal dry amusement. "Normally chapter four is—"

"Ross!" Lady Helen marched down the hallway, her black bombazine skirt shimmering and rustling like a dark cloud in a strong wind.

Mr. Thornbury stepped all the way back to the opposite wall. As far away from Elinor as the passageway allowed.

For a fleeting second, Elinor regretted the loss of his touch. Then the full realization of her kiss's indiscretion hit her. Angry with herself for her usual inability to conform to the expectations of proper behavior, she could only glare at Lady Helen.

Lady Helen confronted her. "I knew it was a mistake to invite you here. If you interfere in any way with my son's betrothal, there will be consequences."

"Mother—"

"You are wrong, Lady Helen." Elinor blushed uncontrollably. She needed to stem the older woman's misconceptions about her relationship with her son and swiftly deny that any personal confidences existed between them. "I am resolved—I have no intention of interfering in your son's affairs." If only the disparity between her words and her blushing cheeks was not so obvious.

Lady Helen clutched Ross's arm. "You must keep away from *that woman*. There are already shocking rumors about her shameful behavior now that she is a widow. We have no need for her disgraceful society."

Elinor froze; speech eluded her.

Mr. Thornbury lifted his mother's hand and patted it, his natural charm regained. "A simple misunderstanding. Mrs. Colton only expressed her gratitude for her nephew's care." His mischievous grin appeared. "The only lady whose society I am interested in tonight is your friend Lady Welton." He bent to kiss his mother on the cheek. "After what you told me about her skills at whist, I'm dying to be introduced. Come, we must return to our other guests." He turned his head to address Elinor. "Please forgive me." He paused. "Again. Wait here while I make arrangements for the carriage." He firmly led his mother down the hall.

The older woman glared over her shoulder.

Elinor's thoughts raced like an out-of-control team of horses, ready to pursue Lady Helen for further explanation of the older woman's comment. *Tell me, what shocking rumors?*

❧

"I'm looking forward to the purchase of fine buttons," Berdy said, his head lowered to peer at his yellow-striped waistcoat. "I understand some of the finest button makers in all of England will be at the fair today. I'm planning on large brass buttons with scrollwork—like the insides of a fusee watch—for m' second-best waistcoat." He poked his waistcoat at the location of the planned buttons. "Where is Ross? If he's late, we might miss the buttons."

The mention of Mr. Thornbury's name reminded Elinor of her well-intentioned, but brief, losses of propriety in his presence. *She kissed him.* Not like his rakish kisses, which were nothing more serious than his outrageous teasing. She'd kissed an unmarried gentleman of recent acquaintance. Her kiss of gratitude must have appeared like behavior more suited to a romantic heroine in a three-volume novel than a respectable widow. Since she didn't want to sully her reputation, and according to Lady Helen, rumors had already begun, she resolved to be proper to a fault today. Otherwise, her actions might create a scandal impossible to escape.

Now more than a week after being chased at the evening soiree, she waited with Berdy for Mr. Thornbury's carriage to transport them to the Barnaby fair. They would be joined by separate carriages carrying Lord Parker and Mr. Drexel, the Allardyce family in their carriage, and several other carriages for transporting the Thornbury's house party. Peering toward the window, Elinor wondered if time and familiarity would dull her unexpected, yet seemingly predictable, response to Mr. Thornbury's charm. With any luck, he'd be a proper gentleman and not tease her with silly kisses. She'd be luckier still if he kept his promise to mention his varied business achievements to Berdy—the very reason she accepted his invitation to join him and his guests at the fair today.

"Silks too," Berdy addressed the Gothic window, craning his neck sideways for the first sight of Mr. Thornbury's approach up the drive. "Ross mentioned the possibility of new silks. That Ross is truly a bang-up blade, don't you agree?"

She hoped Mr. Thornbury would be a bang-up, boring blade today. She didn't dare mention any subject that might lead him to comment upon her kiss of gratitude or give him the chance to tease her with his handbook's devilish *chapters*.

"Elli, are you listening to me?"

"Of course, buttons. Oh look, here he comes." Once greetings were exchanged, they climbed into Mr. Thornbury's landau. Initially pleased to discover the previous week had granted her the mantle of composure, she discovered that within minutes this composure dissolved as Mr. Thornbury discussed the festival with Berdy. She found it difficult to look at him, because for some stupefying reason, her eyes were drawn to his seductive mouth. That feature seemed different from William's, yet she couldn't describe the precise differences. Her cheeks warmed, and she tried to concentrate on the blur of green scenery outside the carriage, to no avail. Finally, it became impossible to ignore the truth any longer. She had been using some silly comparisons to William as an excuse to mask her physical attraction to Mr. Thornbury. An attraction probably felt by every female of his acquaintance, so she shouldn't worry about it overmuch. Her attraction to him had no relationship—in any way—to her feelings for William. This realization eased her restless mind. Now she wouldn't feel guilty every time she glanced in admiration at Mr. Thornbury.

During their long journey to the fair, Berdy provided detailed commentary upon every feature flying past the carriage. Then, after a couple of hours, they reached an open field south of Macclesfield that had been transformed into a local fair. A brief shower had ended, and even though they arrived in the late afternoon, the sun still shone. Bright multicolored banners whipped in the breeze above the townsfolk strolling along rows lined with vendors. Shouts describing customer testimonials mingled with loud promises of satisfaction. Up ahead, a platform had been erected for the day's speeches, and later for the display of the evening's fireworks.

The landau jostled with other carriages, gigs, and carts for the best viewing position. Eventually, the carriages from Blackwell joined a broad semicircle of carriages just off the main road. Because of their late arrival, their carriage joined a line of vehicles at the back. The coachman, George, folded the top of the landau for an unimpeded view of the festivities. He then left to join a small group of servants heading toward the fireworks platform. A Catherine wheel had been promised for the evening's illuminations, and no one wanted to miss that glorious spectacle.

Behind the sea of carriages in front of her, Elinor stood to observe the crowd. The local men, women, and children were all in boisterous high spirits. Most of the newly arrived quickly exited their carriages to join the infectious celebrations.

After waving to some of her friends standing next to a nearby curricle, she caught Mr. Thornbury offering Berdy spirits from a silver flask. The two men turned their backs to her and drank liberally. Berdy hiccuped, causing Mr. Thornbury to slap him across the back. When they turned to face her, both men wore a what-did-we-do smile.

Mr. Thornbury had clearly become a great hero of Berdy's, but their conversation, at least in her presence, kept to frivolous topics, like cravats, and didn't include any serious subjects, like professions. She was not quite sure what to make of their friendship. Berdy should choose his own future; she knew that theoretically. She could even give justice to Mr. Thornbury's drunken accusation about leading strings. Except the thought of Berdy making his own life's decisions caused a knot of fear in her stomach. Glancing at the two men sharing a jest, she hoped Berdy might associate with more suitable companions in London, gentlemen his own age with serious pursuits. She exhaled a long sigh.

Mr. Thornbury winked at her. "Happy?"

Soon. She must introduce Berdy to other young gentlemen soon. "Tolerably so."

Mr. Thornbury addressed Berdy. "You should leave to examine the goods. Don't want to miss any new silks." He moved to open the carriage door for Berdy to exit.

Berdy failed to budge. "Saw a few silks from the carriage when we arrived, but I must admit disappointment. Once this fair was full of fashionable goods. Now it's all wax dolls and gingerbread nuts."

"Mr. Thornbury," she said, "perhaps this is a good time to tell Berdy about your businesses. For example, the number of opportunities suitable for a gentleman's son in engineering, architecture, or the construction of canals. We'll be in London this spring, and I hope Berdy will investigate these professions as potential livings."

"Of course, Mrs. Colton. What would you like to discuss?"

She patted Berdy's knee to get his attention. "I know in order to build a canal you need to obtain an Act of Parliament. Can you explain the process to us?"

Before he could reply, the sight of Dr. Potts's daughter running up to their carriage distracted everyone. Miss Potts valiantly held on to her bonnet in the stiff wind, and Elinor thought she resembled a young sitter in a Reynolds portrait, all pink cheeks and breezy youth. Miss Potts recognized Berdy first and waved. When she reached the carriage, Berdy made the formal introductions.

Upon hearing Mr. Thornbury's name, Miss Potts

widened her eyes. "*You* are Mr. Thornbury?" she asked in a tone of hoydenish admiration Elinor guessed was unintentional.

"Pleasure, Miss Potts," Mr. Thornbury said with effortless gallantry.

Miss Potts openly stared at him. "It is a great honor to meet you at last. Um, our carriage is right over there." She pointed behind her shoulder without turning. "Father asked how your foot got on, Mr. Deane. He'll join us in a moment, after he pays his respects to the widow Selby."

Elinor peeked at the two men, both smiling at the lovely girl outside the carriage. Berdy appeared overly slender in comparison to the solid frame of Mr. Thornbury. His figure seemed to fill the old landau. Now it seemed inconceivable that once she had considered him "almost handsome." He was so handsome it was difficult for any woman to look away. The memory of his soft lips pressing against hers in the hallway returned. And, of course, she started to blush—couldn't stop it.

Mr. Thornbury glanced at Elinor with a bemused expression upon his face. "Ah, I see by your cheeks you are reading my handbook again. Starting on chapter four, or is it five?"

"Oh." She stifled a giggle. *Curse his boots.* Her blush expanded.

He winked.

Miss Potts glanced over her shoulder, then leaned closer to Elinor. "I overheard Father mention his handbook too. Have you read it, Mrs. Colton?" She giggled. "Is it terribly naughty?"

"I've read it, and it's not a book for proper girls," Berdy admonished, fidgeting in his seat.

Mr. Thornbury raised his eyebrows.

"Berdy!" Elinor said. "That's a shocking fib. You have not read it. I doubt anyone has, for that matter." She glanced at Mr. Thornbury. "Nobody should read it."

Berdy reddened. "Well, no I haven't, but Dr. Potts warned me about it. He said he read it, so I'm as good as an expert." He leaned close to Miss Potts. "Now since you asked about my limb, I'm pleased to tell you that m' foot—"

"As the lady of the house," Miss Potts said to Mr. Thornbury, all but ignoring Berdy, "I would like to extend an invitation to dine this week. I am sure Father would be delighted with your company. Perhaps Tuesday?" A smiling Miss Potts coiled a ringlet around her forefinger.

Elinor blinked, repeatedly. Miss Potts was just sixteen, and here she was batting her long eyelashes at the man and inviting him to dinner, flirting with a gentleman at least fifteen years older than she was. And a dangerous gentleman to flirt with, too. Mr. Thornbury looked particularly handsome today in a dark blue superfine coat and nankeen-colored trousers. He gave Miss Potts one of his lanky grins that involved only one side of his mouth, then leaned back in the seat and crossed his long legs. Elinor noticed his shiny black boots rested a mere inch away from her kid shoes. While formulating a request to move his boots, she found her wanton gaze traveling up his body, but this upward movement stopped and lingered upon the watch fob nestled deep within the folds of his butter-colored trousers. She jerked her glance to the side, irritated by her physical attraction to his person, and for not being able to control her blushes in his presence.

Neither hers, nor Miss Potts's, reactions to Mr. Thornbury surprised her. Her brief acquaintance with him had schooled her in the behavior of rakes. They project their considerable masculine allure upon all females and earn the title "Rake" because—unlike other men—their charms enjoyed a great deal of success. Berdy's father was reputed to be a rake, and unlike her sister, she had resisted his masculine allures. So if she tried very hard, she should be able to resist this one rake, despite her recent failures. She peeked at him again. *Heavens*. She hoped this knowledge would protect her against Mr. Thornbury's rakish charm.

Dr. Potts approached their party and had evidently heard his daughter's well-pressed invitation to dine. He greeted everyone, then said, "The invitation is, of course, meant for you, dear lady, but Mr. Thornbury may attend."

Before Mr. Thornbury could respond to the Potts's invitation, Berdy struggled to stand and offered to accompany Miss Potts to the fair. "Can a fellow offer you some gingerbread nuts?"

Dr. Potts agreed to his daughter's silent entreaty to accept. Only Elinor's protestations about Berdy's foot went unheard as he hopped off with the aid of a cane in the company of Miss Potts toward the festivities.

Next Lord Parker and Mr. Drexel strode up to the side of the carriage. "Two," Lord Parker said, "up for

some country ale served by a fetching wench?" He
glanced toward Elinor. "Pardon, ma'am. I—"

"Mrs. Colton," Dr. Potts interrupted, "may I escort
you to the booths? From there we can keep an eye on
the children." He held his hand up to block the light
from the low sun, or to shield Mr. Thornbury from
his view.

"Thank you, but I prefer to stay awhile. There is
a matter of business regarding Berdy's future that Mr.
Thornbury promised to discuss with me."

"Right then," Lord Parker said. "Two, we'll see
you in a tick." He and Mr. Drexel ambled off toward
the fair's booths.

Dr. Potts waved a hand in dismissal. "Ah, surely
I can give you similar advice? As I have done these
many years."

"I am grateful for your advice, sir," she said. "And
for your advice to Berdy last week about the professions available in medicine for a gentleman. However,
in this case, I seek information about the technical
opportunities available in commerce and engineering. Mr. Thornbury has some recent expertise in
this subject."

"Not trade." Dr. Potts scowled, his perfect posture
straightening even more. "Deane would do well to
enter the church, stand before the bar, or join the
navy. Indeed, many young gentlemen find fame and
fortune in London."

She grinned wistfully at the thought of Berdy strolling the deck of one of His Majesty's ships of the line.
"I don't believe he must enter a profession suitable for
the son of a peer. He is a gentleman's son, and I have

witnessed many good livings made by gentlemen in industry, especially around the Midlands. And industry may be the future for our impoverished young gentlemen. There is no harm in inquiry, is there?"

"Very well. I'll take my leave then." Dr. Potts bowed. "Mrs. Colton, Mr. Thornbury." He headed off in the direction Berdy and Miss Potts had taken.

"I thought they'd never leave," Mr. Thornbury said, moving his boot so it touched her slipper.

That's when she made a tactical mistake. In an effort to stop his boot from touching hers, she innocently suggested a change. "You'll find more room for your feet if you move to this side of the carriage. The seat is long and has plenty of room."

For an instant his eyes darkened. "At your command," he drawled, making a lightning-fast jump from one seat to the other, causing the carriage to bounce.

The landau was substantial, with plenty of room for four people. He could easily have sat with space between them, as she expected, but he sat next to her. His thigh shoved up against her leg, and she flinched at the touch of hard muscles acquired by hours spent on horseback.

"A noticeable change from our meeting at the lake, when you requested I sit five feet away," he crowed, like a cock entering a new coop and finding only hens.

She tried to sound calm. "Can we return to the subject of Berdy?"

"Very well. His talents? Besides cravat knots." He took another drink from the flask.

She quickly countered. "He's interested in all forms

of machines. That dandy horse, for example. Moreover, he can spend hours looking at steam engines." She caught his grin. "Not just silks."

"His political abilities? Could Deane persuade an angry group of landowners to accept a canal or turnpike across their property?"

She considered his question for a moment. "I don't know the answer, but I do know Berdy has consistently surprised me. I believe he is capable of anything he sets his mind to."

"Fair enough. I will consider your request. In return, I ask you to reconsider the lease we discussed."

She jerked at the transient touch of his shoulder and wiggled to put distance between them. "Mr. Thornbury, please. I must admit that I have reconsidered my objections, but I still have concerns about the smoke and soot."

"Yes, but now I only request you join me in touring a foundry southeast of Manchester. I believe it is important for you to see the reduction in smoke produced from a taller chimney fitted with a new smoke catcher. A lesson I admittedly learned from my own chimneys. You see, I recently increased the height of my drawing room's chimney. The taller flue has greater draft, so the room no longer becomes filled by a smoky haze."

The snake of guilt coiled around her heart. Hope sounded in his voice, and she didn't want to disappoint him after his assistance to Berdy. Besides, here was her chance to get his opinion on a few issues in regard to the foundry. For example, the number of families with children that would be employed.

However, she first needed to make her objections clear. He should harbor no expectations of her approval before their journey. "Please don't mistake me, I am grateful—"

"Gratitude, an underappreciated quality." He twisted to face her, and whatever mood had touched him earlier, the rogue was now firmly in place.

She recognized mischief's fire in his eyes, no doubt fueled by the spirits in the silver flask. "I know the power of your charm around women. I know you are aware of it too. So I'm not going to let you kiss me, if that is what you want."

"Ha! You won't let me kiss you…don't you enjoy kisses of gratitude?"

"Yes. No. Listen. Gentlemen have used masculine wiles on me before to get what they want. I'm not a green girl. Keep your *gratitude* kisses to yourself."

"I have no intention of kissing myself." He gave a deep, resonant chuckle. "No kisses then. My masculine wiles must be rather rusty. Don't you agree?" He took another drink from the silver flask.

"No, of course not—I mean—yes—heavens." She scooted to the opposite seat, gentle panic heating her cheeks and fully aware that more outrageous innuendo would likely follow.

"So I'm not rusty?"

"No."

"No," he mimicked triumphantly, jumping to join her on the other seat.

She shuffled close to the carriage's door. "Please, let's not repeat a conversation where every answer is no."

"Agreed. We'll try yeses this time." His arm slid along the top of the seat behind her back. "Much more positive. Ready for chapter...let's see, chapter four, yes?"

She began to chuckle softly. "Mr. Thornbury, enough of this game. Whatever the rules are, I'm sure you've won. Stop teasing me with your imaginary chapters."

"Ah, but since you have not yet agreed to visit a new mine, we have nothing else to talk about except *The Rake's Handbook*. I'm sure you're eager to know what is in chapter ten."

"I already know. *The End*." By now she had scooted as far as possible, and her arm was wedged against the side of the carriage.

"Not The End. I wrote the book, remember. Chapter ten is not The End, it is only the end of volume one."

"Volume one. I really—"

"Since you're one of those naughty, impatient readers who skips chapters, I'll submit to your weakness and read chapter ten."

She shoved his shoulder as hard as she could. After briefly leaning sideways with her push, he righted, his mischievous grin appearing again. She laughed heartily—couldn't help it. Never had she met a man like him; his charm proved unstoppable. "Suddenly I have great admiration for your mother." She turned in the direction of the festivities and tried to calm herself.

It was one of those things women *knew* without looking. He was behind her and examining her—closely. She jumped at the touch of his light fingertip on her shoulder. "Yes?" she asked without turning to face him.

No reply. The touch of his finger returned and traced up her back, leaving a prickling trail of its presence. She heard a soft rushing sound and realized he was blowing on her hair. Then the finger returned to join his other fingers as he cupped his big palm around her neck. Without thought, she leaned into his warm hand before she turned around to discover his face within inches of hers. "P-please move back. I don't want anyone who passes this carriage to get the wrong impression."

"We are off to the side, quite alone, and isolated from sight due to the high sides of this carriage. But you're right," he said with a soft laugh, "a wrong impression would compromise my gentlemanly reputation."

"Your repu—"

"You will come with me to the new chimney. Yes?"

Heavens. "You will help Berdy. Share your business interests. Yes?"

"Yes." He framed her face with his hands and kissed her soundly. The kiss was long enough to taste the brandy and feel the unexpected softness of his lips. He pulled his head back; his expression revealed surprise, similar to what she was feeling.

She tried to speak again, but stopped when she caught sight of his lips. She never should have looked at his mouth. Her mind blanked. He drew a deep breath, and she instinctively gulped air before they rushed forward into a spontaneous kiss. She should gather her wits now and refuse him. Ask him to stop. Push him away. *Say something.*

"Allow me to thank you," he whispered, his lips resting on hers while his thumb traced lazy circles under her ear.

Perhaps she moaned—someone moaned. He twisted her around to face the carriage's side, and she felt the heated touch of his beguiling lips on the back of her neck. Caught by his warm hands and seduced by his wandering kisses under her ears, she fought to gain control of conscious speech. His lingering kisses brought back exquisite responses within her she had either forgotten or buried. She also caught his smell, one she easily recognized, the heavy scent of a man before sleep, sharing brandy-laced whispers under a blanket.

His hot breath warmed her skin, and she let her head fall to the side. He moved his head forward over her shoulder while he continued to kiss her neck. His deep chocolate-colored hair fell loose and glowed like brushed sable in the weak light of the late afternoon.

Reaching up, she caressed the soft hair at the top of his head and threaded her fingers through his locks. She heaved a blissful sigh. Then the stubble on his jaw scraped her cheek, thrilling her heartbeat into a run. She even brushed, on purpose, against his whiskers several times. His mouth surrounded her earlobe and teasingly bit it, before his moist tongue entered her ear and lazily traced circles around its perimeter. Another soft moan escaped with her breath. "Ahh."

She tried to face him, but he stopped her and replied in a broken voice, "In this chapter, you don't turn around."

One of his hands moved around in front of her,

and his palm spread outward, covering her waist. He pulled her full against him, and the incendiary heat between them flared. The pressure from his mobile lips assaulted her neckline, while his hand gently cupped her breast. Her soft moan mingled with his low growl, and the sound escaped into the air above them.

He moved his hand slowly, lightly tracing the outline of her breasts over her wool gown. His long fingers unbuttoned several buttons around her neck and pulled the gown lower over her shoulder until one breast was covered only by her short stays and chemise. He found the swell at the side of her breast, and he rubbed his palm back and forth where the curve began. Then he cupped her full breast—*hard*.

"Oh," she cried, warmth claiming her body. Any attempt at speech was over. Lost in the fog of passion, she passed control of her physical responses to his deft touch. He finally moved his hands to her shoulders and turned her to face him. Even in the light of a gathering dusk, she could see his potent gaze, and another long sigh escaped her. He leaned forward to brush his clever lips back and forth over hers. With their lips barely touching, he paused. His face filled her vision, and she focused on the stubble covering his cheek. She didn't move; her heartbeat raced. What was he waiting for?

Did she say "yes"? Maybe she did, without saying the word.

He covered her mouth with an urgent, rhythmic kiss. He kissed her deeply, pulled back until his lips lingered, then returned deeper. Pulled back and kissed deeper. Her wits melted into extinction. The stubble around his skillful lips scraped her skin, causing an inferno within, and her heartbeat echoed around her. She opened her mouth in a blatant invitation, and received his tongue deep within her mouth. He withdrew it, plunged again, and made seductive circles over her tongue.

Heaven, heaven, *heavens*.

He lowered her below the elbow-line of the carriage and onto the squabs of the seat. His broad chest covered her in warmth. Lost in their rhythmic kiss, he freed several ties and tugged at her stays. The garment dropped a few inches, giving him enough room to reach under her chemise and free the top of one breast to the cool air. Helpless and wanting his touch, she arched again as he took the top of her breast into his mouth. His tongue played lazy circles over the swell of flesh. She stroked his hair, while a pounding noise grew louder, like rolling thunder, and she arched to its beat.

An unfamiliar voice rang out, "Tom, my lad, clap yo'r eyes on th' bonny moon."

This was followed by laughter, and she opened her eyes. More than a dozen men and women stood ogling them over the side of the carriage. Part of a large crowd heading for the road and moving around them like a rock protruding in a swift stream.

"*Hell's fire.*" Mr. Thornbury reflexively sat up. In the next few seconds of panic, he pulled up her half stays and managed to straighten her gown.

"I reckon yo' ha' yo'r own fireworks there, gov," said one man.

The crowd responded with a hearty cheer.

She heard several complaints about the fireworks

spoiled by "the bloody rain." So without their promised Catherine wheel, everyone had headed for home in the direction of the main road.

"Ay, and I seed his are all bust too," someone yelled. Raucous laughter exploded amongst the crowd.

Dr. Potts and Lord Parker ran to join the gathering mob around the carriage.

She sat dazed, uncomprehending, breathing hard. Above all of the shouts and laughter, she heard, "Seems we missed all the fun." Dozens of people stood fixed in place around the carriage and whispered to their neighbor.

Mr. Thornbury's raised voiced boomed over the crowd, "Ladies and gentlemen, Mrs. Colton has just agreed to become my wife."

Twelve

Ross turned to find Mrs. Colton's face a bright scarlet.

"How dare—"

He automatically held out his hand, for some reason he didn't comprehend. "I apologize. Failed to think properly—couldn't—think properly. Tried to save your—our—reputations."

She glared at his palm and clapped her mouth shut.

Ross noticed several ladies standing fixed around the rail of the carriage, unable to call forth speech.

While a grim Dr. Potts gripped the side of the carriage so tightly, his knuckles reddened. "You, you, you," he spat out before he quickly led his daughter away.

Deane moved forward through the retreating crowd and climbed with difficulty into the landau. The others in their party arrived only to hear the news from the gossiping mob. Mr. Allardyce's face reddened too, and without comment, he hurried back to stop his daughters from approaching. Ross's other house guests wished the couple well and headed to their carriages for the return journey to Blackwell.

The sunlight had faded into early dusk, but Ross could still discern Mrs. Colton's anger. Her stiff movements as she righted her gown, coupled with a dark glare worthy of his mother's best disapproving stare, persuaded him to hold off awhile before he attempted another remark upon their current predicament.

Deane failed to catch his aunt's angry countenance and appeared quite pleased with the news. "Engaged to Ross. I couldn't be happier. Told you he was a bang-up blade. Yes, dash it all, I suppose you know that already." Deane embraced Mrs. Colton and planted a loud kiss upon her cheek. "Capital fellow, Elli, capital. I wish you both happy." He leaned over and shook Ross's hand at least five times up and down. "Well, this is news, indeed." He reached into his pocket and pulled out an object for Mrs. Colton. "Here is a most excellent gingerbread nut. Consider it an early wedding gift. But a gingerbread nut can't compete with betrothal news, now can it?"

Mrs. Colton stared at the sweet in Deane's hand.

The coachman returned from the festivities, and Ross jumped out to assist him in raising the top of the landau. Not an action he would normally do, but it did spare him the sight of Mrs. Colton's barely constrained anger. Yanking on the black folding head harder than he planned, Ross whipped the top out from George's grip. He ignored his coachman's surprised expression and fastened the latches on his side. After his latches were closed, he took a deep breath of the soft dusk air and watched the light gray clouds darken with the approach of nightfall. Caught in the fog of temptation, he'd failed to behave like a proper gentleman.

He'd put the foundry at risk, and he'd endangered his mother's sanity. *Damn, he was an idiot.*

George snapped the final latch into place, climbed up on his seat, and gathered the ribbons.

His coachman's actions roused Ross away from his atmospheric contemplations, and he joined the others in the carriage. They soon got under way on their return journey to Pinnacles. He settled back into the comfort of the landau's thick squabs, his much-tried body seeking rest.

Deane, in spite of his words to the contrary, embarked upon the wonders of gingerbread nuts.

"Enough!" Mrs. Colton exclaimed seconds later.

Choking on the word "diaphanous," Deane raised his brow and turned to Ross, a silent male question to another male about an inexplicable female response.

Mrs. Colton reached out to squeeze Deane's hand. "I apologize. I fear I have the headache from all of this excitement. Mr. Thornbury's proposal was never accepted, you understand. He and I have many things yet to discuss."

"But…" Deane turned to Ross again in mute inquiry.

Ross was unsure of the meaning behind her use of the word "many," but he did want one fact to be known. He had not planned to become engaged to Mrs. Colton, but a true gentleman must be ready to save a lady's reputation at all times. Once several citizens had witnessed their indiscretion, he'd failed to see any other way to lessen the scandal, other than announcing their betrothal. But her terse words and rigid manners persuaded him to save his explanations for a later date. Doubtless she'd praise him for his quick thinking once she was at leisure to consider her current situation. "Your aunt and I must make arrangements before any formal announcements are made—"

"But you will publish the news soon?" Berdy said. "Elli?" Without a reply from her, he addressed Ross. "You must tell me everything. You *do* mean to wed, don't you?"

"Berdy, please." Mrs. Colton's mouth remained open, so she probably intended to say something.

"I keep my promises," Ross added, pulling his stare away from the allure of her well-kissed lips and the location of the hiding dimple. "Your aunt and I reached an agreement, a tentative agreement, but an agreement nevertheless. We celebrated our success with a little affectionate kiss, that's all."

With that statement from him, her mouth closed, and her expression might be described as *wry*.

"Kissing in public, how scandalous," Deane exclaimed. "I'm sure this fair will be remarkable for many and be remembered for years to come."

"Years and years," Ross answered.

The slightest of grins finally broke across Mrs. Colton's face.

Deane leaned forward and whispered to Ross, "Things we must discuss, what?"

Ross had no idea what a young man with aspirations to become a Pink of the Ton needed to say to him, but he knew well enough to save that request also for another time.

Deane continued speaking without reply or provocation. "I can't wait to wear m' new silk waistcoat at your wedding. The stripes are a splendid sky blue, very modest, and the buttons are made of silver lattice work." The young man straightened. "Of course, I will join you both when we walk down the aisle... I can see—"

"Please," Mrs. Colton said with tight-lipped restraint. "Why don't you tell me about the fair?"

Her question proved successful, as the two adults continued their journey without exchanging words. Only the sole efforts of the youngest in their party kept the mostly one-sided conversation flowing smoothly.

During the return journey to Pinnacles, Ross found the leisure to contemplate his announcement. For some reason, he couldn't help but rejoice in his good fortune to have Mrs. Colton—Elinor—as his bride, since he enjoyed her spirited company. While being a gentleman and saving her was his first thought upon their discovery, he now recognized the prosperous lands he would gain upon marriage. With the joining of their estates, together they would build Blackwell into one of the great properties of Cheshire.

Still, he harbored a slight uneasiness that affection motivated his proposal. An obvious conclusion, since his friends' wager had surprisingly irritated him, and today he readily gave in to the attraction that flared between them. His famed control of passionate situations had deserted him entirely. These ruminations were interrupted by a vague haberdashery question from Deane. Ross replied, "Yes, I admire curly brimmed hats too."

Ross liked the idea of marriage to Elinor. All in all, he should have considered this engagement before. Indeed, he should have presented it to her earlier as a marriage of convenience. He needed to respond politely to one of Deane's questions again. "No, you are right, white satin is inappropriate for that time of day."

Ross began to realize he truly liked Mrs. Colton. No, not liked, he was fond of her, not overly fond, nor in love—just fond. He glanced in her direction again. The widow appeared overset, biting her lower lip until it disappeared under the upper. The sight created a strong desire to embrace her. Tease and kiss her until he achieved his desired wish—a small "oh." Annoyed by this thought, he congratulated himself on his decision to postpone their betrothal discussion to a later date when his sanity returned. So when she accepted his formal proposal, he'd remain calm and proper. For the remainder of the journey, instead of considering his mother, Lucy, or the foundry, as he should, he contemplated his bothersome desire to provoke the appearance of her frolicking dimple.

After their arrival at Pinnacles, he invited Deane on a journey the following week to observe gears used to lift heavy weights, similar to those planned for his foundry's wench. Deane eagerly accepted his invitation, and Ross exited the carriage to hold the door open. Deane scuttled out of the landau as best he could, but Mrs. Colton lingered behind. More than likely formulating the right words to chastise him.

He seized her hand and gently pulled her from the carriage. "We have much to discuss. I'll call upon you tomorrow afternoon, sweetheart."

❧

An early morning mist claimed the courtyard as Ross mounted the broad back of his dappled gray and adjusted the reins in his gloved hand. His morning ablutions had left his hair wet, so the light wind quickly chilled him. Off in the distance, he heard his mother's voice calling him. Explanations were the very, very last thing on earth he wanted now. First, he needed to make sense of yesterday's remarkable events.

He spurred the gray toward his tenants' farms to check upon the new hedgerow repairs. While he regretted being caught in an unseemly position, the announcement of their betrothal must go a long way in stemming any scandal. Although gossip may flare up for a time, he was confident it would settle down once they were wed.

It began to drizzle, so he pulled his hat firmly down on his brow.

Focus, Ross. Six months ago he had paid for hedgerow repairs, so he'd better damn well get back to work and make sure the job had been completed to his satisfaction. He glanced at a small shrub planted in a spot where one day it would fill a hole in the hedge above it. The green plant seemed alive—good.

When he returned to the house, Rowbottom informed him his mother requested his presence in the drawing room. By the expression on his butler's face, Ross understood avoiding her was not an option.

Mother. How would she respond to his recent news?

His mother might have two very different reactions upon hearing of his betrothal to Mrs. Colton. First, she might object to the match because she deemed Elinor a frivolous chit, but by now she must have reached a similar conclusion about Lucy.

The widow's earlier denial of the lease probably created an even larger impediment to his mother's acceptance of the alliance. After hearing about Elinor's refusal to sign, Lady Helen had remained silent for a full two days.

He next considered his mother's opposite reaction to the situation. She might be delighted over his engagement. She had pleaded for him to wed, and now her long-sought-after wish of his marriage would come true. The other advantage, and probably the strongest argument in Elinor's favor, was that his mother would achieve her greatest dream—grandchildren.

Since his mother never mentioned reasons for him to wed, other than love and grandchildren—love being impossible for him. He gained confidence that Lady Helen would likely approve of the match due to the possibility of grandchildren. He grinned, his mind eased. Now he looked forward to witnessing her happiness when she learned of his impending marriage. "Mother. *Motherrr*," he yelled through Blackwell's hallways. He found her in the formal drawing room, sitting with pen and paper at a small table, the green leather surface obscured by numerous furniture catalogs.

Upon his entry, Dr. Potts rose and nodded a brief greeting. The doctor's gray wool coat matched the sunken gray color of his cheeks and the hair at his temples.

Ross nodded in return and took a chair next to his mother. Putting his arm around her shoulders, he pulled her close and kissed the top of her head. "Ah, there you are, dear. Trying to avoid me?" He settled in his chair and stretched his long legs out in front of him.

"Honestly," Lady Helen said, shaking her pen. "What will the servants think about all your bellowing? They will say I raised you in the local tavern."

"I'll take my leave of you now, Lady Helen," Dr. Potts said, stepping forward to stand next to Ross's chair. "Sir, may I have a word with you before I leave?"

"Of course." He waited, curious about the doctor's request.

Dr. Potts frowned. "I mean a private word."

"Ah." He expected some news of his mother's health, so he followed the physician out of the room into the hallway. "Yes?"

Dr. Potts gave him a fulminating stare. "You must break off your engagement to Mrs. Colton. Immediately! I fear the shock has caused your mother great harm. Despite her brave speech, her spirits are not strong. For the last twenty minutes she has only mumbled on about furniture. I cannot get a single salient response from her, and I fear for her mind."

"Sir, the engagement is my business. Mother is pleased with the news, I'm sure."

"So you are fixed upon matrimony?" Dr. Potts lifted his chin.

Ross stiffened his posture. "Yes, I am."

"I warn you." The doctor glared at him again. "Whether or not your handbook is satire or not, the people around here gossip about little else. Some people, a very few, consider it a lighthearted jest, while others consider it vulgar and totally inappropriate that a person living within our vicinity could pen a book like that. If you wed Mrs. Colton, she will become tainted too and thus isolated from Polite Society. So unless you want a future of madness for your mother, and Mrs. Colton secluded forever, you must call off. Do you understand me?"

Ross struggled to contain his fury.

"If you do not immediately dissolve this engagement, there will be other severe consequences as well. Consequences in regard to your foundry. I suggest you think about your actions carefully." Dr. Potts strode to the entrance without taking his leave.

After waiting a minute for his anger to cool, Ross dismissed the doctor's reckless threats, except those related to his mother's state of mind, and returned to the drawing room. Since his mother had already heard about his engagement from someone else, he stood silently for several minutes, carefully watching her for any sign of distress. To him, she appeared well. There was no evidence of the return of her low spirits; therefore, the evidence proved the doctor's concerns had to be unjustified. Unjustified too in regard to Mrs. Colton. Why would one little satirical tome be taken so seriously, as to cast off a popular neighbor, and a widow to boot? The doctor's threats made no sense and sounded like overblown rubbish.

Lady Helen eventually waved him forward. "Don't just stand there. Give me a hand."

"What do you want me to do?" He kissed the top

of her head again and noticed she worked upon a diagram of furniture placement.

A frown covered her brow, a well-recognized expression of why-don't-men-understand-the-obvious? "You must clear off the console table, then help me move it to the opposite wall."

"Mother, please, call the servants. If I help you move furniture, the servants will think you raised me in the local tavern."

Lady Helen snatched the shepherdess figurine out of his hand. "Don't break the Staffordshire." She cradled the statue in her arms and placed it on a table far away from his reach.

He grinned. "This room looks fine. Why change it?"

"My new Gillow pieces," she said, placing her hands on her hips. "If we are to order mahogany furniture, I have to know what sizes to order. I can't purchase a fifty-two-inch sideboard and expect it to look well on a twenty-foot wall, now can I?"

"More furniture now? I thought we agreed to wait for the foundry's first profits."

"Since you've decided to wed Mrs. Colton for her funds, I will no longer have to wait until this estate is fully on its feet, or the foundry is profitable, before I acquire new pieces."

"Mother. Money is not the reason for my betrothal." He strode forward to tenderly embrace her. "How shall I put this? Yesterday, Mrs. Colton finally changed her mind and considered granting us a lease. A congratulatory embrace ensued, followed by...what followed is not important. But the town observed our affectionate gratitude. In fact, had we advertised the encounter by broadsheets, we could not have gotten better attendance." He raised a hand. "No, it's not what you think. I only gave her a…friendly kiss. So her reputation was compromised. I had no choice but to announce our engagement."

Lady Helen smiled weakly. "A peck on the cheek is not that scandalous. Mrs. Colton is a widow, so her reputation is not as fragile as if she were a young girl. You must not do anything rash. Apologize, but do not feel you have an obligation. I'm sure she will wish for the same."

"Ah, well…more than cheeks were pecked. My mind is set. In your heart you know it's the proper course of action. My inappropriate behavior and announcement created public expectations, so I will privately offer for Mrs. Colton later. As a gentleman, I must marry her immediately."

"Nonsense. She already had one husband, and women don't want two. Did you kiss her against her will? Of course not. Mrs. Colton must take responsibilities for her strumpet-like behavior."

"No, I gave you a vow to behave like a proper gentleman, so I must offer for her. Come now. I thought you'd be pleased. Marriage won't be that bad. I'll be the noble knight saving the queen from the dragon. Of course, I'm both the knight and the dragon, but it's the saving part that matters." He wondered how Elinor would behave toward him when he called upon her in the afternoon. Would she blush and flutter into his arms or vow undying love? Being female, she might expect him to use the "love" word. *Humph*. She would have to wait until men walked on the moon, because that would never happen. "What possible objections can you have to the match?"

"What about Lucy? Mr. Allardyce will claim breach of contract. We could find ourselves in the midst of scandal…the disgrace. Please, I want to remain welcomed in the neighborhood."

"You will be welcomed wherever you go, for your own sake. Everything will be fine, I promise. The marriage settlement with Allardyce had yet to be publicized, and the man was a friend as well as business partner." Ross expected nothing more detrimental than a difficult and embarrassing conversation. Allardyce had the right to seek a breach of contract suit, but he considered that possibility to have long odds, since the betrothal had not been announced. He had no regrets as far as Lucy was concerned, because she deserved a younger husband, a more respectable man, a gentleman who could show the appropriate deference to sleeves.

"The engagement with Lucy was never announced, even to our friends," he said. "We are far from the City, and no one outside of our two families—except Drexel and Parker—know of the intended betrothal. Allardyce is my friend, so when I cry off, I'm sure he will be reasonable."

Lady Helen shook a finger at him. "Listen to me. Plenty of women admire you. It's not as though you were a regular libertine—a cat chasing a mouse—in your case the mice seem to be chasing the cat. If you wait a few years and give up this absurd notion of marrying either Mrs. Colton or Miss Allardyce, I'm confident that with a little effort you will find love.

My efforts to furnish Blackwell can wait, because love is more important." She hesitated, moved to retrieve the shepherdess, and cradled it in her arms. "You are my son. Whomever you choose for a wife, I will welcome—for your sake. But I cannot wish you happy now."

"Why?"

She kept her gaze on the sheep resting near the feet of the shepherdess. "I—I do not know how to say this." A slight tremor claimed her whole body. "I will never have grandchildren."

"Pardon?" He noticed the figurine shake in her embrace.

"Mrs. Colton is barren. She was married for a long time and produced no offspring. Dr. Potts has just reassured me of that fact. He is her physician, after all, and he should know these things."

"Mother! You did not—"

"You will have *no* children." The statue slipped from her hands and fell to the floor. The figurine burst into pieces, leaving a pile of white paste rubble. The only recognizable parts being half the shepherdess's torso and one little sheep with three missing legs. Falling upon her knees and close to tears, she gingerly picked up and held the legless sheep. "No grandchildren."

"We'll buy another," he whispered, pulling her to her feet. He took the sheep from her hand and called Rowbottom to quickly remove the pile. With his arms firmly around her, facing away from the rubble, he led her to the sofa. "Please, tell me about your new furniture. What will this pile of lumber cost?"

She did not reply. Instead, she twirled one of her

long curls around her finger. Several minutes passed before she picked up her embroidery and started to stab it with the needle. She tried to speak, stopped, and took another minute to assemble her thoughts. "I seek your forgiveness, son. I don't know what came over me."

"No forgiveness is needed." Seeking a subject to lighten her mood, he said, "You did not answer my question."

"What question?"

He swept his free arm in a half circle toward the room. "The cost of the lumber to fill this stadium?"

She slapped his shoulder. "You." A pleading look entered her eyes. "Three hundred pounds."

"You jest!"

"I know the amount is a large sum, but each piece is mahogany and mahogany from the West Indies. Furniture like that is worth the expense, I can assure you."

"We'll see, my dear, we'll see." He stood and placed his hand on the console table. "Shall I move this table or leave it?"

"Leave it." She took up her needlework again. Before he exited the room, she said, "Ross, you are my son. I believe Mrs. Colton is to blame for luring you on. But this is the last time I will say it. I hope you find happiness with this marriage."

Ross remembered Elinor's reddened expression and angry words in the carriage. "Your good wishes may be premature. She could refuse my offer." Suddenly he considered the possibility Elinor might reject him. Nothing could explain his sudden anger at the thought of her refusal, not the loss of her lands, nor the loss of their reputations. He failed to understand his discomfort, so he ascribed it to a manly aversion to rejection. Gentlemen like to win, and he could think of no reason for her to refuse him. As his wife, her life would surely be better than social ostracism. Their union would not be a love match, but many marriages were arranged for other reasons, such as the joining of estates. No, it was unlikely she'd refuse his hand, since marriage was the proper thing to do.

"Refuse! You?" Lady Helen jumped slightly in her seat, her spirits greatly improved. "That will never happen. You're the catch of the county, and I've seen the way women look at you. Besides, you are the grandson of a duke, and one day you'll be the wealthiest man in the neighborhood. She will not refuse your offer, of that I'm certain."

Thirteen

THE WALNUTS HAD SOURED. SITTING AT THE BREAK-
fast table, attempting to enjoy a bumpy piece of
her favorite butter cake, Elinor hastily swallowed
to remove the taste of bitter walnuts. She had been
caught in an embarrassing embrace with a reputed
rake and seen by the entire county of Cheshire.
"Entire county" might be an exaggeration, but only
a small one.

Engaged, heavens.

Other than standing before the congregation on
Sunday morning and shouting, "Pardon, Reverend,
while I kiss my neighbor," there was no greater public
forum for her ruin. She had played with fire. She
excused her behavior as childlike affection or normal
physical attraction and got burned. No doubt everyone in the village would hear of her recklessness soon
enough, followed by immediate censure. Once again,
like her mourning period, she'd find herself cast into
seclusion from society. Only this time, there would be
no foreseeable end.

What would she say to him today? The only possible

answer was "no." Her fidelity and love for William demanded it.

Picking up her knife, she teased the offending walnuts from the dense cake onto the white porcelain plate. She then pushed them over the lip to drop on the table. Finally, she moved her plate a few inches to hide the bitter nuts from view. The remaining cake felt dry on her tongue, so she gulped her tea, hoping the scalding brew would remove the taste of horrid cake and make her troubles tolerable.

Berdy entered the morning room the very minute she could no longer wait for his appearance and remain sane. Watching him eat his meal, she wondered how to explain the situation, and if the words would spill out before she cast up her breakfast. She tried to remember every detail of yesterday's transgressions, but failed. Her recollection of the fair's events had been purposefully forgotten, shoved back, entombed. Just flashes of unwanted memories intruded, like the sight of his blue eyes betraying the fog of shared desire. She gathered up her courage and attempted a casual tone. "How do you feel today?"

"Funny thing that, m' head hurts this morning." He scratched the back of his head before rubbing his rosy cheek where a light ginger-colored whisker growth shadowed his jaw. "I'm not sure why. Must be the excitement of your betrothal yesterday." Before she clarified her current situation, he spoke again. "I really must remember to compliment Cook on this cake. I've never tasted better." He tossed another, larger piece into his mouth.

"Cook meant it to be a lighter cake, but two of

the eggs were off. Love, I need to speak to you."
She twisted her napkin into a long cylinder before
recounting some, but not all, of the incidents in the
carriage he had not witnessed. Despite her nervousness, she was pleased her voice sounded even and its
cadence instructive, as if the events were just facts.

Berdy dropped his jaw, his mouth open wide.
Thankfully, it appeared empty.

"You need to understand the behavior of men like
Mr. Thornbury. His actions, according to his judgment, were normal, but these behaviors leave a trail
of victims behind. Rakes use allure to make ladies
forget their obligations to others, and entire families
suffer the consequences. That is why you must never
become a rake. Let's end this subject, please. We shall
never speak of the fair again."

He nodded in firm agreement, but seemed more
interested in smearing butter on his cake with a vigor-
ous back and forth movement of his knife. "Don't
blame yourself. A true gentleman must take all of the
responsibilities—the *swine*."

Whenever her high spirits had led her too far from
propriety in the past, William had kept her from the
precipice. Following her most frequent transgressions,
like speaking too freely or giggling in public, William
would discreetly wrap his arm around her shoulders to
quell any further unladylike behavior. "That's enough,
luv," he'd whisper in a slight Yorkshire accent. Only
this time her benevolent guardian had not been around
to rescue her. Her history of spontaneous indiscretions
would easily reinforce society's belief she was capable
of this current improper behavior.

Now with Berdy apprised of the situation, all she had to do was confront Mr. Thornbury in the afternoon. She leaned over to kiss Berdy's cheek. "You will be glad to hear that your trip to London will start sooner than expected."

Berdy jumped to his feet. "What? Do you mean it? I'll be here when you wed, of course."

"Don't worry about my affairs. Nothing will happen without you by my side." She let out a protracted sigh. "You'll leave immediately, within the week. I'll write to your aunt Amelia today. She will be delighted to have you lodge with her. Company in the City can be thin this time of year, especially with the weather being so warm."

"Capital! I can't wait to fall in with Father. Learn the ropes, what?"

"Berdy, you must—"

"Not now. No objections. I cannot ignore him when I'm in London. He's m' father." With a final shove of the last piece of his cake into an already distended cheek, he excused himself and hurried upstairs for the stated purpose of a thorough wardrobe inventory.

She sat at the table and remained unmoving. Her spirits were so remarkably low, she needed another pot of tea before she could continue with her plans for the day.

Sometime before noon, Henry was announced. Thoroughly soaked from the rain, his many-caped greatcoat dripped from every fold.

She observed his impassive face, but noticed his gaze never met hers for any length of time. Rare for a lawyer who routinely obtained a confession from his opponent after just a prolonged stare. Instead, he glanced in rapid succession from the rug to the fire, to the desk, and to the windows. She curtsied before offering him the wing chair closest to the warm hearth. "I am surprised to see you here so early." Then she returned to the refuge of William's chair and another cup of tea.

"Yes, I apologize." Henry suddenly changed his behavior and fixed her with an unwavering glare. "I've heard disturbing news from the vicar, so I came in haste. You must set the situation to rights." He coughed, looked at his boots, then the hard stare returned. "I understand you and Thornbury were observed...observed in a compromising position at the fair. And members of the town witnessed this... exhibition. Since I have previously given you excellent advice and warned you to avoid Mr. Thornbury's advances, I am here to seek clarification. Because of my warning, I believe this rumor to be a gross falsehood. Probably another woman was misidentified as you."

She closed her eyes, took a deep breath, and rapidly explained the situation. "Yes, the rumor is true. My reputation is compromised." Even though she was still furious over Mr. Thornbury's public announcement of their engagement, she now realized her anger had been unjustified. She had not been coerced or her hands tied. Moreover, during the carriage ride back to Pinnacles, it occurred to her that his pronouncement was the only course of action he could have taken at the time. She should be grateful for his quick-witted response and accept the generous offer of his hand. "I've no excuse, but I hope someday you'll see it in your generous nature to forgive me." She pulled her soft Indian shawl tighter around her shoulders.

Henry extended both arms. "How could you? I warned you about this rake, the very person who wrote the book on the subject, and now look at the results. You realize that after your marriage he will continue to have dalliances with other women, mistresses too. Rakes never reform. I wish you had been wise and heeded my counsel. If you had, you might have avoided this scandal."

The sad tone of his last words caused her heart to sink under the additional weight of his grief.

He began to pace in front of the fireplace. Drops of water fell from his hair and sizzled on the hearth's hot stones. "I don't know what to do about this unpleasantness. It's not my place to call the man out. That should be Deane's job."

"No!" She rose, crossed the room, and grabbed him by the sleeve. "There will be no duel. Do you understand me? Why do gentlemen have this ridiculous fixation with duels? Honestly, I'm a grown woman—a widow no less. I will remain here at Pinnacles and try to avoid venturing into town, so this unpleasantness, as you call it, will be of short duration. I have to believe that."

Henry used both hands to smooth his wet hair behind his ears, but one lock escaped and stood straight out on the side. "Then you must marry. You realize, of course, that Thornbury instigated this situation to obtain your property by marriage? I can legally protect you from many things, but under the terms of William's estate, Thornbury would control your real property."

Of her many mixed thoughts since yesterday, she had not considered the legal ramifications. However, she quickly dismissed Henry's accusation. The event in the carriage was spontaneous—no preconceived gain of a pecuniary advantage was involved. The moment was one of pure celebration mixed with natural physical attraction, and an expression of fondness generated from reaching a mutual agreement, nothing more.

"You must marry," he said. "Think of the outrage if you don't. People have forgiven you for your peccadilloes before, but this is too much. No one will attend you, and you will be forced to move to hide your ignominy. Perhaps disappear into a big city like London or relocate to another country."

"No, I will never leave Pinnacles—never."

"Then you must send Deane away for his own good, at least until you wed. Had you listened to my warning, this action would be unnecessary. For his sake, send him to London and his father now."

Picking up her fallen shawl, she threw it around her shoulders and returned to the overstuffed chair. She already resolved to send Berdy from Cheshire, for his sake, but she could not immediately speak of his departure with any degree of composure. She smoothed the shawl's fringe flat against her knee until the tassels lay straight. "Yes. I am sending him to London directly, but not to his father. That—parent—would only set a bad example for a young impressionable man."

Henry knelt before her, covered her hand with his

damp one, and she caught the scent of his wet wool clothes. "I hoped one day we would marry," he said softly. "I would step in and take Thornbury's place, but an attorney in my situation cannot afford even a hint of bad connections." Deep furrows appeared around his mouth, making his face appear older.

While she had never considered marriage to Henry and avoided dealing with his previous hints, she regretted that he suffered by her actions now. "Yes, I understand. The loss is mine, Henry, and I'm truly sorry."

He glanced down at her with regret written in his green eyes. Then, after a long silence, he collected his greatcoat, hat, and gloves before striding toward the door. When he touched the door catch, he paused. "I wish you had listened to me, my dear. I won't see you again before I too must leave for London on business." He exited the room.

Henry had forced her to realize the strong arguments for the marriage, but she remained steadfast in her decision to refuse. She accepted the blame for the situation and planned to live with the isolation of censure. To do otherwise would be like losing more of William. Her throat seized, and her mouth possessed a sudden metallic taste. Henry also made his position in regard to her situation clear. She would have to survive the scandal alone, without his assistance. She sipped her tea and found it had become cold.

She snuggled back deep into the chair's cushions. Amongst all this confusion, she clung to her sole anchor, the memory of William's love. She tried to imagine what William would do if he were in her shoes and faced her current difficulties. No doubt, he'd charm the town into laughter, and the scandal would be quickly forgotten. If only William were here to make everyone laugh.

She glanced at her chest, and at William's mourning brooch pinned over her heart. After removing the brooch, she examined a lock of his soft hair sealed under glass, isolated from her touch. Small plaits of his light hair looked so smooth and orderly, it gave her comfort to be gazing on him again. Even if it was just a tiny piece of the funny, complex man she loved. She turned the brooch over, and on the front a painted sepia figure in her likeness gazed out to a ship on the distance horizon. A small dog lay at her feet. The diamonds along the brooch's border represented her tears, the dog represented her fidelity, and the ship out to sea represented William's voyage. In the sky above, an angel carried a banner with the words: "Not lost, gone before."

❧

That afternoon, Elinor sat on a tight-weaved oilcloth in the tall grass amongst the apple trees. The sunlight burned her nose, the bees buzzed loudly, and even this far from the garden, the too-sweet scent of China roses filled the afternoon air. The cacophony from the bees serenaded her uneasy feeling of being bound in a tumbrel and headed for the gallows. Since she refused to wed after yesterday's scandal, society and her friends would soon be lost to her. If only scandal would burst through the row of roses, so she could battle it head-on—a tangible object to defeat. She bit off a hunk of tart apple and tucked the bitter piece into her cheek, picked up her novel, and continued to read.

Minutes later she glanced at the trees and realized she had no memory of what she just read. Her mind remained fixed upon her predicament. *What if she changed her mind and accepted Mr. Thornbury's proposal?* Her imagination orchestrated that future like a symphony composed of many musical variations. First, the pleasing effects of simple scales. Berdy would remain in Cheshire, and her reputation would be restored. Second, her future might resemble the discordant sounds of ill-played chords. Mr. Thornbury might abandon her to resume his old life as a rake. Finally, her future's symphony reached its crescendo. Henry might be right, and Mr. Thornbury was scheming to obtain her real property by marriage. Unsettled by the disharmony, she sought comfort by touching her mourning brooch, while the tumbrel's wheels continued to turn.

Around three o'clock, Mr. Thornbury appeared without being announced.

Her book dropped from her hands. "Oh." The sight of his striking figure and jocular grin gave her the same rapid pulse and confused thoughts his presence had always created. Her anger grew enough to be discourteous. She had enough of his outrageous charm for a lifetime.

He seemed to have better control, for he approached her and executed a low bow. "Good afternoon, Mrs. Colton, er…may I call you Elinor?"

She nodded. "Of course, Mr. Thornbury."

"In the dock, am I?"

"I don't know what you mean." She focused on the book in her lap.

"That bad, eh?"

"Mr. Thornbury, if you are going to apologize, please do so and take your leave." Right then she decided to throw her book at him if he gave her one of his beguiling smiles.

"Call me Ross, please." His fine linen shirt billowed out several inches from between his cream waistcoat and navy breeches, suggesting he hadn't the time to compose himself after his ride.

For some inexplicable reason, she found the sight unnecessarily funny. She bit her lip and scowled in an attempt to maintain her level of anger, but it was hopeless and took too much effort. *Oh, bother.*

He observed her glance at his shirt. "Don't suppose I can drop my breeches and tuck my shirt under properly, can I?"

She giggled and understood she couldn't stop if she tried. "If you did, no doubt you would be discovered by the entire town hiding under the apple tree behind you."

He spun to view the tree, then turned back, sporting a wily grin. "And all of Manchester up in its branches."

They laughed together.

His happy demeanor regrettably banished the majority of her anger. *Damn the man.* She'd have to learn to live with her attraction to him but somehow find the will to resist his charms, even in private.

He leisurely stepped over to the large apple tree. When the fruit did not immediately yield, he forcibly tugged it from the tree. After close examination, he tossed the small apple into a wicker basket placed near the trunk. "Too green." He returned to the heavy oilcloth and sat a respectable five feet away.

With her anger somewhat abated, she regrettably found herself pleased to see him. While their acquaintance had been of short duration, she hoped she could always count upon his lively company in the future.

"Elinor, I…" He raked his dark forelock back into place. "I must apologize for my boorish behavior at the fair. To announce our engagement was the only way to remedy—"

"Please." She waved her hand like a fishtail. "You needn't say more. I'm a grown woman and should have stopped you. The consequences are mine."

"Ah, you are too generous. Please give a gentleman the opportunity to apologize."

She nodded. "Of course, apology accepted. But you must know I had been warned about your behavior before our first meeting. Warned that something like our current situation might happen. Even warned not to be seen in your company."

"Excuse me?" His black brows lifted. "Do you mean *all* of the ladies in the county were warned of my arrival?" He chuckled. "Lock up the women. Thornbury is coming."

"At the risk of flattering your vanity," she said with a grin, "yes, we were warned."

That famous smile brightened his handsome face. A smile only a few men possessed. A smile that seduced every person into agreement. "Ah, madam, you know me well. Tell me, was your intended, Mr. Browne, the man who warned you?" In apparent indifference, he brushed his right hand back and forth over the tops of the long grass at the edge of the cloth.

She exhaled a resigned sigh. This expectation of her eventual marriage to Henry must have been commonplace. "Mr. Browne is not my intended, although he is a close connection."

He squinted up at the sun. "From what he told me weeks ago, a *very* close connection."

"Pardon?"

He faced her directly now. "Because of my abhorrent behavior at the fair, I understand Mr. Browne has withdrawn his offer of marriage?"

She tucked a wayward curl behind her ear, and another extended sigh escaped her lips. "Mr. Browne and I have no understanding; however, my actions have hurt others."

He nodded and fell silent. They sat without speaking, listening to the bees hum in the distance. Minutes later, he knelt at the edge of the cloth and faced her. "I…" He inhaled loudly. "I formally offer you my hand in wedlock. I'm not the husband you desire. I understand that. But we should wed. You know it is the proper course of action. I…*admire* you and know we will suit. Moreover, I will join you in taking responsibility for young Deane. If you agree, together we can find a suitable living for him." By the end of his speech, he was breathing fast.

Gratitude swelled in her breast upon hearing his offer to assist Berdy, making her unable to think or immediately respond. Stealing a peek at his face to discern if he was serious, she discovered genuine goodwill in his expression. Maybe even a touch of softness in the depths of his sapphire eyes. Certainly a nervous fidget about his whole person. They remained silent again while he plucked grass.

Regardless of his promised assistance to Berdy, she was somewhat surprised by his current declaration and disappointed that he planned to continue this farce. "I understand your generosity toward my reputation is what led you to that sudden announcement yesterday, but I cannot agree to marry you. I'm sorry." Her throat seized, keeping her from further explanation.

He jerked his head to examine her countenance.

Once again she caught his fleeting expression of sadness. She expected him to delight in gaining his freedom from a forced engagement. Her spirits, which had lightened with his charm, now failed her entirely. His happiness, his mother's, Berdy's, and Henry's all rested upon her decision. A sharp pain grew near her heart.

He contemplated the oilcloth or was lost in thought.

She needed to explain why marriage was impossible. Make him understand she was incapable of being a proper loving wife to any man. Marriage required more than just physical attraction to be successful. Only speech failed her. By her own actions, she had isolated herself and caused others distress. She turned her head as her hopeless situation overwhelmed her, and a regrettable bout of tears began. She covered her face, refusing to let him see her cry.

He held a pressed linen handkerchief close to her cheek.

Automatically waving a hand to refuse his offer, she

kept her face covered with her other hand. With time she became more agitated; any chance of a positive resolution to her predicament had decidedly flown. Squarely facing the consequences of her refusal, she felt a tear or two spill over her fingers. Now her days would be spent like the small boy she'd met at the colliery—alone.

Without a sound, he slid next to her and wholly enclosed her within his arms. "My dear, Miss Leaf." He offered her the handkerchief again.

She hiccuped once before snatching his handkerchief and covering her face. She didn't want him to discover her confusion, but most importantly, she did not want to observe his disappointment. The additional weight of his grief bought on more tears.

"Please, sweetheart, I won't force you to wed me. You know that."

She nodded, while her face remained covered. "Yes."

"Then why tears?" His embrace tightened.

"I will lose everything dear to me." She sniffed. "From the scandal." She hiccuped again. "Must send…Berdy to London." Further explanation failed, and several minutes were required before the continued comfort of his unmoving hug stopped her tears.

"That's better," he said, leaning sideways to plant a chaste kiss upon her cheek. "Don't worry about Deane. You have raised a fine young man." When she failed to respond, he asked, "Something else worrying you? Tell me."

"You won't be angry?"

He playfully squeezed her. "No, never."

She dropped the handkerchief to scan his face in an attempt to discover his feelings, but she found nothing more than a small resolute smile.

"Tell me."

"I—I cannot marry again. I cannot bring myself to even consider it, nor pretend my heart is not taken. And…and I will not give up my freedoms." She turned her head upward to face him and catch his response.

His small smile remained unchanged, but his eyes widened. "I won't make demands on you, if that's what worries you. Your freedoms—for the most part—will remain intact. After marriage, our current indiscretion will be quickly forgotten, and together we can build Blackwell into the estate it was meant to be."

"No, by freedoms I don't mean…relations. I mean my independence. My ability to make decisions about my property—my future—everything, really."

"Well, if you accept me, I promise you will not lose those freedoms. And of course, my dear apple fancier, we can explore every chapter of *The Rake's Handbook*." Now the smile transformed into a decidedly lighthearted grin. "Chapter titles like 'Early Morning Amusements' and 'Sports on the Road.'"

Remarkable. His rakish charm remained undaunted at all times, even with a tearful woman in his arms. "I hoped you'd forgotten that nonsense." She composed herself and even managed a tentative smile. "And you forgot to mention the *Field Guide*."

"Ha!" An eager, boyish expression crossed his features. "No, we will rush through them all to the last chapter—the official begetting part."

The shock of his intentions, and the outcome if she accepted his proposal, opened a new door in her heart. Inside she discovered her lost or suppressed hopes. Her never spoken, deepest longings soared.

She might have children.

Some women considered barren did conceive when married a second time. It sounded plausible to her. Wrapping her arms around her shoulders, she knew William would want her to have children. He would want her to marry and be happy with a child. And married or not, nothing would change in regard to her feelings for William—those precious memories she wore inside her soul. And whatever happened to her on the outside could never alter them. Much to Elinor's chagrin, fresh tears filled her eyes. She resolved never to contemplate these thoughts again.

"None of that," he said, rocking her in a strong embrace again. "I will stop teasing you, I promise. Nothing can be that bad."

"Oh, yes it can." How could she convince him her situation was as bad as it could possibly be? "With Berdy gone…he will fall under the influence of his father. You know the consequences of bad company. He will become a habitual gamester. I'd do anything to stop that—anything."

"Anything?" He paused and faced the apple tree. "Please accept my proposal. We will announce our engagement, and then you and Deane can travel to London together. Remain there for a year, and when you return, all will be forgotten by our neighbors. At that time, if you still wish it, we will quietly dissolve our engagement."

The thought of leaving Pinnacles, combined with his kind offer, only quickened more tears.

His arms tightened around her shoulders. "I'm a hardened rake, you know, and we are inexperienced with *real* tears. I'm quite put out."

Her tears stopped, and she chortled into his neck-cloth. "You—put out—impossible."

"That's my girl. Although I must admit disappointment you don't wish to become my wife. In fact, I plan to waste away from my unrequited *tendre*. That is the proper behavior for a gentleman in one of your three-volume novels, correct?"

She shoved him hard. When she looked up, she did not see laughter in his eyes. Instead, the warmth in his gaze stunned her.

His smile disappeared, and he wore an expression she had never seen before. "Elinor," he whispered, "I want this. I promise to be a devoted husband. Please be my wife."

"No, I am William's wife." For some reason, when the word "no" escaped her lips, she felt guilty and provokingly exposed. Under his fervent gaze, her thoughts grew even more confused, while her body became warm and wanting.

Within a heartbeat, he rushed forward to cover her mouth. They both stiffened at the contact of their lips. Once the kiss ended, he reached out to cradle her face within his palms. "Please."

She weaved her fingers through his soft hair before brushing it back off his forehead, as she had seen him do countless times. She meant to stop him, make it a brief peck, a kiss of friendship, but she was foolish.

This was not friendship, and she knew it. But she remained uncertain whether it sprang from longing, lust, or loneliness.

His lips brushed across hers to signal his need, and somehow her need was the same. His body stiffened as his tongue plunged to claim her mouth, while warm air passed between them in a rushed exchange. Breaths became ragged, and she grabbed his collar to steady herself as they kissed. He enclosed her within a tight embrace before lowering her onto the hot oilcloth.

The delicious kiss slowed, and their lips caressed with tenderness, not want. The stubble on his chin brushed her lips, and her rhythmic breaths slowed to match his. His broad torso created an erotic crush of her breasts, and the firmness of his thighs added to her pleasure. Their glances met, and she gasped at the carnal entreaty seen within the dark blue depths of his eyes. Their unspoken plea spurred a similar desire.

Mere inches separated them, and she watched him move his heated gaze to the left and right, as if he were memorizing her features. His firm lips brushed lightly across hers, and she welcomed the unbearable physical happiness of the long kiss that followed. He rolled onto his back and pulled her on top of his chest, while his tongue sought hers. The kiss was all encompassing. Mutual gasps accelerated the relentless deep movements of lips over lips and tongue sweeping tongue.

When the kiss ended, he struggled out of his coat and laid her upon the soft silk lining. Then he hovered above her on stiff arms before lowering himself to suck and nibble her neck, his long fingers tugging at the shoulders of her gown. With a soft bite on her earlobe, he cupped her breast through the light muslin.

Exhaling an extended sigh, she let her head roll sideways, allowing him greater access to kiss the base of her neck.

His hand moved to the other breast and swept back and forth along the bottom of the swell before enclosing it with his warm palm to shove it upward. The force pushed their bodies forward several inches as if joined.

"Oh," she gasped in liquid, languid joy.

He returned to her mouth to plant a lengthy kiss, while his hands tugged her bodice lower, imprisoning both of her upper arms.

Her breasts were pushed high and held there by her short stays. She moaned softly.

He stilled.

Leaning backwards on his knees, he gazed at her chest. "This is some chapter. Don't remember which one now." He slowly lowered his head before his mouth claimed the first breast. His hand found the other breast, and he began to knead and trace circles with a light touch of his palm.

Heavens. Lust heated her cheeks, and she eased the fire by rolling her head on the cool silk lining of his coat. Pulses of pleasure claimed her, and time escalated to a sudden urgency. *Now.*

Lifting his head, he surveyed her exposed body from her breasts up to her mouth.

She did not want him to stop his heated caresses, so her forearms flailed wildly up, putting voice to her desperation. They latched on his neckcloth and tugged upon the knot.

He batted her hands away. "Impatient reader." He unbuttoned his waistcoat and untied his cravat knot. As he pulled the neckcloth off, the white linen slipped down the side of his neck with a swish. He twisted the cravat ends slowly around each fist, snapped it tight, and bridged the taut linen over her breasts.

She inhaled sharply.

He slid the ribbon back and forth across both peaks at the perfect tempo to escalate desire.

Arching her back to increase the pressure, she reached out to clutch his upper arms.

Then he quickened the pace.

The sweet friction across each breast continued until she wanted all of him, so she reached for the buttons on his tented falls. A second later, she focused on his watch fob, and the initials carved into the sparkling citrine. The initials were not her husband's—not William's. A sharp pain impaled her, caused by the wretchedness of guilt and betrayal. With the effort of reining in a runaway team of horses, she escaped the march of desire and rolled away from him.

With an extended groan, he collapsed to her side a mere foot away and lay on his back, his breaths hard and uncontrolled.

A foot separated them, but that foot might have been as wide as the Thames. In refusing him, she more than likely lost his friendship too. This was all her fault. She let her attraction flare, possibly fueled by either goodwill created by the benevolent fallacy of children or a selfish desire to seize a moment of happiness. Confused, she wanted to scream or cry or both. Instead, she ended up hitting her skirt in a gesture to remove one blade of grass, her thoughts and emotions a jumbled mess.

Once his breathing had been restored to normal, he rose to his feet. "Accept my apologies again. Clearly a record for one man in one day."

The sardonic tone of his voice unsettled her. "Don't... Don't... Forgive me." She stood and clutched his lapel. "Ross, I don't know what to do. There must be some way to keep Berdy in Cheshire and escape society's censure. Please, Berdy must remain here."

He kept his eyes focused on her forehead, his lips pursed. After a long, penetrating stare, he strode off toward the stables. Fifty feet away, he turned around to address her. "My offer was a way—you refused. Handbook closed."

Fourteen

THE PICKAX SWUNG IN A GIANT ARC AND BIT INTO THE black dirt with a thud. Ross stared at the pickax while he tried to recall the mull he had made out of his first proposal. She refused him because she did not want to lose her *freedoms*. As her husband, she must have expected him to behave like an ogre.

Ross straightened and stepped aside. Today he worked at the foundry site, digging the foundation for the main chimney. One of the workmen finished a wood brattice and stepped back, allowing Ross to swing his pickax again and again and again.

He had behaved as a proper gentleman should with the offer of his hand. While his unplanned behavior at the fair had been reprehensible, he honestly tried to mend the situation by his proposal. Granted, he feared her anger the second his pronouncement escaped his lips, but there was no other option. She had a right to be angry. *Hell's fire*. His mother was right; he counted two people in that carriage. Elinor also allowed their attraction to flare—twice.

With a toss of his pickax to the side, Ross and the

man grabbed shovels and started filling the empty basket with loose dirt. An unspoken competition escalated between the owner and the workman. However well built, the man was no match for Ross. No one could best him this day.

She refused his offer of marriage. He couldn't decide whether to laugh or to weep over her refusal, but men did not weep, so he laughed. "Ha!"

The workman paused to wipe his black brow with a filthy rag. "Aye, so that's 'ow it is. S'ovel away, laddie, s'ovel away. Yo'll beat the devil today."

He realized the lease was lost, and with it the steam engine too. But he refused to abandon his plans. Another engine would not be available for months, so in the long run, he might have to consider horses or even a steam locomotive to haul his goods on a railroad. He knew of at least twenty steam engines in use today, mostly hauling coal, but the cost of the steam locomotive and tracks would be expensive. His first remedy, to dig a new canal, would also be costly. Regardless of which method he chose, the profits wouldn't be as great as using the river. But he'd earn them in the long run—he'd damn well see to it.

The basket was quickly filled with earth and hauled to the surface by a temporary crane. Within minutes, it returned to the bottom of the pit, stacked high with bricks and new boards. Ross picked up the pickax and swung into the hard earth. He felt powerful, sharp, like a man who controlled his life. He rejoiced in his physical dominance and single-handedly filled ten more baskets with dirt. When exhausted, he climbed to the surface and perched on the edge of the pit to wait for his rampant breathing to slow. He watched the late afternoon sun sink toward the nebulous horizon.

Females. Eve should have ignored that snake and left that bloody apple alone. Women were to blame for all of man's problems—wars not included. Men were to blame for wars—wait—Helen of Troy. "Ha!" Another alluring female behind all the fuss.

Hell's fire. But men couldn't live without females. A world peopled solely by men would start wars and clear Europe of human life within a decade. Besides, Mother was a female—enough said.

Ross shouted commands to his men. Directions were given in regard to placement of the foundation stones for the foundry, the engine house, and three sand pits. He prided himself on his men's quick obedience, and he went on to complete his business affairs with the aplomb of a master.

His day ended with the acceptance that, as long as he lived, people would gossip about his handbook, a book they likely would never read. He also devised a new plan to handle this one very troublesome widow—avoidance. It would be best to show everyone he had, in no way, been upset by her refusal. Best to put her entirely out of his thoughts. Best to show the world she meant nothing more to him than the soft light of a summer's dusk.

❧

Parker appeared incredulous; he dropped his jaw. "Allardyce set up a bit o' muslin on Edgeware Road. I cannot believe it. Why, the man must be at least forty."

Two days after his failed proposal, Ross sat at the

card table listening to Parker and Drexel argue over whether Allardyce had a paramour hidden away in the City. While the two men dwelled on the lurid details, Ross heard one word out of a dozen. Instead, he stared into the hearth as if he were alone in the room. Orange flames ripped around a dark log in an embrace that scorched the wood and could end only in the log's destruction. How appropriate, his path to future success ended with the scorching finality of Elinor's refusal of his marriage proposal.

Ross told himself all of this flirtation foolishness had just been a ruse to gain the foundry's acceptance, so he should be thankful *his* freedoms would be kept. Marriage was not in his cards. Any thoughts of a more tender nature he quickly dismissed or did not dare contemplate. He tossed back a third brandy.

"Two, are you in your cups?" Drexel queried. "Do you want to stick or twist?"

Ross grumbled as he went through the motions of looking at his damn cards. The game was vingt-et-un, and after glancing at his newly dealt two of clubs, he tried to remember the combined count of his other cards. Was he near twenty-one, or would the two push him over? He needed to devise a new plan to gain the lease, not listen to Drexel and Parker attempt to gammon each other. "Twist."

"I say, Two," Drexel addressed Ross again. "I cannot believe your lucky escape from the parson's mousetrap left you so Friday-faced. Don't tell me you are in love with that ape leader of a widow?"

Ross threw his cards on the table and pushed his chair back. "My motives are entirely pecuniary, I can assure you." He had spent the morning investigating the cost of a railroad to prepare for his journey to London. His last option was to forget the foundry altogether and set cattle out to pasture. But if he remembered rightly, and he wanted to stick to his original plan using the river, he'd have to save her reputation and entice Deane to postpone his immediate journey to London. "According to my calculations, she has as good as agreed to my lease if I restore her good name, and if you can believe it, persuade Deane to remain in the country. I apologized for my actions and did my best as a gentleman to remedy the situation with my offer. So as far as I am concerned, her reputation can go to the dogs. Still, for some reason unknown to me, if I persuade the lad to remain in Cheshire, I'm sure she'd sign anything. At least that is how I remember her wishes. Never truly know with females, do you? But every instinct I have begs me to insist she leave Deane alone. Let the young man make his own decisions."

Parker put down his cards. "Why must the mooncalf remain in Cheshire?"

Ross paced behind his chair. "God only knows. Oh, she is worried he will come under the influence of his father, Ralph Deane. Granted the fellow is a loose screw, but how could any man harm his offspring?"

"Loose screw is putting it mildly," Drexel said, silently twirling a single card between his fingers. "That man gets my vote for the first to sell any member of his family to the devil. I'm told he and his pals have a neat little business going on, fleecing green coves. Their accomplices lure them into a little tavern east of Covent Garden, get them foxed, strip them naked, and steal every shilling. No wonder she fears his influence. A rotten egg that man is. He does not deserve the title of gentleman."

Parker appeared concerned, his voice taking on a righteous edge. "How horrible! He will probably force Deane into the navy, or worse. The boy will end up hanged or transported. I have a bad feeling about this, yes, yes, a bad feeling."

Ross returned to his seat. "Right." He picked up his cards. "The three of us can surely find a way to rescue Deane from his father—and his aunt."

"I have it," Parker exclaimed. "Knew I could do it, what? All you have to do is adopt the boy."

Drexel gave a bark of laughter. "Deane's got too many parents as it is, cabbage head. I have a better idea. Let's go back to the scheme of saving her reputation. This will smooth the waters all around. To achieve this exalted goal, I will sacrifice myself on the altar of propriety and wed her. We'd be neighbors, ol' man. Don't see how any woman could refuse a generous offer like that."

"Oh, don't you?" Ross replied tersely. "I have learned more lately about proper ladies than I ever desired, and I'm convinced you lack the same knowledge. For example, do you know the meaning of the word *ruched*?"

Drexel shook his head. "No."

"Well, I do."

"Important?"

"Something on puffs, puffed sleeves," Ross explained.

"Not important then. A ladies, thing?"

Ross nodded. "Yes, but you must care about this puffed thing to make them happy."

Drexel wagged both brows. "I'll make her happy." He picked up a card. "Hah, twenty-one," he exclaimed, flinging his cards into the center of the table.

"Lucky at cards, unlucky in love," Ross said, watching Drexel lean across the table to gather his winnings.

Drexel peered up at him, his arms surrounding the pile of coins. "Sore loser." He glanced at Parker. "Deal the cards again, man."

"Yes, yes." Parker turned to ask Drexel if he needed a card, but immediately faced Ross again. "I have it! We will convince either that Potts or Browne fellow to marry her. Then, after the ceremony, we will reveal our hand. She will be so grateful, she could not help but sign the lease on the spot." A self-satisfied smirk appeared on his mouth.

"You are the most bacon-brained creature that ever lived," Drexel stated.

Ross stared at his cards. "I believe that Browne character already offered, so I am beginning to think she wants to remain shunned by Polite Society."

Parker stiffened. "I still think my idea is a good one. We will convince the good doctor then. Might be easy. As I understand from Maggie down at the Lion, the fellow is in dun territory, so he's looking to wed a lady with a substantial fortune."

"If she refused my offer," Ross said, "and Browne's, why would she agree to the Potts fellow? She says she can never marry again, because she is in love with her late husband."

Parker held up his cards to examine them, but his hand immediately dropped to the table. "How could she love a dead man? I mean, the cove was probably a fine fellow, but he is dead now, isn't he?"

"God save Mrs. Parker," Drexel remarked, shifting in his seat to face Ross.

"Leave my mother out of it," Parker exclaimed.

Ross and Drexel burst into laughter.

Parker glanced under the table.

Drexel hastily sat upright and said, "If marriage is out, that means our only course of action is to make the locals, the entire county of Cheshire, believe *you* are the villain. She'll then become an innocent victim of your wiles and will become so grateful, she will sign the lease."

With a completely stolid expression, Ross said, "I cannot imagine how you can make me out as the villain."

Now Drexel and Parker joined in a crack of laughter.

Ross ignored them. "The two of you will end up in Bedlam."

"Nonsense," Drexel said. "You know I am right. The only way to save her honor is to lessen yours. Convince the town you are a famous rake, then they will all flock to her defense, believe me."

Parker frowned at Drexel. "And just how is he supposed to do that? Walk down the high street, seducing every woman in sight? Oh, that reminds me of another song from the Coal Hole. My candle burns bright—"

"No!" Ross ignored Parker's wounded-puppy expression. "No songs." Ross believed he might have outgrown the sensibilities of his friends. "This is important. Now, from information I received on my first day here, the town already believes I'm a famous rake. Never-ending gossip about the handbook, I would imagine. I doubt anyone has read it, either that, or the whole town rushed out to purchase copies. Still, men routinely stop me on the high street with vulgar inquiries. Surprising how one book, written as a lark, changed our lives forever, and not for the better. Promise me you will never say anything to Lady Helen."

"Promise," Parker said, crossing his heart.

Drexel nodded.

"Besides, we all know the rake business is complete fustian." He smoothed his forelock back into place. "It being so undeserved. I mean, it's not as though I ever seduced an innocent. And one married woman, or two, or three, only qualifies you as amorous, not a rake."

Drexel asked for another card. "Three women? You jest. When you were in your prime, more like ten married ladies at a time flocking around you. You must admit you had more than your share."

"Not my fault, was it?" Ross noticed Parker quickly look under the table and Drexel immediately shift in his chair.

Parker dealt himself another card. "It is your teeth, you know. The ladies seem to find your teeth remarkable."

"*Hell's fire.*"

"Well," Parker continued, "if you are not going to walk down the high street, seducing every skirt in sight, we'll just have to come up with another plan to convince the town you are a vile libertine."

Ross glared at Parker. "I told you. Many already believe that balderdash. Your scheme will not work."

"If they truly believed the gossip, then there would be no scandal. You would be blamed and the widow forgiven, but that has not happened. So let me handle it, yes, yes. With their own eyes, everyone will realize the gossip is true. You are the most famous, illustrious, bad apple of a rake. It's the only way."

Ross grabbed his head with both hands and dropped his elbows onto the table. "I am going to regret this…"

Drexel shouted twenty-one and quickly collected the pot. "Deal again, my good man." He turned to Ross. "Whip said the very thing to me once too. Promised he would handle it, and you know how that episode ended—badly. I almost had to marry that Lydia chit."

Parker stopped shuffling the cards. "*Almost*—that is the important word to remember here—*almost*." He resumed shuffling and then dealt the cards. "Despite the little hiccup of the dueling pistol, my scheme would have worked like grease through a duck. Moreover, in the end, my brilliance got that Long Meg married off, yes, yes. Two, do you want to stick or twist?"

Ross asked for a card, and the game resumed in silence.

Parker was evidently scheming, as several exclamations of, "No that won't work," escaped his lips.

In the middle of the round, Lady Helen entered the room.

The men immediately rose to their feet. Drexel

appeared off balance and needed to hold onto the table to stop from falling to the floor.

Lady Helen excused herself for interrupting their play and left the room.

Ross turned to Drexel. "Why can't you stand? Just what are you up to?"

"He is cheating!" Parker shouted.

"On the contrary. Guaranteeing a win, that's all," Drexel said.

Parker fell onto his knees and crawled under the table. "No, no, he is using his feet. Oh, he is not doing it now, but that is why he fell over."

"What?" Ross bent to examine Parker under the table.

Parker grabbed the toe of Drexel's shoe, and Drexel tried to shake him off. "It is all the crack," Parker said. "A fellow points his toes at the various o'clock positions to count cards."

Drexel managed to free his shoe. "How can you count aces with your feet, now really?"

Parker said, "The trick is to count the aces by placing your right foot on the floor in a different position each time an ace is played. That way you know the probability of an ace remaining in the deck, and your opponent's chance at hitting twenty-one. For the first ace, he probably placed his toes in the nine o'clock position, the second ace at the twelve o'clock position, the…" Parker stared at Drexel's shoe. "No, that won't work. A fellow's ankles could never do the fourth ace—the six o'clock position—unless they're broken. I know, he moved his foot as far left as possible and moved them slightly thereafter. That would do the trick."

Mr. Allardyce entered the room.

Parker attempted to stand, resulting in a loud bang from under the table as he hit his head.

Ross greeted Mr. Allardyce and invited him to join the game. Mr. Allardyce refused and indicated his family was now ready to leave. He then bade farewell to Parker and Drexel. Ross promised to join him in the drawing room in five minutes to express his gratitude to the family.

Mr. Allardyce nodded stiffly and left the library.

Ross needed to say his good-byes in the drawing room. He had no intention of going outside to bid them farewell. Allardyce had not been reasonable, as he had expected. Charybdis was the price of calling off his engagement without a breach of contract suit, and he couldn't bear to see his filly go.

Parker waved his hand. "Marry this chit, marry that chit, too many ladies to marry, if you ask me." His eyes bulged, and he slapped his thigh. "That's it! Of course, why did I not think of this simple solution earlier? The Smedley girls."

Drexel tapped his fingers on his cards. "Not those hoydens."

Parker ignored him and turned to Ross. "You've heard me speak of them. They're my cousins, wild about theatrics and all that nonsense. They will help us, I am sure. Yes, yes, a bit of playacting is just the ticket."

"It *is* Bedlam for you." Ross glared at him. "I refuse."

Fifteen

By mid-morning Elinor felt a little more optimistic than the previous day, when she had refused Mr.
Thornbury's offer of marriage. Putting on her leghorn
bonnet with the sky-blue ribbons, she planned to
return a novel she had borrowed from a friend, Mrs.
Long. Setting out toward the village, she hummed a
favorite Scottish song. The day was a chilly one, but
the sun shone, and that made all the difference. She
passed familiar cottages on the way into town, her
arms swinging in rhythm with her favorite tune.

Ahead, one of her friends, Mrs. Applewaite, and
her towheaded child dallied in the front garden with
identical watering cans. Mrs. Applewaite poured water
upon a tall white foxglove, and the toddling child
mimicked her mother's action. As Elinor prepared
to shout a greeting over the fence, Mrs. Applewaite
noticed her presence and hurriedly waved the child
into the house. The door shut with a bang, and the
clang of the thrown bolt echoed across the yard.

Elinor froze, insensible to every sound or movement
around her. She couldn't breathe or step forward. The

lace curtains moved, but she could not turn to look fully at them. Her heart stilled on the spot, and the fortitude to continue her journey melted in the chilly wind. She shut her eyes to stop her tears, as her world spun before her. Then she ran home to Pinnacles. Mrs. Long's novel dropped somewhere along the road.

An hour later, she sat at her vanity and examined the effects of washing her face with cold water. The swelling around her eyes had lessened, but her nose remained red.

She closed her eyes. If only William could make her laugh now.

Once no physical sign of her morning's misadventure lingered, she headed to Berdy's room to inquire about the progress of his latest wardrobe inventory. Evidently, his upcoming journey to London required numerous inventories to avoid any fatal wardrobe mistakes. She entered his bedroom and discovered every horizontal surface covered in apparel. Numerous hats lined the top of the bed, while not a single inch of the counterpane's embroidered roses were visible under the sea of shirts.

Berdy stood by the washstand piled high with a dome of white neckcloths. He held out a cravat. "Too soiled? Brummell would not be pleased. What do you think?"

"I think you have too many neckcloths," she said, pulling on the end of the yellowed cravat.

Berdy's grip remained firm on the other end. "I do not own too many cravats for m' stay in London. Why, Brummell—"

With the soft scratch on the door and entry of

the housemaid, Berdy became distracted enough that she gave a swift tug, and the cravat was hers. The housemaid informed her Dr. Potts had called, and waited for her in the drawing room. She tied the long white cravat around her waist and headed down to the drawing room.

Dr. Potts stood with his back to the fire, his hands joined behind him. Despite the lack of his natural smile, he greeted her with warm compliments. Once he caught sight of the cravat around her waist, he grimaced.

She welcomed him and moved to open the damask curtains covering the mullioned windows overlooking the garden.

"I am surprised to see you today," she said. "Will you examine Berdy's foot again?" She sat on one of the large wing chairs, and motioned for him to take a seat. "His limp is only slight, but I am concerned about his upcoming stay in London. He will want to walk much more than he does now. Do you think this will compromise the healing process?"

"Examine?" Dr. Potts shook his head. "Forgive me. I don't think I understood your question. It is early, and yesterday was a difficult day for me. I have not slept for days. To answer your question, no, I do not believe walking will interrupt the healing process. However, moderation is the key. I recommend you give Deane a strong warning not to overdo it. He should return to his lodgings the minute he feels any pain." Dr. Potts leaped to his feet and started to pace before the fire.

She was at a loss to understand his obvious turmoil.

Perhaps he needed to communicate some delicate information about the health of someone else?

His pacing escalated before he strode to her chair and knelt. "I want you to marry me." He hesitated and appeared to compose his thoughts. "Forgive me. It has been a long time since I've proposed. Mrs. Colton—that sounds silly—Elinor, would you do me the honor of becoming my wife?" He took her palm into his and did not seem to know what to do with it. So he absentmindedly passed it between his hands like a hot coal. "Please."

Gratitude overwhelmed her; what a wonderful man. He asked her to marry him, not for love obviously, but to save her reputation. He must have heard about her difficulties before rushing over to lend his assistance.

"I am aware of your current situation, and my offer of marriage will protect you from scandal. I promise you will find me a caring, attentive husband. If you agree, we can immediately release Thornbury from his obligations. His time would be better spent dealing with his mother, make no mistake."

Upon consideration, Dr. Potts would make a suitable spouse for any woman. He lived nearby and had no need for her land or her wealth. Moreover, his motivation appeared to be genuine affection and concern about her welfare.

"We all know Thornbury's intentions toward women are never serious. Considering his reputation, how could they be? The man is as despicable as that handbook of his. I recently obtained a copy from our lending library, for your sake. The boards were cracked and several chapters missing. But I cannot tell you, since you are a lady, how abhorrent and repulsive the handbook is. It's a reflection of the author's shameful nature, without doubt."

Elinor hid a grin. "Do you remember the titles of the missing chapters?"

He readily answered. "Oh, there are so many depraved titles, but 'Method to Handle the Frolicsome' and 'What to Do When There Are Two' were rather crudely torn from book. While 'Larks and Sprees' and 'Something's A-Miss,' all remained. So you see, I obtained a pretty good idea about the depraved book as a whole."

She pursed her lips. "You have a good memory."

His eyes widened. "I beg your pardon. My dislike of the man got the better of me. I did not mean to offend you."

"No offense taken."

"I'm sure such an abominable gentleman will be pleased to be freed of your engagement," he said, taking her hand firmly between his. "I suppose that didn't sound right. I truly wish for you to marry me. In fact, I planned to ask for your hand in matrimony before this…situation with Thornbury happened. You must believe in my deep affection and regard. Agree to my offer, and I will inform him today about your change in plans. I assume you too have been invited to the entertainments at Blackwell next week. If so, we can announce our betrothal to our friends then."

"The entertainments have been canceled." Elinor patted the top of his long, bony fingers. "Thank you, but you misunderstand my current situation. I will not marry Mr. Thornbury—"

"Wonderful!" He jumped to his feet, hesitated, then watched her. "Truly? Just days ago he told me it was as good as settled. What changed his mind? Why, the man is a jilt. How could he call off, leaving you to fend off people's vicious accusations—the censure?" He knelt before her again. "We will marry. I expect us to marry." He seemed to regret his strident tone. "Forgive me. I ask you again to accept my hand in marriage."

"No, you mistake me. I was the one who called off, not Mr. Thornbury. It seems I'm the jilt." She considered her remarkable situation. Within days she had received two offers of marriage. After Ross's proposal, she had spent several hours asking herself if marriage might be the correct action to take, after all. Wedlock need not be a reflection upon her love for William.

Now, after her cut from Mrs. Applewaite, likely the first of many incidents, if she accepted Dr. Potts, all would be set to rights. Her friends could freely associate with her without drawing disapproval upon themselves. Life would continue as before, only Berdy would have a stepfather. Granted, she didn't love the doctor, but he had never used that word either. "Affection" was the word he chose. As older adults, they could be honest with each other, and she truly did like him. She'd been lucky the first time and married for love, but women rarely got that opportunity. Now she would wed for a position in life—a common event for many women. Or rather the *restoration* of her position in life.

He appeared to expect an answer now, so she tried to ease his mind. "Thank you for your offer. But it is all such a shock you see—"

"Of course." He rose and paced before the hearth again. "I cannot say that I am not disappointed. I had hoped for an immediate reply, but take a few days to consider my proposal. With a little thought, I believe you will understand my offer is the correct action to take. In time, I am confident our union will become a love match."

She was at a loss for words. Why did all these gentlemen expect marriage to lead to affection or even love? She was fond of Dr. Potts, respected Henry, and was charmed by Ross, but these tender feelings were not love. Her manners must have been faulty, the only possible explanation. Because of her behavior, she anticipated losing three of her allies. Masculine anger or mortification over her refusal might taint their future friendship, leaving the years before her ones of grim isolation. Without the comfort and protection of her closest knights, she truly would live her life alone.

The doctor gathered his kid gloves and tall hat. "Please consider my offer. In a day or two I'll return, and we can discuss our future happiness."

⸙

"Elliii." Berdy's howl rent the early morning silence across Pinnacles.

Elinor paused halfway through her arrangement of a bouquet of roses in the entranceway and looked up to the origin of the rumpus. Today Berdy would leave for London and be separated from her for an unknown length of time, but that was no reason to lower her standards and let him continue to wail. "I wish you'd cease making a racket from upstairs while I'm downstairs."

Clump. Thud. Clump. Thud. Clump. Thud. Berdy appeared at the top of the stairs wearing one top boot on his left foot, while the right boot swung from his outstretched hand. "I must find champagne—now—this instant. I've no time to lose."

"Instant champagne? The last time we had champagne was celebrating the completion of Pinnacles. Why do you need spirits at this time of day? Too much claret last night?" Her question ended in a higher tone, a universal motherly enticement to confess.

"It's to polish m' boots. You *must* know fellows need champagne to polish their boots." Berdy held the champagne-deprived boot out for sympathy.

"How silly. I know no such thing." She glared at him with her arms crossed over her chest. "Love, champagne is alcohol and sugar. Boots are leather. Why would alcohol and sugar be good for leather? Seems to me champagne would only render them dry and sticky."

He shook the free boot at her. "Sugar and…rubbish. Nothing to do with that mishmash. It is the effervescence—the life of the champagne. Bubbles. Froth! It brings a shine to your boot no blacking can achieve. Why, I can tell a boot polished by champagne, versus a boot polished without, at twenty paces."

"I doubt you could do any such thing. You shouldn't believe everything you hear. Someone is pulling your boot. If you'd like, I'll ask Mrs. Richards for some blacking."

"No, no, not enough time. Ross said he would arrive around six, then off to London. So I don't want to be late." His torso gesticulated wildly as he hopped into the troublesome right boot.

Several minutes later, after he returned to his room, she heard another wail break the silence. This time it was more of an extended "nooo." She recognized the cause of that sound—wrinkles in his cravat.

Ross arrived promptly, and Berdy bounded out to greet him, unable to get his salutations and gratitude out fast enough.

Ross smiled, patted Berdy on the back, and both men headed toward the carriage.

This is the moment she feared most. The moment both Berdy and Ross left Cheshire. And she didn't know when, or if, either of them would return to stay. Panic seized her heart as she stood in the doorway, watching them stride away. Desperation welled up within her, and she yelled Berdy's name far too indecorously for a lady.

Berdy appeared rather sheepish before hobbling over, lifting her an inch or two off the ground, and swinging her around. "Don't be sad. I'll be back soon. I promise." He kissed her cheek.

When her feet were returned to solid ground, she straightened his collar, even though it rarely needed straightening. "I know, love. If you are in any trouble, write to me immediately. Promise me, please."

"Of course." He peeked over his shoulder at the carriage. "I promise to write frequently, but you must be patient. I'll have so much to do in London, a considerable amount of time may pass before I can write." After another quick kiss on her cheek, Berdy ran to the carriage, jumped in, and began to wave his arm out the window.

If she could have commanded speech, she would have told him to write anyway, no matter how busy he was, but she could not. Her throat closed, and tears swelled around her eyes. The carriage failed to leave. Yet Berdy continued to wave, and as long as she was able, she waved back too.

Finally, after Berdy's box had been properly stowed, Ross strolled into view from the other side of the carriage, bowed, and intoned a formal "madam."

"Ross," she said. The sound of his forename startled both of them into silence for a moment. "Thank you for inviting Berdy to accompany you into Town. I'm forever grateful for your attentions to him."

With an abbreviated bow—and a possible "humph"—he strode forward until he was looking down upon her imperiously.

Blushing wildly, she could not look him in the eye.

He stilled for what felt like hours, then his countenance softened. "I understand you are having difficulties with some of the townsfolk in the village. Even though my handbook is closed…I never meant it to end in this manner." He turned toward the carriage to leave. "I want you to believe that. Farewell."

She grabbed his elbow. "Ross."

With a slow turn of his head, he peered down at her.

"I—I do not want our handbook to end," she whispered.

"Pardon?"

"Oh, let me explain." Her stomach performed somersaults. He could tease her or read her any imaginary chapters he wished. All she wanted was his friendship—a simple request.

"Well?"

"I—I...our friendship..." With her mind muddled, how could she explain? "Please return soon."

His stiff posture loosened, and he grinned. "I do not have time to chat now." He bent to bestow a chaste kiss upon her cheek.

"Ross, please."

He gave a carefree chuckle. "Later, sweetheart." He barked instructions to his groom and climbed into the dark green carriage.

She watched the chaise disappear down the road. The reflection of the early morning's sun obscured the view through the back window, thus preventing any final glimpse of the carriage's occupants. She stood in the drive for several long minutes after it had disappeared from sight. The intense sunlight burned her cheeks, and today's clear blue sky irritated her. Today was an awful day.

Would she see either of them anytime soon?

Several feet away, she noticed a glove amongst the pebbles in the drive. She picked up the gray glove, too large to be one of Berdy's gloves, and realized Ross must have dropped one of his. The soft kid glove had a ruffled nap, so she smoothed it back into place. She then held the glove to her nose, and the scent began a wave of fond memories. Ross's broad shoulders providing comfort just by standing nearby, his smile outshining every light in the room, and the warm taste of brandy-tainted kisses. She slipped the glove down her fingers and cradled it in her other hand. The warm glow this gesture created she ascribed to friendship. However, her actions might also be described as those of a lover, a frightening conclusion she dismissed as a mere fantasy created by low spirits.

Sixteen

"MADAM, I HOPE YOU ARE WELL."

Elinor stood in the study, reading the first sentence of a letter that had just arrived. Her glance raced down to the salutation and noticed the strong *R* in the word "Ross." *Why had Ross written her from London?* Seconds earlier, when the letter had been placed into her hands by Mrs. Richards, her spirits soared. Here was her promised letter from Berdy—her first since he left for London a month ago. But Berdy did not write the letter, so her hopes suffered a Phaëthon-like death and spiraled down to Earth. The letter dropped from her hands and landed on the desk in front of Nelson's inkwell, almost directly under the paws of the weeping lion. Then aware of her desire to hear from Ross, she snatched up the letter, moved to her favorite chair, and began to read.

Madam,

I hope you are well. You will be pleased to hear your nephew arrived safely in London. I heard his name mentioned in my club and decided to make a morning call. I found him in rooms off Harley Street under his father's care. While I cannot say Mr. Ralph Deane was delighted with the arrival of the young man, the expression on young Deane's face indicated he was truly happy and was where he wished to be. So happy in fact, I took this liberty to inform you of his safe arrival lest he forgot. The last words I heard from Mr. Ralph Deane in regard to his son were, "Tell Mrs. Colton I will teach him everything he needs to know." So Deane is in the hands of his father, who will undoubtedly see that the young man comes to no harm. I have reminded Deane to write you as soon as possible. He assured me he would do so.

You have my constant hope for your continued health and happiness.

Ross Thornbury

Males. So Berdy resided with his father, after all. Perhaps her opposition to this plan was the reason Berdy failed to write of his arrival in a timely fashion. She admitted she expected changes from her original plan, but she could do nothing now except be resigned to the situation. Paternal affection and responsibility must ensure Berdy came to no harm.

She read the letter again to find any hints about Ross's well-being, or what he thought of her, but she found none. For some unknown reason, she held the letter to her nose and inhaled the sweet smell of the lavender mixed into the writing sand used to blot the ink. Even though the letter was not as long as she wished, she knew Ross had done her a great kindness by writing. After perusing his words a third time, she decided his hearing was satisfactory, as he was able to remember Mr. Ralph Deane's words upon parting. Also, his intellect remained sound, as he correctly predicted Berdy's neglect in writing her. Other than a preoccupation with her health, it was a considerate letter overall.

She smoothed the paper flat on the polished top of the large desk, carefully rolled the letter, and tied it with a piece of blue silk. She picked up her traveling desk kept on a bookshelf behind her, lifted the baize-covered top, and carefully placed the letter on top of the gray glove. Letting her imagination run free, she pleasantly daydreamed about the meeting in London between Berdy and Ross.

໔∾

A full month after the arrival of Ross's letter, she was tying up her roses to protect them from the wind and cold weather, when Mrs. Richards ran outside and handed her a letter from Berdy. Dropping her twine and grabbing the letter, Elinor hurried toward the house and opened the letter immediately upon reaching the protection of the flagstone loggia.

My dear Elinor,

I just arrived safely in London and have been occupied with experiencing all that London has to offer. What does that Dr. Johnson fellow say, "Tire of London, tire of life, because London has affordable life"? That might not be the exact words, but very like. Did you know that people don't really polish their boots with champagne? I must admit disappointment, but you will be pleased to hear that my cravat knot, The Circumbendibus, is a great success. I receive many admiring glances and gestures as I stroll London's streets. Father has taken me to a few of the clubs and establishments he frequents, and you will not be surprised to hear that I have been successful at cards. In fact, my luck has been so exceptional, many have remarked upon it. I am confident I shall win ten thousand and return home a wealthy man. It is regrettable you cannot be here to witness my success.

> With great affection,
> Berdmore

Males. If the letter from Ross bordered on tolerable, Elinor could think of no words to describe this one other than "absolute disaster." In her mind, a coiled serpent of trouble lurked in every sentence, ready to strike upon the last word. If Ross's letter revealed his intellect remained sound, this letter indicated Berdy's cravat knot had strangled his wits, and the vacant carcass paraded through the streets of London. If she were a man, she'd be off to London this instant. But if she were a man, she might also laugh it off as just a youthful indiscretion. Instead, she harbored a feminine foreboding, telling her something was amiss.

She took a deep breath and stared at the roses

thrashing against one another in the wind. For the tenth time that minute, she reminded herself Berdy's father would care for him. His father would see no harm befell him—guide him. Well, not exactly guide him as she would, he was a man after all, and therefore, certain tolerances must be granted.

She dashed into the study to write her reply. She congratulated Berdy upon his good fortune and implored him to keep the connection with Mr. Thornbury. Putting her pen down, she felt remarkably better. Somehow she knew, even if Berdy forgot the connection, Ross would not.

She returned to the garden and tied up the roses tight.

The following week, Elinor was surprised to receive another letter from Ross. *So soon?* Her heartbeat careened as she broke the wafer. She took a deep breath and collapsed into her favorite chair.

Dear Madam,

I hope this letter finds you well. Please do not be alarmed that it contains bad news, young Deane is well. I write merely to inform you that your nephew has experienced a change in residence and a change in heart. He is no longer living with his father and is residing with me. I can only say London was not up to Deane's expectations, and his father desires he returns to Cheshire soon. Unfortunately, his circumstance is much reduced, so Deane requests to remain here at present. I will endeavor to bring him home when my business requires I return to the

neighborhood in two weeks. We both send you our
best wishes for your happiness.

Your servant,
Ross Thornbury

Should she laugh or cry? Run to London or stay
at Pinnacles? Berdy split with his father—in reduced
circumstance—what did it all mean? From past
experience, she knew Mr. Deane had never desired
Berdy to reside with him in London, yet how could
he abandon his son? Perhaps he even had a hand in
Berdy's difficulties? No, that behavior was unthink-
able for any parent.

After an hour of contemplating myriad questions,
she was more confused about what happened to
Berdy than after her first read of the letter. Finally, she
realized Ross must have gone through considerable
trouble and expense to save Berdy. She knew the two
men had become friends, but... She forced herself to
concentrate on arranging the flowers in a vase next to
her. She refused to think about a possible motivation
for Ross's actions, other than saving his young friend.
Especially a reason that might involve her.

Now she had to wait two weeks until her mind
was set at ease by their safe return. Of course, she
must remember to reimburse Ross for any expenses he
may have incurred on Berdy's behalf. Taking up her
pen, she started a letter to him, requesting the sum of
money required to pay off Berdy's debts.

After she affixed the wafer to the letter, she heard
the crunch of gravel from outside, announcing the

arrival of a visitor. The housemaid informed her Henry called and was waiting for her in the drawing room. Being late in the day, it wasn't his usual hour to call. So what event caused him to alter his routine?

Upon entering the room, she found Henry still struggling out of his many-caped greatcoat. "My dear," Henry intoned, followed by a deep bow. His straw-colored hair was windblown from his ride, but he made no effort to check it in the glass. He sat across from her and scooted to the edge of his chair, his green eyes alight, while he rapidly spoke. "I've just heard the news about Deane. I can't say I'm surprised. I always knew—"

"What do you know?" How did Henry hear about Berdy's plight so soon?

"Deane *ruined* himself with bad company. While I'm ignorant of the details, other than he was found naked in the bowels of Covent Garden. I am unsure if he was truly without clothes or metaphorically naked. Still, I rushed over to hear the story from you. The entire neighborhood is tattling on about the scandal."

She too leaned forward in her chair, eager to learn more details about Berdy's fate. "How can the neighborhood know of Berdy's situation, when I have just received the news from Mr. Thornbury myself? Pray, how did you hear of it, and what do you know?"

Henry shook his head in small defense shakes. "Mrs. Thornbury wrote her friend, Mrs. Norton, who, of course and rightly so, immediately brought the matter to my attention. I am here today to offer my sympathies and assistance."

"Wonderful," she said, grateful for his kind offer. "I'm pleased you would consider helping Berdy in his moment of distress."

"You misunderstand me, my dear. I've come to help *you*, not young Deane."

"I don't understand." Upon hearing his qualification to assist only her, a lead knot settled low in her stomach. "I assumed you would offer to fetch Berdy from London."

He stood and set his hair to rights in the mirrored glass over the fire. "That is all very well had we been betrothed. Since we're not engaged, I have no right to meddle in Deane's concerns. Surely you can imagine what people would think?"

She dropped her head a little. "Yes, I understand. Could you assist me by making sure Mr. Thornbury is reimbursed for his troubles?"

Once more he glanced at himself in the glass. "But I would have to travel all the way to London."

Her lead knot spread upward, making her heart feel heavy too. "What sort of assistance and sympathies did you have in mind?" She retreated deep into the cushions of her chair and had to restrain herself from complaining about the sour-apple smell of his excessive pomade.

"Why, I can supply the assistance of sound masculine advice."

She bit her tongue. "And the sympathies?"

"The same, my dear, the sympathy inherent in all masculine advice. Well, not *all* gentlemen. I would never trust Thornbury's advice, for example."

She possessed little tolerance for Henry's opinions

at the moment, and strode to the door. "And that advice is?"

"You must insist Deane remain in London. Even if it means never seeing him again."

"What?" Now this was too ridiculous. Henry's lack of support for Berdy's situation did not surprise her, but his lack of empathy for a fellow human in distress troubled her deeply. "Your hair is too… You should check your hair in the glass before you leave." She reached for the door's catch. "Please excuse me, Henry, but I must make plans for Berdy's return." She exited the room and shut the door, leaving him to escort himself out.

❧

Ross collapsed onto his sofa and watched Henry Browne exit his London rooms at Long's Hotel. The front door closed with a bang, and Ross heard Browne's footsteps descend to the flagstone pathway outside. As the sound faded, he heard another set of quicker footsteps approach.

Seconds later, Lord Boyce Parker burst into the parlor without waiting to be announced. "Hallo, hallo."

Ross saluted his friend with a wave of his hand. "Hallo." He nodded toward the sideboard. "Help yourself, but keep it down. Young Deane's nerves have not recovered quite yet."

Parker tiptoed over to the cut-glass decanter and poured himself a sherry. Then he tiptoed back to sit in the chair next to the sofa. "Right ho, mum's the word. What did that Browne fellow want?"

"Nothing of consequence."

Parker leaned back and crossed his long legs. "He's a lawyer, right? My father told me they are always up to mischief. Didn't that Shakespeare fellow say we should shoot all the lawyers?" Parker took a long gulp of sherry. "Was is shoot or drown? I mean, there must be plenty of ways to kill a fellow. I wonder which one Shakespeare used?"

"I think his comment was hypothetical."

"By the frown on your face," Parker said, "Browne must have threatened you. Continued problems over that foundry business?"

"Always. Seems a railroad will be too expensive, so I'll need to get that lease signed."

"Browne knows about the cost of a railroad?"

Ross rose and helped himself to his fourth glass of sherry. He must remember to get some brandy; the sherry's sweetness irritated him today. "No, he offered to pay my expenses for Deane's recovery on behalf of Mrs. Colton. Unfortunately, she is having a rough time at the present and wants the boy home. Browne's officious, but I'm now convinced he means well." In fact, Ross had probably made a fool of himself by seeking Browne's promise to look after Elinor. He even went so far as to suggest his investment group could use Browne's legal assistance in the future.

Parker put down his glass and studied him.

Ross felt like he was under a microscope. "What?"

"So Mater is fending off the irate locals, and your widow is…what exactly is a rough time?"

"None of your business."

"Ha, ha. You know in your heart you will eventually have to take my advice and use the Smedley girls. So we must return to Cheshire and let loose the hounds of war." He waved his arm. "Well, not hounds of war exactly, more like the hounds of foolishness. The squire's too busy with his hunters to provide adequate paternal oversight."

Ross rose and stood by the fire.

"You know I'm right," Parker said, raising his glass.

Peering into the fire, Ross kicked a loose coal near the scuttle. "No. I know nothing of the sort."

"Listen. You can bring home the mooncalf, parley your neighbors away from the Mater, and rescue the lovely widow. All with just a few minutes of playacting."

Ross dropped his fist on top of the mantel. "I can do all that without the assistance of the Smedleys."

"Not rescue the widow," Parker said, tossing back the last of his sherry. "You said yourself you doubted the townsfolk had actually read the handbook, so they must give it the same veracity one gives gossip— entertaining, but false. We could pass out copies of the handbook at the local market day, but that might be expensive. No, they must see your vile character with their own eyes."

"Stop."

"How are you going to change people's minds about the widow? Plead with them?" He lowered his voice to mimic his father's pedantic tone. "'Please be civil to her, it was all my fault.' Ha! Like to see you try. Yes, yes, I want a front-row seat for that performance. I'm telling you, it will take just one gossiping matron to see you with the girls, and your name will be gleefully sullied all over town."

"And that helps Mrs. Colton how?"

"Because you are so obviously vile, the widow must have done the right thing by refusing you. Yes, yes, she will become the town's heroine."

Ross glared at him. If he agreed to Parker's little farce, he hated to think of his mother's reaction if she were told. But his news from Blackwell indicated Lady Helen had retreated to her rooms soon after his departure. So he doubted she would ever hear the news of Parker's playacting. If she did, he could always explain the situation. He'd rather walk on hot coals than explain, but he could if necessary.

Lord Parker raised both hands. "Do you have a better plan?"

❧

The five Smedley girls, ages sixteen to twenty-two, climbed into the large carriage for their journey to the town's central square. Their cousin, Lord Boyce Parker, and his friend, Mr. Thornbury, would ride in the curricle behind them. The eldest sister, Miss Hope Smedley, pointed to the exact location where she wished the two youngest sisters to sit. Her orders were obeyed without question, because the girls were not listening to her. The five sisters were all dressed as tarts, and the other four were busy comparing costumes.

Days before, it had taken some time for Lord Parker to gain Mr. Smedley's parental consent for his scheme, even though a lady's honor would be saved. The girls' father, an easygoing country squire, agreed to the outing upon the condition no names would be used, so the sisters would remain anonymous. He also insisted the girls' nurse would accompany them every foot of their journey.

All of the sisters expected their performance to be superior to what they had ever done before, because now they had a real audience. An audience that promised to be more susceptible to fine acting than Uncle John with his listening horn, a sleeping nurse, a disapproving mother, or silly Aunt Sarah.

Once the two conveyances started forward and the girls were alone in their carriage, conversation turned to the performance ahead of them. The girls were to act like harlots, merely by dressing like tarts and strolling in public accompanied by Mr. Thornbury. Then they would join their nurse and return to the posting house. They should reach their home in the next county before nightfall.

Alice yanked up the window to stop the breeze from blowing the feather on her bonnet across her face. "That Mr. Thornbury is a little terse, granted, but a very nice man. I wonder why the unknown lady wants to call off and does not wish to marry him? It must be his age. He is very old, perhaps thirty."

"I am worried about you," Elizabeth said pointedly. "I fear you need spectacles." The artist of the family, no detail escaped her sharp eye.

Jane, the ginger-haired sister, nodded. "Oh, I agree completely."

The two other young ladies murmured in general agreement.

"I mean, it is not as if he was objectionable in any way." Elizabeth pointed out. "In fact, he is painfully handsome. Just why does the lady wish to refuse him?"

"She is refusing him," Jane said, "because like Alice here, she cannot see him. *God's carrots*. Did you see the thighs on that man?"

Four pairs of eyes widened in identical astonishment. Jane ignored them and continued. "I wish my beau's thighs looked like that in pantaloons. They were so broad—"

"Thighs!" Elizabeth exclaimed, shaking her head. "You must be blind, too. No, it's his buttocks."

Collective gasps ricocheted throughout the carriage. Furtive glances were exchange from left to right, then right to left. Everyone started to giggle.

The sisters replied in turn. "Oh my word."

"Don't be vulgar."

"I'm going to tell."

"Did you see them?" Elizabeth asked. "How could you ignore those buttocks? I would love to have him sit for my next watercolor."

Anne, the wisest sister said, "I never stood behind him."

"I apologize for the vulgarity," Elizabeth said, leaning forward into the center of the carriage. "But his buttocks were just like butter cakes or those London muffins Cook was trying to replicate. You know, Mogg's muffins, nicely curved and—um—delicious to look at."

The sisters gasped again before exploding into various types of giggles.

"Muffins?" Jane replied, taking her turn to lean forward. "No, those muffins are soft, and believe me, there was nothing soft about those buttocks."

The other sisters gasped.

Jane wagged her finger. "Those buttocks were perfectly round and firm. I'll bet they are so hard, a shilling would bounce off them."

"I agree with Jane," Anne said stolidly. "His backside cannot be compared to cakes or muffins. It's so-so troublesome. Besides, our cake rings are all fluted."

Four young ladies burst into identical whoops of laughter.

"No," Elizabeth joined in, "he has perfect buttocks." Waving her hand, she sliced a curve through the air. "Prominent, and you know how each cheek can get that little hollow in the side when the gentlemen are particularly fit. Buttocks with a hollow like that might be called fluted."

"Just like those naughty Greek statues in the British Museum," Jane said.

"Ladies, please," Hope pleaded. "You are all being vulgar, and I fear we are not helping Boyce."

The girls sat for a minute in guilty silence.

Jane whispered to Elizabeth, "Why are you making such a funny face?"

Elizabeth grinned. "Since I am acquainted with all of the available beaus within forty miles, and I am the second sister to be out, I believe I will set my cap for Mr. Thornbury. He really does have a lovely smile, does he not? Besides, he is the finest specimen of our acquaintance. Wealthy, kind, doing what he did to save some lady—although the nature of the matter escapes me. So I plan to do everything in my power to *reel* him in."

"Oh, yes," Anne said, "a wise decision. I'll help you reel him in. I suggest we invite him to supper."

Each sister replied in turn. "I will invite him to play whist."

"I will invite him to stroll in the garden."

"I will invite him to ride Father's hunter."

"But he is still old," Alice stated, struggling to make her bonnet's feather stand upright. "And next year he'll be even older."

"See, I was right," Elizabeth said. "She needs spectacles."

"No, she needs a brain," Anne said.

Jane held up a finger to her lips. "Shh, Mr. Thornbury's coming. God's carrots. If one day he becomes my brother-in-law, I will always think of him first as the muffin man."

Seventeen

STROLLING DOWN THE FLAGSTONE PAVEMENT IN FRONT of the local marketplace, Elinor stilled. *Heavens.* She had forgotten about the bazaar held on the last Saturday of the month. All she set out to accomplish this morning was to visit one of William's closest friends, the Reverend Hill. Now she found herself in front of sixty women strolling past tables within a cavernous marketplace. They all turned in unison to stare at her, as if orchestrated by some unseen conductor. Her mind raced. *Should she run or hide?*

The formidable dowager, Mrs. Harbottle, turned to face the ladies in the marketplace, her gray curls bouncing with her quick movements. "Can you believe she means to attend the bazaar today? I mean, now really."

"Shh." The sound echoed amongst small groups of women.

Elinor backed up against a wide stone column and shuffled halfway around to face the town square, so she would be hidden from their view. Surely after a few minutes, her presence would be forgotten, and she could walk past the ladies without being seen. She held her breath, waiting.

∾

Ross opened the carriage door to allow the Smedley sisters to alight. It took longer than expected, because a feather became stuck in a door hinge. Parker stood behind him, grinning widely—*the devil*. If only this daft plan were over this minute, Ross could start drinking himself to the blue devils. But first, all he had to do was convince the townspeople that the tittle-tattle spewed by his neighbors was true—he was a rake.

He acknowledged to himself that there was some justice to this farce. Elinor would be absolved of any indiscretion, and the blame would be shifted to him. Besides, as the saying goes, *nosce te ipsum*, know thyself. This "charade" would truly be the last nail in the coffin of his failed "proper gentleman" masquerade.

As he paused to speculate whether Elinor's suitors could guarantee her happiness, his attention was regained by five expectant smiles. "Ladies, I'm grateful for your assistance in this matter."

Standing before him, five sisters stood dressed according to their individual ideas of what a tart would wear. The outfits varied from the low-bodice country maiden, complete with a milk bucket, to the washerwoman with a hiked-up skirt tucked into a broad black belt. One short young lady wore an old ball gown, which Ross decided had more to do with her lack of a suitable frock than to her belief that harlots dressed like members of the *ton*. All of them had apparently dipped into the same face powder, because ten cheeks sporting identical red dots framed five broad grins.

A tall girl with long features to match, Miss Alice sneezed after a feather fell on her nose. She batted the feather back into place.

Miss Hope, not a day over twenty-two, took charge. "Mr. Thornbury, we are all delighted to help someone who is a friend of our dear cousin Boyce."

"He is our favorite cousin," Alice added.

Miss Hope frowned at her sister before she spoke again. "While the exact nature of your assistance is unclear, I believe it had something to do with releasing a lady from a premature betrothal without scandal attaching to the lady."

Miss Elizabeth gave her opinion. "You are obviously a very nice man, aren't you, Mr. Thornbury? I am sure you did not want to marry this old harridan anyway, correct?"

Ross grimaced at Parker. "If you say so, Miss Elizabeth. Parker, you are a fortunate man to have such lovely relations. All of these young ladies are remarkable."

Miss Elizabeth beamed.

"Now, ladies," Ross said, "here is my plan. Upon my signal, all you have to do is slowly stroll by the town hall. There is a bazaar being held today, and several distinguished ladies will be present. After a pass or two in front of the hall, this charade should be over. I will join you and Parker at the posting house, where our carriages have been readied for our return journey. I do not know the details Parker has told you, but we are doing this as a service to a lady, and each sister will receive a new bonnet for her assistance. Any questions?"

The five sisters clapped in approval. Then the dairymaid asked, "Should we—I mean—what should we *do*?"

Ross tried to think of something the young ladies could do that would keep them in the courtyard for several minutes, but his mind blanked. If only one matron saw them, it would be enough for gossip to quickly spread. "I will pretend to be reading a book aloud, and you all can pretend to be listening."

"I think she means," the washerwoman said, "we would all like to *act*...like tarts."

Ross impatiently brushed his forelock off his brow. His thoughts ran wild, trying to imagine what respectable young ladies knew about acting like harlots, but he forced himself to stop. Instead, he faced the certainty that this was the last moment he possessed some control. The last stop before the edge of the cliff. The last chance to finally use his brain to end this scheme. But without an alternative plan to assist Elinor, he must march forward and take his chances. "Point taken. Perhaps a small—very small—amount of acting might be in order."

Four of the women sported mischievous grins, looking like horses ready to bolt into action.

Miss Hope gave them all a disapproving stare. "Now, girls, remember we are respectable young ladies. Actresses, yes, but ladies first." She lectured in the universal tone used by elder siblings to instruct the younger ones. Then she pointed to each sister in turn. "Elizabeth, you play the indifferent tart, Jane, you play the silly tart, and I'll play their keeper. Alice and Elizabeth, you can have a subtle fight over our hero's attentions." She nodded at him. "Ready, girls? Remember, great acting involves using your eyes and moving your arms. Oh, and don't do anything untoward."

All of the girls nodded in agreement, but Ross noticed the twinkle in their eyes did not fade.

Miss Elizabeth giggled. "I have always wanted to be an actress. This is much more realistic than acting in front of nurse."

"Er...right," Ross said, acknowledging his private doubts that Parker's cousins could convince anyone they were London harlots.

"Isn't this exciting?" Miss Anne looked at each of her sisters in turn for an affirmative response.

Ross and the five ladies started to stroll, one sister clinging to each arm, and the others strolled in front of him. For some unknown reason, the girls blinked at everyone they passed on the pavement.

Ross glanced ahead of them as they approach the town square and saw Elinor leaning full against a stone column. Upon his first glimpse of her after so many months, his heartbeat stopped. Her altered looks were not lost upon him, as he noticed she was thinner by at least a stone. The plump, laughing lady of the lake now appeared thin and ashen. Even the excessive formality of her sapphire gown, instead of the light-colored gowns she wore at the parties held at Blackwell, announced a newfound seriousness. Trying to hide his panic caused by her unexpected presence, he needed to think of some explanation or casual way out of this muddle. *Think, man, think.* With his mind in a whirl, and at a loss for a solution, he stopped strolling. He must appear like a bacon-brained half-wit, standing there staring at her with his jaw dropped, so he feigned reading a book to the washerwoman. His heartbeat became so loud, he could not hear his own words.

The four other sisters stopped too. Only they did not attend him. Instead, as if choreographed by an unseen hand, they bent at the waist in unison and pretended to adjust their stockings.

Gasps were heard from the direction of the bazaar.

Elinor took several steps forward, as if she were to greet him, then stopped in place, her mouth open and her face scarlet.

He stepped toward her, but the tall Miss Hope blocked his exit and began to trail her index finger down the side of his cheek. *Hell's fire.* Now he wholly regretted this tomfool plan. With a mock smile planted on his face, he imprisoned the tall lady's hand against his chest before she could "act" again, but her other hand wandered up and down his arm. Next the short-est Miss Smedley, wearing an overdramatic scowl, strode over and snatched his free hand before holding it to her breast.

The first lady giggled.

He glared at the sky.

The milk bucket dropped.

Elinor's body trembled slightly, enough for him to notice. She then lowered her head to focus on her clutched hands. Whatever sounds or movement were made by the five girls, Elinor's head remained lowered and her gaze unmoving.

He broke free and reached her in three long steps. "Please, let me explain."

"No," Elinor almost shouted. "I don't want to interrupt your…business. Good day." She shuffled backward and appeared to be in some distress. "Good day," she repeated as she started to run in the direction of the church.

With penitent humility, he yearned to fall at her feet and beg her forgiveness. Forgiveness for causing her public embarrassment. Scoop her up in his arms to cradle her softly. Soothe her wretchedness with a silly rhyme or tease out one of her fetching smiles until she gave him a wide-eyed gasp followed by a single "oh." An exclamation that had always coaxed the dimple to play in the corner of her mouth.

If he wouldn't look like such a sodding idiot, he'd kiss the hem of her gown and allow her the satisfaction of kicking him to the opposite side of the square. No, he'd grant her leave to kick him to the other side of England. She needed to marry Browne or Potts or some gentleman who would guarantee her happiness.

He herded the sisters together, and they all retreated to the posting house.

❧

Elinor did not get far before several ladies at the bazaar stepped in front of her. Her body stilled, but her senses remained on guard. She held her breath.

Mrs. Harbottle, who in the past had been her severest critic, gave her a single righteous nod.

Mrs. Applewaite moved forward and gave her a quick hug. "My dear Elinor, I always knew that man was a scoundrel. He is even worse than that earl who ran off with the opera dancer."

"Dear Mrs. Applewaite," Mrs. Long said, "that event never happened and truly was just gossip."

"But no one saw him again." Mrs. Applewaite shook her head. "And he had a large estate to run."

Mrs. Long pulled on her glove. "That's because his ship sank."

"Well." Mrs. Applewaite crossed her arms. "Even so, he still was a scoundrel."

"Ladies," Mrs. Harbottle pronounced. "Those who believed that Mr. Thornbury's vile handbook was nothing but gossip, I told you it was true, but you did not believe me. It is painfully obvious that every time that man smiles, scoundrel is written all over his face."

"Indeed," Mrs. Long remarked, running over to embrace her next. "Our little neighborhood is not safe with such a creature like Mr. Thornbury in our midst. First that foundry business and now this—this— behavior. You have my full support now that you have called off, dear. No woman in her right mind should marry such—a villain." Surprisingly, all of the ladies nodded in agreement.

Soon a small crowd of ladies gathered around Elinor. Simultaneous conversations erupted, in which she heard Ross repeatedly called a rake, a villain, and several other words, including blackguard, miscreant, libertine, reprobate, rapscallion, and rogue. As she surveyed her indignant friends surrounding her, the only word that came to her mind was "hero."

Eighteen

INSIDE THE SMALL ELIZABETHAN ALEHOUSE, UNDER A low-timbered ceiling, forty or so men drank liberally. Ross suspected Drexel was faking eagerness to hear the Banbury story of a cock and a bull escaping Parker's lips, but he ignored them and called for more ale to banish the memory of yesterday's rout.

"Yes, yes," Parker said. "The girls were overjoyed with their performance. Suddenly—suddenly you understand—the jaw of every lady in town dropped to the floor. You should have seen their faces."

Drexel, seemingly desperate to hear Parker's words, leaned close to him across the long wooden table of the local establishment, the Sleeping Lion.

Ross glared at Parker. "I thought you were to remain at the posting house."

"Would not have missed that performance for the world," Parker said.

"Humph." Ross stared at the water ring his glass left on the shiny dark table. He lowered the glass and made another circle close to the first. Then he repeated the process until the silvery rings resembled a watery chain. Parker's damn farce better have worked, and Elinor saved from grief. If he heard otherwise, he planned to wring his friend's neck.

At the table next to their party, several local farmers whispered. A few heads lifted to stare, sneers written across their red faces. Then—to a man—each spat upon the floor. Meanwhile, the landlord and six others standing at the bar kept their voices unnervingly low. Regardless, Ross heard an equal measure of the two words "handbook" and "foundry."

Ross tried to ignore all of them. His steward informed him earlier that his reputation was being sullied all over town. As a result, several of the foundry's loans had been called in. Taking his glass, he swiped his carefully produced watery rings into oblivion. Now he must travel to London to arrange quick payment of these debts. While this did not worry him too much, his steward also recounted some mischief at the site, nothing major. One of the brick walls had been knocked over, and the hoist mechanism of the winch used to lift the foundation stones had been tampered with. He expected to stay in London until all of this nonsense faded, and the men returned to their herds or harvest.

"Tell me more," Drexel requested, winking at Ross.

Parker leaned closer to Drexel, resulting in the two men appearing nose to nose. "A Smedley—won't tell you which one—developed a small *tendre* for ol' Two here."

Drexel leaned back in his chair. "Don't bet on that leg-shackle anytime soon. Two's heart is taken by the widow, and I do believe it's true love."

Ross froze, not daring to respond. If he did, he might start a brawl with every man in the room.

Parker gulped a mouthful of ale, foam lingering at the side of his mouth. "No, no, he can't be. He just burned his bridges with the widow."

Drexel raised his glass. "I will take that wager."

Parker held out his palm, ready to shake hands. "Right. What is the bet?"

"His heart," Drexel said, batting away Parker's offered hand and snickering at his own wit.

"Fustian!" Ross exclaimed. *Damnation*. They were right. He did love Elinor. The realization hit him the moment he saw her in the town square. He would never reveal it to anyone though, since he truly believed romance was for younger men, gentlemen optimistic about their future. His past aged him to a point where he considered himself too old for romantic love. Old because he felt unworthy of regard, and old because he had squandered the advantages given to him in the past. In his future, Elinor would return to her home and marry one of her suitors. While he would gain much-needed humility and hold close the memory of his one love that arrived too late.

❧

Berdy held out both palms, all ten fingers spread wide. "The foundry's steam engine is a full ten horse power. All that gobs of power is needed to run the steam hammers, drills, and cranes. You should have seen it, Elli. A single beam engine, the spinning regulator based upon centrifugal force—"

"Force?" Elinor smiled at the budding engineer

sitting across from her in the study, now sipping Madeira. He had spent the day with Ross, visiting a distant working foundry, and tried to recount all of the technical wonders he witnessed as fast as he could. He sat forward in his big wing chair, legs wide, flinging both arms in all directions with each sentence. His glass of Madeira traveled in a dizzying arc that captured her attention. What would be the first victim to be baptized by Madeira: waistcoat, carpet, or chair? "Force is a technical term I don't understand. Tell me about Ross's business plans instead?"

"Business plans? Plans are not important, unless they involve more machinery, of course. Ross showed me a strong steam engine like the ones he plans to build. These small engines will change the world, I'm certain. Then he demonstrated the action of sun and planet gears—"

"Gears. No more talk of gears or force. I must see them in action first, before I can give them due credit."

After Berdy's return from London, he had remained silent for days. Gradually his free-flowing speech resumed, but it was unlike his conversation before. Gone were his eager speeches about cravats, men of style, or a successful marriage. He even decided his yellow-striped waistcoat might be too vulgar. Now, after this trip with Ross, his enthusiasm returned to its old levels, except his conversation focused upon rational subjects, not neckcloths. The future might contain one or two additional flare-ups of a Berdy Rash Scheme, but she expected them to fade with time. Elinor dropped her needlework. A simple motion, but for some reason it felt like she had shed a mantle of iron. "Why don't you go upstairs and have Wilson remove your boots so they can be cleaned? When you're finished, come back down, and we'll play a game of chess."

"M' boots are fine," he said, clearly unwilling to stop until whatever he had on his mind spilled out. "We also visited the site of Ross's foundry. Using his own crane, Ross demonstrated how the mechanical force—work—is transferred to the winch's gears. Steam power will eliminate the necessity for a large workforce. Elli, you won't believe this. Ross mentioned the equipment at his foundry was vandalized last week. And when we pulled up in the curricle, Ross's steward had just caught one of Mr. Burton's men tampering with the winch again."

"Why would Mr. Burton's men do that?"

"To stop the foundry from ever being built, I imagine. The nerve." The glass of Madeira completed its arc and landed on the arm of his chair with some force, baptizing everything within a foot, including his trousers.

She gasped. "Vandalize the site, on purpose, deliberate mischief? I doubt anyone could be so vile."

Berdy ignored his wet trousers. "The ruffian also called Ross a villain—a villain. Unbelievable. I thought the opposition over the foundry ended long ago. You will sign his lease, right? I surely hope so. I cannot wait to see the construction start again. Anyhow, Burton's man said some very foul things, I can tell you. His words made m' blood boil. I almost stepped forward to plant the man a facer, but Ross seemed unconcerned and sent the man about his business."

"Berdy—"

"Don't worry. We didn't come to blows." He put down his empty glass and leaped from his seat. "Save me some cake at tea. I am quite famished. I will be upstairs reading the *Technical Repository*. It has an article about strong steam—"

She held up her hand. "If you tell me about the *Technical Repository*, I will have to read you *The Mirror of Graces*—or better yet—*Fordyce's Sermons*."

"Gad, not that book." He ran to the door. "Remember the cake."

"I will. I suggest you clean your trousers," she said before the door closed. She pulled the bell for a servant to help clean up the Madeira. Ross a villain? *How unjust.* She fought an urge to stand in front of the congregation on Sunday and read them a sermon about judgment and tolerance. "Villain, indeed." The man had given up his betrothed to save her reputation, and physically saved Berdy from who knows what—Newgate?

Her sense of injustice grew, so there was only one thing she could do now—clean. Whenever she started fretting and desired to compose sermons, she lost herself in housework. Now would be a good time to mop the flagstones or polish the bookshelves in William's study. Wax and rub every surface until she could see her reflection. She gave the bellpull another tug.

Mrs. Richards appeared hesitant to fetch the beeswax, as if she might protect her mistress from whatever trouble assailed her by failing to hand over the wax.

Elinor stood firm, polished for two hours, then collapsed onto William's chair. While she caught her breath, she touched William's mourning brooch. *William*. She unpinned the brooch and turned it over to reveal his hair under the glass. A simple gesture she had repeated daily. But the first thought that came to her mind—this time—was the discrepancy between the small plaits of hair, and the remembered softness of his locks when he lived. This was followed by a similar memory of caressing Ross's forelock as it fell over her shoulder. His hair too felt soft and sweet to the touch. She peered again at William's hair locked behind a wall of glass. It seemed so very wrong for a loved one to turn into mere gold, glass, and hair. William seemed to fade from her into an object, just an object. No lover to caress. For some unknown reason, today she realized that injustice even more.

By the first light of the next morning, she rose with the same determination to find a compromise with Ross about the lease, as she had while polishing William's desk. Of course, she needed to thank him again for Berdy's rescue. Then perhaps subtly inquire about his friends at the bazaar. She did not exactly understand what had happened at the bazaar that day, or if it had been planned. But she did recognize the results from his efforts, the restoration of her friends.

A true compromise was the only tangible way to thank him properly. She expected they would have a serious discourse in regard to her concerns about the smoke and then reach a mutual agreement. If this strategy failed, she would appeal to his generous nature to keep his friendship with Berdy. A reasonable request, surely.

Upon her arrival at Blackwell, Rowbottom indicated

Mr. Thornbury was not, at present, in the house. He pointed south and suggested she try the pinery.

It was general knowledge the previous owner had built a modern pinery to grow pineapple, but she had never seen it. Once she passed the planting beds of the home farm and took several wrong turns, ending in storage sheds, she glimpsed an all-glass roof just behind the old cruck barn and headed in that direction.

Standing before the pinery, she was surprised to see how long it was, probably twice the length of a normal glasshouse. The early morning sun played off the panes in a shimmering light that frolicked on the wall of the neighboring barn. Once she stepped inside, she inhaled warm, wet air smelling faintly of slate. Before her, long empty rows of raised iron shelves stretched the length of the room. She walked to the other end and passed through the door leading to the pinery's interior room, a glasshouse within a glasshouse. Here, under the shelves of ornate iron framework, large evaporating pans were visible, and she could feel the wet heat. Next to the door, a large pile of black potting soil, covered by a brown oilcloth, gave the room an earthy smell. Like the outer chamber, most of the rows were empty, but in the center row grew two large pineapple plants.

Ross was on his knees, inspecting an evaporating pan directly under the plants, but straightened upon her approach. Presumably because of the heat, he wore only a lawn shirt, and his sleeves were rolled up to his elbows. She noticed the dark hair on his lower forearm laying against his light skin, and the room grew warmer.

"Good morning." He pointed to the largest plant. "Come see Mother's joy. There is still one fruit left. Look here."

She peered at a plant resembling an unfriendly fern. Nestled in the center, a pineapple was recognizable. For such a visibly unimpressive fruit, she wondered what all the fuss was about. She had never tasted pineapple, mainly because she doubted whether something that ugly could have a pleasant taste.

Ross seemed surprised by her lack of enthusiasm. "Well?"

"Lovely."

He chuckled. "Keeping this little weed happy is a financial strain, but Mother won't let me sell the plants off. I don't understand why they make her happy, but they do, so there's an end to it."

Heavens, she was delighted to see him. Her heartbeat escalated like every time she had been in his company. "I… Um…I would…I don't know how to say this, but…"

His eyes focused steadily on her now.

She smothered an unbearable desire to walk right up to him and stroke his hair. *How embarrassing.* Growing increasingly befuddled, she gave up trying to assemble words together and smiled instead. For the moment, this was the best she could do.

"I take it you are pleased with Deane's return. Is that the reason for your visit?"

"Oh. Yes. I'd like to thank you for all you've done for Berdy's sake—"

"I've done nothing." He grabbed one of the pointed leaves and began to stroke it.

She bit her lower lip and tried to recall the purpose

for her visit. "I…you must have intended to shock everyone at the bazaar."

"You have no proof. I suggest, for all parties concerned, the less said the better." He tilted his head to peer at her with a serious expression; however, he couldn't hide the frolic dancing in his sapphire eyes.

She exhaled her held breath in a soft whoosh. For some unknown reason, she wanted her suspicions confirmed that the performance at the bazaar had been planned for her benefit. Then, if he put forward any other information, she would welcome it, although she would never directly solicit an explanation. "Did you know I would attend the bazaar?"

A wry grin played at the corner of his mouth.

Did she hear him whisper "females" under his breath?

Ross straightened his shoulders and stood like he was about to testify in a witness box. "I can honestly say I was woefully unaware of your attendance." He gave a desultory laugh. "No idea, I can assure you. Now if you will excuse me, I must return again to London on business in regard to the steam engine order. Apparently"—he frowned down at her—"changes will have to be made."

"So you *will* leave." Elinor knew he referred to arrangements to transport his engines, but she wanted to know when he would return. She smiled sheepishly, realizing here was her opportunity for a serious discussion about the lease. "I believe we might discuss the iron foundry further, if you'd like?"

He froze and searched her countenance. "Are you in earnest?"

She inhaled deeply, then held her breath. "Yes."

The sunshine smile beamed across his face. He dropped the pineapple leaf and examined her. "Would you consider the trip I mentioned to a foundry farther northeast? The steam engine near Buxton has the new smoke catcher on a considerably taller chimney flue. This added length dissipates the smoke to a greater degree than the colliery chimney we visited."

She nodded in agreement at his easy request. "Yes, I will visit the Buxton works with you."

They exchanged grins and let the silence stretch.

She became spellbound. He was too handsome, too charming, and too kind to those she loved.

"How about Thursday?" he asked.

"Yes."

"We will have a long travel day ahead. I'll pick you up early. Six?"

"Agreed."

"Agreed." He started forward to escort her back to the house.

She didn't move toward the door when he held out his hand to demonstrate the ladies' prerogative of going first. Fixed in place and unable to leave, she became overwhelmed by gentle panic—her mind blanked, her pulse climbed, her throat dried. She wanted his extended arm to close around her waist, so she could caress the smooth hair on his arm below his rolled-up sleeve. After this thought, she harbored no doubts she was the most foolish woman in the world.

Without any effort to move on her part, he let his arm fall to his side. "Well, then? Something else you would like to discuss?"

She tried gathering her wits, knowing enough to avoid any sight of his hair if she wanted to complete the task. Except now her vision fixed upon his jaw, where a light whisker growth shaded his chin. Why hadn't she noticed his lips before? Their slight rose color was an unusual contrast to the dark line of rough stubble.

Ross impatiently brushed his hair back from his forehead. "Let me escort you back to the house." Again he motioned for her to lead the way. "There's a significant amount of work I must complete today in regard to the estate."

She smiled at him in a manner she feared must have resembled the worldly intelligence of a two-year-old spying a favorite toy. Somehow his eyes had become dear eyes, very dear eyes, dear eyes indeed. "If we agree to a lease after our trip to Buxton, will you remain in Cheshire? I know both Berdy and I would like you to stay."

He paused and examined her face for a long minute. Then returned to stroking a single spear-like leaf on top of the pineapple.

Since he failed to answer her question, perhaps he was considering his reply. Hesitant to leave his captivating presence just yet and fearing he might leave Cheshire for a long time, she tried to keep the conversation upbeat and flowing. "Besides heat, what do pineapples need to thrive?"

"What we all need: food, water"—he stared at her again—"attention."

She took a step toward him to show her interest and demonstrate her gratitude. "It looks prickly."

"Some are. Depends how you touch…the plant."
He chuckled. "A wise man is gentle with them." He
stepped closer to her but continued to stroke the leaf.
His eyes briefly closed while he switched to caressing
the leaf in small circles with his thumb.

Mesmerized by his stroking finger, she wanted
to sound intelligent and racked her brain for a
sensible horticultural comment. "Do pineapples
require pruning?"

"No…that would tickle, don't you think?"

Caught by his hypnotic movements, and tickled
herself by his deep voice, she mouthed the next horticultural word that came to mind. "Grafting?"

"Ouch."

"Oh." The pinery became meltingly hot, a sublime
wet heat. "I've never eaten pineapple."

His eyes bespoke laughter, or something else.
"Never eaten…it's sweet like…sweet."

"And the flesh?" The word *flesh* made her breath
come in rapid pants.

His glance passed over her skirt. "Firm, but if you
press the bare fruit just so—it releases juice. Your
fingers can become quite sticky." Now he began to
pant too.

Heavens. "What next?"

Mischief teased her from within those blue eyes of
his. He stopped stroking the plant and stepped to close
the distance between them. "What comes next are the
most important chapters in husbandry."

"And that would be?"

"Plowing and propagation."

"No." She chuckled softly.

He nodded.

"Ross, will you remain in London? Never come back?" she whispered, looking at the small hollow in his throat, a feature that made her eyelids heavy and spoke of her desire.

A muscle in his cheek twitched.

She froze, her silent blazing desire broadcast by rapid pants and probably every feature of her being. "Please stay."

He failed to answer.

"Please." She answered the question she saw within the light of his blue eyes. "Yes."

He moved fast, spun her around, and pulled the laces of her gown and then her stays.

Reaching behind in a frantic gesture, she helped loosen her laces. Desire racing through every one of her veins.

In less than a minute, he managed to pull her bodice down to just above her stomach. He picked her up, laid her on the oilcloth covering the pile of dirt, and lifted her skirts to her waist. Next he tore at his shirt, pulling it over his head.

"Oh," she exclaimed, quickly unbuttoning the six buttons of his falls and shoving his breeches to his knees. A few seconds passed before he covered her fully with his torso. With unbearable delight, she spread her fingers over his chest and stroked his dark hair.

A slithering growl rumbled upon her neck, then he covered her lips with his. Their lips slid repeatedly in the kiss's heated mimicry. His tongue plunged to taste her, and she returned the pleasure to find he tasted of the lemon that laced his morning's tea. They kissed each other's features in return, forehead, cheek, nose, ear, shoulder. A bliss-filled eternity of wandering, mutual kisses.

He caressed her breast, and she arched into his palm, desiring him to feel all of its aching fullness.

His moist breath warmed her breast a moment before he claimed it with his skillful mouth. While he sucked and nibbled, she stroked his soft locks, letting his hair slide between her fingers.

She glanced over the top of his dark head to the sunlight streaming through the glass panes of the roof. *Heaven remembered.* "Plowing and propagation?" she whispered. "I've always enjoyed them." She felt his chuckle upon her breast, and realized nothing was more enjoyable than a man's amorous laughter against her skin. Soon her heart hammered, and she gasped in desire.

His talented hand moved between her legs and circled with the same slowness he had caressed the plant.

She felt liquid and sweet. She continued to stroke his body's contours, learning the feel of the soft hair covering his chest, the taught muscles of his abdomen, and the weight of his privates against her thigh.

"I enjoy plowing," he managed to say before moving up to kiss her again. The delicious silence broken only by her giggle and one of his ragged moans.

Joy seized her spirit. With her hand, she surrounded his member from the base of dark curls and down its length, flicking her finger over the slight ridge near the tip.

He lifted his head and gave her a look of

astonishment. "We'll get to the seed bit and miss the plow bit if you continue to do that." He quickly pressed her center, found what he sought, and thrust deep. They both moaned when he pulled back and thrust again, the force moving them together across the warm earth.

She rejoiced in his long, deep strokes and became even more stimulated by the liquid slap of their coupling as they climbed to the inevitable. Her bunched gown billowed between them with each thrust. She gasped, lifted her heels high, and gave a final shove with her hips to drive him deeper still before bliss triumphed in a succession of quivers.

He lifted himself upon stiff arms and thrust them forward another foot on the pile before a groan wrenched from his chest. He collapsed upon her, his weight resting on her chest, and his member still intimately filling her.

For several minutes, no words were exchanged between them. Then he pulled away from her and rolled off the earthen pile to stand. He turned his back and busied himself with the buttons of his breeches.

Rising to rest upon her elbows, she watched him. The relatively cool air evaporated the warmth he left between her legs and within her heart. Meanwhile, the distinctive smell of sex mingled with the musty smell of steam-heated earth.

Once his breeches were buttoned, and other clothing set to rights, he stood with his back to her, unmoving, staring at the floor.

Why didn't he speak? Why no fond words, a lover's final caress, or tender care rendered to refasten her garments? Like a sudden slap on the face, she felt humiliated by her physical exposure. She brought her legs together, sat upright, and attempted to dress herself. With her gown's laces mostly out of reach, she managed to loosely tie her dress. She removed the pins from her hair, twisted her locks into something suitable, and anchored the plaits firmly in place.

Ross remained still.

Heavens. What if his mother had visited her pineapples? She had never done anything so reckless in her life—and she was a minister's widow. All of her previous actions, which she had dismissed under the bias of attraction to a handsome man, were now seen for their true worth—she had desired this lovemaking since he found her fishing at the lake. Guilt assaulted her conscience, and Ross's never-ending silence only made it worse. *What had she done?*

She understood his silence could mean only one thing; he was not going to offer her marriage. Men never did a second time—everyone knew that. Male pride never allowed exposure to rejection twice. Yet some sliver of hope, brought to life by the joy of their shared ardor, died from his continued silence. She felt sick.

Being a male, he probably crowed over another quick conquest. Her wanton behavior must have confirmed his worst accusations that she was some lust-driven widow, or a belief she had manipulated him into the encounter. Heat ran up her back and spread over her cheeks. *She needed to flee.* Before he could sense her movement, she ran from the pinery.

Nineteen

DAMNATION, HE WAS AN ASS. ROSS FELL BACKWARD ON the large pile of earth, his spent body seeking rest. He should have fastened her gown, at least, while he searched for the right words to propose. Only this time, ready words had escaped him. She refused him the first time he attempted this proper-gentleman farce, and everyone knew ladies never accepted a second proposal. Besides, men would rather stand naked in the streets than expose themselves to rejection twice.

Hell's fire. Her soft plea for him to remain in Cheshire had rendered his blood hot, and he charged through the deed like old times, except afterward he never felt so vulnerable, so shattered. He could not adequately explain what she meant to him—could not explain even to himself.

She fled his presence as fast as those well-shaped legs could carry her, and he did not have the strength to make her stay. Ironic, that. He had always considered himself strong; everyone depended upon his strength. In the midst of John's illness, his strength kept both

John and his mother from falling apart, but now? *Now he needed strength*.

The strength to run after her to request forgiveness, and the bravery to offer his hand regardless of her expected reply. He laughed at the absurdities of his situation. Tomorrow he would call upon her and apologize—an all-too-common occurrence in their relationship. His apologies had failed in the past, and there was every reason why this one would be no different. He had no idea what he would say to her, no idea how to express his feelings, no idea how to make her happy.

He lay unmoving and let a warm burst of steam smother him. In the future, she'd probably greet him coolly before their arranged visit to the foundry and then sit beside him on their journey with the same tight smile his mother wore when one of the housemaids created an accidental mess. Pounding the dark earth with his fist, he felt better, so he pounded again until dirt baptized everything within five feet.

The next day, Ross paid a morning call to make his apologies. With a flushed face, Elinor stood before him like a statue, heard his apologies, and stared like he was a lunatic. When he finished, he started toward the door, and she escorted him out without saying a word.

He returned to Blackwell, explained to his mother that business called him to London immediately. He wrote a short note to Elinor, postponing their travel plans for Thursday. Then he gathered his papers and left that very afternoon for an extended stay.

❧

"How would you like to go fishing today?" Elinor asked Berdy on a warm autumn morning. "We can pack a picnic."

"Capital idea. I know how much you enjoy fishing." Berdy grinned. "We can also discuss m' new plan for the future."

Elinor decided to wait until her mind settled before she inquired about the details of his plan. So she left to gather the fishing equipment, and an hour later they stood next to the dense reeds on the south side of the lake. A light morning mist still hung in the air, but the day promised to be a sunny one. They climbed onto a low rock wall some distance from the water's edge and sat in silence for several minutes, watching the mist clear.

She contemplated the dark green water lapping upon the muddy shore. "Three years ago I sat here with William," she said, her voice unavoidably wistful. "I had everything I could ever desire, William, you, and a happy future for us all. Now I have—"

"You still have me." He reached out to clasp her hand. "And a future."

She gave his hand a squeeze. "I was about to say, now I have everything too. Only the nature of everything has changed somewhat. I have you, your future, and my memories."

He squeezed her palm in return. "Together we'll survive this. Please don't fret."

She pulled her hand free. "I'm not fretting. With all of these happy memories, I'm a grateful woman. See the thick tuft of reeds over there?" She pointed to a dense clump ten feet wide. "One time, William's line got tangled in that grass. He claimed if it wasn't for those reeds, he would've landed the biggest pike ever." She smiled and stared off into the distance. "And see that large flat rock half-submerged? That is where I first…"

Where she first met Ross, she was going to say before her throat closed. He had left Cheshire two months ago and still remained in London. When he had paid a call at Pinnacles the day after their love-making, she stood shocked, mortified, incapable of responding to his apology. She was unable to explain why she behaved as she did. Now her inability to speak or even acknowledge his apology might have alienated him forever. Whenever he did return, she must keep her promise and join him to evaluate the new smoke catcher. But she swallowed hard upon the thought that he might send her a letter, canceling their trip. Her behavior may have irrevocably torn their friendship.

A startled heron took flight from the water's edge, and they watched the bird disappear over a stand of timber.

Berdy turned to face her. "I've been thinking. What do you think about emigrating to America? We could make the journey together. Johnson from school emigrated, and he lives happily in New York. The Indians now live far to the West, I'm told."

"America? No." The old familiarity of being broadsided by a Berdy Rash Scheme returned. Glancing at his expression, she saw the depth of his sincerity and realized she might have misjudged him. "This decision is not a result of your father's behavior, is it?"

"No, that situation was my fault. I didn't listen to him. He never wanted me in London. I realize that now. First I thought I unwittingly exposed the schemes he used to earn a living, but now I've realized he taught me a valuable lesson learned from his own mistakes. Life as a gamester is an unsuitable profession for anyone." He inhaled deeply. "The only cost of his lesson was a brief loss of m' pride, but it made me a wiser man. So he acted like a parent should, surely?"

She did not fully understand him or actually believe in his father's motivations, but she recognized his generous spirit of forgiveness. "I hope one day you'll thank him."

He smiled sheepishly. "One day." Berdy tossed a pebble far into the center of the green lake, and they watched the ripple spread into an ever-increasing circle. "You know, in America we can put the past behind us and start afresh. Think of the adventure we'll have. If I left without you, I may never see you again. Not for years, at least." The tone of his voice was both sincere and optimistic about the future.

Her heartbeat rose at even a hint of their separation. "Are you truly considering America?"

He reached for her hand again. "Yes, I am. Dr. Potts is all for the idea. He even recommended it, so I've given it serious contemplation. This week I plan to ask several gentlemen, who have acquaintances that emigrated, about the opportunities in America. I need a complete picture of the challenges we might face before making a decision."

He spoke slowly, adding the appearance of *thought* to the enthusiastic stew of a Berdy Rash Scheme.

Moreover, he voluntarily suggested seeking a profession. A comment that rendered her a tad giddy.

"I'm glad to hear you are giving the matter serious thought," she said, hoping the more contemplative Berdy before her would remain. "Yet, America, so far." She patted his warm hand again. Her choices seemed simple: the warm life she held in her palm or the memories associated with this rock, this bush, or this house. One choice looked forward with optimism; the other looked backward to the comforts of the past. Of course, if she found herself unwed and with child, America might be the perfect refuge for them both.

The light mist in the center of the lake fully disappeared under the heated rays of the morning's sun.

"Let me know what the gentlemen say about America," she said. "I cannot imagine leaving Pinnacles, but our absence doesn't have to be permanent. We can always return to England someday." She faced him and smiled. "Maybe we created another happy memory here today? The beginning of our new future. I hope so."

After a successful morning fishing, they started home, each proudly holding one end of a stringer displaying three pike and one tench. Up ahead, Henry and Dr. Potts hailed a greeting, dismounted their horses, and joined them on the footpath home.

"My dear Elinor, Deane." Henry gave them a curt nod. "I feel it is my duty to warn you not to venture out into society just yet."

"Come now, Mr. Browne, charity please," Dr. Potts said with a brief bow in their direction.

Henry scowled at Dr. Potts. "Everyone has heard

of Deane's reckless behavior in London." He glared at Berdy. "Gambled away his money and discovered naked outside an alehouse."

She glanced at Berdy. She never inquired about his troubles in London, because she did not wish to embarrass him. Now there was surprise on his face, nothing more. "I don't believe Berdy has spoken of his adventure to anyone."

Berdy gave her a heartfelt smile.

"I wonder how society"—she paused—"how did the two of you hear of it?"

Henry moved one step closer than Dr. Potts. "From Mrs. Thornbury, of course. She wrote to her friend, the vicar's wife, who then told me."

She turned to address Dr. Potts. "How did everyone else hear of it?"

Dr. Potts rubbed his chin and nodded in Henry's direction.

Henry appeared busy tugging on his waistcoat, which had risen to his ribs after his dismount. "I fail to see how the news communicated is more important than the nature of the scandalous behavior. The point is, between the"—he cleared his throat—"impropriety with Thornbury at the fair, and now Deane's disgrace, you can't expect to be warmly welcomed by your neighbors any time soon, either of you. No, I'm sure forgiveness will take years and much effort."

She and Berdy exchanged sympathetic glances.

"Mr. Browne is mistaken," said Dr. Potts, calmly ignoring Henry's agitation. "Your neighbors no longer find you at fault and will gladly welcome you. They readily remember your many acts of kindness throughout the parish. Recent events have proved you have been ill-used by Thornbury, and the blame has fallen upon his shoulders, and rightly so." He straightened to full military attention. "May I call upon you tomorrow?"

She flashed him a warm smile. The doctor and his daughter had informally dined every fortnight for the last five years, and she was pleased he intended to resume the tradition. Except she hoped enough time had passed that he would not embarrass either of them by mentioning his proposal. "Yes, I know Berdy will appreciate the company of Miss Potts, and I would be delighted to have you call."

"If you don't object, I plan to arrive alone," Dr. Potts said. "There is an important proposition we need to discuss, remember?" A tender smile broke across his tanned aquiline face.

Henry stopped fidgeting with his waistcoat, glared at Dr. Potts, and took another step forward. "I'll call the following day, for I have your best welfare in mind. To prove my sincerity, I have voluntarily gathered several opinions from the local gentlemen on what actions should be undertaken. The consensus is both you and Deane should move far away to the south of here. I'm told life is better in the South. Perhaps if you choose your destination wisely, your ignominy might not follow. You can then return here in a year or two." Straightening his shoulders, he appeared quite pleased with himself.

"What an interesting idea, Henry," Elinor said, giving Berdy a wink. "Actually, we are considering moving west, not south. America perhaps."

Henry stumbled backward.

"America is the perfect country for a young man like Deane," Dr. Potts said with a nod at Berdy before he addressed her. "But you should remain here, dear Mrs. Colton. Your many friends would truly miss you."

"Yes, but for the near future, Berdy and I will stay together."

They reached a fork in the footpath, where Dr. Potts then took his leave. He mentioned a sick widow needing his attention and headed off down the other footpath.

Henry watched him disappear with a scowl across his handsome face. "Regardless of *his* opinion, my suggestion of moving to the South for a year or two is the better option."

Together, Elinor and Berdy started walking again, leaving Henry behind. "I must remember to consult Mr. Thornbury about your suggestion," she said. "I have always found his advice invaluable."

"As have I," Berdy added enthusiastically.

"Thornbury," Henry exclaimed. Pulling his horse's reins to close the distance between them, he scowled at her. "I doubt that man will be able to give you advice. His hands are full at the moment, dealing with the displeasure of his neighbors. The good doctor and I have just passed Mr. Burton, Mr. Mabbs, and others on the way to call upon him today. It seems Thornbury has returned from London and was seen at his foundry. Mr. Burton intends to confront him about it, of course."

"Confront him about what?" Elinor asked.

"Why, the foundry," Henry replied. "Burton, Mabbs, their tenants, and others—even I—do not wish a large number of laborers to live in the vicinity. Workers are low people given to drunkenness and filth."

"They toil in a foundry, so soot from charcoal is inevitable," she said.

"Still, we will be overrun by Methodists."

"Half of Macclesfield is Methodist silk weavers and button makers. You don't object to them, do you?"

Henry hesitated. "No, but these workers will reside close to us, not far off in a town like Macclesfield, where you cannot choose your neighbors. We'll be forced to put up with their noisy habits of drunkenness and keeping bulldogs."

"You own greyhounds. How does that differ from bulldogs?"

Henry stopped walking. "The breed of dog is not important. You surely don't support Thornbury's foundry?"

"At this moment, I'm trying to be fair." Her opinion had fluctuated so many times within the last months, she didn't know if she approved of the foundry or not. Persuasive arguments could be made for each side. Perhaps she could make her final decision after visiting the second chimney in Buxton. Then once a few issues were cleared up with Ross, the final decision should be obvious. She and Berdy continued walking toward home.

Henry remained fixed in place. "I'm all in favor of foundries, just not in the vicinity of my grounds. Besides, the local gentry have every right to protect their property, the very reason they travel to the site now. So Thornbury will have trouble on his hands."

They were a good fifty feet ahead of him by now.

Henry yelled, "But he brought it upon himself, didn't he?"

When she and Berdy reached the gravel drive to Pinnacles, they exchanged knowing glances. Berdy handed her his end of the stringer and headed off toward the stables. She entered the house, handed the fish to Mrs. Richards, and emerged minutes later to find Berdy waiting in the gig by the front door.

Henry had followed them up the drive and stood unmoving, his brows knitted. "The two of you are not thinking of interfering in gentlemen's business matters, are you?"

She climbed into the gig and spread a blanket across their laps. "I have no intention of interfering in Mr. Thornbury's business matters. We plan to drive out and greet our neighbor, that's all."

Berdy leaned forward and pronounced to Henry, "I plan to ask him about your idea of moving to the South, versus m' idea of emigrating to America. I will attend him closely, for there is no man on whose discretion and wisdom I trust more. Don't you agree, Mr. Browne?" Berdy didn't wait for an answer. Instead, he urged the mare down the drive.

Henry hurriedly mounted his chestnut and followed them.

Once the gig crossed the river and reached the beginnings of the foundry, they came upon a group of fifty or so men gathered around the chimney's foundation. She recognized a half-dozen members of the local gentry joined by a larger number of their tenants and freeholders.

The amount of work already completed at the site surprised her. The men stood several feet away from the stone-lined foundation. Suspended above the foundation was a tall wooden crane. One end of the crane's rope was tied around a load of bricks, while the other end went through a pulley and wrapped around a winch that would be turned by a pony walking in a circle. Behind the crowd were small walls, piles of bricks, and several wells scattered around the site.

They leaped from the gig and approached the crowd. Several men spoke at once, so she could not understand them. However, she caught a fleeting glimpse of Ross. He held his head high and gave the arguing men as good as he received in return.

A dozen men turned once she and Berdy were recognized, but even their additional presence on the scene did not stop the heated discussion. One man leered at her, but Berdy stepped between them, his hands raised, ready to defend her with fisticuffs.

She grabbed Berdy's arm. "No, don't."

Henry stepped forward and confronted the man. "Explain yourself, sir."

Ross turned at the sound of Henry's comment and rushed toward them. His red face a brighter hue than his russet coat. He did not acknowledge her, but he yelled at Berdy instead. "Get her out of here. Now!"

The crowd shouted epithets, and she heard, "Running to a woman."

Another voice shouted, "Defend yourself as a gentleman, sir."

Ross spun to confront the throng of irate men.

His steward, Mr. Douglas, grabbed Ross's elbow. "Don't. You'll be killed, man."

Ross focused on Mr. Douglas's face for a second, uttered a "humph," and strode with open arms into the angry crowd. "As you can see, I have no weapons," he yelled. "Now explain your grievances against me or get off my land."

Someone shouted, "Smithy says 'is well water been blackened since the diggings started."

"That's impossible," Ross replied. "The wells are not deep enough, and only one well had a small amount of water."

She stepped forward to challenge the men. "Smithy's well is over ten miles away from here. Did anyone else see his well water fouled?"

Ross strode to her side, grabbed her arm, and marched her back into Henry's care.

Henry took her arm and faced Ross. "If underground springs are involved, I will make you prove your title to affect the water."

"There are no springs on the site. Besides, my legal man informs me you cannot apply laws meant for rivers, like proving title, to underground water. Is that right, Mr. Browne?"

"Well, yes, but—"

The mob's shouts grew, and Ross strode back into the hostile crowd.

Several voices shouted in unison. "She's in on it. She is as bad as he."

"No!" she yelled, her high voice rising above the shouts of the men.

Several men shuffled back, exposing her to everyone's view.

Mr. Mabbs, his face scarlet, pointed at her. "We all know she doesn't need the profits, but she agreed anyway. If our water and streams are tainted, it will be her fault, and we all know why."

Grumbles, shouts of agreement, and the word "lovers" ricocheted throughout the crowd.

Henry tried to pull her away.

She struggled. "Let me go."

Ross roared at Mr. Mabbs. "Leave her out of this. She is innocent of your accusations."

She pulled herself free. "Mr. Mabbs, I assure you, I have not agreed to anything."

Mr. Mabbs opened his mouth to reply, but was drowned out by the men shouting epithets about fouled water, the presence of laborers, and the disintegration of their farms.

Henry grabbed her arm again. "Come with me. You are not safe here. You must not interfere in men's business."

She looked at him incredulously, jerked herself free, and stormed into the center of the crowd. "All of you would like to be told what to do with your property?"

Ross appeared at her side, lifted her off the ground, and carried her toward the gig. His thunderous expression excluded any opposition.

Someone yelled, "Don't let them get away."

Glancing in the direction of the speaker, she saw a rough-looking man cock his arm to throw a brick in their direction. She struggled to the ground, then managed to shove Ross forward.

Ross whipped around to face her just as the brick whizzed by her face. Horror crossed his features, and he pulled her behind him. He faced the enraged crowd squarely again, with his arms held wide to protect her. "Sod off," he yelled. "Your business is with me. What kind of monsters are you to threaten a woman?"

Several men dove at Ross, forcing her to the side.

Berdy joined the fray and tried to pull one ginger-haired bully off Ross, who by this time sported a bleeding lip.

Elinor rushed over to pull Berdy away, but fisticuffs flew, and Berdy hit the ground before she could reach him.

Suddenly Henry grabbed her from behind, imprisoning her arms, and dragged her away from the crowd. She struggled but was painfully held fast. "Let me go."

Ross escaped the mob and pulled her free. Before he could address Henry, a thrown brick gave Ross a significant blow to the head. He stumbled a step or two backward and tripped over the low wall surrounding a well. For an instant, their glances met. It was not horror at the realization of his situation that she saw in his eyes, but a quick softening as he beheld her.

Ross disappeared into the well.

She screamed.

Twenty

BERDY REACHED THE EDGE FIRST, FELL TO HIS KNEES, and peered down. His action dislodged a stone that fell into darkness. It took an extraordinarily long time before they heard the first sound of a metallic clang, followed by a plop after the stone fell into water. Berdy looked back at Elinor and shook his head.

She flung herself into the crowd of men, swinging her fists at any target foolish enough to come within reach. She landed several blows before her arms were restrained. "You criminals," she shouted. "I will prosecute you. You will all hang for this." She gulped for air while struggling to free herself.

Her threat seemed to divide the crowd's opinions. She heard reckless shouts of "His fault," "She's right," and "Brought it upon 'isself." The men stepped away from the well and separated into small groups engaged in heated arguments.

Henry grabbed her arm and yanked to free her. "This is no place for a lady. Come with me."

Once released, she snatched her arm away. "No." She ran to Berdy, who was still examining the well.

The entrance was darker than Hades, and she could discern only the first ten feet into its depths due to the overcast sky. She listened but could hear no sound other than the crowd arguing behind her. Several men joined them at the edge to peer down.

Berdy assumed command and shouted orders to Mr. Douglas. "You four men take the winch and lower me into the pit." Without waiting for an answer, Berdy handled the crane's mechanism with familiarity. Obviously during his visit to the site, Ross must have taught him how to use the hoist.

Mr. Douglas and two gentlemen manned the winch and yanked enough slack in the rope to position the basket to the side.

Berdy jumped into the basket. "Now ease me down. Keep that rope free. We want that line straight. Mr. Douglas, careful with that pulley. Hurry, gentlemen, hurry."

Once Berdy was aligned over the pit, Mr. Mabbs and several others threw their full weight into the wooden spokes. Everyone's shouts were soon drowned out by the creaks and groans emanating from the winch, pulleys, and ropes. The basket lurched downward, and Berdy disappeared from view into the blackness.

Elinor clutched her hands. *How could Berdy find Ross in the darkness at the bottom of the well?* He had not taken a lantern. "Can you see anything? Are you all right?" she yelled down the pit.

A faint "yes" echoed in return.

The basket must have reached the bottom, since Mr. Mabbs and the others stopped turning the winch and joined her at the side of the pit. The group stood in tense silence. She stared directly into the eyes of each gentleman, but not a single one held her gaze.

Mr. Douglas attempted to alleviate what must have been her obvious distress. "Thank heavens this well had several feet of water at the bottom. The presence of water would help break his fall."

They heard metallic noise from deep within the well. The noise was followed by silence. Musty, rank air rose from the depths and smelled like a crypt, the stench of death. Several uneasy minutes passed. By now, all of the men who had not left for home were crowded around the well's opening.

Mr. Mabbs turned to Mr. Douglas and spoke in an officious manner. "Why weren't the wells filled in once the level of groundwater was determined?"

"Scoundrels have looted material and bricks from the site," Mr. Douglas explained, his face reddening. "And I doubt they were removed because of need, but by men eager to stir up trouble, eh, Mr. Mabbs?"

Mr. Mabbs stilled, possibly contemplating his own culpability.

All conversation ended amongst the crowd, and the minutes stretched endlessly in complete silence.

Suddenly the heavy rope twitched to the side, and a clang of metal preceded Berdy's faint cry, "Up."

The men ran to the winch and pressed their weight against the spokes.

She stared again into the well's blackness, but her vision blurred. She wiped her tears away just as Berdy's head came into view. The basket rose to the top in jerky movements, and she waited—for what seemed like hours—before it appeared close enough to see its occupants clearly.

Berdy's clothes were covered in mud, and he held the limp body of Ross propped up against the side of the basket.

She gasped and then quickly covered her mouth.

She could not tell if Ross was alive or dead, but his eyes were closed. Moreover, he was muddy from head to toe. When the basket became even with the ground, she saw blood on Berdy's cheek, then blood mixed with mud on Ross's shoulder, arm, and face. She stifled a scream and held her breath.

Mr. Mabbs and Mr. Douglas heaved the basket to the side, and several men shouted simultaneous yet contradictory orders.

Berdy's shouts rose above the others. "To the gig. The gig. Quickly, men. Hand him to me in the gig."

While four men pulled Ross from the basket, Berdy ran to the gig.

Without thought, she ran forward to embrace Ross. Her gesture caught the men off guard, and they stepped back, so she ended up falling to the ground under Ross's weight. He felt lifelessly heavy. She sat holding him, and the sound from the madness surrounding her faded.

She had been here before.

She and William had indulged in a spirited ride. William turned to his right, and without warning, his horse reeled to the left. William lost his balance and plummeted headfirst into the road. The fall killed him instantly. She spent hours sitting in the mud cradling him, watching the warm color of life fade from his cheeks.

Holding his body.

She tightened her grip around Ross, her gaze never leaving his face.

Seconds later, the men yanked him from her, and the emptiness of her embrace shocked her into action. Ross was not dead—yet. She jumped into the gig before the men handed Berdy Ross's body. Berdy pulled him across their laps, the majority of Ross's weight resting on Berdy, while she grabbed the mare's reins.

Berdy instructed Mr. Mabbs to send a volunteer to Dr. Potts's house to inform him of their situation.

She suggested Dr. Potts should be directed to Pinnacles. "It's closer to the doctor's house, so he will reach his patient faster." While true, the action also reflected her unwillingness to hand Ross over to his mother. She firmly believed Lady Helen lacked the strength of mind to oversee his care properly.

Berdy insisted Lady Helen be notified, and Mr. Douglas nodded.

She gazed up at Berdy, tears filling her eyes. Tears of fear for Ross, but also pride at Berdy's decisive actions. But then the insensate man in her lap regained her attention. "He's still unconscious. Did he speak at all?"

Berdy struggled with the task of keeping Ross from tumbling off the gig.

She wanted to pull more of his weight onto her lap, to remove some of the pressure off Berdy, but she would be unable to control the horse if she did.

"No, not a sound," Berdy said. "It was black. Couldn't see m' hand directly in front of m' face. I called out, but no response. Ended up wading in the muck until I found him. The bottom of the well has a foot or two of foul water, so I splashed around until I found a leg. Then I grabbed a boot and hauled him into the basket. You know the rest. He never spoke, not even a groan. Is he alive, do you think?"

She glanced at Ross's head in her lap. In repose, he looked like a young child sleeping, except for the muck and blood. His dark hair was matted in mud, but one perfect lock around his ear escaped the dirt. It looked so soft as it lay sweetly curled behind his pink ear.

A pink ear—not gray—she clung to that hopeful sign.

With tears now trailing down her cheeks, she asked Berdy to examine Ross's chest to discern if he was breathing, but the gig jerked too much for him to tell. Then she found blood oozing from a wound on his shoulder. She pulled back his torn coat, and fresh blood appeared. "He's bleeding!"

Using one hand, Berdy managed to unwind Ross's simple neckcloth, bunched it into a ball, and pressed it against his wound to stop the flow of blood.

Twenty minutes passed before they reached Pinnacles, and they waited another two hours before Dr. Potts appeared. The entire time, from the gig to the sofa, Berdy had kept pressure upon the wound with Ross's cravat.

She didn't dare peek to see if the bleeding had stopped, for fear it would start again.

When Dr. Potts pulled the balled neckcloth away to examine the wound, fear drove her backward until she stood against the wall. Her breathing became irregular, and she struggled for air, but she forced herself to remain silent until Dr. Potts completed his examination. With her hands behind her back, she pressed her wet palms on the cool wood paneling to steady herself.

Meanwhile, Berdy sat patiently in a high-backed chair and sympathetically glanced either at her or at Ross.

After completing his inspection, Dr. Potts lifted his head. "He has a possible fractured skull and this large puncture wound. Normally, I would be concerned over his lack of consciousness, but perhaps this is a blessing, considering the severity of the gash on his shoulder." The doctor pulled several tools from his leather chest and quickly sewed up the wound. Berdy and Dr. Potts then carried Ross to a servant's bed on the ground floor.

Months ago when she had punctured her finger, she remembered her medical books suggested a wound should be cleaned before the application of any bandage or poultice. *Why didn't Dr. Potts clean the wound first?* She withheld her question, since he was the expert—she wasn't. Perhaps desperate measures were required to save Ross's life. Besides, any interference from her might interrupt his immediate care.

Berdy helped remove the remainder of Ross's clothing, and the muddy, blood-soaked clothes were soon carried from the room.

She dropped her chin on her chest and concentrated on inhaling slowly.

Dr. Potts wiped his brow and rolled down his sleeves. "He lost a fair amount of blood, so no leeches or lettings. Bleedings might be danger…" Dr. Potts paused, then turned to face her.

A guilty blush warmed her cheeks. He'd probably stopped midway in his diagnosis to save her from distress. Dr. Potts must have discovered her affection for Ross by now.

The doctor pulled her gently away from the wall. "You must prepare yourself. There is little hope of recovery unless his brain injury heals, and he wakes. Has his mother been informed?"

Berdy nodded. "I received a note that Lady Helen was out calling upon friends when Mr. Douglas arrived at Blackwell. She should be informed of her son's accident by morning, at the latest. No doubt she will rush to Pinnacles as soon as possible."

Dr. Potts nodded. "She will more than likely insist he be removed to Blackwell tomorrow. I will volunteer to stay with our patient until her arrival."

Elinor took tentative steps toward the bedside. "Thank you. May I bathe him to remove the mud?"

The doctor paused. "It is not necessary for you to do so."

"I must." She instructed her servants to bring hot water, soap, and an upholstered chair for Dr. Potts's comfort during the long night ahead. With Berdy's help, she washed Ross's head, chest, and arms. Then Berdy left the room, and she and Dr. Potts sat quietly, each absorbed in their own thoughts. The only sounds heard in the room were from the large fire in the grate and the chimes from the clock in the hallway outside the door.

Close to midnight, Dr. Potts stood and came to her side. "I suggest you retire for the evening, for your own good. Don't worry about Mr. Thornbury. I will have a servant notify you if there is any change."

She glanced at his weary face, lines of concern written across his shadowed brow. "Thank you, but I will remain. I want to be present when he wakes."

The doctor returned to his chair, only to fidget endlessly. Ten minutes later, he mentioned instruments he might need from home—if Ross should wake—so he took his leave. He assuaged her panic upon his farewell by promising to return in the morning, before Lady Helen had a chance to remove Ross to Blackwell.

She returned to her chair, pulled a blanket around her shoulders, and began her long watch through the night.

She loved Ross.

Whether rake or gentleman, Ross had claimed her heart, without her loving William less. Now she stood gifted with a second chance at happiness. Over a year ago she could never imagine feeling romantic love. Now she faced the reality. A reality forced upon her by Ross's possible loss. She realized, rather ruefully, at least now she wouldn't be obsessively thinking about William all of the time.

Her attention returned to the man she loved stretched out on the small bed. She rose and added fuel to the fire, so the room would remain warm. Then she waited, her distress growing with each hour. Finally, unable to continue sitting in her chair, she moved to the bedside, her heartbeat pounding in her ears, a sharp pain near her heart.

Ross lay on his back; no trace of mud in his hair or body remained. Other than a pale face and a few small cuts, he appeared perfectly normal. His dark lashes rested upon his pale cheeks, and his chest rose ever so slightly with each steady breath.

She pulled the blanket away from his shoulder and examined the white linen wrapped from his upper arm to his neck. The cloth looked clean, but a small patch of darkness appeared under the linen, indicating the presence of blood.

Reaching up to smooth his dark hair from his brow, as she had observed him do so many times before, she secretly hoped he would wake with her touch, but he did not. Her tears began, and she needed to confirm he lived by a caress of his warm skin.

Finally exhausted and heart weary, she lay beside him on the small bed and arranged the covering so he would remain warm. She slid her arm across his and settled in to watch him through the remainder of the night. Watch his chest rise and fall with each whisper of life, knowing that tomorrow, when his mother claimed him, she might never watch him again. With each hourly chime from the hallway clock, she went through the futile motion of stroking his hair back from his brow.

He never moved or registered her touch in any way.

Close to dawn, in a moment of careening desperation, she tried to wake him with words. She told him of her love and teased him with the scandalous banter he enjoyed. Rhyming jests were never Ross's humor, but he was a master of the sly, outrageous remark.

These retorts came naturally to him and always brought out his stunning smile. She had been delighted every time she'd cast out a seemingly innocent word into conversation, only to find him rise to the bait with the most brazen innuendo. If only he would do that now. "Ready to read volume two of *The Rake's Handbook*? I cannot imagine what it suggests."

No response. No smile. No serene countenance expostulating the naughtiest retort ever. He failed to move.

"I need you awake for chapter ten, dearest, your favorite chapter. Do you think you might like to read it more than once?"

No reply.

With her strength gone and spirit defeated, she stroked his brow. After each soft caress, she whispered, "Please wake, love."

⚘

Searing pain ripped Ross apart. He did not recognize the day or the place. Pain ruled, and he must escape its fire-like grip.

Was he dying or dead?

Gradually, he became aware of his circumstances. He lay on his back upon a high plateau big enough only for him. If he rolled two feet, he would plunge into the watery blackness surrounding him. In the distance appeared several tall ships on fire, and beyond them, the horizon stretched out in every direction, creating a uniform line. Dawn began to break; the morning light forced the black clouds upward.

He felt a familiar presence surrounding him: John, his younger brother. John, the auburn-haired boy with an infectious smile. Ross welcomed the presence of the brother who remained foremost in his thoughts. Here and now, in this place, his memories became real. He saw John at five years old, twig in hand, protecting Mama from a dragon the knights had failed to kill. Then John at eighteen, fresh from school, joy skipping across his face when Ross agreed he could join him on the Grand Tour.

And once in Italy, what example had he set for his brother? Instead of setting an example of a true gentleman, or behaving in a discreet manner that was usual for him, he openly acted like the worst of men—a rake. His actions unwittingly confirmed the exaggerated behavior contained in his satirical handbook, written in a drunken wager. Such books were commonly published for the amusement of London's swells. Only John must have never fully understood the satirical part. Proud of his older brother, he likely believed the overblown seductions in the handbook were real, something to emulate. And Ross's appalling actions in Venice were nothing more than a silent confirmation of that vile behavior.

On the Grand Tour in Venice, while he "punted" in a gondola with a raven-haired contessa, what did he expect John to do? Wait alone in their rooms, sit in a café drinking himself into oblivion, or find a woman? A significant female conquest to impress his older brother.

He remembered John missing for days. Then finding him given up for dead at a hospital, the victim of an irate husband's knife attack. Then the memory of John's fallen expression when Ross told him the knife had likely scored his heart and pierced his lung.

He remembered his desperate promises to save John. Flee back to England and recover—together.

In London, he held what remained of his brother's once

stout body steady while he was bled. Then the memory of John looking directly into his eyes, without recrimination, pleading for life as his blood flowed unrestrained. John smiled up at him, sighed, and died in his arms.

Why? Because all John ever wanted was to be like his older brother.

He could join John in his harbor from pain, and free himself from guilt. Hold him in his arms again. All he had to do was roll off the plateau into the blackness of hell's own fire. "John!"

Twenty-one

At dawn, Elinor moved to a chair set close enough to the sickbed to hold Ross's hand. She didn't give a shilling if anyone caught her thus, for she had no intention of not touching him, not stroking the top of his fingers or caressing his cheek. He had spent a restless night, calling out his late brother's name, but he never woke. Even with her caress and the new day erupting in violent birdsong and searing sunlight, he failed to regain consciousness.

Berdy entered softly around seven o'clock. "Did he wake?"

"Oh, love," she managed, rubbing her sore eyes.

He pulled a chair next to her, leaned over, and embraced her.

The warmth coming from his body comforted her, and her head fell to his shoulder. She began to openly sob. "What if he never wakes?"

"Shh."

Her agony grew with the passage of time, because the illness endured. Obviously breathing and alive, Ross appeared to be sleeping, so she expected him to open his eyes at any moment. Only this was a false expectation. Unlike William's accident, death was not sudden. It lingered in the atmosphere, teased her with its presence, and fed her tears. She had no thoughts about how to save him and no thoughts about what she could do. No thoughts.

They sat in silence until the sounds of a heavy carriage became apparent from the crunch of gravel outside. She pulled back from Berdy's embrace, panic consuming her. Lady Helen would take Ross—take him—and she might never see him again. In desperation, she turned to Berdy for help.

"Come now," he said. "Dry your eyes. I'm sure his mother would never consider moving him in his current condition. The wound may open."

He's right. She had not thought of that. Maybe she would have more time, after all.

"Let's go meet her together," he said.

The Thornburys' large black carriage stood in the drive, framed by the glorious pinks and oranges of the new morning light. Perhaps the chilly air was the reason the older woman failed to exit the carriage. The window dropped, so Elinor and Berdy approached.

A grim Lady Helen faced them, but she was unable to speak at first. A minute or two passed before Ross's mother choked out a response to their perfunctory greetings. "Does my son live?"

Lady Helen's ashen face and trembling hand were visible from outside the carriage, and Elinor regretted the bad feelings the foundry had created between them. "At the moment he is alive, but not conscious. He also lost a fair amount of blood."

"Will he live? I must know. What did Dr. Potts say?" Lady Helen asked in a broken voice, a sound that indicated the questioner was not strong enough to bear the answer. Looking down, she bunched her cap and hair together on her forehead with a balled fist.

Lady Helen's distress affected her, and she too could no longer speak.

"When brought here," Berdy said, "the wound was covered in mud and filth. Dr. Potts sewed him up and indicated we should not disturb him. I'm sure Ross just needs rest to heal and will be pluck in no time. It's a gash in the shoulder. People don't die from that, do they?"

Ross's mother said nothing. With her head lowered, she looked like she was inspecting the carriage's floor. After she recovered enough to speak, she addressed Elinor directly. "I insist my son is removed to Blackwell as soon as possible. I've also sent word to our family surgeon in London and requested that he attend my son. I have great confidence in his abilities, since he worked diligently to save John, my youngest. There is no medical man I trust more."

"Goes without saying you wish the best for your son," Berdy said. "But if he is moved, the wound might open, and he'd start bleeding again." He grabbed Elinor's hand and gave it a firm squeeze.

Lady Helen paused. "No. The decision is mine. I want him home." She scowled at Elinor. "As his mother, I have his best interests at heart and shall attend him until... I must stay with him every minute until he is well."

She took a deep breath. "I hope in the future you

will let Mr. Deane and myself call upon Mr. Thornbury to inquire about his progress?"

The older woman's jaw set. "No. I will not allow you in the sickroom. Your presence cannot assist his recovery in any way. I am the person who cares for him, so all decisions are mine."

Her breath caught, and Berdy tightened his grip on her hand. She believed a clinging mother's desires for her children were often misguided. But the sight of Berdy, holding her hand and gently kicking the gravel with the toe of his boot, restored her to her senses. The older woman was a mother like her, and she would have acted the same. "Yes, it's such a disappointment, you see. I'd like to see him, well, I'd just like to see him again, that's all."

Berdy put an arm around her shoulder and squeezed. "Dr. Potts promised to care for him wherever he was, remember? Lady Helen, I hope you do not object if I ride over tomorrow and receive an update on his condition? Ross has many friends, you understand."

Lady Helen gave a single nod.

Elinor replied softly, "Thank you. Thank you."

The window squeaked shut, and the black carriage lurched forward on its return to Blackwell.

In the sky above peeked one of the most radiant sunrises she had ever witnessed. The pink sky still claimed the horizon, but farther up it melted into the light blue sky of the new day. She glared upward and silently cursed. *Bloody pink sunrise announces a lie; it does not promise to be a perfect day.*

Ross's ear was pink, not pale like William's. She clung to that fact. Hours had passed after William's fall from his horse, but she made no motion to leave him. Alone in the road, she held him, vowing never to move. After they were discovered, and Dr. Potts called, she feared never seeing William again. She clutched him tightly and stroked his cheek. Trying to remember every detail about a man of whom she already knew everything. Why? Because they would take him from her arms forever. The same fate befell her now. Ross would soon be lost too.

Within the hour, Dr. Potts arrived, and several servants loaded Ross into his carriage for transport to Blackwell. A breath, a second, a heartbeat, and Ross was gone.

She could think of only one action—wait at Dr. Potts's house for him to return. It was the fastest way to receive the latest information concerning Ross's condition. She grabbed a book and took a seat on a garden bench in front of the doctor's home. Her wait proved a long one, and she failed to remember a single word of her novel. Darkness shrouded the house when Dr. Potts finally returned. She ran to meet him before he had the chance to enter his home. "How does Mr. Thornbury fare?"

"Elinor!" He started, taking a full step backward. "Mrs. Colton, I beg your pardon. I must admit surprise in seeing you here."

His unknotted cravat and air of weariness—quite unlike him—worried her. "Does he live? Is he awake? How is the wound? Has it festered? Does his mother relent and allow visitors?"

Dr. Potts held his palm high. "Please. The answers to your questions are no. His mother is not allowing visitors and remains by his side. I have done everything for him, believe me, but there is no change."

"What treatments have you given him?"

"He was bled, of course. I also—" He stopped; a frown appeared on his long, aquiline face.

Her heartbeat began to race. "Since his large loss of blood yesterday, you indicated it would be unwise to bleed him."

"Bleeding is the standard treatment for cases such as this," he said in an icy tone, walking around her, heading for his front door.

"Will you treat him tomorrow?"

He sighed and looked skyward. "Lady Helen's surgeon is expected any day. I will attend him until her London man can take over." He stepped across his threshold and held the door half-open so she could not enter.

She pushed her palm on the door to keep it from closing. "But no more lettings, lest he die from loss of blood? That is possible, correct? My medical books—"

"Of course." He forced the door shut.

She returned home, her mind fixed on the fact that Ross had been bled again. She knew bleeding was important to relieve bad humors, but surely there was a limit?

The following day began with her desire to pray for Ross's recovery, so she and Berdy headed into town. Once they reached the village's high street, they saw the farmhouse-like church set some distance back from the street. Today the sun glinted off the long windows, sending shafts of light across the small burial ground close to the road. William had been reverend of this beautiful Unitarian church, and now he rested peacefully within its iron gates.

While Berdy set out to call upon the current reverend, she headed inside to visit her husband's monument. The normal cacophony of birds, horses, and rustling trees ended upon entering the chapel and closing the giant oak doors. Silence and heavy cold air surrounded her. As she walked down the aisle toward William's monument, her footsteps tapped loud enough to be discourteous.

Halfway to the altar, she stopped and faced north. Set into the wall was a marble bas-relief of William's side view with his name, date of birth, date of death, occupation, and "beloved husband" carved below. She reached out to touch his likeness. The white marble felt cool under her fingers, and for the first time she noticed a slight darkening from the oil on her hands where they had repeatedly touched the elevated parts of his profile. She stroked the top of his head and then let a finger linger on his jawline. His high-collared coat, which was no longer fashionable, she remembered with a smile as one of his favorites.

She rested all of her fingers on the engraved *W*, stared at his profile, and spoke to the man she would love forever. "William, I love again. His name is Ross, and you would like him. Since we were so in tune, that had our roles been reversed—you survived while I had not—I would be pleased if you had found a second love. I realize you would wish the same and that you are happy for me. I understand that now. William, I need your strength today. Ross may die, and I cannot bear the loss of two—"

She heard a commotion from the direction of the front door and turned to see a group of young girls entering the chapel with their matronly teacher. Many of the girls had been favorites of Elinor's when she helped teach at the parish school. Seeing them again filled her with an aching wish to return to the old days.

"Girls, girls, quiet, please," the teacher said, corralling one young lady who had already started to march down the center aisle. The teacher clapped her hands several times, and the gaggle of girls moved into a tight herd around her skirt. "Now, girls, Henrietta, pleeeease, thank you. Now, girls, remember, show your respect by being perfectly silent. Susan, did you hear me? Right then, follow me." The teacher turned to the far aisle from Elinor and headed toward the altar. The shuffle of footsteps mingled with giggles and whispers of almost-obedient young ladies.

Halfway down the chapel, the children caught sight of her. One of them shouted, "Look, it's Mrs. Colton."

A young girl clutching a bouquet of roses smiled at Elinor, and she returned the smile. The girl started to walk in her direction, but a steady hand from her teacher momentarily stopped her. The small child twisted out of her teacher's grasp and attempted to run toward Elinor, but the teacher got a better grip and stopped the girl from advancing. The child twisted and squirmed again with more effort, determined to reach her. Then taking advantage of the teacher's momentary distraction, she slipped from under her arm and ran to Elinor. The other young ladies took the opportunity to escape, leaving the teacher lunging in all directions for errant children.

Young Margaret reached her before the teacher was able to call out for her return.

"Good day, Mrs. Colton. Do you remember me?"

She tilted her head and gave the child a tender smile. "Of course I do, Margaret. You are dear to me and quite unforgettable."

A heartwarming smile crossed the young girl's face. Margaret held her roses inches from Elinor's nose. "I've come here today to give Grandfather these roses. He died in the war with the American colonies. But you do not have any flowers for Mr. Colton." She pulled a perfect bloom from her bunch and handed it to her. "Please take this, as I know Mr. Colton must have a flower. They are for remembrance, right?"

Elinor pursed her lips. "That's right. Yellow is... was his favorite color of rose. Thank you."

The young girl giggled and skipped back to the group of girls, now moving forward in a collective herd to the altar.

Elinor closed her eyes and mulled over her thoughts. She had once taught Margaret lessons, and now Margaret taught her by example. A lesson about determination, exemplified by the child's steadfast effort to reach her, despite her teacher's demands and physical restraint. Elinor placed William's rose at the base of his plaque before she ran outside to find Berdy.

Berdy was nowhere near the gig, so it cost her precious minutes before she found him. They made their farewells to the reverend, and it wasn't long before they found themselves speeding out of the village in the direction of Pinnacles.

After returning home, she flew into the study, heading for William's books. She resolved to stop depending upon her knights, like Henry, and teach herself about medicine. Ross once told her she could understand the contents if she tried, and she had no intention of letting him down. She charged over to the bookshelves and started pulling out every medical book in her possession. Silently thanking William's passion for books, she glanced at the pile of medical tomes before her: *Quincy's Lexicon*, *Mothersby's Medical*, *Hooper's Compendium*, Hunter's book on gunshot wounds, and many others. She arranged them by relevance to Ross's injury and began to read.

Very quickly, a plan emerged to find the appropriate treatment. In each book she would look up the word: brain, coma, putrescence, septic acid, and suppuration. Some physicians hailed the effects of Peruvian bark; others claimed it had no beneficial effect whatsoever. By late afternoon, pages of her treatment notes spread across the polished desk. She read each remedy several times and compared remedies among authors.

By the end of the day, her treatment plan solidified. Any remedy or practice that was not universally agreed upon by every author was eliminated. What treatments remained were carefully cross-checked and common themes identified. She had a remedy to treat him internally for fever and externally for inflammation. Backup treatments were also written down should his wound fester.

At first light, she roused Berdy out of bed, gave him twenty minutes to dress and bring the gig to the door.

Berdy rubbed his eyes. "So Lady Helen will let us visit him? Cheer up, Elli, that must mean he is doing better, right?"

"No, I don't think he is doing better. That's why we are going now. If Lady Helen tries to stop me, I'll twist out of her grasp and run upstairs, or do whatever it takes to see him." She could still recall little Margaret doing the same to reach her.

"Gad, I'll help."

"Dr. Potts should be there by now, so I expect he will support us and insist we are both allowed in. But I have little hope Rowbottom will even allow us to get that far."

"Maybe we should sneak in the entrance at the back?"

She began to sigh, but willfully stopped herself. "No, we'll just go forward and fight."

Twenty-two

AT THE HALFWAY POINT ON THEIR JOURNEY TO Blackwell, Berdy suddenly said, "I've got it! I will yell 'fire,' and everyone will rush out of the house. Then you can slip in and see Ross undetected." His explosive revelation almost put the gig into a ditch.

"Berdy, that's irresponsible." Elinor clutched the seat with one hand, and with the other hand, held on to the back of her poke bonnet, leaving the ends of the pink satin ribbons to whip around her face. "Think of the panic you'll cause. The fire brigade will be sent on a false alarm. No, that is a very bad idea, indeed." Elinor thought his suggestion qualified as the worst Berdy Rash Scheme ever.

Her censure didn't even slow him. "The brigade won't be called if I stand in the front of the house and yell 'elephant.'"

"Elephant! In Cheshire?"

"Elephants are frightening. People will run out of the house fast."

She huffed. "No, they won't. If everyone is upstairs in the sickroom, why would they run downstairs and outside if an elephant is waiting for them? Why would anyone, anywhere in the house run outside, for that matter?"

"Right." He gave the ribbons an urgent flick. "I could shout that the elephant is heading upstairs."

"Elephants cannot climb stairs—"

"We must do something. A man's *life* is at stake."

"Be serious, please," she said. "Some people even like elephants. So we will ring the bell and simply not take any refusals."

He shook his head. "No, Rowbottom will refuse us entry before I can say, 'My good man.' I've got it! We'll ask to call upon Lady Helen. Rowbottom probably lacks instructions along those lines."

His suggestion was a good one. Elinor peeked at him again, her understanding of the new Berdy much improved. In the future, his Berdy Rash Schemes would likely fade in number, and the mature Berdy— the man who shouted forceful directions at the foundry—would eventually prevail. Her newfound pride in him gave her a brief sense of ease.

They traveled in silence for the next ten minutes. Once they arrived, she marched up to Blackwell's giant front doors and yanked on the bell. The possibility Ross might be overbled returned to gnaw at her, and she used this fear to fuel her resolve.

Rowbottom answered and gave the expected response to visit the patient. "I am afraid that is impossible, madam." Yet the valued servant remained in place and failed to close the door. Kindness shone in his steely blue eyes.

She stood fast. "Lady Helen Thornbury please,

Rowbottom. We wish a private word with her. I assume the visitation denials apply only to calling upon her son."

Rowbottom nodded, grinned, and informed them Lady Helen had not left her son's side. He then led them to the drawing room. Elinor sat on a chair farthest from the door, so it would be harder for the servants to throw her out when directed.

Berdy stood behind her chair with his hand resting on her shoulder.

Silently fighting the lump forming in her stomach, she refused to recognize her panic. Instead, she told herself the lump was nothing more than tenacity, and she must use it well.

Lady Helen appeared twenty minutes later, failed to greet her guests, and stood before Elinor. The older woman was stoic in a black gown with a white fichu tucked into her sash. "This is all your fault. First you spread vicious, untrue rumors around town that my son wrote a vulgar handbook. Then you led him on like a strumpet for your own purposes. I understand you planned to break his heart and never approve of the lease. If he dies, it will be on your conscience."

Elinor jumped to her feet. "No!"

Berdy strode forward to stand between the two women. "Please calm yourself and take a seat, both of you. None of that is important now." He addressed Lady Helen. "Besides Elinor and myself, I speak for others when I ask how Mr. Thornbury does today. Indeed, Mr. Mabbs, Mr. Burton, and several neighbors have inquired about his health."

A lock of hair escaped Lady Helen's cap, and she

brushed it behind her ear without seeming to care about the outcome. Her spirits collapsed and appeared too low to put up additional resistance. She stood unmoving, dull weariness marking her features. Then she fell upon a yellow sofa like her legs lacked the strength to hold her upright. "I've been told of the circumstances surrounding his accident." She stared at Elinor now sitting across from her. "I understand you tried to protect him, and he received his wound attempting to save you. Is my information correct?"

Elinor's heart sank; Ross must not have improved. "Berdy is right. Does that matter now? All I can say is Mr. Thornbury acted like a true gentleman, and I will do everything possible to ensure the criminals responsible for his injuries are brought to justice. My relative, Mr. Browne, will assist me in this endeavor, I'm sure."

Lady Helen nodded, then stared into the blazing fire. The firelight outlined deep furrows carved across her brow.

Normal compassion compelled Elinor to reach out and embrace her, but she refrained, knowing her sympathies would be unwelcome. "How is he?"

His mother continued her vacuous stare at the fire. "Dr. Potts is with him, but I must admit preference for my medical man. Unfortunately, his trip from London is delayed, and he might not arrive for several days. I had hoped the bleedings would have a positive effect by now."

Elinor jumped to her feet. "Bleedings?" She rushed to kneel before the older woman. "Something is amiss. Dr. Potts recommended no bloodletting due to the large amount your son lost in the accident. Plenty enough blood to release the bad humors. And even yesterday, he promised me the bleedings would stop. Please, for your son's sake, take me to him. We must insist these lettings stop together, you and I." She grabbed Lady Helen's hands and pulled them both to their feet.

In the process, one of the older woman's black gloves slid off and dropped to the floor. The horror expressed in Lady Helen's wide, unblinking eyes as she stared at her glove indicated Elinor's words had hit their target. Perhaps the identical concern had flowed through her mind.

Together the women rushed upstairs and entered the sickroom with such a velocity that the door was thrown back against the wall with a bang. Berdy followed close behind.

A rancid smell assaulted Elinor first before she noticed Ross lying on a large bed. His head, shoulder, and arm being the only part of him not covered.

Dr. Potts stood by the fire and scowled at them.

The local leech man, Mr. Gulch, sat by the bedside and tended to the bloodletting.

Elinor ran to Ross. "No! Stop immediately." She turned to Dr. Potts. "You promised no bleedings. He'll die from loss of blood, and it will be your fault. You are murdering him, sir. I insist you stop this instant."

Ross's mother joined Elinor's side. "Yes, two hours ago you said we were finished with the bleedings. Now the leech man has arrived and is practicing his trade without my knowledge. The leeches must be removed immediately. I will have your head if he dies."

Dr. Potts stepped toward her. "Elinor. I need your—no—I request the honor—no—let me explain—"

"Remove them," Elinor screamed. "Now!"

The doctor sneered at each of them in turn, hesitated as if weighing his options, and ran from the room, knocking over two chairs in the process.

Berdy tripped over one of the falling chairs as he chased after Dr. Potts.

The two women exchanged startled glances. Lady Helen tried to pull a leech off Ross's arm, but it held fast.

"Don't," Elinor cried. "I know from my medical books that if you pull them, the heads only latch on stronger. Remove your creatures now, Mr. Gulch."

Mr. Gulch frowned. "But I 'ave not received a shillin' for—"

Elinor clutched his coat. "Remove them!"

He shrugged her off and tenderly stroked a slimy, engorged leech. "No fee, let 'em drink, I say. My pets must feed. Unless I am paid." He held out his palm.

Elinor had no money on her person, and she did not dare waste a single second. Even if Lady Helen went to obtain the funds, how much more blood would be lost in that time? Elinor took off her brooch and held it under Mr. Gulch's nose. "It's gold and diamonds. Worth more than your bloody leeches. Remove the beasts. Now!"

Mr. Gulch snatched the brooch, squinted at the stones, then grabbed a leech. "There's a trick to remove 'em. Stick your nail under the sucker like this, then flick the dears up."

Elinor shook his arm. "All of them. Hurry!"

Mr. Gulch quickly removed the leeches, placed his pets in a jar, and scurried from the room.

Ross appeared quite blue, and very little blood trickled from the leech's puncture wounds on his arm.

Behind her, Lady Helen instructed the upstairs housemaid to remove the blood-soaked rags. She turned away at the first sight of the pretty china bowl half-full with her son's lifeblood. "I can't—I can't stay anymore." She started toward the door.

Elinor grabbed her shoulders, pulled the woman back into the room, and turned to face her directly. "You're his mother. You must stay." She embraced Ross's mother. "He'll be all right."

Tears flowed across the older woman's cheeks as she dropped her head again. "I cannot—too painful."

"We will save him. You and I together, agreed?" Elinor stepped back and shook her. "*Helen*. Vegetable acid. Do you have vinegar in the house?"

Startled, the older woman looked up. "Of course, but—"

"Have some fetched, please." Elinor moved to Ross's shoulder and started to unwrap the linen bandage.

"What are you doing?" Lady Helen asked.

Elinor stared at her hard, an unmistakable sign to the older woman not to be missish. "Get the vinegar first."

"Yes, yes." Ross's mother left the room for a moment and then returned. "Rowbottom will retrieve all we have from the kitchens. But why vinegar?"

Once the last bit of linen was removed, both women recoiled from the sour smell. Lady Helen spun to face the window.

Elinor ignored her and fought her own rising tears. "Yesterday I read all of my husband's medical books, and vegetable acids are the best easily available treatment to heal a festered wound. Wine is slightly less efficient, and other recommendations, like gastric acid, will take too much time to acquire." She grabbed the older woman's shoulders, shook her, and spun her to face the bed. "We must work around the clock—together."

Lady Helen stared at the red gash on her son's shoulder. An angry red line streaked across his broad chest, aiming at his heart. The older woman grabbed her hand. "You read all of your husband's books, gave Mr. Gulch your brooch," she whispered. "Why?"

Elinor inhaled. Her actions must be focused on treating the wound, *only* treating the wound.

Seconds later, Lady Helen squeezed her hand and nodded. "Thank you."

Standing close, the two women looked at each other, Elinor noticed no evidence of their previous opposition in the older woman's eyes. For her, it was the moment she no longer considered Ross's mother just an acquaintance, but an ally.

Rowbottom returned, carrying water, soap, and a large bottle of vinegar.

Elinor cleaned the shoulder area as best she could, while Lady Helen stood by Ross's side, stroking the top of his hand.

"Thank you, Rowbottom," Elinor said. "Please send for the surgeon and a message to Mr. Browne. Berdy's pursuit of Dr. Potts concerns me, and I fear for his safety."

Lady Helen nodded at Rowbottom, who hurriedly left the room. "There is no hope, is there?" she remarked unsteadily.

By now Elinor had dabbed his shoulder with vinegar, but without a response from the patient. She looked up at his mother. "I wonder how much to use? My books varied in specifics." Without an obvious answer and frightened by the rancid smell, she poured some of the vinegar directly into the wound.

"Hell's fire." Ross opened his eyes and threw his arm in a wild arc in an attempt to touch his wounded shoulder.

"Thank heavens." Staggering joy made her feel like jumping, but it swiftly ended at the sound of his moan. "No, no, don't touch the wound. Lady Helen, please restrain his hand."

"He lives," Lady Helen replied, her knees slightly buckling. A mixture of joy and tears animated her weary face.

Tears filled Elinor's eyes too, and one dropped onto Ross's chin. She brushed them away and tried to focus.

"Madam," Ross rasped. "Sprung a leak…hope not…my account." Kindness shone in his eyes.

Her breath caught. She became consumed by an overwhelming desire to embrace and kiss him, even in front of his mother.

Lady Helen grabbed his hand to imprison it within hers, kissed his palm, and then rested her cheek on the back of it.

Ross turned his head to look at his mother, the effort made him grimace. "Let go. Let me sleep."

Elinor tried to catch his expression, but he tilted his head to the side and shut his eyes. "Don't sleep," she said. "Not yet. I must change your bandage first." She applied more of the vinegar remedy.

When the acid touched his wound, he jerked in a twisting motion. "*Hell's fire.* What are you about?"

"Saving you," she replied. "And if you move again, you'll damage yourself further. Lady Helen, please pour some barley water. All of the medical books agree that a full recovery is related to the patient's strength of constitution, so we must make sure he is strong before he sleeps."

Lady Helen removed her remaining glove and moved toward the widow to pour a glass of barley water.

Ross lifted the corner of his mouth and whispered to Elinor, "Need me to be strong, eh?"

For the first time in days, she felt relieved enough to smile. Before his mother turned around, she planted a swift kiss upon his brow.

After ingesting a full pint of barley water, Ross felt restored enough to have some soup. But his strength did not last long. With each spoonful of broth-like soup, it became harder for him to swallow. Finally, he waved her away, closed his eyes, and slept. The effort must have exhausted him, because he did not wake even when she wrapped his injury in clean linen.

The two women retreated to their chairs, and Lady Helen pulled her chair close. "What shall we do now?"

Elinor took her hand, and the older woman squeezed hers in return. "Replenish your vinegar supplies and have the kitchen staff make more barley water should he wake. Also, the vinegar treatment should be continued every hour. Other than that, all we can do is wait and pray."

Lady Helen smiled at her. "Thank you." Then she picked up her needlework. "I will join you tonight. From now on, I will never leave his side, for any reason."

After additional supplies of vinegar, bandages, and barley water had been organized upon a table close to the bed, Elinor settled in her chair for the long night ahead. After the next application of vinegar, Ross still did not wake, once again raising her fears. She moved her chair to sit as close to the wound as possible, so if it began to smell, she could treat it immediately.

Sometime after midnight, Ross shouted, "John."

His shout woke Elinor, and she held her breath, hoping he'd wake. He didn't speak again, nor did he wake, so she smoothed back his dark hair and poured more vinegar onto the linen. When she returned to her chair, she noticed his shout had awakened his mother.

"He must have loved John very much," Elinor whispered to her. "Your youngest?"

Lady Helen nodded. "He died," she said in a monotone voice, like the mere speaking of the words constituted a confession. "My son, my shame." She let out a long, shuddering sigh.

A heavy pain crushed Elinor's heart. Here Ross's mother struggled with guilt from the death of one son and now had to deal with the possible loss of the other. No mother should ever have to face such a reality. While she did not know the details of John's death, for some reason the older woman seemed to be blaming herself. "I don't understand."

After days spent worrying about her son's life, Lady Helen's speech became unguarded and perfunctory. "I didn't stay to see him properly nursed. He became weaker with every cure. Finally, his heart stopped, I've been told. I blame myself because I failed to warn him about the dangers of reckless behavior. With his father gone, that lesson becomes a mother's duty, especially when the children are boys."

Elinor regretted her thoughtless question. Lady Helen had suffered enough. "Please don't say any more. My husband died in a fall off his horse, turning to respond to one of my silly jests. In my grief I blamed myself. A natural response to the loss of a loved one, no matter the situation. Later, I realized blame is a useless notion. William would not approve of it either. He'd want me to hold close only the happy memories."

Lady Helen surprised Elinor by flashing her a searing glare. "The loss of a husband is not like that of a child. You don't know what it is like to lose a child. A mother never recovers. Never. John was my responsibility."

"Not your fault," Ross said in a raspy voice.

Both women rushed to his side.

"I led him to hell when I didn't fully explain the handbook," he said. "I took him to Italy. I abandoned him in the evenings. *Hell's fire.* I didn't warn him of the dangers."

Lady Helen collapsed, sobbing into the coverlet, lost in her grief.

"I failed to take care of him." Ross turned his head to look at Elinor's face, now mere inches away. His dilated blue eyes were navy colored, and without words, they pleaded for her recognition of his guilt.

"In both our cases, choices were made by others we could not control." Elinor bent and placed her cheek upon his. "I too know what it is like to fear the loss of a child. Berdy might have lost his life in London. The outcome of his troubles might have been very different if you had not been there. You saved him, and for that I will be forever grateful." She kissed his forehead. "You said these words to me once, and they were true," she whispered. "It will be all right. In the future, I hope together we can talk about our loved ones and share happy memories."

Lifting her head, Lady Helen became animated. "She cannot understand the depth of our grief. Ross, you must explain, you must tell her—"

"She knows," he said softly.

"No, you must tell her, you must—"

He reached for his mother's hand and grimaced as he pulled it near. With extreme slowness and pain etched upon every feature, he kissed Lady Helen's hand. "Let's take Mrs. Colton's advice and remember only the happy memories. Instead of silence, we'll change and speak of them frequently, because they are too important to lose." He attempted a small smile before closing his eyes. A long sigh followed.

This time Elinor did not succumb to her fears when he closed his eyes. He needed sleep now. The obvious pain he suffered trying to meet Lady Helen's demands taught her a valuable lesson, and she vowed never to use the words "you must" to Berdy again. Consoled by Ross's peaceful sleep, and the promise of the surgeon's arrival in the morning, she used her remaining strength to rush home and discover the outcome of Berdy's pursuit of Dr. Potts.

∽∾

"Elliii, you'll never *guess* what happened," echoed from the direction of the upper story. "Down in a tick."

Elinor strained to remove her heavy woolen cape, and when Mrs. Richards appeared, she asked for a pot of tea. With slow steps, she entered the book-filled study and collapsed into the refuge of William's overstuffed chair.

"You will never *believe* what happened." Once again, the words echoed throughout Pinnacles.

She was still pulling on the fingers of her kerseymere gloves when tea arrived. The housemaid repositioned a round tea table next to her, set down the tea things, and Elinor nodded in thanks. Odd sounds and bumps emanated from the ceiling above her. The bumps ceased, but she sat unmoving, staring at the steam gently rising from the pretty teapot's spout.

The study door flung open. "You will never guess," Berdy pronounced, his glance falling on the tea. "Tea—oh, good—cakes."

She gave him a blank stare.

Upon reading her expression, his smile faded. He pulled her up from the chair and gave her a heartfelt hug. "I apologize. How is he?"

"Alive." The sound of her voice startled her out of her dreamlike trance. "And awake."

Berdy leaned backward to examine her face. "That's good, right? It means he'll live."

"No, unfortunately there are no guarantees. Now, tell me what happened."

His face brightened. "A tale to tell, for sure. Dr. Potts galloped away as I reached the stables. Tom was rather put out about saddling Molly, but I insisted. I couldn't have been more than ten minutes behind him. I reached the turnpike, and do you know what happened?"

She gave him the smallest of grins, encouragement to continue.

"I thought to m'self, what if I caught him? What should a fellow do? I mean, it wasn't as if Ross was dead yet." He grimaced. "Oh, sorry."

She collapsed back into the chair's deep cushions. "So what did you do?"

He yanked on the bottom of his green waistcoat. "Pointed Molly in the direction of Henry's house. I figured a man of the law would know the proper procedures in a case like this. Clever thinking, don't you agree?"

She smiled openly now. "Clever, indeed. I'm glad you asked Henry to assist you. Sometimes his words sound harsh, but he truly doesn't mean them. I know he has your best interests at heart."

"Not now." He waved his hand. "So Henry was late, as usual. I mean, he is a lawyer. And by the time we reached Dr. Potts's house, guess what happened?"

"I have no idea."

"Guess."

"No violence, I hope. Henry is well? He didn't try to fight the villain, did he?" She leaned over and poured them each a cup of tea; the scent of tea laced with orange oil filled the air.

"How can you think of tea at the best part of m' tale?"

"I need tea to survive. Go on." She handed him a cup, which he immediately placed back upon the tea table. Probably because a good deal of arm waving might be needed to complete his story.

"Gone! Flown!" He waved his arms. "Both Dr. Potts and Miss Potts fled. The valuables missing, the servants unaware the family had flown." He slapped his thigh. "Very sinister goings on, what?"

"Go on."

"Go on? There's nothing more to tell." He waved his arm. "They fled. Dr. Potts is guilty of attempted murder."

The evidence now supported her worst fears. Dr. Potts's behavior was no longer a misunderstanding that could be easily cleared up. He truly must have tried to kill Ross, but the question remained—what was his motive? "So what did you and Henry *do*?"

"We went to the local magistrate, Mr. Collins, of course. We explained the circumstances in every detail."

"And?"

He picked up his teacup and grabbed a cake. "Gad, now m' tale gets boring. Mr. Collins told us to return home and promised to look into the matter himself. I tell you, I'm impressed with the fellow." He raised his teacup and gulped the brew before stuffing a large piece of raisin cake into his mouth.

"Maybe you should study law in America. I understand standing before the bar might be expensive, so you must inquire about the costs." She bit her lower lip. Once the words "you must" escaped, she regretted them. To witness Lady Helen order her grown son taught her a lesson. She must let Berdy decide his future for himself. Any of his plans, going to London, to America, she'd support.

He poured himself another cup of tea. "We are not going to America."

"Oh?" Would a Berdy Rash Scheme appear, or had he obtained information in regard to America's unsuitability for their future home? "I'm relieved to remain here in England, but what changed your mind?"

"Ross. He saved me, you see. In London I found myself rather...blue-deviled." A slight pink tinged his cheeks. "I guess you heard about m' troubles. After I recovered, we had another talk, man to man. He showed me his ledgers, so I could learn about the necessary funds needed to manage everything from a large estate to a small household. Then we discussed my ambitions, and how I might achieve them."

Her smile faded.

"No, don't worry. Not m' bacon-brained ambition to be a rake or gamester. Ross set me straight on that score. So when I pulled him from the pit, I changed my mind about America and made a vow to help him. I'm not a medical man; besides, you succeeded in that capacity. He asked before if I would join one of his business interests—pick a project to study. Now I'm going to choose engineering. Both Mr. Allardyce and Mr. Brunwell are his associates, and either man will be an excellent person to apprentice with, I'm sure." He blushed slightly. "That way I can repay m' debt. It's a debt of honor, you know. I expect to help Ross with the planning of his foundry, turnpikes, and canals." He waved his hand. "Everything, really."

"Oh." She fought a tear of joy and laid her hand on his free arm. "Thank you." The older, wiser Berdy had spoken, and she rejoiced in this Berdy's more frequent appearance.

"Once Ross's foundry is on its feet, I'll be skilled enough to support m'self elsewhere, if need be. Yes, I have a grand future ahead of me."

She knew full well she owed Ross unending gratitude for Berdy's grand future. Beaming at him now, she let a tear of happiness fall down her cheek. "I know you will. Your future sounds wonderful, and I'm glad it includes more than just your skills at tying a cravat."

He quickly put down his teacup. "I may not be a gamester or rake, but I will always be a dandy." His brows lifted in reproach, and he reached up to straighten the ends of his cravat. "Cravats are still important. The skills involved in inventing a new cravat knot will go a long way in helping me design complex machinery. Think, Elli. For a fine cravat knot you need imagination, a clear understanding of the possible variations, and the knowledge of the proper fit." A broad smile crossed his face. "Most of all, the ability to experiment by trial and error." He held his arms out. "Gad, they really *are* similar, aren't they?" He straightened in his chair. "Think of it. Think of what I will accomplish. We are living in grand times. By harnessing coal and steam, it's men like me who will move us out of the medieval times and into a new future. And I'll wager that future will be full of machines."

Twenty-three

"GORHAM, NO MORE OPIUM," ROSS ANNOUNCED.

The Thornburys' family surgeon, Dr. Gorham, frowned. A short Scottish man dressed head to toe in plaid and sporting a remarkable set of side-whiskers, he lowered his head to look at him over his spectacles.

Ross threw back the wool blanket and rose to a sitting position. "I know opium fights bad humors, but damnation, it doesn't work, because I'm in a bad humor." The room wheeled around him. Shafts of white light from the windows spun by, followed by the dark burgundy color from the walls. He clutched Dr. Gorham's arm for support.

The doctor moved to face him and, with a strong clasp of both upper arms, steadied him until his dizziness faded.

Lady Helen entered the room, carrying a basket of thread. "Is my son being troublesome?"

"No more than usual," Dr. Gorham replied, grinning at Ross and stepping behind him to adjust the new linen bandages around his arm. "If you'll excuse me, I have done all I can do for today. I will check upon you tomorrow. Your mother has kindly informed me that there is a lovely fish lake on Blackwell's grounds, so I must acquaint myself with your northern fish. I understand they are a lively breed and give good sport. Not as lively as Scottish fish, naturally, but not at all as slovenly as London fish."

Ross could focus better now. "Excellent. You fish, I stand and walk."

"But is that wise?" Lady Helen asked, dropping her ball of thread.

Dr. Gorham replaced the opium draught in his leather medical case. "He's ready to leave the sickbed, as long as he spends most of the day resting." He then bowed and left the room.

Ross remained in a sitting position until his dizziness faded. "Mother, I want Mrs. Colton here."

"No. You are in no state to receive visitors."

"We owe Mrs. Colton a debt of gratitude."

Holding her head high, Lady Helen wagged her forefinger. "Yes, of course, but—"

"I have asked her to read me some of John Donne's work while I recover."

His mother lifted a single brow. "So be it, but I don't want her here for a week at least. There is tittle-tattle already amongst the servants, and I don't want more scandalous rumors to spread."

"Fustian."

"Boy, you *are* grumpy today."

"You would be cross too if you had been in an opium daze forever. Now please bring her to me." He took a reckless gamble and placed both feet upon the floor. *Mothers.* He stared off into the fire and watched the rising heat blur the armorial crest on the iron plate built into the back of the chimney. A lion rampant came in and out of focus.

Lady Helen resumed her needlework. "Now may not be a good time for her to call. I heard Mrs. Colton and Deane are moving to America. At least, that is what Mrs. Fulsom told me at church yesterday."

He struggled to reach the bellpull. "Rowbottom! Rowbottom, in here this minute." He yanked on the pull, but needed to lean against the wall to steady himself.

Within minutes, a serene Rowbottom appeared in the doorway. "Yes, sir?"

"Rowbottom, send a footman with a note to Mrs. Colton. Ask her to call at her earliest convenience."

Rowbottom bowed deeply, an unusual gesture signaling his approval. "Right away, sir." He glanced at Lady Helen before leaving the room.

"What do you need her for?" Lady Helen asked, probably knowing full well the answer.

"Maybe she needs my advice."

Her solemn expression vanished, and a crack appeared at the side of her mouth. "Advice for what?"

"Just advice. I'm sure my advice is better than that clodpate Browne's advice. Besides, maybe Browne is making a nuisance of himself. Maybe Deane needs urgent masculine guidance. Maybe she knows nothing of the dangers in America."

His mother stifled a small laugh.

"What?" He waved his good arm. "Those are all plausible."

Lady Helen bestowed upon him her brightest smile. "My dear, why don't you just admit you are in love?"

"Lov—I wish to get dressed now. Send Locke in. Also please see if we have some of those pineapple cakes available. Mrs. Colton has never tried pineapple cakes, and I think she would like them."

She laughed. "Of course, I'll ask Cook." She strolled over to the door and turned. "Advice, indeed."

"Excuse me?"

"Oh, nothing." She walked through the doorway. "Nothing at all."

Once the door closed, his dizziness returned and forced him to stumble to a chair. Who was he kidding? *He must shout his love from the rooftop.* Now Elinor and his happiness were joined. A man could never voluntarily walk away from true love, or his life would be lost. Lost like it had been for the last couple of years—anxiety for a loved one, a dull sort of plodding forward day by day. His winter of discontent stretched to a lonely life of discontent.

Hell's fire, not if he could help it. John would not like it either; he knew that now. So he must convince her they were well suited. Only he could fully appreciate her high spirits, provide masculine guidance to Deane, and together help each other survive their shared loss of a loved one.

Behind the flames in the fire, the iron lion's paws were raised, claws out, a clear challenge.

Damn lion. He would just have to prove to Elinor that he loved her. He could just say the words, tell her of his passion. Somehow, using words alone sounded weak. Something females would do, but not gentlemen. Talking was too…exposing…too much in the realm of feeling and not of action. Besides, everyone knew he was all about action. Then he recalled his mother's warm expression whenever a family member openly expressed their love. A sanguine glow had settled around her, and he did not want to deny Elinor a similar glow. He must tell her aloud that he loved her. Except after that, he had no idea how to communicate everything he felt, everything he hoped for, everything he wanted for her—no idea whatever. But from what little he knew about romance and females, it would have to be big. He must pronounce his love by a grand gesture.

∽

Elinor grinned at Henry's continued solemnity as he spun her across the black-and-white marble floor in a lively waltz. *How could any human being present not have a smile upon their face?* She enjoyed this evening's ball, held in the Macclesfield assembly rooms, more than the one held a half a year earlier. There was less of a crowd, due to the cold weather, so when she turned to speak, there was every chance her partner heard her conversation.

In the middle of a twirl, she dropped her head back to delight in the sparkling crystal chandeliers overhead. Later she looked down to enjoy her favorite sight, the ladies' beautiful skirts swirling in circles until they blended into one. She also enjoyed the abundance of friendly society present that evening. If any of them had heard silly rumors about her in the past, today they appeared unconcerned.

After their waltz, Henry chose two empty chairs far from the orchestra.

"Do you have news of Dr. Potts?" Elinor asked once they were seated.

Henry adjusted his silver-striped waistcoat, which resulted in a great deal of squirming. He made a final tug then addressed her. "The fugitives have not been apprehended. While the authorities are on the lookout at all major ports, Dr. Potts and his daughter have not been seen. Since they had a head start, they must have already landed on the continent." He picked up her hand and patted it. "Now, here is the part of the story I must discuss with you, however painful it may be. Bleedings are considered normal, so there is no recourse on that account. However, you and I know better, and the doctor's bloodletting was extreme. Thornbury, when asked, claimed he could think of no reason why Dr. Potts wished him harm. So the current general consensus is the value of Potts's house and lands would be severely diminished by Thornbury's foundry. Inquiry into the doctor's state of affairs revealed a significant mortgage on his property. He also left debts everywhere and even embezzled funds from his daughter's inheritance. That is the basis for further investigation by the authorities."

"Poor Miss Potts. Is there any way we can assist her?"

"No, but don't worry about them. Dr. Potts has a small annuity for his services during the war, and many of our countrymen find it is much cheaper to live in France than here in England." He patted her hand. "The point I wish to make is, I believe Dr. Potts wished harm upon Thornbury because of you, my dear."

Elinor blushed and pulled her hand free.

"I was there," Henry continued, "when Potts

requested the honor of calling upon you to pose a question. Surely you too considered he might ask you to become his wife?"

"Yes."

"I firmly believe he had plans to acquire your fortune by marriage. It is the only way he could respectfully pay off his debtors. Did Potts have any reason for this belief? Are you to wed Thornbury?"

Her throat seized, so she couldn't reply.

"I understand," he said. "I believe my theory is the correct one, but I'll refrain from making it generally known, for your sake. However, if you do marry Thornbury, all sorts of tittle-tattle and rampant speculations will arise again."

She nodded, keeping her gaze focused on her bouncing knee.

"I will, without fail, continue to protect your best interests. You'll always have my support and guidance. Even if you do wed *that man*."

Elinor grinned. "Thank you, Henry. I owe you so much. I'm truly blessed to have you as a friend."

"I see that villain Mabbs approaches. I don't see how he has the nerve to request a dance. I'll save you. Shall we stand up for the next waltz?"

Needing a minute of repose, she begged Henry to divert Mr. Mabbs. The quiet vestibule called, so she entered the empty alcove and leaned against the cool marble of Apollo's plinth. Turning to catch a glimpse of the couples dancing the latest waltz, she noticed Apollo wore a new stone fig leaf. Nothing to straighten here, as his marble leaf was well carved and seemed to cover much more than necessary. Apollo could only be pleased with the prominent arch of his new leaf. Glancing up at the statue's expression, she now considered it quite smug. She chuckled to herself. Yes, all men would be pleased with that enormous leaf.

Her thoughts turned to the memory of her tall stranger. Ross hadn't answered her short note indicating she would attend the ball tonight, so perhaps he never received it, or perhaps he had not recovered enough to dance. She glanced up at the statue. Apollo would make a remarkable dance partner, indeed.

"Madam, once again I catch you gazing wantonly at that man's fig leaf," Ross said.

Elinor whirled to face him. "I—I, oh," she managed before the twinkle in his expression robbed her of breath.

He performed a deep, gentlemanly bow. "My dear Miss Leaf, may I have the honor of the next waltz? Although you may have to put up with a partner who can lift only one arm. To remedy the situation, I plan to hold you about the waist with both hands. I expect to enjoy that."

"I'm shocked. What will people say?"

Ross chuckled and held out his good arm. "They'll be shocked too. Then they will promptly enjoy the ball twice as much as they did before. It will also give them a reason to engage in outrageous tittle-tattle. In fact, our scandalous behavior might make the evening remarkable for many. Come, come, we don't want to disappoint them."

She eagerly placed her hand on his offered arm, and his muscles tightened upon her touch. Joy surged through her.

Once in the center of the grand room, they waited while other couples assembled to join them for the next waltz. Meanwhile, the small orchestra made curious noises that in no way resembled music.

Ross wiggled an eyebrow up and down.

She blushed and hid her smile behind her pale, rose-colored silk fan. He then stared at her with an odd expression—one that might be described as a leer—*a leer*. Leering on the dance floor in front of her friends; what a wonderful man.

The musicians pulled together musically and started the first notes of the waltz. Couples either found the proper waltz position easily or utterly failed, resulting in a somewhat comical display of flailing arms. Ross slid both of his hands around her waist, and she rested her palm on his good shoulder. Together, they entered the swirl of candlelight, music, and the movements of the other dancers. She barely noticed them this time, her attention captivated by the man before her and the fierce expression of warmth in his eyes.

"Now to the point." He cleared his throat by a small cough. "Madam, you are going to receive a proposal here and now. I can no longer delay. I had planned to wait, but upon consideration, a vow on a dance floor is more private than in a house with my mother in residence. You can refuse me if you wish, but I'm afraid it will cost you, since I shall repeat my offer daily." His words came at a rapid pace, necessitating a deep breath. "If you would like a private proposal, you'd better stop me now. I'm a hardened rake, after all, and I'll likely be up to all sorts of bad behavior here on the dance floor."

Comprehension deserted her. She could only grin and rotate dizzily in the arms of the man she loved.

Ross spoke even faster. "To the point. I ask you—no—request you—no. Damn, this was easier the first time." He took another deep breath. "Madam, you are aware of my great regard—no. What an ass."

She giggled softly.

"Madam, please."

"Yes?"

He took a misstep and quickly righted his footing. "Damnation, I bet that dunderhead Browne's proposal was smoother."

"I think it is going very well so far." Her smile was almost genuine.

He grimaced. "You're enjoying this, aren't you?"

"Immensely. You, suffering gentle panic."

"Pardon?"

"Nothing of the least importance. Continue."

"Why don't you refuse me now?"

"You haven't asked me."

Two couples approached close enough to hear their conversation. Ross scowled at them and waltzed her to the empty side of the dance floor. As soon as this was accomplished, several other people moved in their direction. Whatever look Ross gave them, they immediately retreated.

She saw the matrons watching them, as they had done at the summer assembly. Mrs. Harbottle glared at her, so she smiled back and raised her arm to cheerfully wave at the woman.

"Where was I? Ah, why are you here and not sailing away to America?"

She shook her head. "That doesn't sound like a proposal—"

"I've a speech prepared, but you could save us time and just say 'yes.'"

She smiled coyly. "I could. But I want to hear your speech."

He winked. "Is this what marriage will be like?"

She gave a short burst of laughter. "You must offer first before you find out."

"No, no. It's all wrong here. Later, lovely lady, later. Oh look, now that Browne fellow approaches."

Henry and Ross exchanged the briefest of bows. "Good evening, sir," Henry said. "Since you and Mrs. Colton are obviously on such excellent terms, I expect you will abandon your plans for a foundry. I will therefore immediately cease my efforts on the nuisance lawsuit. I must admit I am relieved."

"Actually, Mr. Browne, I need your legal expertise. My investment group would like to dig a canal to service the Macclesfield area. Perhaps from somewhere around Marple to Bosley."

She squeezed Ross's arm in silent approval.

Henry nodded. "Of course. I'm just pleased this foundry scheme has ended."

"No, we'll build it at another location," Ross said. "That way, when the new canal is completed, we will have a route to move our new engines to our customers." He glanced at her. "No children will be employed, I promise. Now if you will excuse us, we have some waltzing to do." Without waiting for a reply, he spun her into the center of the dance floor.

Whirling in his arms, she rejoiced in the comforting embrace of the man she loved.

"Where was I?" He spoke in a low voice, so the other dancers would not hear him. "Madam, due to my physical restrictions—temporary, I can assure you—and the restrictions of propriety due to our gallivanting in a public place"—he took the opportunity of a fast twirl to whisper in her ear—"madam, consider yourself thoroughly *kissed*."

"Oh," she replied, her heart skipping a beat before escalating into a rapid gallop. "Sir, consider yourself thoroughly"—she gave him a coy smile—"*kissed in return*."

His eyes widened in pretend shock before he passed his mouth close to her ear. "Madam, consider your figure…*worshipped*."

"Oh. That is the most scandalous thing ever said on the assembly floor. And a comment like that demands a reply of a similar nature." She waited a minute or two until they swirled over to the edge of the crowd, then expressed her desire. "Sir, consider your cravat *torn off*."

"Madam, I may faint. But high spirits like yours deserve a proper mate." He surveyed the room with a sly expression. "Consider your bodice *rent*."

"On the assembly floor," she exclaimed, gathering everyone's attention for a moment. She felt a blush stealing up her cheeks with the thought of his hands and mouth on her breasts. "Sir, and here I took you for a gentleman."

"No, not a gentleman. Failed at that endeavor, almost got me killed too. Therefore, I'll be a rake forever." He leaned close. "*Your* rake forever."

This time she leaned to whisper in his ear. "Now that you mention it, who were those women at the bazaar?"

He stepped back, holding her at arm's length. "Are you too warm? Shall I retrieve some refreshments?"

She laughed loudly. "Who?"

He shrugged and failed to answer her question for a minute, before he spun her into the crowded floor. "Parker's cousins acted as tarts to assist me in my misguided—very misguided—attempts to protect you."

"Parker's cousins." Her eyes widened. "The milk-maid was a nice touch." They chuckled together as they performed an extra-fast whirl across the floor. "Although I was suspicious. Men don't usually read books to tarts, do they?"

"Ah, caught."

"Now that I think of it, his cousins must be the dark-haired ladies like Parker. Who was the red-head then?"

He chuckled. "Maybe one real tart snuck in."

A loud giggle escaped her. "They say reformed rakes make the best husbands. But what are unre-formed rakes?"

"Husbands with happy wives? Still, consider me an *exclusive* rake. Exclusive in regard to relations, but by nature I'll probably continue to partner the matrons in the cotillion, and say outrageous things dangerously close to the wallflowers. Oh look, I must smile at Browne's new dance partner first, don't you agree?"

"I like your version of a rake best. He'll let me begin with a thorough examination." She leaned close. "Consider your fig leaf *peeked*."

"Madam, we'll do more than peek." His radiant smile beamed, eclipsing all of the light in the room. "I've something to show you."

"Not now."

"You, my love, are being an impatient reader. The final chapter in *The Rake's Handbook* must be savored slowly." A look of sublime satisfaction danced in his eyes.

"Not in the middle of the assembly floor."

He stopped waltzing and started to unbutton his waistcoat. "Now there's an idea."

"No!" She flung herself at him, grabbing his hand to stop him.

"You really must contain yourself in public."

"You devil."

He leaned close enough his lips brushed her cheek. "Your devil, madam, and no one else's. In fact, you cannot even begin to understand what subject matters your devil has in wait for you." He lowered his eyelids. "We'll become quite heated after reading the later chapters of my handbook."

Her heart thumped in her chest as she grinned at the man who meant everything to her now. She needed to hold him, kiss him senseless, but not here with the town's matrons watching their every move.

He took a deep breath and held her closer than propriety allowed. He tried to speak, looked upward, and then whispered, "I should have waited. Tomorrow, my love. I'll show you tomorrow."

Twenty-four

"WHAT IS THE NATURE OF YOUR SURPRISE?" ELINOR asked.

A brisk sunny day greeted them as Ross gathered her for a carriage ride to Blackwell. He ignored her question, handed her up into the carriage, and placed a plaid blanket around her knees before they set off. In unison, they clasped hands and intertwined their fingers. She felt the heat of his warm palm even through two layers of kid gloves. "Where are we going?"

He chuckled before giving her hand a squeeze. "I knew you would ask me that."

"I—we—there are important subjects to discuss."

He leaned over, kissed her on the neck next to her bonnet's blue silk ribbons, and then resumed stroking her arm.

Males. Hopeless at conversation, just when you need to talk. She glanced at Ross abstractly staring at her fingers and realized he would remain silent. How could he be reticent when they needed to discuss Berdy, their living arrangements, the foundry, the wedding, and his mother? *Males.* She weakened at the sight of his dark hair against his white collar as he turned to peer out the window. *Males.* Wonderful, strong, loving men. Both similar in many ways, one gentleman kind and proper, the other kind and wicked. Why had she been gifted with the privilege to truly love a man a second time?

Elinor snuggled up to his warm body, and rested her palm on his deep green velvet coat. After a prolonged sigh, she shut her eyes. When she opened them, they had arrived at Blackwell's stables.

Ross bounded out of the carriage and reached up to help her down. "Come, come, you must see this."

"See what?"

"Naughty, naughty girl, this way." He tucked her arm under his and started off toward back of the house. "What a beautiful day."

Once they reached the rear of Blackwell, she discovered many changes had taken place since the garden party. The sloping lawn had been graded into terraces, supported by short walls of new fieldstone. A wide gravel path separated the terraces into two large arcs of dark, freshly dug earth. Approaching the first terrace, she saw a half-dozen rosebushes taking benefit from the day's glorious sun. This early in the year, most of the roses resembled bare canes with few leaves, but one must have come from a glasshouse, since the plant had several fragile blooms.

"How lovely," she said in a soft voice.

"My gardener is quite put out at being able to find only one plant with flowers. But as you can see, we are ready for spring. I've also ordered fifty more canes to be delivered. By next summer, the rose garden will have taken its first step toward becoming the most glorious sight in the neighborhood." He leaned close with a devilish smile upon his face. "Of course, this does mean the air around your home will become a nuisance. I'm afraid the wind will blow the scent of roses right into the house." He winked.

She grinned wryly. "You will have so many roses, you should start a new business. Use the old salt-evaporating pans down by the river to make rose water." She giggled. "Thornbury's rose water, for the lady who has everything"—she looked into his eyes—"like me."

He kissed her cheek and patted her hand. "Excellent idea, madam. Now stay there please. I shall be right back."

Striding to the table on the terrace, he returned with a full glass of water. "My first attempt at being the proper lover females desire, so be easy on me." He took a deep breath. "Once upon a time there was a young student who applied for a vacancy in a famous academy of philosophers. In answer to his request, the head of the academy sent him a glass of water so full—the addition of a single drop would run over the side. The young man sadly realized this message was the philosopher's way of telling him he was too late. There was no room at the academy—no room." A wistful light shone in his eyes.

She understood the metaphor. *Her heart must be full of William's love.*

Ross continued speaking. "Peering through the water in the glass, the young man noticed a rose at his feet. He plucked a petal"—Ross did the same from the plant before him—"then carefully floated the petal so not a single drop escaped." He lowered the velvety white petal until it touched the water and let go. The petal floated gently across the water's surface. "The young man handed the glass back to the head philosopher. He was then immediately accepted into the academy for his demonstration that room can be found where least expected. I know you will always love William, but I ask for room in your heart for me too, because I love you." He tossed the water and the petal across the ground then set the glass down. He grabbed her hands. "Will you do me the honor of becoming my wife?"

A soft, fulsome joy radiated through her. "Yes." Her eyes started to water. "Yes, room." She laughed. "Always room in my heart for you, my love."

Reaching into his waistcoat pocket, he pulled out a gold brooch.

The sunlight bounced off the gold and diamonds of William's mourning brooch. Somehow he had rescued it from the leech man. "How…"

"You were right. It cost a small fortune to recover this, but I hope you approve of my alterations. Look carefully."

She gazed at him in wonderment. Upon examining the brooch, she noticed the tight plaits of William's hair remained. Yet resting along the side lay one of Ross's sable curls. The bottom of his curl was held together with seed pearls, making his hair resemble a dark stalk nestled amongst the wheat-colored plaits.

"Oh." Words failed her.

"Someday I hope you will tell me about him."

She was able to nod. William's memory was safe in her soul, and her gratitude for the honor of that love still warmed her. "And you tell me about John."

"Yes, I would like that." He spoke softly. "So in my heart the phrase, 'not lost, gone before' has an additional meaning. With your love, I can be myself. I don't have to pretend to be someone I am not. I truly am—*not lost*."

Now even an "oh" was beyond her capabilities. Warm tears obscured her vision as she began to laugh.

Ross gathered her into his arms. He wiped her tears away with his thumbs and kissed her resoundingly. "Hell's fire, we will have to wait three weeks for the banns to be read. Three weeks! I can no longer wait to—express my love."

Elinor wiped the last happy tear away with the back of her hand. "We can always go fishing or for a carriage ride or, where is that pinery?"

"Madam, it is clear you and I shall suit."

She laughed. "I know we will, my love, I truly know."

He surveyed the area. "Just how far away is that pinery? Come, come. I'll need plenty of time this morning." He grabbed her hand, imprisoned it under his arm, and strode briskly toward the glasshouse.

"Ross, someone will see us."

"No, Mr. Douglas and the others are at the foundry site today. We'll have the pinery all to ourselves." He stopped to kiss her deeply, then urgently pulled her toward the pinery. "Besides, Mother would find us anywhere in the house." A reckless grin emerged. "Exactly what is that thing around your neck?"

"Pardon?"

"Your gown. Looks like I'll have a devilish time removing it. What is that cloth muddle around your neckline?"

Elinor peeked at her bright blue muslin gown, and found nothing more than lovely cording at the bust line. Above that, fine white muslin went all the way up and gathered in a ruffled edge around her neck. She reached her hand up and felt the delicate ruffles that framed her face.

"Yes, what do you call those?" He jabbed his finger in the direction of her neck.

"Ruffles?" she asked.

He groaned. "What *type* of ruffles?"

"Just ruffles, I suppose."

He smiled brightly. "I can't think of anything I'd like more than to free you of those damnable ruffles."

They reached the pinery and hurried into the inner chamber with its musty steam and soft pile of dark earth. He flung his cravat and waistcoat up in the air and started to disrobe her. "Time to read you the final chapter in *The Rake's Handbook*. In fact, we will read it often."

She giggled. "I expect we'll write the next book together. I've mentioned this handbook before, remember? You said it needed a new title."

"Ah, yes, some handbook on marriage."

"I've come up with a new title, and I'm sure this handbook will become immensely popular too."

A dark brow lifted. "So what's the new title?"

"*The Cornucopia of Connubial Bliss.*"

Watch for Sally Orr's next Regency adventure

When a Rake Falls

Coming soon from Sourcebooks Casablanca

LORD BOYCE PARKER FELT A SUDDEN URGE TO SING. The wooden platform grew smaller as the balloon gained altitude. Seconds later, the fields and hedgerows below resembled the irregular squares of a mottled green chessboard.

"We must land and soon," the girl said. "Once I get you safely on the ground, we have plans for some scientific experiments today."

"But I hired this balloon to go to France."

"No! Time is of the essence. The valve must be opened." She squinted like she was studying the best way to reach the draw line controlling the valve. Leaning forward as if to attack, she widened her stance.

Her actions caught him off guard, and he crouched in anticipation of repelling her charge. *Who would move first?* He returned her narrow-eyed stare.

She jumped forward to her left. He leaped to his right.

At the last second, she dove past him and attempted to grab the line. Picking her up by the waist, he carried her to the opposite end of the swaying basket and held her there. Squirming to free herself, she only managed to turn sideways. "You're a madman."

"Beg pardon?"

"Who but a madman would...*sing* all the way up?"

Acknowledgments

A big thank-you to all of the RWA contest judges for their comments on this story. Special recognition to Christie Ridgway, Nicola Cornick, and Caroline Linden for their generous advice. I'd also like to thank the wonderful Chris Sterner, Wendy Kitchen, and Susan Winer for their invaluable assistance.

About the Author

Sally Orr, PhD, worked for thirty years in medical research, specializing in gene discovery. One day a cyber-friend challenged her to write a novel. Since she is a hopeless Anglophile, it's not surprising that her first book is a Regency romance. She lives with her husband in San Diego, surrounded by too many nonfiction books and not enough old English cars.